Praise for the novels of
JACK CAMPBELL

"Jack Campbell has written the most believable space battles I've ever seen anywhere. He takes distances and relativity into consideration to a degree I've never seen before."
—David Sherman, coauthor of the Starfist series

Praise for
THE LOST FLEET: DAUNTLESS

"A rousing adventure." —William C. Dietz

"Jack Campbell's dazzling new series is military science fiction at its best. Not only does he tell a yarn of great adventure and action, but he also develops the characters with satisfying depth. I thoroughly enjoyed this rip-roaring read, and I can hardly wait for the next book."
—Catherine Asaro, Nebula Award–winning author of *Alpha*

"A slam-bang good read that kept me up at night . . . A solid, thoughtful, and exciting novel loaded with edge-of-your-seat combat."
—Elizabeth Moon,
Nebula Award–winning author of *Engaging the Enemy*

THE LOST FLEET
FEARLESS

JACK CAMPBELL

ACE BOOKS, NEW YORK

THE BERKLEY PUBLISHING GROUP
Published by the Penguin Group
Penguin Group (USA) Inc.
375 Hudson Street, New York, New York 10014, USA
Penguin Group (Canada), 90 Eglinton Avenue East, Suite 700, Toronto, Ontario M4P 2Y3, Canada
(a division of Pearson Penguin Canada Inc.)
Penguin Books Ltd., 80 Strand, London WC2R 0RL, England
Penguin Group Ireland, 25 St. Stephen's Green, Dublin 2, Ireland (a division of Penguin Books Ltd.)
Penguin Group (Australia), 250 Camberwell Road, Camberwell, Victoria 3124, Australia
(a division of Pearson Australia Group Pty. Ltd.)
Penguin Books India Pvt. Ltd., 11 Community Centre, Panchsheel Park, New Delhi—110 017, India
Penguin Group (NZ), Cnr. Airborne and Rosedale Roads, Albany, Auckland 1310, New Zealand
(a division of Pearson New Zealand Ltd.)
Penguin Books (South Africa) (Pty.) Ltd., 24 Sturdee Avenue, Rosebank, Johannesburg 2196,
South Africa

Penguin Books Ltd., Registered Offices: 80 Strand, London WC2R 0RL, England

This is a work of fiction. Names, characters, places, and incidents either are the product of the author's imagination or are used fictitiously, and any resemblance to actual persons, living or dead, business establishments, events, or locales is entirely coincidental. The publisher does not have any control over and does not assume any responsibility for author or third-party websites or their content.

THE LOST FLEET: FEARLESS

An Ace Book / published by arrangement with the author

PRINTING HISTORY
Ace mass-market edition / February 2007

Copyright © 2007 by John G. Hemry.
Cover art by Pat Turner.
Cover design by Annette Fiore.
Interior text design by Kristin del Rosario.

ISBN: 978-0-441-01476-7

ACE
Ace Books are published by The Berkley Publishing Group,
a division of Penguin Group (USA) Inc.,
375 Hudson Street, New York, New York 10014.
ACE and the "A" design are trademarks belonging to Penguin Group (USA) Inc.

PRINTED IN THE UNITED STATES OF AMERICA

10 9 8 7 6 5 4 3 2 1

To Stanley Schmidt,
a great editor, a great writer, and a very decent human being.
Thanks for helping so many writers, including myself,
become better at our work.
And I have no doubt that despite this dedication,
Stan will continue rejecting anything I send him
that doesn't meet his standards.

For S., as always.

ACKNOWLEDGMENTS

I'm indebted to my editor, Anne Sowards, for her valuable support and editing, and to my agent, Joshua Bilmes, for his inspired suggestions and assistance. Thanks also to Catherine Asaro, Robert Chase, J. G. (Huck) Huckenpöhler, Simcha Kuritzky, Michael LaViolette, Aly Parsons, Bud Sparhawk, and Constance A. Warner for their suggestions, comments, and recommendations. Thanks also to Charles Petit for his suggestions about space engagements.

ONE

SHIPS appeared against the black of space, squadrons of destroyers and light cruisers flashing into existence, followed by groups of heavy cruisers, then the divisions of battle cruisers and battleships, massive platforms for the deadliest weapons mankind had been able to create. In the distance a bright speck of light marked the star humanity had named Sutrah, so far away that the people living on the worlds near that star wouldn't see the light announcing the Alliance fleet's arrival for almost five hours yet.

The Alliance fleet, which had jumped into normal space here, appeared to be incredibly powerful as its formations fell toward Sutrah. It seemed impossible that something so strong could fear anything. But the Alliance fleet was running for its life, and Sutrah, deep within the enemy territory of the Syndicate Worlds, was but a necessary stepping stone on the way to ultimate safety.

"WE have detections of Syndicate Worlds light warships at ten light-minutes, bearing ten degrees down to starboard."

Captain John "Black Jack" Geary sat in the fleet commander's seat on the bridge of the Alliance battle cruiser *Dauntless*, feeling over-tensed muscles slowly relax as it became apparent he'd once more guessed right. Or the Syndicate fleet commanders had guessed wrong, which was just as good. No minefields had awaited the Alliance fleet as it exited from the jump point, and the enemy warships so far spotted posed no real threat to his fleet.

No, the major threat to his ships remained inside the fleet itself.

Geary kept his eyes on the three-dimensional display projected before him, watching to see if the neat ranks of the Alliance formation would dissolve into chaotic pursuit of the Syndic ships as discipline gave way to a desire to get in on a kill.

"Captain Desjani," he directed the commanding officer of the *Dauntless*. "Please broadcast a demand to those Syndicate warships to surrender immediately."

"Yes, sir." Tanya Desjani had learned to hide her reactions to Geary's old-fashioned and (to the thinking of modern times) softhearted concepts like granting the option of surrender to an enemy force that could be easily destroyed.

He had slowly learned why she and the others in the fleet felt that way. The Syndicate Worlds had never been known for the humanity of their rulers or for concepts like individual freedom and justice that the worlds of the Alliance held dear. The unprovoked, surprise attacks by the Syndics, which had started this war, had left a bitter taste that still lingered, and over the century since then, the Syndics had taken the lead in a race to the bottom when it came to win-at-any-price tactics. Geary had been shocked to learn that the Alliance had come to match the Syndics atrocity for atrocity, and even though he now understood how that had happened, he would never tolerate it. He insisted on abiding by the old rules he'd known, rules that tried to control the rage of war so that those fighting it didn't become as bad as their enemies.

Geary checked the system display for at least the tenth

time since sitting down. He'd already memorized it before then. The jump point his fleet had exited was just under five light-hours from Sutrah. Two worlds in the system were inhabited, but the nearest of those to the fleet was only nine light-minutes from the star. It wouldn't see the arrival of the Alliance fleet in this system for another four and a half hours. The other inhabited world was slightly farther away from the fleet, a mere seven and a half light-minutes from Sutrah. The Alliance fleet wouldn't have to go close to either as it transited Sutrah Star System en route to another jump point on the other side from which it could make the leap to another star.

Around the depiction of the Alliance fleet on the system display, an expanding bubble marked the area in which something like a real-time picture of events could be evaluated. Right now, the fleet could see what the closest inhabited world had looked like four and a half light-hours ago. That was a comfortable margin, but it also allowed a lot of time for unanticipated events to pop up and surprise you when the light from them finally arrived. The star Sutrah itself could've exploded four hours ago, and they wouldn't see the light from the event for almost another hour.

"Red shift on the Syndic ships," a watch-stander announced, unable to keep disappointment out of his voice.

"They're running," Desjani added unnecessarily.

Geary nodded, then frowned. The massively outnumbered Syndic force they'd encountered at Corvus had nevertheless fought, with only one ship ultimately surrendering but three others annihilated. *The Syndic commander there cited Syndic fleet regulations as requiring that suicidal action. Why are the Syndics here behaving differently?* "Why?" he asked out loud.

Captain Desjani gave Geary a surprised look. "They're cowards."

Geary managed not to snap out a forceful reaction. Desjani, like so many of the other sailors and officers in the Alliance, had been fed propaganda about the Syndic enemy for so long that they believed it all, even when it didn't make sense. "Captain, three of the Syndic ships at Corvus fought to the death. Why are these running?"

Desjani frowned in turn. "Syndics follow orders rigidly," she finally declared.

That was a fair assessment, reflecting everything Geary had once known and what he'd seen now. "Then they've been ordered to run."

"To report on our arrival in Sutrah System," Desjani concluded. "But what's the point of that? If they've got light units posted at the other jump points, and we can see that as of a few hours ago they did, what advantage do they gain by having someone right here? Their report still goes out at light speed, and since they can't get through us to the nearest jump point, they won't be able to jump out quickly."

Geary brooded over the display. "True enough. So why?" He took another look at his fleet's formation, still holding together, and breathed a prayer of thanks to the living stars. "Wait a minute." Within a solar system, directional references were always made to the world outside a ship so other ships could understand them. Anything above the plane of the system was up, anything below it down. The direction toward the sun was right, or starboard, (or even *starward* as some urged), while the direction away from the sun was left, or port. Using that standard convention, the Syndic light warships had been below the position of his fleet and were now fleeing up and slightly to the left. Why would they run in a way that brought them closer to his fleet? Unless running in that way had another purpose.

Geary drew an intercept line from his ships to the Syndics, the curving course tracing through a region the Syndics hadn't gone through. "Get me a real good look at this area. Fast."

Desjani gave Geary a startled glance but passed the order on. Geary was still waiting for the reply when he saw three destroyers and a heavy cruiser suddenly break formation, leaping forward under full acceleration to intercept the fleeing Syndics. *No! You fools!* Without waiting another moment, Geary keyed the fleet command circuit. "All units, alter course up three zero degrees. I say again, up three zero degrees. Immediate execute. There are mines along our projected track."

He took a moment to identify the units that had broken formation. "*Anelace, Baselard, Mace, Cuirass!* Break up from your current course immediately! Up three zero degrees. You are entering a minefield."

Then all Geary could do was stare at the display. The Alliance fleet was spread across light-minutes of distance. The farthest ships wouldn't receive his order for another two minutes. The ones in greatest danger, those three destroyers and the cruiser *Cuirass*, wouldn't hear it for at least a minute. At full acceleration they'd cover a lot of ground in that minute.

A watch-stander on the bridge of *Dauntless* was making her report in a loud voice. "Anomalies detected along the track indicated. Assess better than eighty percent probability of stealth mines in the area. Recommend avoidance course now."

Desjani held up a hand to acknowledge the report, then gazed at Geary, her eyes filled with admiration. Geary realized that the eyes of the other officers and sailors on the bridge reflected the same amazement as well as the hero worship he really hated seeing, even after months of it. "How did you know, Captain Geary?" Desjani asked.

"It was just too obvious," he explained, shifting uncomfortably in his seat under the regard of the other officers on the bridge. "The warships positioned far enough from the jump point to avoid incoming enemies but close enough to warn off friendly shipping. Then that course they took, which seemed aimed at taking us through a certain area when we pursued." He left off something they both knew, that if this fleet had been the same one he'd brought into Corvus, most of his ships would be rushing headlong into that minefield right now, instead of only four lighter units.

The widespread formation of the Alliance fleet began

bending in the middle as the nearest ships reacted to the order, then as the order reached farther ships, they responded, too. The overall image almost resembled a manta ray, Geary realized, flexing up in the middle with the "wings" still drooping lower.

He waited, seeing the three destroyers and the cruiser maintaining their courses, as if the pursuit was all that mattered. Geary checked the time. Five minutes had passed. Give it one minute for the order to arrive at the speed of light, then another minute for him to finally see whatever course change the ships started. That left three minutes, which was way too slow a response in an emergency. "*Anelace, Baselard, Mace, Cuirass*! Alter course upward immediately, maximum turn. We've detected a minefield across your tracks. Acknowledge order and start turn immediately!"

Another minute. "How far away are they from those anomalies?" Geary asked, trying to keep his voice level.

"On current track," Desjani tapped her own controls rapidly, running the calculation, "they'll be in among them in thirty seconds." Desjani's voice was calm, disciplined. She had seen a lot of Alliance ships die, a lot of Alliance sailors die, in her fairly short career. Geary had only gradually learned that, and realized that now Desjani was drawing on her experience to numb herself to what seemed inevitable.

Thirty seconds. Too late to even try broadcasting another order. Geary knew some of the commanding officers in his fleet weren't really qualified for command, knew that many others still clung to the idea of all-out glorious charges into the enemy without hesitation or thinking. It would be a long time before he could, hopefully, teach those warriors the value of fighting wisely as well as bravely. But even knowing that, Geary wondered what insanity had led those four captains to ignore his orders and his warning about the minefield. Their minds must be fixed on their chosen targets, oblivious to anything else as they tried to close to engagement range.

Maybe the ships would survive in the minefield long enough for another warning to work. Trying to keep his voice from betraying desperation, Geary called them again. "*Anelace, Baselard, Mace, Cuirass,* this is the fleet commander. You are entering a confirmed minefield. Alter course up immediately. Maximum turn."

They were entering the minefield now, he knew. The light from the four ships was half a minute old, so the ships that he could see proud and intact were already in the minefield, might already have hit mines. All he could do was stare at the display, waiting for the inevitable, knowing there was nothing that could save the crews of those ships now but an actual miracle. He prayed silently, wishing for that miracle.

It didn't happen. Exactly one minute, seven seconds after Desjani's warning, Geary saw his display reporting multiple explosions as the three destroyers leading the charge ran into the dense minefield. The small, relatively frail destroyers simply disintegrated under the hammer blows of the mines, shattering into fragments of men, women, and ships that the smart fuses of unexploded mines simply ignored.

A few seconds after that, Geary saw the *Cuirass* finally trying to turn. It was far too late, though, as momentum carried the cruiser into the mines. One punched a crater amidships, then a second blew away a good part of the stern, then the optical sensors on the *Dauntless* momentarily lost sight of the cruiser as the debris field from it and the destroyers blocked the view of the destruction.

Geary licked lips suddenly gone dry, thinking of the sailors who'd just died to no purpose. He blocked out emotion, concentrating on the mechanics of his next task as he studied the display. "Second Destroyer Squadron, you are to make a cautious approach to the vicinity of the minefield in search of survivors. Do not enter the minefield without approval from me." Odds were there wasn't a single survivor. The four ships had been destroyed so quickly it seemed unlikely anyone could've reached a survival pod.

But it was necessary to ensure no one was left behind to the tender mercies of the Syndic labor camps.

A slow minute passed. "Second Destroyer Squadron, aye. Proceeding to search for survivors." The voice of the squadron commander was subdued.

Geary took another look at his formation, all on the new course, rising above the plane of the Sutrah System, coursing above the minefield area now prominently labeled with danger signs on the display. "All units, alter course two zero degrees down at time one five."

Everyone was looking at him, perhaps expecting some speech about the heroism of the crews of the four ships. Geary stood up, his mouth a thin line, shook his head, and walked off the bridge, not trusting his voice. The dead shouldn't be spoken ill of. He didn't want to publicly lash the commanders of those ships as vainglorious fools who'd murdered their crews.

Even though that was exactly what had happened.

VICTORIA Rione, co-president of the Callas Republic and a member of the Alliance senate, was waiting for him at the entry to his stateroom. Geary nodded to her with one quick jerk of his head, then entered without inviting her inside. She came anyway, standing silently while he glowered at the starscape that decorated one bulkhead. She didn't have any command authority in the fleet, but as a senator she was a senior enough representative of the Alliance government that Geary certainly couldn't just throw her out. Besides, the ships of both the Callas Republic and the Rift Federation, which made up part of his fleet, would listen to orders given by Rione if she decided to buck Geary. He had to be diplomatic with this civilian politician even when all he wanted to do was yell at someone.

Finally he just glared at her. "What do you want, Madam Co-President?"

"To hear you relieve the anger that is devouring you at the moment," she replied calmly.

He slumped for a moment, then slammed his fist into the starscape, making it shimmer briefly before returning to normal. "Why? Why would anyone be so *stupid*?"

"I saw this fleet at Corvus, Captain Geary. The Syndic tactic would've worked perfectly there, before the training you insisted upon taught the fleet better discipline."

"Is that supposed to make me feel better?" he asked bitterly.

"It should."

Geary rubbed his face with one hand. "Yeah," he agreed wearily. "It should. But even one ship . . . and we just lost four."

Rione gave him a penetrating look. "At least they presented an object lesson on the value of following orders."

He stared back at her, wondering if she was serious. "That's a little too cold-blooded for me, Madam Co-President."

She shrugged. "You have to be realistic, Captain Geary. Unfortunately, there are some people who refuse to learn until they see errors literally blow up their faces." Her voice fell, and her eyes closed. "As happened just now."

So she was affected by the losses. Geary felt a surge of relief. As the only civilian in the fleet, the only person not under his command, Rione was the only person he felt able to confide in. He was beginning to discover he also liked her, an unfamiliar feeling for him after the isolation of being in a time a century removed from his own. After the isolation of finding himself among people whose culture had changed in many ways large and small from the one Geary had known.

Rione looked up again. "Why, Captain Geary? I don't pretend to be an expert on the military, but those four ship commanders had seen that your way of doing things worked. The way the fleet used to fight, back in your time. They'd seen a large Syndic force destroyed to the last ship. How could they possibly believe that charging headlong at the enemy was wise?"

Geary shook his head, not looking at her. "Because, to

the great misfortune of humanity, military history is very often the story of commanders repeating the same unsuccessful way of fighting again and again while their own forces are destroyed in droves. I don't pretend to know why that is, but it's a sad truth; commanders who don't learn from immediate or long-term experience, who keep hurling their forces forward as if causing the same useless deaths time and again will eventually change the outcome."

"Surely not all commanders could be like that."

"No, of course not. Though it seems they tend to collect in the highest ranks, where they can do the most damage." Geary finally looked over at Rione. "Many of these ship commanders are good, brave sailors. But they've spent their entire careers being told how to fight one way. It'll take a while to overcome all of that hidebound experience and convince them that change is not a bad thing. Change doesn't come easily to the military, even when that change is a return to the professional tactics of the past. It's still change from the way things are."

Rione sighed and shook her head. "I've seen the many ancient traditions that the military holds dear and sometimes wonder if it thereby attracts too many of those who value lack of change over accomplishment."

Geary shrugged. "Maybe, but those traditions can be a tremendous source of strength. You told me some time back that this fleet was brittle, prone to break under pressure. If I can successfully reforge it stronger, it'll be in no small part because of the traditions that I can draw on."

She accepted his statement without any sign of whether or not she believed it. "I do have some information that may help to partially explain the actions of those four ships. Since we left jump space and the communications net became active, some of my sources have reported that rumors have been spread through ships. Rumors that you, having lost your fighting spirit, would rather allow Syndic warships to escape to fight another day than risk engaging them."

Geary found himself laughing in disbelief. "How could anyone believe that after Kaliban? We tore that Syndic flotilla apart. Not a one got away."

"People will believe what they wish to believe," Rione observed.

"You mean like believing Black Jack Geary is a mythical hero?" he asked sourly. "Half the time they want to worship me, the warrior from the past who's going to save this fleet and the Alliance by winning a war a century old, and the other half of the time they spread rumors that I'm incompetent or afraid." Geary finally sat down, gesturing Rione to a seat opposite him. "So what else are your spies in my fleet telling you, Madam Co-President?"

"Spies?" she repeated in a surprised tone as she sat down. "That's such a negative term."

"It's only negative if the spies are working for your enemy." Geary rested his chin on one fist, regarding her. "Are you my enemy?"

"You know I distrust you," Rione replied. "At first it was because I feared the hero worship that could make you as big a threat to the Alliance and this fleet as the Syndics. Now it's because of that, and because you've proven yourself a very capable man. That combination is very dangerous."

"But as long as what I'm doing is in the best interests of the Alliance, we're on the same side?" Geary inquired, letting some sarcasm show. "I'm worried about what that mine ambush says about our enemy, Madam Co-President."

She frowned at him. "What does it tell you about our enemy that you did not already know?"

"It says the Syndics are thinking. It says they're being smart, like when they tricked this fleet into taking their hypernet to the Syndic home system so it could run into a war-ending ambush."

"Which would've succeeded if not for the unlooked-for presence of the century-old hero of the Alliance, Captain Black Jack Geary," Rione stated half-mockingly. "Found on the edge of final death in a lost survival pod, like an ancient king miraculously returned to life to save his people in their hour of greatest need."

He grimaced back at her. "To you that's funny, because you don't have to live with people believing you're that person."

"I've told you that you *are* that person. And, no, I don't find it funny at all."

Geary wished he understood her better. Since being rescued, he'd been in the military environment of the fleet and had been badly surprised by some of the cultural changes wrought by a century of bitter war. But his only direct contact with civilian culture in the Alliance was Victoria Rione, and she kept much hidden. He couldn't tell how much had changed back home and in what ways, and he really wanted to know.

But Rione isn't likely to help me better understand Alliance civilian culture if she thinks I could use that knowledge to make myself more of a threat to the Alliance government. Maybe someday she'll trust me enough to unwind about such things. Geary sat forward, working the controls on the table between them that still seemed a bit unfamiliar, even after months in this stateroom. An image of Sutrah sprang up, next to a larger display of the stars near Sutrah. "We're going to go through the rest of this system very carefully. I assume the Syndics laid similar minefields near the other jump points, but we can spot them and avoid them now that we know to look."

Rione pointed to symbols on the display. "Two Syndic military bases? Are either a threat?"

"They don't look like it from what we can see. Obsolete, to all appearances. What we'd expect in a system not on the Syndic hypernet." He let his gaze rest on the depictions of the Syndic bases, thinking about the hypernet that had changed things so much since what he thought of as his time. Much faster than the system-jump-faster-than-light method, and with unlimited range between the gates of the hypernet, it had revolutionized interstellar travel and left countless star systems to wither like broken twigs when they weren't judged special enough to justify the expense of a gate.

Geary punched the update key, and the latest information on Sutrah System was presented. The only change was in the positions of the light Syndic warships, which had lured his four ships into the minefield. Those Syndics were still running, heading away from Geary's forces at velocities edging toward .2 light speed. They'd been accelerating so fast that their inertial compensators must be badly stressed and their crews pinned to their seats by leakthrough. Chasing them would be futile, since they could simply keep heading away while the Alliance fleet sooner or later had to proceed to one of the jump points out of Sutrah, but Geary still felt a tide of anger sweep over him at the sight of the Syndic ships, knowing vengeance was out of the question in this case.

But the Syndic ambush bothered him for reasons beyond that. Rione didn't seem to understand the implications. The survival of the Alliance fleet depended upon Geary making the right decisions and the Syndic command making the wrong decisions. If the Syndics had lost their overconfidence and begun carefully planning, then even Geary's best moves might fail to keep the Alliance fleet at least one step ahead of Syndic forces strong enough to deal the Alliance forces a death blow.

Though even the little blows could add up. Out of the hundreds of ships in the Alliance fleet, the four lost here weren't critical. But the fleet could be nibbled to death over time by taking such losses at star after star, and there were a lot of stars between the fleet and home.

He glanced at the display, wishing Sutrah were a lot closer to Alliance space. Wishing Sutrah had somehow miraculously gained an unguarded hypernet gate. Hell, as long as he was at it, why not wish he'd died on his ship a century ago, so he wouldn't be in command of this fleet now, with so many lives and ships depending upon him?

Snap out of it, Geary. You had every right to be depressed when they thawed you out, but you're past that now.

The communicator chimed for his attention. "Captain Geary, we've spotted something important." Captain Desjani's voice held some emotion he couldn't quite identify.

"Important?" If it was a threat, surely she'd have just said that.

"On the fifth world of the system. It looks like a labor camp."

Geary gave Rione a glance to see how she was taking the news, but Rione didn't seem to find it remarkable, either. The Syndicate Worlds had a lot of labor camps, because the Syndicate Worlds devoted a lot of effort to dealing with real or imagined internal enemies. "Is there something special about it?"

This time he could clearly identify the strain in Desjani's voice. "We're picking up communications from the camp that indicate it holds Alliance prisoners of war."

Geary stared at the depiction of the fifth world in the Sutrah system. Nine light-minutes from its star, still a bit over four light-hours from the Alliance fleet. He hadn't expected to be going near the inhabited worlds of this system, hadn't anticipated any delays.

It looked like his plans would have to change.

I *hate these meetings*, Geary thought for perhaps the hundredth time, which was impressive, given that he'd only had to attend about five of the things so far. Inside the briefing room, the conference table was actually only a few meters long. But thanks to the communications net connecting the ships of the fleet and the latest virtual presence technology, the table now seemed to run off into the distance, seat after seat occupied by commanders of his ships. The most senior officers were apparently seated the closest to Geary, but all he had to do was look at any officer, no matter how far down the table, and they'd loom close, identification information helpfully appearing right next to them.

Granted, the conferences had an odd rhythm to them. The fleet had been drawn into a much tighter formation for the conference, but because of light speed limitations on the communications, the farther-off ships were still twenty or even thirty light-seconds off. Those were the smallest ships with the most junior commanders, of course, the ones who were expected to watch, learn, and keep their mouths shut, so the delayed-action nature of their interactions had little impact. But even for closer ships there could be several seconds' delay between question and answer, so the participants had learned to speak, pause, speak, pause, allowing time for interjections and comments to arrive.

Captain Numos, commanding officer of the *Orion*, was staring down his nose at Geary, doubtless still seething over his own poor performance at Kaliban, which of course Numos blamed on Geary rather than himself. Near Numos sat Captain Faresa of the *Majestic*, her expression as acidic as usual. Geary wondered why Faresa didn't somehow dissolve the table surface just by glaring at it. In welcome counterpoint to those two, Captain Duellos of the *Courageous* lounged in his chair, apparently relaxed but with alert eyes, and Captain Tulev of the *Leviathan* sat stolidly, his dismissive gaze fixed on Numos and Faresa. Farther down the table, fiery Commander Cresida of the *Furious* grinned openly at the prospect of more action, while not far from her appeared to sit Colonel Carabali, the senior surviving Marine in the fleet and another capable and dependable officer.

Actually sitting next to Geary was Captain Desjani, the only other person physically present in the crowded room. Co-President Rione had begged off attending, but Geary knew the officers of the ships from the Rift Federation and the Callas Republic would provide Rione with a full report of everything that happened. He suspected she'd avoided being here in person in order to see what he'd say in her absence.

Geary nodded brusquely to the assembled officers. "First of all, let us pay respect to the crews of the destroyers *Anelace, Baselard,* and *Mace*, and of the cruiser *Cuirass*, who are in the arms of their ancestors, having died in the line of duty in defense of their homes and families." He felt a bit of a hypocrite to not add in a denunciation of the behaviors that had led those ships to their deaths, but that still seemed out of place.

"Are we sure that there were no survivors?" someone asked.

Geary gestured to the commander of the Second Destroyer Squadron, who cleared his throat and looked unhappy as he answered. "We conducted a thorough search. The only survival pods located were all badly damaged and inactive."

Numos spoke, his voice harsh. "We should've pursued those Syndic Hunter-Killer ships and made them pay for destroying those ships and killing their crews!"

"How would you have caught them?" Duellos asked in a drawl that clearly conveyed contempt.

"A full-scale pursuit at maximum acceleration, of course."

"The youngest officer in the fleet knows the laws of physics wouldn't allow us to catch those ships without chasing them halfway to the next star and burning up nearly all of our fuel in the process."

Captain Faresa intervened, her voice sour. "An officer in the Alliance fleet shouldn't give up before starting. 'Attempt the impossible, and you will achieve it.'"

The way the quote was delivered sounded depressingly familiar. Geary glanced at Captain Desjani, who nodded at him, unable to suppress a proud look. Another "quote" from Black Jack Geary, doubtless taken completely out of context if he'd ever actually said it at all, and used to justify things that the real Black Jack never would've supported and certainly didn't support now. "I'll have to look up just when I said that and what I meant," he replied, keeping his voice even. "But I agree completely with Captain Duellos. Pursuit would've been futile. I have to place responsibility for this entire fleet above my desire for revenge, and I'd expect any other officer to do the same."

"The fleet has grown used to expecting the fleet flagship to lead the way into battle!" Faresa stated as if that somehow proved an argument.

Geary bit back a vicious comment. *Just because the fleet's grown used to expecting stupidity doesn't mean I have to be stupid.*

But Desjani answered for him, her pride clearly affronted by an implied insult to her ship as well as to Geary. "*Dauntless* was in the center of the formation at Kaliban, right where the Syndics aimed their attack," Desjani noted in a formally stiff voice.

"Yes," Geary agreed. *Though to be honest, because of the way I'd set up the battle with my fleet's firepower concentrated on the aim point of the Syndic attack, being in that position probably was the safest place for* Dauntless. He didn't say that, though. He didn't because he knew he'd have to keep *Dauntless* safe all the way home to Alliance space, fleet traditions be damned. *Dauntless* still carried the Syndic hypernet key, though few knew that besides Geary and Captain Desjani. Even if every other ship in the fleet was lost, getting that key back to Alliance space would give the Alliance a crucial advantage over the Syndics. Not that Geary intended sacrificing every other ship if there was any other possible way to get *Dauntless* back.

Numos looked as if he were ready to say something else, so Geary stabbed a finger at the display of Sutrah System hovering above the conference table. "I hadn't intended bothering to divert from our transit of this system to deal with the inhabited worlds, but as you all know, we've learned something that changes those plans. We have indications that there's a labor camp on the fifth world that confines Alliance prisoners."

"Indications?" Captain Tulev asked shrewdly. "You don't think this is certain?"

Geary took a deep breath. "We've already been tricked once in this system. It would've been easy for the Syndics to fake the message traffic that makes it seem there's Alliance personnel in that camp." He easily sensed the rebellion rising around him. "I fully intend going there and finding out for sure. But we have to be alert for another ambush."

"Bait to lure us near the fifth planet?" Colonel Carabali asked, her eyes narrowing in thought.

"It's possible. We'll be able to spot any minefields during our long approach to that world no matter how stealthy they are. What else could be there that we'd have to worry about?"

The colonel shrugged. "You can mount truly massive weaponry on a planet like that, but it has to climb out of the gravity well and deal with the atmospheric effects to get at space targets. Besides, if they try to engage us with that kind of stuff, all we have to do is stand off and throw big rocks at the planet."

A studious-looking ship captain spoke up. "You mean massive kinetic energy projectiles."

"Yeah," the Marine colonel agreed. "That's what I said. BFRs. It's not that I'm thrilled about sending my boys and girls down to the surface of a Syndic-occupied world. We don't have nearly enough ground troops to secure the kind of perimeter we need for safety. But the entire planet will be hostage to the Syndics' good behavior, and we don't really have any alternative."

"We have to send the Marines down?" Geary asked.

Captain Desjani nodded. "After a few incidents much earlier in the war we determined that the Syndics would hold back some of their prisoners, especially any they thought of high value. The only way to confirm we've picked up everyone is to have our own personnel access the Syndic camp records for everything from body counts to food rations to make sure our count matches the numbers they seem to have."

"All right." That made sense, even if Geary didn't like the idea of sweeping the fleet close to the fifth planet and slowing down so his shuttles could pick up the prisoners. "I assume the Syndic shuttles aren't to be trusted, and we have to depend on our own." Everyone nodded this time. "Everyone with shuttles on your ships prepare them for some heavy use. I'll ask Co-President Rione to deliver our ultimatum to the Syndics regarding the prisoners."

Numos gave Geary a look of exaggerated disbelief. "Why should she be involved?"

Not sure why Numos had developed a dislike of Rione, Geary answered bluntly. "She's our most capable negotiator."

"Her blunders at Corvus nearly costs us the *Titan*!"

Geary felt anger rising in him. The Syndic betrayal at Corvus involving merchant ships supposedly delivering supplies to the Alliance fleet hadn't been Rione's fault, hadn't been anyone's fault, really. Surely Numos knew that. "That's not my assessment."

"Of course not! Since Co-President Rione has been spending a great deal of time alone with you in your stateroom, I'm sure you think—"

Geary cut off Numos with a fist slamming to the table's surface. Out of the corner of his eye he could see the outraged faces of the commanders of ships belonging to the Rift Federation and the Callas Republic. "Captain Numos, you are out of order," Geary stated in a deathly low voice.

Captain Faresa stepped in with characteristic certitude. "Captain Numos is only stating what everyone—"

"Captain Faresa," Geary stopped her with a glare. "I never thought to see the day when officers of the Alliance fleet would behave like gossips in a schoolyard. Both you and Captain Numos obviously need to review the personal and professional standards to which an officer is expected to adhere." Faresa's face had gone white, Numos's red, but their eyes glinted with the same hatred of Geary. "Co-President Rione of the Callas Republic is a member of the Alliance senate. She is to be treated with the respect that position requires. If you feel yourselves unable to provide due respect to a senior civilian member of the Alliance government, then you are obligated to submit your resignations from the fleet. I will not tolerate insults aimed at any officer or any representative of the Alliance government in this fleet. Is that clear?"

Geary took a long breath and looked around the table, unable to be sure how this latest speech had been received. Captain Tulev, his face grim, was nodding in agreement, though. "There's been too much gossip, too many rumors. Insults aimed at those in command," Tulev added with a glance at Numos. "Rumors that encouraged ship commanders to adhere to the old traditions of all-out pursuit, with consequences we have seen this day."

A chill ran around the table at the direct reference to whatever might have motivated the captains of four ships to ignore Geary's orders and leave the formation to chase the Syndic warships. Captain Numos swallowed, his mouth working, then finally got out some words. "I had nothing to do with that, and if you're implying—"

"He's implying nothing!" Geary snapped. "He's bringing to our attention that encouraging ships to ignore orders, that attempts to undermine the commander of this fleet, can have serious consequences. I'm aware of the rumors Captain Tulev speaks of, and let me assure you that if I ever discover that anyone encouraged the commanding officers of the *Anelace, Baselard, Mace,* and *Cuirass*"—he recited the names slowly to make sure their impact was felt—"to act in the way they did, I will personally make sure that whoever that is will wish they'd died an honorable death with the crews of those ships." As he finished speaking, Geary let his gaze rest on Numos, who reddened so much more that he looked like he'd suffered a radiation burn. But Numos sat silent, having apparently realized that Geary was in no mood to be antagonized further.

"Now," Geary continued in a calmer voice, "at our present speed we're about forty hours from the fifth planet. Make sure the shuttles are ready. I have a plan here for distributing the Alliance personnel we pick up from the planet among the ships of the fleet." It had been absurdly easy, just a matter of calling up the intelligent agent on his system and asking it how to add five thousand more personnel to the ships in the fleet. Since that was a simple but tedious exercise in math, comparing berths and complements of personnel and support facilities on all of the available ships with the numbers needed, the computer had handled it within moments. It was the sort of thing fleet commanders had required staffs for in the old days, but the ability of automated systems to handle administrative and command tasks had eliminated much of the grunt work those staffs had handled. On top of that, Geary had learned that after the terrible losses suffered year in and year out in this apparently endless war, the need for as many officers as possible to be available to crew replacement ships had led to the cannibalization of the remnants of the old staffs.

Technically, as fleet commander, Geary was still authorized a chief of staff, but that officer had died along with the former fleet commander Admiral Bloch as a result of Syndic treachery during negotiations. He was also authorized an aide, but Geary was damned if he was going to pull a junior officer out of a combat job to act as his personal servant.

"Look at the plan," Geary continued, " see what it says your ship can handle, and let me know if there's any problems with it. I want to know, so don't just suck it up and hope you can handle more than your ship is able to carry safely. There appear to be between three and five thousand prisoners by initial estimates, which we can handle. We'll worry about identifying skills in any fleet personnel who were prisoners and getting them to ships that need them later.

"Colonel Carabali."

The Marine nodded.

"Prepare your Marines. I'd like to see your plan for handling this no later than five hours before we reach the planet.

"Are there any questions?" Geary asked the entire group.

"How will we handle the Syndic military base on the fifth planet?" someone asked.

"That's yet to be determined," Geary advised. He could see dissatisfaction rippling around the table. To many of his commanders, the only good Syndic was a dead Syndic, and no opportunity to kill Syndics should be passed up. "I'll remind you that the installations in this system are obsolete. It costs the Syndics to keep them running. Leaving those installations intact means Syndic funds spent on them and means Syndic troops trained and committed to them. If that base turns out to be a real threat, we'll take it out. Otherwise, I'm not interested in doing the Syndics a favor by removing it from the list of things they need to worry about."

He paused, trying to remember what else he'd planned on saying. "We won't know if this is real until the Marines see Alliance prisoners of war at that camp. Everyone needs to stay alert." He couldn't imagine even the Syndics would risk the population of a habitable world in order to try to destroy a few more Alliance ships, but then he'd seen a lot of things since he'd been rescued that he had never imagined. "We have a chance to do a great good for people who never expected to be liberated. Thank the living stars for that, and let's do our ancestors proud."

The crowd dwindled with the usual amazing speed as the virtual images of ship captains vanished like popping soap bubbles, both Numos and Faresa disappearing on the very heels of Geary's dismissal. Captain Desjani, with a meaningful glare at the place where those two had apparently been sitting, shook her head and then excused herself before leaving the compartment the old-fashioned way by walking out.

As Geary had hoped, the reassuring image of Captain Duellos remained at the end. Duellos also indicated the places where Numos and Faresa had been. "I wouldn't have said this before, but those two are a danger to this fleet."

Geary sat back, feeling weary and rubbing his forehead. "You wouldn't have said that before what?"

"Before four ships of this fleet set off on an insane charge." The image of Duellos seemed to walk up to Geary and take the next seat. "Valiant! Glorious! Brainless! I have no proof, but I know Numos was behind that."

"I figure he is, too. But," Geary admitted bitterly, "the lack of proof is a problem. My command of this fleet is still far too shaky. If I start sacking commanding officers, especially one with Numos's seniority, without being able to prove misconduct I might find way too many of my other ships valiantly and brainlessly dashing into minefields."

Captain Duellos looked down and grimaced. "The lesson of those four ships was a powerful one. No matter what lies Numos encourages, everyone will remember that you were right to warn those ships off and to avoid chasing pell-mell after a few Syndic HuKs."

Geary couldn't help a snort of derision. "You'd think being right would gain me a little more credit than that. What do you think? Will everyone follow my orders when we approach the fifth planet?"

"At this point, yes."

"Do you have any idea where that nonsense about Co-President Rione came from?"

Duellos looked mildly surprised. "I assumed you two were on friendly terms, but even if you're extremely friendly, it's no affair of mine. Co-President Rione is not an officer or sailor under your command, and a personal relationship with her has no bearing on your performance in command."

Geary stared for a moment, then laughed. "Personal relationship? With Co-President Rione?"

This time Duellos shrugged. "Scuttlebutt declares that you spend time together alone."

"For conferences! I need her advice." Geary laughed again. "By our ancestors, Victoria Rione doesn't like me at all! She makes no bones about it. I frighten her because she worries I'll turn into Black Jack Geary at any moment and sail this fleet home to depose the elected leaders of the Alliance and become god-emperor or something."

"Co-President Rione is a shrewd and intelligent woman," Duellos observed with absolute seriousness. "She's told you she doesn't like you?"

"Yes! She—" Come to think of it, Rione had several times expressed distrust of Geary, but he couldn't remember at the moment her ever saying she didn't *like* him. "Yeah, I think so."

Duellos shrugged again. "Whether she does or not makes no difference. I say once more, she is not your subordinate, not in the military at all, and any personal relationship with her is perfectly appropriate. Should one occur."

Geary couldn't help a third laugh as he bade farewell to Captain Duellos, but as he began to leave the room, he paused in thought. Surely Rione's spies in the fleet had reported to her the rumors about a relationship between her and Geary. Why hadn't Rione told him of those rumors when she'd spoken of the other rumors?

Could the iron politician he'd dealt with actually be embarrassed by the rumors? But if so, why had she continued visiting him?

Geary leaned one arm against the bulkhead for a moment, staring at the deck, remembering the first days after he was revived from the survival sleep that had kept him alive for a century, a span of time in which everyone in his life had died in battle or of old age. The shock of learning that everyone he had once known and loved, men and women, were long dead had led him to wall off the idea of new relationships. The ice that had once filled him seemed almost gone, but it still occupied that one place, afraid to retreat and let warmth grow again.

He'd lost everyone once. It could happen again. He didn't want it to hurt so much the next time.

TWO

THE fifth planet looked like exactly the sort of place made for a Syndic labor camp. Too far from its sun to ever know a true summer, most of the world seemed to be featureless fields of tundra that on rare occasions ran into bare, jagged mountain ranges rising like islands from the sea of low, tough vegetation. Glaciers extending from the poles appeared to hold a good portion of the planet's water, with only shallow, small seas dotting the areas not covered by ice. Looking at the dismal place, Geary didn't have any trouble understanding why Sutrah hadn't been deemed worthy of the expense of a hypernet gate. Unless the fourth planet was an absolute paradise, which it certainly wasn't since it was a shade too close to its sun and probably unpleasantly warm. Sutrah was just the sort of place that had ceased to matter when the Syndic hypernet was created.

Once, using the system jump drives that could take ships from star to star, anyone going anywhere had to traverse all of the star systems in between. Every one of those systems was guaranteed a certain amount of traffic passing through en route to other destinations. But the hypernet allowed ships to go directly from one star to another, no matter how far the distance between them. Without the ships passing through, and without any particular value other than as the homes of people who had suddenly found themselves living in nowhere, the systems off the hypernet were slowly dying, with everyone who could migrate moving to hypernet-linked systems. The human communities on the fifth planet of Sutrah were fading even faster than usual. Judging from what the Alliance sensors could see, fully two-thirds of the former habitations on the world were now vacant, showing no signs of heating or activity.

Geary focused back on the depiction of the labor camp on the fifth planet. There were mines nearby, which might represent actual economic value but also might exist solely as a place to work the life from the prisoners in the camp. There weren't any walls, but then there didn't have to be. Outside the camp was nothing but those empty fields of tundra. Escape would simply be suicide, unless someone tried to get out through the landing field, and there walls of razor wire did exist.

He became aware that Captain Desjani was waiting patiently for his attention. "Sorry, Captain. What do you think of my plan?" Geary, uncomfortable with trying to place his fleet in orbit about the planet, had put together a plan calling for the fleet to slow down, dropping the shuttles as it passed closest to the world, then looping around in a wide turn outside the orbits of the fifth planet's small moons before returning again to pick up the shuttles as they returned with the liberated prisoners.

"The pickup would go quicker if we put ships in orbit," Desjani suggested.

"Yeah." Geary frowned at the display. "There's no sign of minefields, we can't see any major defensive weaponry on the planet, and even the Syndic military base there seems to be half shut down. But something's still bothering me."

Desjani nodded thoughtfully. "After the Syndic attempt

to use merchant ships on suicide missions against us, it's understandable to be worried about undetected threats."

"The Syndics had time to lay that minefield trap for us. That means they also had time to try to conceal that labor camp or even try to move the prisoners in it. But there's no sign they did that. Why? Because it's bait far more attractive to us than those light warships near the jump point? The sort of thing we can't pass up?"

"Yet there's no sign of an ambush this time. No sign of anything that could strike at us."

"No," Geary agreed, wondering if he really was just being hypercautious. "Co-President Rione said the Syndic civilian planetary leaders she talked to seemed scared witless. But not a single military officer was available to talk."

That made Desjani frown. "Interesting. But what could they be planning? If there was anything hidden, we should've spotted it."

Geary tapped some controls irritably. "Let's assume we do go into orbit. The fleet's so big we'd have to be way out from the planet."

"These moons will be an annoyance, but they're not much bigger than asteroids. Any formations running past them can dodge easily enough since they're traveling in a loose cluster and on fixed orbits."

"Yeah, and we have to swing past the moons anyway, even with my plan." He scowled at the display. Nothing he'd learned of the war since being rescued seemed to be helping, so Geary cast his mind back, trying to remember the lessons imparted to him by experienced officers long dead, the sort of professionals who'd been killed in the earliest decades of the war along with everyone they'd managed to teach their tricks of the trade. For some reason the sight of the small moons triggered memories of one such trick, a single ship hiding behind a much larger world to lunge out on a passing target. But that didn't make sense. The moons of the fifth planet were too small for anything but a few light units to hide behind, and even suicide attacks by such small ships would fail against the massed

might of the Alliance fleet, concentrated in a tight formation to minimize the distance the shuttles would have to
travel.

But what had the commander of that other ship said? *"If
I'd been a snake, I could've bit you! I was right on top of
you, and you didn't even know it."*

Geary grinned unpleasantly. "I think I know what the
Syndic military is planning, and why those civilians on the
fifth world are so scared. Let's make a few modifications
to this plan of mine."

THE fifth world, which Geary had now learned had been
given the poetic name Sutrah Five in typical Syndicate
Worlds bureaucratic style, lay only thirty minutes away
now at the Alliance fleet's current velocity. Under his original plan, the fleet would have begun braking and swinging to port now, setting up a pass over the planet and
inevitably crossing through the space where the moons of
Sutrah were orbiting.

He glanced at the five moons again. They orbited in a
cluster, only a few tens of thousands of kilometers from
each other. Once upon a time they'd probably been a single large chunk of matter, but at some point tidal stresses
from the fifth planet, or perhaps the near passage of some
other large object, had torn that single moon into the five
fragments.

Geary tapped his communications controls. "Captain
Tulev, are your ships ready?"

"Standing by," Tulev reported, his voice betraying no
excitement.

"You may fire when ready," Geary ordered.

"Understood. Firing projectiles now."

On Geary's display, large objects detached themselves
from the bulks of Tulev's ships, hurled forward by propulsion and guidance packs that boosted their speed a little
higher than the nearly .1 light speed of the fleet.

Co-President Rione, occupying the observer's seat on

the bridge of the *Dauntless*, stared at Geary. "We're firing? At what?"

"Those moons," Geary advised. He noticed Captain Desjani trying to hide a smile at Rione's surprise.

"The moons of the fifth world?" Co-President Rione's voice expressed skeptical curiosity. "Do you have some particular dislike of moons, Captain Geary?"

"Not usually." Geary got a perverse satisfaction out of knowing that Rione's spies in his fleet hadn't heard about this operation.

She waited, then finally unbent enough to ask more. "Why are you launching an attack on those moons?"

"Because I think they're weapons." Geary tapped some controls, bringing up magnified images of the moons, their surfaces resembling those of asteroids. "See this? Signs that excavation activity was conducted. Well-concealed, so we had to look for it to find it, but there it is."

"On a small, airless moon?" Rione asked. "How can you tell it's recent?"

"We can't from here. But all five moons show the same signs."

"I see." Whatever else could be said about Rione, she thought quickly. "What do you think was buried inside these moons, Captain Geary?"

"Firecrackers, Madam Co-President. Really big firecrackers." The images representing the massive kinetic energy projectiles, or 'big rocks' in Marine terminology, were steadily pulling away from Tulev's ships on a curving trajectory aimed at the moons. Despite the incredible amount of damage they could inflict, such weapons couldn't usually be used because they were too easily dodged by anything able to maneuver. But the moons were on fixed orbits, following the same track around the fifth world that they'd coursed for innumerable years. It was strange to think that after today those moons would orbit that world no more.

Geary activated the fleet command circuit. "All units, execute preplanned maneuver Sigma at time four five."

The time scrolled down, and every ship in the fleet turned itself, using their propulsion systems to reduce their velocity and simultaneously altering course to starboard to pass Sutrah Five on the side away from where the moons of that world had their dates with the projectiles launched by the Alliance fleet. Geary watched and waited, taking pleasure in the intricate ballet, all of those ships moving in unison against the darkness of space. Even the lumbering and partially misnamed fast fleet auxiliaries like *Titan* and *Witch* moved with what seemed unusual nimbleness.

Twenty minutes later, as the decelerating Alliance fleet was still approaching Sutrah Five, the huge solid metal projectiles launched by Tulev's ships slammed at a speed of just over thirty thousand kilometers per second almost simultaneously into the five moons of Sutrah.

Even the smallest moon was massive by human standards, but the amount of kinetic energy involved in each collision was enough to stagger a planet. Geary's view of the moons was obscured as the *Dauntless*'s sensors automatically blocked the intense flashes of visible light from the collisions, then by a rapidly growing ball of dust and fragments, some large and some small, flying outward from the points of impact.

Geary waited, knowing Desjani had already passed orders to her watch-standers on what to look for. It didn't take long for the first report. "Spectroscopic analysis shows unusual quantities of radioactive material and traces of gases consistent with very large nuclear detonation devices."

"You guessed right," Desjani noted, her eyes showing the complete trust in him that bothered Geary. He didn't like seeing it in her any more than he liked seeing it in so many others in this fleet, because of his certainty that sooner or later he would fail that trust. They believed he was perfect, and he knew otherwise.

"Explain, please?" Rione asked in a crisp voice. "Why would the Syndics have placed large nuclear weapons inside those moons? Some of those large fragments will impact on Sutrah Five. "

"That was a risk the Syndics were willing to take and one that I judged I had to take," Geary advised heavily. "Given the unpopulated nature of much of the world, the odds of anything being hit are tiny. You see, Madam Co-President, the Syndics knew we'd have to do two things to liberate the prisoners on that planet. We'd have to go close to the planet, and we'd have to get the fleet into a tight formation so our shuttles wouldn't have to fly any longer distances than necessary to handle picking up and distributing the people from the labor camp."

He pointed to the spreading cloud of debris. "When we were close to those moons, or rather to where those moons used to be, they'd have set off those big nuclear explosives inside them, blowing them into dense interlocking fields of heavy fragments. We could have lost a good number of ships to that, even big warships that happened to be too close."

Rione's eyes glinted with anger. "No wonder the civilians I spoke with were frightened."

"I doubt the planetary leaders knew exactly what was going to happen," Geary suggested. "But they surely knew the Syndic leaders in the system were going to do something."

"Something that would've subjected them to the same risk of bombardment by fragments of the moons and a retaliatory barrage by the fleet." Rione's face was grim. "Captain Geary, I know that under the laws of war you're now justified in conducting an orbital bombardment of installations and cities on Sutrah Five, but I ask you to show some mercy to the civilian pawns living on that world."

Geary could almost see the disdain on Desjani's face at the suggestion, but he nodded. "We will retaliate, Madam Co-President, but I won't slaughter helpless civilians. Please recontact the civil authorities on Sutrah Five and tell them to immediately evacuate all industrial, mining, and transportation centers. Any space facility or field is also to be evacuated. Tell them I won't decide how much to destroy, including more than what's on that list, until I see what sort of greeting our Marines encounter at the labor camp." He let his anger show now, anger at the thought of what might have happened. "Make sure they understand that if there's any more problems at all, there will be hell to pay, and they'll be the ones receiving the bill."

Rione nodded, smiling thinly. "Very well, Captain Geary. I will ensure your orders to them are understood and that they know their lives hang on the thread of their cooperation with us."

Desjani shifted as if uncomfortable. "The military base, too, right, Captain Geary?"

Geary checked, seeing that the part of the planet holding the base was within line of sight of the fleet right now. "I assume it's already been evacuated?"

Desjani frowned and checked, then frowned a little more. "No. A partial evacuation seems under way."

"Partial?"

"Yes. There's some columns of ground vehicles, but most of the occupants appear to be family members. Few uniforms noted." Desjani quirked an eyebrow at Geary. "It looks like the Syndic troops are planning on crewing their positions to the end." She didn't seem bothered by the idea.

Geary was. He rubbed his chin, thinking. "Ground vehicles. Nothing else has been spotted leaving?"

"Let me see." This time both of Desjani's eyebrows went up. "Ah, yes. Several air vehicles departed over half an hour ago, headed toward the nearest mountain range. The system has maintained a track on them."

"The top commanders, headed for a buried command bunker to ride out our retaliation in safety and comfort," Geary stated.

Desjani nodded.

"I want to find that bunker."

She grinned.

"I assume we've got kinetic rounds for orbital bombardment that can penetrate a fair distance into solid rock?"

"Yes, we do, sir," Desjani replied with positive glee. Geary had telegraphed a desire to blow away Syndics, and her world was a happy one.

A swarm of shuttles had left the Alliance fleet, descending on Sutrah Five like a cloud of huge insects falling on their prey. Overhead, the ships of the Alliance fleet were concentrated into a tight formation that nonetheless covered a large sector of space above the planet. Geary knew that the inhabitants of Sutrah Five were looking up right now in fear, knowing that his fleet could rain death upon them and render the entire planet uninhabitable in very short order.

The landing force virtual display floated next to Geary's seat, with the ranks of images from Marine officers presented like trading cards for his selection. He could, with the movement of a finger, talk directly to any of the Marines and see through their eyes, thanks to helmet-mounted sensors. But the only officer he called up was Colonel Carabali, not wanting to jump the chain of command, even though the command and control system made that entirely too easy.

"The reconnaissance shuttles have detected no signs of nuclear or other weapons of mass destruction at the labor camp site," Carabali reported. "We'll conduct another sweep, then land the recon teams."

"Have you confirmed Alliance prisoners are present in predicted numbers?"

"Looks like it, sir." Carabali grinned. "From up here they seem pretty happy."

Geary sat back, smiling himself. He'd encountered a lot of situations since being rescued that he'd never expected, and most of those had been unpleasant. Duty had been a heavy burden. But now there were thousands of people who'd never expected liberation, viewing the shuttles of this fleet overhead, people who might've already spent decades as prisoners with no hope of release. This fleet, *his* fleet, was going to rescue them. It felt good.

If only the Syndics didn't try anything else. It was still possible for thousands on the verge of being freed to die in that camp.

"Recon shuttles down," Carabali reported, echoing the information on Geary's own display, which he'd focused on the camp. "Teams deploying."

Geary gave in to temptation, calling up one of the recon team officers. A window opened with a view from the officer's helmet, showing bare dirt and battered structures. The sky was a washed-out pale blue verging on gray, its appearance as cold and drab as life must have been in that labor camp. No Syndic guards were visible, but the Alliance prisoners had formed up into ranks, their officers in front, waiting with anxious and dazed faces as the Marines dashed past them, searching for any signs of danger.

The Marine Geary was monitoring stopped in front of one formation of prisoners, facing the woman standing before them. "Are there any concealed weapons you know of? Any unusual activity?" the Marine demanded.

The woman, well past middle age, thin, her skin almost leathery from long exposure to the environment of Sutrah Five with inadequate protection and probably a prisoner for most of her life, spoke with careful precision. "No, Lieutenant. We were confined to quarters and couldn't observe outside activity last night, but we heard the guards leave in a hurry before dawn. We've searched every part of the camp and found no weapons. The camp data office is in that building." She pointed.

The Marine paused for a moment to salute. "Thank you, Commander."

Geary pulled his attention away from the view, forcing himself to close the window showing that particular Marine's point of view. He had a duty to keep his eye on everything going on around the fleet.

"It looks quiet," Desjani remarked. "The only activity we can detect on the planet are the columns of evacuees heading away from target sites. There's a moon fragment coming in about three hundred klicks west of the labor camp," she added, pointing to the display. "It'll mess up everything around the impact site, but the camp will just hear a distant bang and feel a breeze."

Geary read the data for the impact. "And maybe feel the ground tremor. Every time we've thought things looked quiet in this system it's just meant the Syndics were planning something else nasty. What could we be missing this time?"

Desjani pursed her lips in thought. "The Marines are checking the prisoners for exposure to delayed-effect biological agents. The prisoners should've spotted anything buried in the camp. The only Syndic ships in the system besides a few cargo ships are the three sets of HuKs we've been tracking since arrival, none of which are within a light-hour of us. I wouldn't put it past them to blow the planet to hell in hopes of getting more of us, but there's no weapon that could do that."

A window popped up before Geary, and Colonel Carabali's image saluted. "I'm sending in the main landing force, Captain Geary. No threats detected." On his display, Geary could see the bulk of the shuttles coming in to land, many just outside the boundaries of the camp to find sufficient room. Marines spilled out, looking reassuringly efficient and deadly in their battle armor.

Yet Geary found the sight worrisome. Practically every Marine in the fleet was down there. If something happened to them, he'd have lost a very important combat capability, as well as the most reliably obedient component of his fleet. A moment later he mentally lashed himself for thinking of the losses in those terms instead of as the deaths of a lot of good men and women.

Co-President Rione seemed to share Geary's disquiet. "This seems too easy after all the other mischief the Syndics have pulled in this system."

Geary nodded. "But there's nothing in the camp. The prisoners said they'd searched it, and they'd know if there was anything unusual."

Colonel Carabali reported in again. "We've taken the data building and are checking the files now. All prisoners had implants linked to a tracking system and a virtual wall around the camp to keep them from going anywhere they weren't allowed. We're in the process of deactivating the implants and the virtual wall."

"Good." Geary's eyes went back to the display. "Once the virtual wall is down, the prisoners will be able to leave the camp boundaries to board those shuttles," he remarked to Desjani.

"Damn!"

Geary spun in his seat, shocked by the sudden and un-characteristic outburst from Rione. She was pointing at the displays. "*Outside* the camp, Captain Geary. You're all looking at threats inside the camp, but most of your shut-tles are grounded outside the camp!"

Geary felt a hard lump in his gut as he realized what Rione was saying. He punched the controls to call Carabali. "Outside the camp perimeter, Colonel! The pris-oners couldn't go there, which means they couldn't search there. We've focused our own search on the camp itself. But a lot of the shuttles are outside the camp, and the pris-oners will be brought to them there."

Carabali gritted her teeth. "Understood." Geary watched the Marine command and control net light up as orders flew from Colonel Carabali to the rest of the Marines. Units headed out to secure a wide perimeter started backtracking and spreading into search patterns, while some of those inside the camp headed out to search closer in.

"We still should've detected nukes," Desjani stated an-grily.

"Yeah," Geary agreed. "But something else could've been buried there."

"We've got delayed action mines," Carabali reported, her voice cool. "A mix of lofting fragmentation and chem-icals. They're older models but still hard enough to spot that we wouldn't have seen them if we hadn't done a special sweep of that area. My mine experts say they're probably set to blow once they detect enough human presence around them. We're using high-energy pulses to fry the triggering mechanisms and render them harmless."

"What about even farther out?" Geary asked.

"We're sweeping now." A trace of anger entered the calm professionalism of Carabali's tone. "I'll provide a full report of my failure to anticipate and identify the threat so you can take whatever disciplinary action you deem appropriate, sir."

Geary couldn't suppress a sigh, catching a glimpse as he did so of the now-impassive face of Co-President Rione. "Thank you, Colonel, but we missed it, too, and share in any blame. You can thank Co-President Rione for figuring it out in time."

Carabali's voice held a tinge of self-mocking humor this time. "Please pass my respects and thanks to the co-president, sir."

Geary turned to look at Rione. "Did you hear that?"

Rione inclined her head in acknowledgment. "I'm used to examining the possible meanings of words. There are times even the devious mind of a politician can be useful, aren't there, Captain Geary?"

"There are indeed," Geary agreed. He saw Captain Desjani grinning, too, and realized Desjani's opinion of Rione, or at least her opinion of Rione's value, had just increased dramatically.

"We have a match on prisoner numbers and Syndic data," Carabali announced. "My troops are screening the former prisoners now and will begin loading as shuttle areas are reported clear."

Geary tapped a control, bringing up a projection of the entire surface of Sutrah Five. Target identifications were plastered across the map. Geary zoomed the display in on the biggest cluster, the view automatically changing to actual imagery of the site. The capital of the planet obviously had lost considerable population in recent decades. Most of the industrial sites targeted were cold, shut down long ago. The spaceport was shabby and decrepit. As Geary checked other targets, it became clear why the Syndics had risked a retaliatory bombardment of this planet. The place was what the Syndicate Worlds leaders would no doubt call "excess inventory," with no industrial, resource, or military value to speak of. *Only about a hundred thousand human beings still trying to scratch a living out of the place.* "Captain Desjani, do we have target data on Sutrah Four?"

Desjani didn't quite suppress a fierce grin as she fed the data to Geary. Geary studied it, noting that Sutrah Four seemed to be doing a lot better than its sister world in this system. *Okay, we can't let the Syndics think this is something they can get away with. But I don't want to slaughter civilians, which may be what the Syndics are hoping for, since that'd be great propaganda.* Geary tagged the big spaceports on Sutrah Four, the big military base on that world, the center of the government complex in the capital, and for good measure all of the orbiting facilities. Switching back to the display for Sutrah Five, he tagged the biggest spaceport and the still-working industrial areas.

Then Geary paused, looking at the military base. Zooming in on the image, he saw intelligence assessments scrolling next to it. The convoys of civilians were still heading away, but most of the military seemed to still be at their stations. *Where's those so-called leaders?* Pulling the scale out, Geary spotted the targeting information. Optics designed to gain detailed information across billions of kilometers hadn't had any trouble spotting the entrance to the command bunker where the high command had taken shelter. Geary felt himself smiling grimly as he tagged that location for a kinetic round designed to penetrate deeply on impact.

By the time he was done deciding the fate of two worlds, the first shuttles were lifting off from Sutrah Five, and the Alliance fleet was looping back through the space where the moons of Sutrah Five had once been. Many of the smaller pieces of debris from the destruction had been snagged by the gravity of Sutrah Five and might someday form a tenuous ring around the planet.

"Captain Geary," Colonel Carabali reported, "all personnel are loaded. The last shuttles should be off the surface by time one six."

"Understood, Colonel, thank you." Geary turned and sent the targeting commands to the combat system, which evaluated the targets, the weapons available on every ship, and launch angles before spitting back two seconds later a detailed plan. Geary skimmed it, checking how much his retaliation would draw down the fleet's supply of kinetic projectiles and seeing that he'd have plenty left, even if *Titan* and her sisters weren't able to manufacture new ones. He paused on the estimated ground casualties section. "I need to send a message to every Syndic in the system."

Desjani nodded, gesturing to the communications officer, who rapidly set up the circuit, then gave her a thumbs-up back. "You're ready, sir."

Geary composed himself, checking to make sure the last Alliance shuttles had lifted before transmitting. "People of the Sutrah Star System, this is Captain John Geary, commanding officer of the Alliance fleet transiting your system. You've been betrayed by your leaders. Their sneak attacks on this fleet and on the forces liberating Alliance prisoners of war grant us the right to conduct retaliatory bombardments of your worlds." He paused to let that sink in. "In exchange for the possibility of harming a few of our ships, your leaders placed your homes and your lives in our hands. Fortunately for you, the Alliance fleet does not war on civilians." Not anymore, anyway. Not while Geary was in command. Hopefully his "old-fashioned" attitudes would someday wear off on the other officers.

"We will launch retaliation strikes at targets of our choosing on Sutrah Five and Sutrah Four. A list of targets in or near civilian areas will follow this message so evacuation can proceed before impacts. We aren't required to provide that list, but our war is with your leaders.

Remember that we could've wiped all life from this system and been justified by the laws of war. We choose not to do so. The Alliance is not your enemy. Your own leaders are your enemies.

"To the honor of our ancestors," Geary recited. He'd been told the old form for ending a broadcast of this type was rarely used anymore, but clung to it. He still believed in it, and somehow it helped anchor him in this future in which honor had taken on sometimes alien meanings. "This is Captain John Geary, commanding officer of the Alliance fleet. End transmission."

Rione spoke from behind him. "Thank you, Captain Geary, for acting to minimize the suffering of the populations of these worlds."

He looked back at her and nodded. "You're welcome. But it's what I would've done anyway. It's what honor demands."

"The honor of our ancestors," Rione replied, no trace of irony in her answer.

Captain Desjani stood up. "The shuttles from *Dauntless* will be docking soon. I should be at the shuttle dock to greet our new arrivals."

"I should, too," Geary agreed, standing as well and trying to conceal his reluctance. It really was his duty to greet the newly liberated Alliance personnel, even though he'd much rather have gone to his stateroom to avoid the public spectacle.

"May I accompany you?" Rione asked them both.

"Of course," Desjani replied, seeming startled by the request. Geary realized she probably had been surprised, since Rione had every right to demand to go along with them and had instead asked permission. He wondered whether the request reflected political calculation to win Desjani over or sincere deference to the captain of a ship. Geary found himself hoping it was the latter.

The three of them walked to the shuttle dock, Geary and Desjani exchanging greetings with every crew member of *Dauntless* they passed, Geary getting real satisfaction out

of the number of personnel who saluted him. His campaign
to return saluting as routine seemed to be working.

"Does it please you to be saluted?" Rione asked in a
noncommittal voice. "Salutes seem much more common
now."

Geary shook his head. "I don't need it for my ego, if
that's what you're asking. It's what saluting implies,
Madam Co-President, a level of discipline that I think ben-
efits this fleet." He didn't add outwardly that he thought
the fleet desperately needed such discipline if it was to
hold together and continue to defeat Syndic attempts to destroy it. The leap from a salute to getting this fleet home
safely seemed a huge one, but Geary did believe the con-
nection existed.

It wasn't until they reached the shuttle dock that Geary
realized this was his first visit to it since he'd been sum-
moned to the compartment by the doomed Admiral Bloch
as that officer left to negotiate with the Syndics. He'd vis-
ited just about every place on the *Dauntless*, so he must've
subconsciously avoided this location. Geary tried to remember how he'd felt then, the ice filling him emotionally
and mentally, and felt relief that he'd managed to overcome much of that under the pressure of being in command. Or perhaps in spite of the pressure of being in
command. But he could stand here now and not be haunted
by the ghost of Admiral Bloch pleading for Geary to save
what was left of the fleet.

He glanced at Captain Desjani, standing waiting beside
him for the shuttles to disembark their passengers.
Normally somber with the pressures of command or showing joy only at the destruction of Syndic ships, she looked
different now. Anticipation of seeing the liberated prisoners had brought an unusual attitude of simple happiness to
her. "Tanya?" Desjani gave him a surprised look. Geary
rarely used her first name. "I just wanted to tell you that
I'm glad *Dauntless* is my flagship. She's a great ship, and
you're a great commanding officer. Your ability and support have meant a great deal to me."

Desjani actually flushed with embarrassment. "Thank you, Captain Geary. As you know, I've been very glad for your presence ever since we found you."

He nodded with a small, self-mocking smile. Desjani was among those who firmly believed he'd been sent to the fleet by the living stars to save the Alliance in its hour of greatest need. Geary didn't think he would ever be comfortable with that level of confidence or belief in him. For that matter, he shared Victoria Rione's fear that if he ever did start to be comfortable with such hero worship, then he'd be well on his way to turning into a greater danger to this fleet than the Syndics.

As if reading Geary's thoughts, Co-President Rione spoke politely. "We are indeed fortunate to have Captain Geary in command."

The shuttles from *Dauntless* swung into the docking bay like huge, ungainly living creatures. No wonder current fleet slang for the shuttles was "birds." The outer hangar doors sealed, the inner doors opened, and after a moment the ramps of the shuttles dropped.

The Marines assigned to *Dauntless* disembarked first, moving quickly to take up formation and present arms in a sign of respect. Then the group of newly liberated prisoners who had been designated for *Dauntless* began leaving the shuttles, looking around as if uncertain this was really happening, as if they expected to wake up any moment and find themselves still doomed to lifelong imprisonment on a miserable Syndic world far from any possible hope of rescue. All of them were thin, only a few still wore intact uniforms, most having to make do with what looked like cast-off civilian clothing.

Captain Desjani was speaking into her portable communications unit. "All hands on *Dauntless*, the Alliance personnel we liberated will need uniforms. I encourage everyone to contribute whatever they can spare." She looked at Geary. "We'll get them properly outfitted, sir."

"I'm sure they'll appreciate that," Geary agreed, imag-

ining that the exact same arrangement was playing out
through the entire fleet right now.

Geary heard a gasp of surprise from Captain Desjani as
the former prisoners filed past. "Casell?"

A man with tarnished lieutenant's bars pinned to a
ragged jacket turned at the name, his eyes fixing on
Desjani. "Tanya?" A moment later the two were embrac-
ing. "I can't believe it! The fleet shows up here, and you're
with it!"

"I thought you'd died at Quintarra," Desjani exclaimed.
To Geary's shock, the iron-willed captain of the *Dauntless*
seemed to be blinking away tears.

"No," Casell denied. "Half the crew survived, but we all
got picked up by the Syndics." His eyes finally focused on
Desjani's uniform, his jaw fell, and he stepped back.
"Captain? You're a captain?"

Desjani grinned. "There were a lot of battle promotions.
This is my ship." She turned to Geary. "Sir, this is an old
friend of mine, Lieutenant Casell Riva."

Geary smiled in greeting, extending his hand. After all
the too-youthful senior officers Geary had seen, the fruit of
hideous losses in battle after battle that had forced the fleet
to promote quickly, it was odd to meet an older junior officer. But there were no promotions in labor camps. "It's a
pleasure, Lieutenant. Good to have you aboard. I'm
Captain John Geary, fleet commander."

Lieutenant Riva, still surprised by the realization of his
old friend's current rank, automatically shook Geary's
hand for a moment before Geary's words apparently penetrated. "D-did you say Captain *John* Geary, sir?"

Desjani smiled proudly, her face glowing. "Captain
John 'Black Jack' Geary. He's alive, Casell. He's our commander. He's bringing this fleet home."

Riva's face took on the look Geary had come to dread,
a mixture of awe, disbelief, and wonder. "Of course," Riva
breathed. "One of the Marines said Captain Geary had
brought the fleet here, and we thought he was speaking
symbolically. But it's true." His face flared with enthusi-

asm. "The Syndics are doomed. Tanya—I mean, Captain Desjani, do you know who was senior officer in the camp? Captain Falco."

Desjani stared at her old friend. "Fighting Falco? He's alive, too?"

"Yes! And with him and Black Jack—" Lieutenant Riva gulped. "I mean, Captain Geary, this fleet will be unbeatable!"

Geary nodded, keeping his polite smile fixed. From what he'd seen of the fleet he'd inherited, any officer with the nickname "Fighting" probably represented everything Geary had been trying to change. But maybe not. He couldn't prejudge a man obviously held in high regard.

A tall, thin man paused dramatically at the top of a shuttle ramp, surveying the scene, then came marching over, his expression demanding. He wore fleet captain's insignia pinned to the collar of a coat that was in pretty good shape compared to what the other prisoners were wearing. People turned to watch, something about the man's presence exerting a pull on attention like a magnet attracting iron. Geary couldn't help thinking of Rione's disdain for "heroes" who led fleets to their doom. This man could do that, Geary thought.

The man halted before Geary and gave him a confident, comradely smile. "I need to see the fleet commander."

Geary couldn't help noticing that the statement hadn't been a request. "I'm the fleet commander."

"A captain!" The man looked around, frowning, as if searching for a concealed admiral. "You must have suffered some serious losses."

"I'm afraid we did," Geary agreed.

The man sighed and looked regretful in a way that somehow implied that if he had been in command that wouldn't have happened. He was, Geary realized, a master at projecting unspoken things that those around would believe had actually been said. "Very well. No rest for the weary, eh?" he asked Geary with another look that implied shared understanding. "But duty is a harsh mistress that cannot be ignored by those with honor. I'll be assuming command, then."

Geary managed to keep his reaction limited to raised eyebrows. "Excuse me?"

The man whom Geary assumed had to be Fighting Falco gave him a look that combined surprise at the question with reassurance. "I think I'm safe in concluding that I'm the senior officer present now by virtue of date of rank. That makes it my duty and responsibility to assume command."

Geary nodded in a way that he hoped acknowledged the man's words without conveying agreement. "The situation may not be what you think it is, Captain . . . ?" he asked, even though he'd already guessed.

That earned him a full-scale frown. A shot aimed at the man's ego apparently had no trouble penetrating the shields of companionable authority he liked to carry. "You should recognize me."

Lieutenant Riva, apparently oblivious to the tension, spoke proudly. "This is Captain Falco, sir."

"Captain Francesco Falco," the man advised. "I assume you recognize the name?"

"Actually I heard it for the first time a few moments ago." Geary didn't know why he had said that, but the renewed frown his words conjured on Falco's face was worth any fallout from it. "Pleased to meet you," Geary added, trying to keep his tone neutral.

"From your age," Falco stated, his expression stern now, "it's obvious that I'm senior in date of rank." He had clearly decided to set Geary straight on who was in charge. "Now, if you'll show me to my stateroom, I'm sure there's a lot to do. Set up a fleet conference as soon as possible." He waited, frowning a third time as Geary stared back with no apparent emotion and no sign of moving. Geary had the clear impression that Falco wasn't used to having to repeat orders. "Who are *you*, Captain?"

Desjani, who from her attitude had noticed the tension, spoke carefully. "Captain Falco, this is Captain Geary."

"Geary? Some relation to the hero, I suppose." Falco had a chiding expression now, like a father dealing with a recalcitrant child. "We all remain in debt to the example given us by Black Jack Geary, but that doesn't mean—"

"No," Geary interrupted. "I'm afraid you're mistaken." Falco frowned deeper this time. He seemed to frown a lot, at least whenever things weren't happening exactly as he wished, and didn't seem used to being interrupted, either. "I'm not related. My name is John Geary."

Falco's expression shifted, locking back into the mode of a comrade who happened to be in charge. His eyes went to Desjani, who nodded. "Captain Geary did not die at Grendel a century ago," she advised as if she were reciting a report. "This fleet found his survival pod on the verge of failing, and managed to revive him."

"Black Jack Geary?" Falco seemed rattled by the information, his carefully tailored expression falling apart into confusion.

Geary nodded. "My date of rank is, in fact, a bit earlier than yours," Geary advised Falco dryly. "Nearly a century earlier, in fact. I thank you for your willingness to serve as the Alliance requires." That was a stock phrase from Geary's time, usually heard just before a particularly unpleasant assignment was handed out. Now it seemed a good way to rebuff Falco in a manner that appeared respectful. "As senior officer present, and as the officer assigned command by Admiral Bloch prior to his death, I will remain in command of this fleet." Part of him was shocked. How many times had Geary wished he could pass command of this fleet to someone else? But not to this man. It wasn't just because Falco had challenged his authority, Geary assured himself. Falco felt like someone who devoted more time to how he appeared to be doing than to actually doing well.

Geary could see Rione watching him, doubtless remembering the many times that Geary had sworn he would turn over command to someone else as soon as he could. But he knew what Rione thought of "heroes." Surely she wouldn't expect him to place the fate of this fleet in the hands of someone such as Falco seemed to be.

The news of who he was dealing with seemed to have knocked Captain Falco totally off balance. He was looking around as if confused. Geary gestured toward Desjani. "This is the commanding officer of *Dauntless*, Captain Tanya Desjani."

Falco nodded quickly, his eyes flicking over to Desjani. Instantly, as if he had needed something to focus him again, Falco's expression shifted back to that of someone in command who was nonetheless a comrade. "It's always a pleasure to meet a brave officer of the Alliance fleet. It's obvious that you run a tight ship, Captain Desjani."

Desjani nodded back politely. "Thank you, Captain Falco."

Geary pointed to Rione. "And Victoria Rione, co-president of the Callas Republic and a member of the Alliance senate."

This time Falco turned, nodding slowly and politely to acknowledge the introduction. Rione, her own face rigidly formal, nodded back. Geary could tell from the glint in her eyes that Rione didn't like Falco at all and wondered what she knew of him. It struck him that Falco had offered a fellow officer a greeting full of compliments, false compliments surely, since Falco had no basis yet for declaring Desjani brave and her ship tight, but acted noticeably cooler toward a senator. He was treating Rione like a rival, Geary realized. Someone who had to be dealt with rather than collected as an admiring subordinate.

Desjani, not being a fool, had apparently noticed as well. Geary could see the tightening around her eyes that indicated the commanding officer of the *Dauntless* wasn't happy at the assumption that she could be won over by some flattery. For her part, Rione gave Falco a greeting noticeable for its lack of warmth. "Your reputation precedes you, Captain Falco."

Geary was wondering exactly what that meant when out of the corner of his eye he noticed the other newly liberated Alliance prisoners. A slow ripple effect was running through them, with group after group turning to stare at him with those same expressions of hope and wonder that Lieutenant Riva had displayed. Geary, trying not to react negatively, noticed that Captain Falco had found something else to frown about. *He doesn't like them looking at me like that. But not for whatever reasons Rione is worried. No, if I judge Captain Fighting Falco properly, he's jealous.*

Great. As if I didn't have enough problems. "Captain Falco, Lieutenant Riva," Geary stated politely, "I need to attend to some business. Captain Desjani's crew will see to your needs, I know."

Falco, his carefully cultivated expressions crumbling in the face of new developments, seemed to have fallen back on an inexhaustible supply of frowns. "Business?"

"A conference," Rione interceded smoothly. "Captain Geary and I must go. On behalf of the Alliance government," she continued, speaking in a voice that carried through the compartment, "I welcome you all back to the fleet."

A ragged cheer went up from the former prisoners as Rione led Geary out of the shuttle bay. Geary imagined he could feel Falco's gaze boring into his back as they left, somehow certain that Falco saw him as a greater problem than he did Rione. But he didn't want to talk about Falco anywhere they could be overheard, so he and Rione walked silently all the way to Geary's stateroom. Not until they were inside did Rione turn to him with a scowl. "That man is a danger."

"I thought I was a danger," Geary noted sourly, flopping down into a seat.

"You are, because you're intelligent. Captain Falco is a different kind of danger."

"Needless to say, I don't know anything about him. Are you saying he's stupid?"

Rione made a dismissive gesture. "No. The long-standing thorn in your side Captain Numos is stupid. In fact, Numos is so dense that I'm surprised he doesn't have his own event horizon. But Captain Falco is smart enough in his own way."

Geary managed not to laugh at the all-too-accurate assessment of Numos. "Did you know Falco before he was captured?"

"Do you think I'm that old?" Rione asked, arching her eyebrows. "Captain Falco was captured about twenty years ago. I've been told of him by older politicians I've met since I became a member of the senate. Captain Falco was, at the time he was captured, a very ambitious and charismatic officer who managed to make bloodbaths look like grand victories. He would also make declarations that defeating the Syndics could only be done if we were willing to abandon the alleged inefficiencies of our democratic system in favor of a temporary autocratic government like that of the Syndics."

No wonder Falco hadn't tried to cultivate Rione. Even if he hadn't read her attitude toward him and known that wouldn't work, Falco probably saw elected politicians as rivals for power. Geary exhaled a gust of humorless laughter. "I assume that means an autocratic government in which Captain Falco would no doubt play a leading role. Why didn't the government sack him for saying that kind of thing?"

Rione sighed. "The Alliance was just as desperate for heroes then as now, and Captain Falco managed to cultivate enough senators to protect him. He also had substantial public popularity. You saw him in there. Falco could charm the scales off of a snake. The governing council was afraid of the public outcry that would follow sacking Falco. But eventually his luck ran out and he was lost along with far too many of our ships. While the fleet mourned his loss for reasons I've never understood, since he'd probably killed more Alliance sailors than he had Syndics, the Alliance government was not terribly saddened even though it publicly expressed sorrow."

"And now he's back." Geary shrugged. "I could see

some of why the fleet liked him. He's one of those people who can stick a knife in your back and leave you thinking he did you a favor."

"I said he was charismatic, didn't I?"

"Too damned charismatic for my peace of mind. Too bad I can't think up an excuse to return him to the Syndics."

"If I think of one, I'll let you know." Rione stared at the bulkhead, her thoughts elsewhere. "Captain Falco will contest your command of this fleet."

"He doesn't have a leg to stand on," Geary stated. "I'm senior to him by at least eighty years."

Rione smiled briefly. "Captain Falco did not take that well."

"I could tell. But at least it's the first time I got any joy out of it," Geary admitted.

"But Falco will try to wrest command of this fleet from you, Captain Geary, regardless of regulations. If you thought Captain Numos and his allies were a danger, that danger has now increased greatly."

"Thank you for your assessment." *Which unfortunately matches my own.* Rione seemed skeptical of his statement, so Geary tried to give her a sincere look. "Your counsel is very valuable. I mean that. I'm grateful for your presence in this fleet."

She gazed back at Geary for a while, her expression hard to read. "Thank you, Captain Geary."

After Rione had left, Geary took a while to call up the records of Captain Falco's battles. Looking at the replays of the battles in the combat simulator, it was far too apparent that Rione's assessment of the man had been accurate. The losses during Falco's so-called victories had been staggering, while there'd been more than one defeat due to simple errors. *Fighting Falco, huh? Funny how that fighting captain managed to survive so many battles where a lot of other Alliance officers didn't.*

There were speeches and news accounts on file, too, showing a much younger-looking Falco dazzling crowds with high-sounding rhetoric delivered with apparently absolute sincerity. Geary found himself wondering if he had misjudged the man, then paid closer attention to what was being said. Appalled, he heard exactly what Rione had described: Falco blaming lack of progress in the war on the government's policies and all but openly campaigning for the role of supreme leader. *I wonder what would have happened if the Syndics hadn't captured Falco. No wonder Co-President Rione was so worried about me when I took command. She thought I'd be like Falco. But fortunately for all concerned, I come from a time when fleet officers simply didn't do such things. It never occurred to me that someone would, let alone that they'd get away with it by appealing to the public.*

Twenty years. Desjani knew Falco only by reputation. She had seemed initially thrilled, but less happy once Falco had begun contesting command with Geary. Desjani's loyalty to Geary was apparently unshakable. Geary wondered how the rest of the fleet would regard Falco. Especially if he and Falco ended up openly butting heads over command of the fleet.

I don't want to be stuck with commanding this fleet, but I can't surrender that command to someone with Falco's record. He'd doom it to destruction and then issue a press release claiming it was a great victory. And if somehow he managed to get the fleet back to Alliance space, he would be the sort of danger to the Alliance government that Rione has worried about.

Unless Falco changed while he was in that labor camp. I have to give the man some benefit of the doubt until I find out how that experience affected him.

That reminded him of the need to deal with the current Syndic threat to the fleet rather than worrying about what Falco might do. With the fleet pulling away from Sutrah Five and heading for open space above the plane of the system where traps couldn't have been placed, there was no longer a possibility of an immediate threat. Even if a Syndic fleet appeared at one of the jump points, there would be close to a day to prepare for action. *But what about the longer term? What are the Syndics doing right now that could hurt this fleet at the next star and the next?*

Geary pulled up the display for this region of space and spent a long time studying it, mentally jumping the fleet from one star to possible destinations and then on again, always eventually running into the same ugly conclusion. He had been doing the same mental projections ever since the fleet arrived at Sutrah, and the answers hadn't changed, no matter how many variations he tried. Even without running simulations, his gut instincts told him that the Syndic net was closing on this fleet. The only way to avoid it was to do something so unpredictable the Syndics wouldn't regard it as worth considering. How could he find something like that which wasn't also suicidal?

His gaze kept coming back to one star. Sancere.

No, that's crazy.

Crazy enough that the Syndics won't believe I'd take the fleet there?

Maybe. I'm certain that as far as the Syndics know, it can't be done the way I want to do it. They're wrong. I know a way.

But how would I convince the fleet to follow me to Sancere?

THREE

THE hatch alert on Geary's stateroom chimed, startling Geary back into awareness of the here and now. He was surprised to see how long he'd spent thinking about the fleet's next steps. Bringing up the fleet display as well, Geary checked the position within Sutrah System. As planned, the fleet had left Sutrah Five and was now following a course that would allow it to head for either of the other two jump points in the system. Only an hour remained before the fleet would launch the kinetic retaliatory bombardment of the two inhabited worlds. There wasn't any rush. Neither the two planets nor the targets on their surfaces could go anywhere except along the predictable and fixed orbits that made them sitting ducks for bombardments. "Please enter," Geary called.

Captain Falco had managed to very quickly acquire a uniform adorned with all of the ribbons and awards to which he was apparently entitled. He'd also gotten his hair trimmed, but Geary couldn't help noticing how the dashing young officer whose pictures he'd seen in old reports had been aged considerably by not just twenty years of time but also the hardships of a Syndic labor camp. Falco gave Geary a friendly, confident smile as he entered the stateroom. Geary recognized that exact smile from some of the records he had reviewed. "I'm sure you'd like to discuss our options for future operations," Falco stated graciously. "My expertise and leaderships skills are at your disposal, of course."

Actually, the thought of discussing options with Falco hadn't even crossed his mind. *Especially since I don't think much of your expertise and don't trust your leadership skills.* But Geary nodded with outward politeness. "There'll be a fleet conference held soon."

"I meant with me," Falco noted. "In private. It's always best to map out a plan of action before the battle, eh? A good leader like you knows that, and I've heard plenty about your achievements in command of this fleet. But even the best commander needs input from those with the skills to support him, so I've taken the time to evaluate the fleet's position and work up a course of action."

The praise left Geary wary, wondering what Falco intended. "That was rather quick."

The understated sarcasm didn't seem to register on Captain Falco, who sat down and pointed at the regional display still visible. "Here's what we should do. The most direct course back to Alliance space is by proceeding to Vidha. From there—"

"Vidha has a Syndic hypernet gate," Geary interrupted. "Since it's an obvious objective for us and easily and quickly reinforced by the Syndics, it'll be heavily defended, and the jump points certainly will be mined."

Falco had one of his frowns visible again. Interrupting him seemed to trigger a frown almost automatically. But he recovered quickly, assuming the expression of a respectful coworker again. "This fleet can overcome any Syndic resistance. Aggressive action is always the best move," he lectured. "I don't need to tell a commander like *you* that. This fleet has the initiative right now, and we must retain it, as you know. *You* understand how important it is to keep the enemy reacting to *us*. Now, from Vidha—"

"We're not going to Vidha." Since Falco seemed unable to take hints, Geary laid it out bluntly, even as he felt some admiration for Falco's ability to make it sound like agreement with Falco's plan was just what a good commander like Geary would, of course, do.

That seemed to take a while to sink in. Unexpected developments appeared to throw off Falco in a way that surprised Geary. Was that an act, designed to cause opponents to underestimate him? But Geary hadn't noted any examples of that debating tactic in the old records he had reviewed.

Eventually Captain Falco shook his head. "I understand there will be Syndic forces awaiting us at Vidha. Like us, the Syndics know that Vidha is the only reasonable objective."

The repeated use of "us" was a nice touch, Geary had to admit.

"Not only because it takes us back toward Alliance space, but because it offers an opportunity to engage and destroy the Syndics surely awaiting us at Vidha."

"I consider that an opportunity to stick our heads into a nest of scorpions," Geary observed. "Accepting battle at the time and place we choose is our best option. Going to Vidha would mean fighting a battle at the time and place of the Syndics' choosing. The best we could possibly hope for at Vidha is to take horrific losses, leaving any survivors easy prey in the next Syndic system we fled to."

Falco frowned, taking a noticeable pause to absorb Geary's statement. "I see. You're looking at it in terms of material factors." Falco made it sound like that was misguided, if not completely unreasonable.

"Material factors?" Geary questioned. "You mean like numbers and types of combatants? Minefields emplaced? Fixed defenses operational and ready to assist mobile forces?"

"Exactly," Falco beamed, projecting admiration for

Geary's insight. "Those are purely secondary issues. You *know* that! You're Black Jack Geary! The moral is to the material as three is to one! With us in command—" Falco hesitated and smiled good-naturedly. "With you in command and myself along, this fleet has overwhelming moral superiority. The Syndics will flee in confusion, and we'll have no trouble crushing them."

Geary wondered if he was avoiding showing how appalled he was. Discounting firepower in favor of "moral" factors? Such things counted, surely, but nothing Geary had seen since assuming command had led him to conclude that the Syndics were so poorly trained, motivated, and led that such nonmaterial factors could carry the day even if the odds were close to equal. "Captain Falco, this fleet fought a substantial Syndic force at Kaliban. They didn't fight well, but they fought."

"I've seen the records of that battle," Falco noted. "You're to be congratulated for your efforts. But look at how few of our ships were lost! The Syndics didn't fight well, because they were overwhelmed by our moral force!"

"They were overwhelmed by our superiority in numbers and our effective use of ancient tactics, which they weren't prepared to deal with," Geary corrected. "What I've seen so far is that the Syndics will fight even when faced with overwhelming odds, even when common sense would dictate avoiding provoking a fleet able to wipe out entire planets."

"Nobody ever said the Syndics were smart," Falco advised with another smile. "Our goal is to engage and destroy the Syndic fleet, so if they rush to their doom, so much the better."

"*My* goal is to get as much of this fleet as possible home to Alliance space," Geary stated. He wondered very briefly if he should tell Falco about the Syndic hypernet key onboard *Dauntless* and immediately dismissed the idea. Based on what he'd heard and seen so far, he simply didn't trust Falco enough to share that critical information. "Hopefully, we'll do considerable damage to the Syndic war effort on the way, but the overriding objective is getting the fleet home."

Falco stared at Geary, seeming genuinely shocked this time. "You can't refuse the opportunity for battle!"

Geary stood up and walked slowly around the stateroom, not looking at the other captain. "Why not?"

"It's . . . this is the Alliance fleet!"

"Exactly." Geary gave Falco a flat look. "And I have no intention of letting it be destroyed to no purpose. That would serve the goals of the Syndics. As I stated before, to the maximum extent possible, I'll fight when and where I want to fight."

"You're supposed to be Black Jack Geary!"

"I am John Geary, and I will not waste the ships of this fleet or the lives of its crews."

Falco's face lost its shock and settled into stubborn lines. "Unbelievable. When the fleet ship commanders vote on—"

"There are no votes for courses of action in my fleet, Captain Falco."

That seemed to startle Falco more than anything else Geary had yet said. Geary was increasingly convinced that, like the late Admiral Bloch, Falco's skills had been centered on political gamesmanship to control the outcomes of such votes rather than on military tactics or strategy. Falco's greatest victories had probably been won in such conferences and not on the battlefield. Now Falco spoke slowly, as if trying to ensure Geary understood something. "Tradition calls for the assembled wisdom and experience of the fleet ship commanders to have a role in deciding the fleet's course of action."

"Tradition!" Geary paced again, shaking his head. "I think I know a bit more about how this fleet used to operate than you do. Try regulations. Try good order and discipline, or unity of command. I'm the commanding officer of this fleet, Captain Falco. I will listen to advice, and I will consider all suggestions offered, but I will decide what this fleet does and does not do."

"You have to show proper respect for the commanding officers of the ships in this fleet!"

Geary nodded. "We're in agreement on that, but showing respect isn't the same as avoiding my responsibility, my duty, to make critical decisions."

"I must insist on following the command procedures that this fleet has developed in the face of constant warfare." Falco looked stubborn and proud, not willing to yield the point. It was the same way he had fought battles, Geary realized, refusing to admit or recognize when head-on assaults simply wouldn't succeed. Oddly enough, he was clearly being sincere about this. Falco really believed this was the right way to do things.

For that reason, Geary controlled his voice, speaking with care. "I have deep respect for the officers I serve with, and deep respect for the traditions of the fleet. I am also obligated to carry out my duties as I best understand them given the rules and regulations of the fleet. I've checked, and those rules and regulations say nothing about votes to confirm command decisions."

"This is not about blind adherence to rules that may be outdated in the face of the threat we face," Falco declared.

Geary recognized the words. Falco had said similar things a number of times before being captured, usually when talking about the government of the Alliance. "For better or worse, Captain Falco, I carry respect for those outdated rules within me, and I insist upon the fleet following them as well."

"I repeat, I insist—"

"You don't have the authority to insist upon anything. I'm the senior officer present. I'm in command. I believe that command procedures based on votes and committees are not a good idea, and I will not follow that kind of procedure. That will not change." Falco made to speak again, but Geary pinned him with a demanding stare. "You've offered one suggestion. Do you have anything else?"

Falco finally stood as well, his face reddening. "I've reviewed the planetary strike plans. The first volley of kinetic bombardment of the two inhabited planets in this system will leave many targets unstruck. We need to eliminate all sources of Syndic power in this system."

"I'm destroying industrial, military, and governmental targets, Captain Falco."

"You are leaving many Syndic workers alive to continue their labors on behalf of the Syndicate Worlds. Their ability to work on Syndic war efforts must be permanently forestalled."

"Permanently forestalled?" Geary asked. "Is that another way of saying they have to be killed?"

Falco gave Geary an uncomprehending look. "We are in a war for everything we believe in, Captain Geary. We cannot let legal niceties prevent us from doing what must be done to protect our homes and families."

"Legal niceties? That's what you call them? You think that's all that stands between us and slaughtering the civilian inhabitants of those two planets, Captain Falco?" Geary asked with deceptive quietness.

For his part, Falco seemed baffled by the question and answered as if speaking to a child. "They are part of the Syndic war machine. Only by eliminating all aspects of Syndic power can we win."

"And you believe such an action represents everything we believe in? That our ancestors will look with favor upon mass murder?" Geary replied.

"The Syndics have done far worse!"

"That's why we're fighting them, isn't it?" Geary waved one flattened hand in a chopping motion. "I will not commit atrocities or permit atrocities to be committed by anyone under my command. There will be one volley of kinetic projectiles fired at those worlds to retaliate for Syndic actions against this fleet. The targets will be military, industrial, and governmental. Period."

Falco seemed torn between amazement and outrage. "I'd heard you'd spared Syndic prisoners, but I didn't believe you were this soft."

"Soft?" Instead of angering him, Geary discovered the

word amused him. "I have no trouble fighting enemy combatants. If you've really heard what happened to the Syndic flotilla at Kaliban, you should realize that. As for treatment of prisoners, I would've thought your last two decades of imprisonment would've caused you to recognize the virtues of handling prisoners of war in accordance with the laws of war." He paused, realizing that further antagonizing Falco wouldn't do any good. But he also guessed that Falco would leap on any sign of perceived weakness. "I was trained to do things that have since been lost through no one's fault, Captain Falco. I've brought that training with me from the past so I can help this fleet fight better. I've also brought with me attitudes that may be regarded as archaic but that I believe in. I believe they'll make this fleet stronger."

Falco stared back, his face rigid. "So you say." He made an obvious effort to control himself. "Perhaps we should start over."

Geary nodded. "That might be a good idea."

"We both want the same thing," Falco noted, the companionable smile back. Geary wondered just what Falco considered that same thing to be. "Together, we can accomplish a great deal."

"For the Alliance?" Geary prodded.

"Of course! But the Alliance needs strong leaders! We can provide that leadership." Falco shook his head, sighing theatrically. "You can see what things are like now. The state of the fleet. The sort of people giving orders to the fleet. That Rione woman. An Alliance senator accompanying the fleet as if we needed politicians breathing down our necks to do our jobs right! I understand she's been a thorn in your side, which is exactly what I would have suspected."

Geary tried to look noncommittal. "You've heard that?"

"From many people. But of course we can work together and neutralize her influence."

"That's an idea," Geary stated in as neutral a tone as he could manage. It occurred to him that Falco might have already had this exact same conversation with Co-President Rione, commiserating over Geary's presence and offering to work together with Rione against Geary. He wondered if Rione would tell him about such a thing if he asked.

Falco leaned closer, smiling like a comrade in arms and brandishing an emphatic forefinger. "When this fleet returns to Alliance space, its leaders will be able to write their own tickets for the future. You know that. We'll have a historic opportunity to shape the way the Alliance pursues this war, and the way the Alliance makes decisions. With that opportunity, we could establish the conditions to finally win this war. You'll need someone with you who understands the current lay of the land. Someone who will help you against the politicians who have done all they can to ruin the Alliance and leave it helpless against the Syndics."

Geary just gazed back, keeping his expression unrevealing. *With me? Why do I think that the instant we hit Alliance space, Captain Falco will be sending out press releases hailing his success in getting the fleet back safely and making me out to be a figurehead at best?* "Captain Falco, you've been in a Syndic labor camp for some time. Your own knowledge is considerably out of date."

Falco's smile was now confident as well as conspiratorial. "I have friends who can bring me up to date. After all, I have a lot fewer decades to learn about than you, eh?"

"Captain Falco, I'm always grateful for useful suggestions. However, my role is to get this fleet home safe. Once there, my job is to defer to the elected leadership of the Alliance, regardless of what I think of the wisdom of their decisions. If I can't in good conscience support legal decisions by the Alliance leadership, my duty is to resign my position in this fleet."

"Preserving the Alliance is more important than the prerogatives of politicians," Falco noted dismissively.

"Captain Falco, in the time I came from, it was understood that preserving the Alliance meant preserving what it stood for. Preserving individual rights and the rights of the electorate." Falco was clearly working hard at trying not to frown again. "I wish to continue working in a constructive manner with Co-President Rione. I would hope for your support in all of my decisions."

Falco eyed him, a trace of wariness in his eyes, even though the smile was still present. "Support doesn't come without a price."

Isn't that a surprise? "I'm afraid I have nothing to offer in exchange for support but the welfare of this fleet and of the Alliance."

"That's all I care about!" It sounded completely sincere, and Geary realized it probably was. Falco believed he could save the Alliance and believed that he could make better decisions than the elected leaders of the Alliance. "The Alliance needs a strong leader! I have to know your actions will work to the short- and long-term benefit of the Alliance, and frankly, right now I'm concerned that you don't realize how serious things have gotten in the many years you were in survival sleep!"

It had been easier to think of Falco as an opportunist. Instead, he was apparently motivated by a genuine and heartfelt belief that he and he alone could save the Alliance. In some ways, that probably made him more dangerous, Geary reflected. No one else could ever meet Falco's ideal of the best leader, a position reserved in Falco's mind for Falco himself, and no action that Falco disapproved of could possibly be right.

Geary tried to speak in as professional and dispassionate a way as he could. "I grant that you are concerned for the welfare of the Alliance. Our opinions on the right courses of action may diverge at times. But fate and my rank have placed me in command of this fleet. I can't in good conscience deny my duty to this fleet and to the Alliance, which requires me to lead this fleet to the best of my ability. I believe we are in agreement that getting this fleet back to Alliance space is critical to the Alliance war effort, and I welcome your support in ensuring that happens."

Falco's smile had vanished again. "You expect me to stand by while you squander opportunities to strike important blows against the Syndicate Worlds? While this fleet wanders around backwaters of the Syndicate Worlds instead of seeking out the enemy? While civilian politicians with no experience presume to tell us how to fight this war?"

"None of those things are happening," Geary stated. "We are engaging the enemy, we are heading for home, and Co-President Rione does not interfere in the decision making of this fleet."

"Extended survival sleep does things to people," Falco observed with enough acid to match Captain Faresa's best. "It warps their judgment."

"And your judgment isn't warped?" Geary asked. "Have you ever made a mistake, Captain Falco? Ever?"

Falco glared back, openly hostile now. "There have been times when I have placed too much trust in some subordinates, but I personally have been able to avoid serious errors. Which is why I should be commanding this fleet, and which is why I will try to convince my fellow officers of that fact."

"I see." Geary took a moment to wonder what would happen if people willing to believe in perfect heroes, as some thought of him, were combined with a man who thought he was perfect. The idea was frightening. "Captain Falco, I have a job to do to the best of my ability. I take that responsibility very seriously. Your duty to the Alliance is to support my efforts. I will not tolerate any attempts to hinder me. If you attempt to undermine or obstruct my command of this fleet, I *will* make you regret it. Do not doubt my honor, Captain Falco. Perhaps it's a very old-fashioned thing, but I do take it seriously."

Falco stared back at Geary for several seconds, then spun on one heel, turning to go. "Captain Falco." Falco stopped in midmotion, hesitating at the tone of Geary's voice. "You have permission to leave." Though Geary couldn't see Falco's face, he could see the other captain's neck redden alarmingly.

Falco whirled back to face Geary as the hatch opened and revealed Rione standing there about to touch the alert button. She paused, watching, as Falco spoke with cold precision, apparently not having yet noticed Rione standing nearby. "This fleet deserves a commander whose personal bravery and boldness matches that of its sailors. If you don't provide that sort of command, I assure you that the fleet will find a new leader." He pivoted back to leave, freezing for a moment at the sight of Rione, then walked brusquely past her without a word.

Rione gave Geary an inquisitive look. "Did your meeting go well?"

"Very funny. What brings you back here?"

"I wanted to inform you that Captain Falco had expressed concern to me about whether you were acting in the best interests of the Alliance," Rione stated matter-of-factly.

"He expressed the same sentiment to me about you," Geary replied.

"Among other sentiments?" Rione asked. "You know what you're dealing with now." She nodded and left as well.

Geary closed his eyes and rubbed his forehead in a vain attempt to relax as the hatch closed. He sat down again, drumming the fingers of one hand on the armrest next to him, then paged Captain Desjani. "Do you have time to stop by my stateroom? I'd like to discuss a few things."

It took Captain Desjani only a few minutes to arrive. She gave him a quizzical look. "You needed to speak privately, sir?"

"Yes." Geary waved her to a seat, sitting forward and waiting until Desjani had sat down, stiff enough in her posture that she seemed to be sitting at attention. *I need to know how other officers feel.* "Captain, I'd like your candid assessment of Captain Falco."

Desjani hesitated. "Technically, Captain Falco is senior to me."

"Yes, but you're the same rank, and he won't be commanding this fleet."

She seemed to relax a bit. "I've only known Captain Falco before this from his reputation and from stories told by older officers, sir."

"I've been given to understand he's well regarded."

"Yes, in the sense of a dead hero. Captain Falco was seen as an inspiring example." Desjani grimaced. "You wish me to speak frankly, sir?" Geary nodded. "If Black Jack Geary was regarded as the fleet's god, then Fighting Falco was a sort of demigod. Officers I've spoken to told tales approving of Captain Falco's fighting spirit and his general attitude."

Geary nodded again, pondering the irony of the fact that the two things Captain Falco had been admired for were the exact two things Geary disliked most in Falco. "He's still thought of as a good commander?"

Desjani thought for a few seconds. "If any captain but you had been in command of this fleet, then Captain Falco would've very likely ended up in command instead."

"How would you feel about that?"

Desjani grimaced again. "At one time . . . I've gotten used to dealing with a commander who wasn't seeking my vote in a fleet conference, sir. You gave me some praise while we were on the shuttle dock if you recall, and that meant a great deal, because you had grounds for making an assessment of me and my ship. When Captain Falco offered praise . . . I knew it couldn't have been earned. The contrast was very clear: one commander who respected what I did and another who saw me as someone he could flatter and use."

Geary thanked whatever had prompted him to say what he had when he had. Perhaps his ancestors were lending him a hand sometimes. "Did you have any other impressions?"

She hesitated, thinking. "He's very personable, sir. I

thought Admiral Bloch was good, but he wasn't in Captain Falco's class at all. And I've had time for a couple of more brief talks with Lieutenant Riva. He and the other liberated prisoners believe Captain Falco is deeply devoted to the welfare of the Alliance. Captain Falco dedicated great efforts in the labor camp to keeping up morale and assuring everyone that Alliance victory would come. Lieutenant Riva thinks many prisoners would have given up hope and let themselves die without Captain Falco's example."

This would be easier if Falco was simply a glory hound, Geary reflected. *But he is an inspiring leader, and he does care about the Alliance. Unfortunately, his vision of saving the Alliance would mean turning it into a reflection of the Syndicate Worlds. May our ancestors preserve us from those who would destroy the things that make the Alliance worth fighting for in the name of defending it.* "Thank you, Captain Desjani. I have reason to believe that Captain Falco intends promoting himself as the rightful commander of the fleet."

That got another grimace from Desjani. "Sir, as I said, if it were any captain but you, if you had not already successfully brought us this far and won a great victory at Kaliban, then Captain Falco would be in command within a few days at the most. He's . . . um . . ."

"A little more charming than me?" Geary asked dryly.

"Yes, sir." She paused. "In truth, sir, if I'd met him before you, I might feel differently. The changes you've brought about were often hard to accept. But you truly have changed how I see senior officers."

Geary looked away, embarrassed by the praise. "How about the other ship commanders? Do you think they'll feel the same way?"

"It's hard to say. There remains a hard core of ship captains who would rather lose fighting in what they see as the 'honorable' way than win by fighting in the more disciplined fashion you've brought. They believe that fighting spirit is the most important element in battle, and that you lack that spirit, sir."

It wasn't anything he hadn't heard before. "So I understand. 'The moral is to the material as three is to one.' Surely there's been enough disasters as a result of that attitude to impress even the firmest believers in fighting spirit as the silver bullet of warfare."

Desjani smiled humorlessly. "A belief doesn't rest on evidence but on faith, sir."

Like the belief in him, or rather in Black Jack Geary, which he had been able to put to good use. Geary nodded. "True enough. Are there enough of these true believers in fighting spirit to give Captain Falco command?"

"No, sir. There's many fence-sitters, still, but that wouldn't incline them to support Captain Falco. Many have been impressed by your performance, sir." She must have seen Geary's self-consciousness this time. "You showed everyone at Kaliban, sir, even though the lessons from that battle are taking time to filter through the fleet. And I have to add, because you asked me to speak frankly, sir, that your moral stands have deeply moved a lot of officers and sailors because they're based on what our ancestors truly believed and would expect from us. We've forgotten so much, or allowed ourselves to forget so much, and you've allowed us to regain those things."

Geary kept his eyes on the deck, too embarrassed to meet her eyes. "Thank you. I hope I can live up to that sort of assessment. Captain Desjani, there may be trouble at the fleet conference I'm about to call."

"There usually is trouble at fleet conferences," Captain Desjani observed.

Geary smiled briefly. "Yeah. But I expect this to be worse than usual. Partly because I expect Captain Falco to be there, trying to throw his weight around, and partly because of what I'm going to propose to do."

"What are you planning, sir?"

"I'm planning on taking this fleet to Sancere."

"Sancere?" Desjani seemed puzzled, trying to recall where that was; then her eyes widened. "Yes, sir. There'll be trouble."

• • •

GEARY walked to the bridge, checking the time and barely arriving before the scheduled launch of the kinetic bombardment. He settled into his command seat as Captain Desjani nodded in welcome as if she'd been on the bridge for hours instead of getting there just minutes before Geary himself.

The planetary display obligingly popped up, the target sites glowing. Geary scanned them again, thinking about the power he had to ruin worlds. Falco had seemed ready and willing to exercise such power, but then after twenty years on a cold rock like Sutrah Five, maybe Geary would've also been eager to bomb the living hell out of the place. "You may proceed with launch of bombardment as scheduled."

Desjani nodded again, then gestured to the combat system watch-stander, who tapped a single control, then entered the authorization.

It all seemed so simple, so clean and neat. Geary called up the fleet display, waiting, then saw his battleships and battle cruisers begin pumping out the bombardment rounds. Just solid chunks of metal, aerodynamic and with special ceramic coatings to keep them from vaporizing from the heat of atmospheric friction before impact. Inheriting a lot of speed from the ships that had dropped them, the kinetic rounds would fall toward their planetary targets, accelerating to even higher velocities under the pull of gravity and gaining more energy every meter of the way. When those simple metal chunks struck the surface of the planets, all of that kinetic energy would be released in explosions that would leave nothing but large craters and twisted wreckage in their wake.

Geary sat, watching the bombardment aimed at Sutrah Five arcing down into the atmosphere, wondering how it looked to those on the planet's surface. "It must be a very helpless feeling."

"Sir?" Desjani's question made Geary realized he'd spoken out loud.

"I was just thinking how it'd feel to be on a planet and see that bombardment coming in," Geary admitted. "No way to stop it, impossible to run fast enough to avoid one of the rounds if you were at a target site, no shelter capable of withstanding the impact."

Desjani's eyes shaded as she considered the idea. "I hadn't really thought about it in those terms. Alliance worlds have felt it, too, and I know I've felt helpless when I've heard about it, not able to have stopped it. But, yes, I'd much rather be in something that can maneuver and fight."

By now the kinetic rounds aimed at Sutrah Five were all glowing brightly with the heat of their passage, dozens of deadly fireflies curving toward the planet's surface. From *Dauntless*'s position, Geary could see part of Sutrah Five covered by night and watch the brilliant display of fiery destruction lighting the darkness of the skies there. "There's no honor in killing helpless people," he murmured, thinking of what Falco had urged.

To his surprise, Captain Desjani nodded in agreement. "No."

He remembered her once expressing regret that the null-field weapons were short-range and couldn't work near gravity wells, and therefore couldn't be used against planets. Geary wondered if Desjani still felt that way.

He zoomed in the scale on his display, getting a good picture of one of the targets, a still-functioning industrial site that, on multispectral imagery, displayed heat from warm equipment and radiation of electronic signals leaking from wiring. There were no signs of people at the location, though, all of them apparently having taken the warning seriously and evacuated. Geary didn't really see the kinetic round come in, as it was moving far too fast for his eye to register, but his mind imagined seeing a blur rocket in followed by an intense flash of light automatically blocked by *Dauntless*'s sensors. Pulling back the scale again, Geary saw shock waves radiating out from a cloud of vaporized material, shattering buildings and making the planet's surface ripple like the hide of a living beast stung by an insect. He pulled back the scale again, much farther, seeing the mushroom-shaped clouds that mankind had grown to know all too well rising high into the skies of Sutrah Five as impacts occurred at multiple sites, smashing in moments all of the industrial and transportation hubs that humans had spent centuries creating on Sutrah Five.

Torn between fascination at the destruction and sorrow over its necessity, Geary selected one special site and homed in on it. The target in the mountain range didn't show as much obvious destruction as other locations, because the kinetic round fired at it had been shaped to penetrate deeply into the rock on impact. The crater was deeper but smaller than at other locations, as if a spear had lanced into the planet seeking a special target. As it had, because this was where the hidden command post had once existed. Geary wondered if the high-ranking leaders who'd been willing to subject others to the risk of bombardment had themselves had time to realize they wouldn't be safe after all.

"I know the Syndic military base is an obsolete burden to them," Desjani remarked, "but it wouldn't have cost us much to eliminate it as well, as long as we were trying to teach the Syndics a lesson."

Geary shook his head, his eyes still on the impact site where the planetary high command had been sheltered. "That depends on what lesson we're trying to teach, doesn't it? Vengeance? Or justice?"

Desjani spent a long time quiet. "Vengeance is easier to inflict, isn't it?"

"Yeah. It doesn't require much thought."

She nodded slowly. Whatever lesson he'd taught the Syndics, Desjani seemed to be thinking a great deal.

On his display, Geary could see the swarm of projectiles headed for Sutrah Four. The people there would be seeing the impacts on their sister world and would know a similar fate awaited many locations on the planet they called home. They would also get to watch the bombardment heading their way for another hour or so, prolonging the suffering of their experience. He wondered if they'd blame the Alliance or the Syndic leaders who had been willing to sacrifice them.

ANOTHER conference, the atmosphere tense because every ship commander present knew that Geary intended laying out his next course of action. Granted, besides Geary himself, only Captain Desjani was actually physically present. Once again, Co-President Rione wasn't in the room. Geary wondered this time if her absence had anything to do with the rumors that she and Geary were personally involved.

The absence of Captain Fighting Falco was a pleasant surprise but left Geary worrying what Falco was up to. Falco didn't seem like the sort to give up easily, and Geary would've much preferred to see any political games being played right before him to having them occur in shadows outside of his knowledge. He hoped that Rione's spies would tell her of anything Geary had to worry about and that she would pass those reports on to him.

Geary looked around the table, knowing he was about to set off a firestorm and seeing no alternative. "Ladies and gentlemen, the Syndics are drawing a net about us. The traps we encountered in this system are clear evidence that the Syndics are predicting our next objectives well enough to prepare for us. As you all know," *or should know,* Geary added to himself, "the Syndics had light ships posted at all of the jump points in this system. As the light from our arrival reached them, three of those ships jumped out. There are three possible destinations through those gates, and all will be warned of our possible impending arrival."

He waited for any comments, but there were none. Everyone seemed to be waiting to hear his proposal. "I've taken a look at our possible objectives from this point, and the reachable stars beyond those, and it's all too clear that the Syndics will be able to channel our options down to the point of being able to trap us with greatly superior forces no matter what we do." He paused, letting that sink in. "I have no doubt that we'd inflict terrible losses on those Syndic forces, but this fleet would be destroyed in the process." That was a valuable offering to their pride, Geary thought, as well as a reminder that this was still about trying to get home.

"The Marine exploitation groups were able to get an outdated but useful Syndicate Worlds star system guide from files left behind at the labor camp." Geary nodded toward Colonel Carabali. "After reviewing that, I believe there's another option, which I think gives us a chance to not only avoid that trap but also to inflict a powerful blow to the Syndics, totally disrupt their plans, and leave us many options for heading back toward Alliance space again." He used his finger to draw a line through the display. "We take the fleet back to the jump point we used to arrive. Not to go back to Kaliban but to jump to Strabo."

"Strabo?" someone blurted after several seconds of silence. "What's at Strabo?"

"Nothing. Not even enough rocks to have developed much of a human presence and now completely abandoned."

The captain of the *Polaris* was staring at the display. "Strabo is almost directly away from Alliance space."

"Yes," Geary agreed. "The Syndics have to believe the chance we'd jump back toward the way we came is very remote. They haven't sent anyone through that jump point since we've arrived. Once they get word that we did, they'll consider a jump to Strabo even more remote. But we're going to throw them off worse than that." He swung his finger again, knowing his next words would trigger a much stronger reaction. "From Strabo we jump to Cydoni."

"Cydoni?" Captain Numos had finally been prodded into challenging Geary again. "That's even deeper into Syndic space!"

"It is. The Syndics will figure out eventually that we've jumped to Strabo, and from there they'll assume we're headed for the other three stars within range of Strabo, all of which bend back to Alliance space. It'll take them a long time to figure out we jumped to Cydoni."

"What possible purpose could that serve?" Numos demanded. "Shall we run to the far side of Syndic space? They won't expect that, will they? Do you have any idea how badly we'll need resupply by the time we reach Cydoni? What's there?"

"Nothing," Geary stated. Everyone was staring at him. "It's another abandoned system. The star's photosphere is expanding, so the one once-habitable planet was evacuated decades ago. No, what counts is what lies beyond Cydoni." He gestured again, trying to make it dramatic. "At extreme jump range from Cydoni is Sancere. Again at an angle away from Alliance space, but the odds seem exceptionally good that our arrival at Sancere would be a total surprise to the Syndics."

"Sancere's the site of some of the Syndicate Worlds' biggest shipyards," Captain Duellos observed in the shocked silence that followed. "But can we really reach it from Cydoni? Jump drive specifications don't say they have that range."

"We can. I've made longer jumps," Geary advised. "Since the invention of the hypernet, you all haven't been dependent on jump drives for long hauls between stars. We had no alternative to using the jump drives in my time, and we learned some ways of extending the range past the official maximum."

"This is insane!" Captain Faresa commented in a baffled voice. "Running deeper into Syndic space, repeatedly, to reach an objective sure to be heavily guarded with our own supplies near exhaustion!"

"It won't be heavily guarded enough to deal with us," Geary stated with a confidence greater than he really felt. There was always that awful chance that he was wrong. But he couldn't admit to that and have a hope of convincing these people. "The Syndics will have had to send strong detachments every which way to try to find us and intercept us. They'll never suspect we've been bold enough to strike at Sancere, even if they have someone who remembers that the jump drives will let us reach there from Cydoni. And resupply won't be a problem. This is a heavily populated major shipbuilding center. It'll have everything we could possibly want."

"Including a hypernet gate," Captain Tulev observed.

"Right." Geary nodded, looking around and seeing uncertainty on most faces. "If they destroy it, it'll prevent reinforcements from arriving relatively quickly. If they don't destroy it . . ." He let the thought hang, deliberately holding it out as bait.

"We can get home. Fast," someone breathed.

Numos gave Geary a narrow-eyed look. "The Syndic hypernet key we acquired from the traitor still exists then?"

"It does."

"We could've gone to Cadiz and used it there!"

Geary felt anger rising at the stubborn stupidity of Numos. "As we decided at the time, Cadiz was too obvious an objective. The Syndics surely had overwhelming forces there awaiting us."

"But they won't at Sancere? How can you take such an insane risk?" Numos demanded.

Geary stared coldly at him. "I thought I was supposed to be too cautious. Are you now accusing me of being too bold?" He shifted his gaze, sweeping it across the other officers. "You know the truth as well as I do. The Syndics laid not one but three traps for us in this system. They've sent word ahead to all of our possible objectives if we continue on our current paths toward Alliance space. The only way to disrupt their plans, to preserve this fleet, is to do something so unexpected, not once but three times, that they'll be scrambling to catch up." He pointed again. "Sancere was a big shipbuilding center even before the hypernet, not just because it's a wealthy star system, but because there's six stars within jump range, not counting Cydoni. Six options, five of which bear back toward the

Alliance. No, I'm not thrilled by the amount of distance we have to make up, but we'll inflict a major blow on the Syndics, we'll ruin their plans to keep wearing us down and trap us, and we'll be able to pick up everything we need to keep going."

"And if all works," Captain Duellos added, "perhaps the hypernet gate we need to get home."

Too many pairs of eyes were still locked on the path Geary had traced. He knew from the expressions that those officers were gauging just how far Geary's plan would take them from Alliance space. "If our objective is to get home," Geary emphasized, "and to hurt the Syndics in the process, then Sancere is the way back to Alliance space."

"This is nonsense," Numos declared. "I call for a vote!"

Geary eyed him coldly. "There are no votes in my fleet."

"If I'm to be asked to charge deep into Syndic territory on a suicidal mission, I should be allowed a say in it! We all should!"

Captain Tulev made a disgusted sound. "You already voted to do that. When Admiral Bloch was in command of the fleet. Or have you forgotten that a vote put us in this situation?"

Numos flushed with anger. "That was an entirely different situation. Where is Captain Falco? What is his advice?"

"You'll have to ask him," Geary advised. "I've already received his input." And discounted it. But they didn't have to know that.

"Where is Captain Falco?" Captain Faresa demanded, seconding Numos as usual.

Captain Desjani answered, her voice as calm and unemotional as if she were providing a routine report. "Captain Falco is undergoing medical tests recommended by the fleet medical personnel aboard the *Dauntless*."

Geary tried not to look surprised and not to smile. He hadn't suspected Desjani could be so devious.

Faresa, however, looked outraged. "Medical tests?"

"Yes," Desjani confirmed blandly. "For Captain Falco's

safety. He was under considerable physical stress in the Syndic labor camp, and of course also suffered from the pressures of being the senior Alliance officer present there. Fleet medical personnel expressed concern following their initial checkup of Captain Falco, asking for a follow-up examination as soon as possible."

"What did Captain Falco recommend?" someone asked.

"His advice to me is between Captain Falco and myself," Geary replied. That didn't go over well, so Geary decided to elaborate. "I will say that Captain Falco hadn't had time to fully acquaint himself with the situation this fleet finds itself in. He also recommended that we launch a much larger bombardment of the inhabited worlds in this system. I don't believe that to be wise, humane, or justified, so I rejected that advice."

"Captain Falco is a fighting commander," the captain of the *Brigandine* finally remarked after another long pause.

"My father died serving under him," the captain of the *Steadfast* agreed.

It was too much for Geary. "A lot of sailors died serving under Captain Falco." A hush followed the blunt comment. "Anyone who wishes to compare my fighting spirit to that of Captain Falco is welcome to contrast what happened at Kaliban with any battle commanded by Captain Falco. Since I believe we serve the Alliance best, and protect our homes best, by both winning *and* surviving, I don't fear any comparison of ship losses on both sides or of casualty ratios."

"I served under Captain Falco at Batana," Captain Duellos remarked in an almost idle tone. "My first battle and nearly my last. My commanding officer commented afterward that as our losses equaled those of the Syndics, it would've been simpler if Captain Falco had only ordered each of his ships to ram one of the enemy ships, thereby achieving the same result with much less difficulty."

"Captain Falco is a hero of the Alliance!" someone else argued.

"Captain Falco is an officer of this fleet," Commander

Cresida replied sharply. "Are we choosing commanders by vote again? Given how well that's worked in the past? Has Captain Geary given any reason at all to doubt his judgment? How many of you would've chosen to die at Kaliban in the name of adding glory to the battle?"

Her words seem to give pause to most of those present, but Captain Faresa sent a particular acidic look Cresida's way. "We don't need to hear lectures from an officer junior to us in rank and experience."

Commander Cresida flushed, but thanks to time delay in the signal from Cresida's ship, Geary got his answer in first. "I'm running this meeting and this fleet," he stated in a hard voice, "and I decide what we need to hear. I welcome input from a capable officer such as Commander Cresida."

More objections were raised. Geary argued them down. More wishes were floated for Captain Falco's opinion. Geary's strongest allies belittled those, using the undeniable fact that Falco was still unfamiliar with the fleet's circumstances. Geary finally held up a restraining hand. "A decision needs to be made. I have the responsibility of making it. The bottom line is this: I will take this fleet to Sancere because that offers our best hope for continued survival. And when we get there, we will inflict a serious defeat on the Syndics in the bargain and avenge *Anelace*, *Baselard*, *Mace*, and *Cuirass*."

More than one commander looked unhappy, more than one looked to Numos for further argument, but a warning glance from Geary kept Numos silent this time. More importantly, the majority of the officers seemed not only willing to go along but convinced by Geary's arguments. "That is all," Geary concluded. "Orders to maneuver the fleet back toward the jump point we used to enter this system will go out within a few minutes."

The crowd shrank within moments, leaving only Captain Desjani and the virtual presence of Captain Duellos. Desjani stood and smiled in a grim way. "Another victory, sir."

"I think I'd rather fight the Syndics," Geary admitted. "Please have *Dauntless* broadcast the change-of-course order. To be executed at," he checked the readouts, "time two zero."

"Yes, sir." Desjani saluted before she departed.

Geary nodded to Duellos. "Thanks for the backup."

Duellos gave Geary a skeptical look in return. "You don't really expect the Syndics to let us access that hypernet gate at Sancere, do you?"

Geary looked down and grimaced. "No. I think the Syndics know they can't afford to let this fleet get home with a working key to their hypernet. It'd give the Alliance a decisive edge in the war."

"So they will take the extreme measure of destroying the gate rather than allow us access."

"Probably." Geary shrugged. "There's always a chance they won't. A very slim chance, but it's there."

"True." Duellos sighed. "If not for that gate, the fleet wouldn't have followed you to Sancere, you know."

"I know."

"But if we make it there, and win, the doubters will have trouble finding an audience." Duellos carefully saluted. "It's a tremendous risk, but you've earned the right to our trust."

Geary returned the salute. "Thanks."

"You're sure the jump drives can get us from Cydoni to Sancere?"

"Absolutely."

After Duellos "left," Geary went wearily back to his stateroom. He didn't need to be on the bridge when the fleet turned since he could watch the maneuver from the displays in his own stateroom. Normally he'd try to be on the bridge anyway, satisfying the need of the crew to believe that their commander cared about their work and how they did it, but after the drawn out and too-often-hostile arguments he'd dealt with, Geary badly needed a break.

He saw Co-President Rione waiting outside his stateroom, knew there'd been time enough for her to be briefed on the meeting by some of the commanders of ships belonging to the Callas Republic, saw the fire barely restrained behind her eyes, and knew he wasn't going to get that break yet.

Rione stood silently until Geary entered, following him inside and waiting until the hatch closed before rounding on him and letting her feelings show clearly.

Looking at her, Geary realized he'd never really seen Co-President Victoria Rione angry before. It wasn't something he wanted to see again. "How could you have done such a thing?" Rione demanded, seeming to bite off each word as it came out.

Geary spoke carefully. "I believe this is the best course of action—"

"You've betrayed this fleet! You've betrayed the Alliance! And you've betrayed me!"

Flinching from the harsh words and anger, Geary nonetheless found his attention fixing on the last sentence. "I betrayed you? How?"

Rione flushed, drawing herself back. "That's . . . never mind. I misspoke. I meant that you'd betrayed everyone in this fleet, all of the officers and sailors who have come to trust that you would use your command wisely! I have not worked against you. I have tried to support your efforts, thinking that you had demonstrated a lack of personal ambition and some minor degree of common sense. I was wrong, Captain Geary. By fooling me as to your true intentions, you succeeded in manipulating this fleet to a place where you can play the hero you've obviously always sought to be! And you've made me an unwitting accomplice in your schemes!"

"I am *not* a hero," Geary snapped back at her. "This isn't about that at all. If you'll just take a moment to consider my reasons—"

"Your *reasons*? I already know what your reasons are," Rione insisted. "You fear that Captain Falco will wrest command of this fleet from you. I heard what he said to you, warning you that the fleet would choose another commander if you weren't bold enough! So to prevent that from happening, you're willing to risk this fleet's destruction! As if the fleet and every person in it is just a toy that you and Captain Falco are fighting over like a pair of jealous toddlers! If you can't have it, no one can!"

Geary kept a rein on his temper with great effort. "Madam Co-President," he ground out, "I extrapolated every possible course of action—"

"Did you? And where are the records of these extrapolations, Captain Geary?" she demanded.

That statement knocked Geary off balance for a moment. "You can access my personal strategic models and simulations? Those are supposed to be under a tight eyes-only security seal."

Rione, looking like she regretted having admitted that, nonetheless nodded imperiously. "Did you have something to hide, Captain Geary? Such as a total lack of records of the simulations you claim justify this decision of yours?"

"I didn't run simulations," Geary roared back. "I could do all of that in my head. Not to the same degree of accuracy as simulations, but well enough to identify the dangers we were facing!"

"You actually expect me to believe that? Do you think I'm stupid as well as gullible, Captain Geary? What were you planning to manipulate me into doing for you next? Do you think I have no pride? Do you think I have no sense of honor?"

He tried to get his temper back under control. "I have not fooled you, I have not manipulated you, I have been honest every step of the way."

Rione leaned closer, her eyes blazing. "I have endured many things for the sake of the Alliance, Captain Geary. But to find that I have been treated in this fashion by a man I had come to assume was above such things is the most humiliating thing I have ever experienced. Worse, the fact that you succeeded in using me to further your aims means these ships and perhaps the Alliance itself are doomed. The people of the Callas Republic, who I swore to serve faithfully, are doomed. I have failed, Captain Geary. You can take satisfaction in that much. You don't need to continue pretending to be unjustly accused."

Geary glared back at her. "Believe it or not, this isn't about you."

"No, Captain Geary. It's not. It's about the thousands of men and women you are leading to their deaths."

Geary looked away, trying to regain his composure. "If you would do me the courtesy of letting me explain my intentions—"

"I've already heard them." Rione pivoted, walked one step away, then swung back to face him again. "The simulations you claimed to have run don't exist. You haven't even tried to claim otherwise."

"I never claimed to have run simulations!"

Rione paused, then a bitter smile curved one corner of her mouth. "So the simple warrior chose his words with such great care? Implying something existed when it didn't?"

"I didn't intend that anyone misinterpret my reasons for this course of action! You just have to take my word for it that I worked this out."

"How convenient," Rione stated in a voice suddenly gone icy. "I only need to take your word again. I hadn't realized you held me in such contempt. Am I really so easy to manipulate?"

"I did not manipulate you! That was never my intention!"

"So you say." Rione shook her head slowly, never taking her eyes off of Geary. "Your real intentions are already clear to me."

"Fine," Geary almost snarled. "Then why don't you tell me what you *think* they are?"

"I already told you. When confronted with a serious challenge to your command of this fleet, you have chosen to do the sort of insanely risky and ill-considered action that you have spent the last few months claiming to abhor. Your intention, Captain Geary, is to prove that you can be as brainlessly aggressive as Captain Falco, thereby ensuring these ships continue to follow you, regardless of what happens to them as a result."

"This isn't brainless," Geary snapped back at her. "I considered all options."

"And clearly disregarded all of the intelligent ones!"

"I don't want this fleet destroyed! If we'd continued ahead as planned, we would've been trapped by superior Syndic forces after having been worn down by more minor losses in every system along the way!" He was yelling at her again, Geary realized, more angry than he could remember feeling since being rescued.

She kept yelling back. "Where is the proof that you considered these options? Where are the simulations you ran?"

"In my head!"

"Do you seriously expect me to believe such a self-serving argument? One that I cannot verify? I'm just supposed to continue trusting you?"

"Yes! I think I've earned the right to some benefit of the doubt!"

"Benefit of the doubt? I've granted you that in the past, Captain Geary, to my eventual sorrow. But you can't offer one solid piece of evidence to excuse this course of action, not one! This decision of yours is totally unjustified by any proof except your assertions. You're supposed to hold on to your command by proving that you're a better man than Captain Falco! Not by proving that you're an even bigger idiot than he is!"

Geary shook his head like an angry bull. "I never claimed to be a better man."

"Yes, you did," Rione accused him. "You spoke of caring for the lives of the sailors in this fleet, you spoke of leading them wisely. You—" She broke off, her face twisted with fury. "How could you do this to me?"

"To you?" There it was again. Geary managed to rein in his temper again with a supreme effort, wondering why Rione's anger was affecting him so strongly. "I did not misuse your trust. I didn't manipulate you. I swear this is my best judgment. To keep this fleet alive and get it home."

"You actually believe that?" Rione demanded. "You can't be such a fool, so you must be lying."

"It's true." He flung an arm out toward the star display. "If you don't believe me, run simulations yourself! See what happens if we kept going to any of the destinations we'd been considering."

"I will! I will run simulations and produce a *verifiable record* of my deliberations. And when I prove the conclusions you claim to have reached were totally wrong, I'll show you the results, assuming that this ship is still intact at that point and not a broken derelict awaiting the arrival of a Syndic salvage crew!"

She swept out, leaving Geary alone with the echoes of her anger and disappointment. He turned to the projection of a starscape on one bulkhead and punched it several times viciously, but though the stars rippled each time, his efforts had no other result.

THE Alliance fleet turned again, hundreds of ships large and small rolling and pitching as their bows swung around. Main drives lit off, pushing the ships onto a new course, arching over the top of the Sutrah Star System's plane and back down toward the jump point where the fleet had entered not long before.

Geary, pleased at the smooth execution of the maneuver even though he knew it had been handled by automated controls, kept his eyes on the Syndic light warships still hanging around the fringes of the star system. The closest enemy warships were almost two light-hours away, so they wouldn't realize the Alliance fleet had made a big change of course until that time. They'd have to wait after that, determining what the Alliance fleet's new objective was, making sure the Alliance fleet was actually heading back to the first jump point, and confirming that it had actually made use of that jump point.

They've got one ship left there, one more there, and three there. They can't send updates to the three possible stars that could be reached through the other jump points without sending a ship each time. They can send a warning to all of them that we seem to be backtracking, or they can send an alert to all when we actually use our arrival jump point to leave the system. But not both, so they'll have to wait until they know we've left. It buys us more time and leaves the Syndics with more uncertainties. It'll also teach them to assume they can use the most "efficient" number of ships to shadow my fleet instead of having enough to deal with the unexpected.

Not that he wanted the Syndics to actually learn from experience with him. They'd learned enough already to seed Sutrah system with unpleasant surprises, and he prayed Strabo wouldn't be the same.

FOUR

SEVEN more hours until the jump to Strabo. Geary arranged the formation for departure carefully. When the fleet arrived at Strabo, it would be in the same disposition as when it left Sutrah, so he wanted to try to set things up so there wouldn't be any more out-of-control charges. With so many commanding officers to deal with, Geary couldn't assess how all would react in any given situation, so he tried to place the ones he had reason to believe he could trust best to the forefront. Unfortunately, there weren't as many of those commanding officers as he would have liked. He glanced at the current fleet formation, wondering why so many shuttles were winging their way between ships.

He looked up as the alert on his stateroom hatch chimed, followed by the entry of Captain Desjani. Geary smiled in greeting. "Good timing. I was just about to call you and ask if you knew what all those shuttle trips were about."

"It's a swap meet," Desjani explained. "Personnel. As the liberated prisoners have been fully debriefed and their particular skills and experience entered into the fleet personnel database, each ship has been checking to see if individuals they need are available. Most of the ships are swapping people right now to get skills they need and transfer surplus skills to other ships that need those individuals more. The fleet database automatically coordinates the whole process."

Geary felt a brief stab of annoyance. Why hadn't he been told? Why hadn't anyone asked for his approval? But then he realized that there'd been no need to tell him or ask approval. He didn't sign off on normal individual transfers between ships and didn't have time to try to monitor such things. The ships could easily handle the task with the help of the fleet database, doing their jobs of keeping themselves at the best possible combat readiness and leaving Geary to keep his eyes on the big picture. "I guess if there were any problems I'd be told."

"Of course, sir." Desjani paused, looking uncommonly uncomfortable. "Permission to request personal counseling, sir."

"Personal counseling?" A private matter? One that Desjani wanted him to offer advice on? "Certainly. Have a seat."

Desjani sat at attention again, chewing her lip for a moment. "Sir, you met Lieutenant Riva when he came aboard."

Geary took a moment to recall the liberated prisoner. "Right. Your old friend."

"Lieutenant Riva was . . . more than a friend, sir."

"Oh." Then the phrasing sank in. "Was?"

Desjani took a deep breath. "We'd been hot and cold, sir. But we'd never broken off completely. Now . . . well, he's here. And he's considerably junior to me in rank."

"That can be a problem," Geary agreed, thinking of fleet regulations and general appearances. "But if he's just an old boyfriend, I'm sure you can remain professional enough."

"He's not—" Desjani flushed slightly. "Seeing Lieutenant

Riva again was a very emotional experience. It took me a while to realize how emotional."

"Oh." *Stop saying that.* "He could be a current boy-friend again?"

"Yes, sir. The feelings are definitely there. On my side, at least. From what talks we've been able to have, I think Cas—Lieutenant Riva feels the same way." Desjani shrugged helplessly. "But nothing can happen while he's on my ship. It'd be difficult enough because of the rank difference now, but if he's under my command, it's simply impossible."

The scale of the problem finally got through to him. "But after just finding him alive again you don't really want to ship him off to some other unit."

"No, sir."

It was definitely a knotty predicament, the sort of personal dilemma that made commanding officers wish they could gaff the problem off on someone else. But handling things like this, or trying to handle them, came with the job. And, unfortunately, in this particular case he had some personal experience of his own to draw on. "Okay, here's my advice. If Lieutenant Riva stays on this ship, you *can't* pursue a personal relationship with him. That's true even if we got him a job working directly for me. He'd be as un-comfortable as you would. And if I judge you right, Tanya, anything you think is professionally improper is going to be doomed." She nodded silently.

"I think he should go to another ship," Geary advised. "Pick a commanding officer you think well of. You'll be able to communicate pretty freely while we're in normal space, and you'll have the distance to keep things appropriate and to deal with the reality of the changes that've taken place since you two last knew each other."

Desjani nodded, then gave Geary a haunted look. "What if the other ship is lost in combat? The ship I sent him to?"

He wondered if there wasn't something he hadn't heard

yet. "Why weren't you and Riva on the same ship at Quintarra?"

"We . . . needed some time apart." She clenched her jaw. "I needed some time apart. The ship Riva chose to transfer to was lost."

Geary sighed, thinking of the guilt Tanya Desjani had certainly been carrying around with her since the battle of Quintarra. "We wouldn't want that to happen again. Listen, Tanya, all I can say is that I'm doing my best not to lose any more ships. Pick a good captain, someone like Duellos or Tulev or Cresida, someone who you know will fight smart, and ask them to take Riva as a personal favor. If you're uncomfortable with that, I'll ask them."

"Thank you, sir."

"And I want you to tell Lieutenant Riva in no uncertain terms why he's leaving this ship," Geary ordered. "Not because you need more time apart or because you want him on another ship. Don't leave him guessing, because if something happens to you, or to him, he'll never know how you really felt."

"Yes, sir." She stared at him, leaving Geary wondering what he'd betrayed of his own past. "I'm sorry, sir."

"It was a long time ago," he replied, looking away. Most things in his life had been a long time ago. "I hope you and Lieutenant Riva work things out for the best, whatever happens."

He sat for a while after Desjani left, haunted by memories of a woman long dead, and wondering why he kept wishing Victoria Rione were here to talk to about it. But Victoria Rione believed Geary had given in to the worst temptations the situation offered and wasn't talking to him about anything. With her off-limits, the last friends Geary had known had all been gone for many, many years.

GEARY strode onto the bridge of the *Dauntless*, frowning as Captain Desjani turned an angry face his way, though the anger obviously wasn't aimed at him. Her watch-standers looked as if they'd all just been given the verbal equivalent of ten lashes with a cat-o'-nine-tails. "What's up?"

"Captain Falco is no longer aboard," Desjani reported. "He arranged transport on one of the shuttles without my knowledge."

Geary glanced at the watch-standers. "We assumed Captain Falco was authorized," one of them explained, his eyes shifting from Geary to Desjani.

Geary sat down, shaking his head. He should've guessed Falco would be able to charm junior officers into doing whatever Falco wanted. "Where'd he go?"

"The *Warrior*, sir."

"The *Warrior*?" Geary would have guessed Numos's ship, *Orion*, or Faresa's *Majestic*. "Who's the commanding officer of *Warrior*?" he muttered even as he worked the controls to bring up that information.

Captain Kerestes. The man's service record was available at a touch, and Geary scanned it quickly. Of course. Kerestes had managed to survive much longer than most officers, so he'd actually served under Falco at the same battle Duellos had mentioned. On the same ship, actually. The inflated language of the performance reports on Kerestes told Geary little, but the fact that he couldn't recall having noticed either Kerestes or *Warrior* for any particular reason up to now led him to suspect Kerestes was not the most dynamic and forceful of commanders.

Geary tapped a privacy circuit and called Captain Duellos on *Courageous*. "What can you tell me about Captain Kerestes? You and he were on the same ship at Batana."

Duellos seemed surprised by the request. "Did he actually do something that merited attention?"

"Captain Falco managed to get to *Warrior*. I'm wondering why he chose that ship."

"Because what Captain Kerestes lacks in initiative and intellect he makes up in slavish obedience. He will do what Falco says."

Geary nodded, trying not to smile. *Don't hold back, Captain Duellos. Tell me what you really think of the man.* "Kerestes isn't a problem in and of himself, then?"

"Don't worry about him," Duellos advised. "Consider Captain Falco to now be the commanding officer of *Warrior* in every way that matters."

"Thanks." Geary hastily checked his planned formation after he had finished talking to Duellos. He'd placed *Warrior* out on one flank to support the lighter units there. Now it was too late to haul *Warrior* in and position her somewhere with less room for Falco to cause mischief. *I'll have to live with it and hope Falco is more willing to compromise than I think.*

Geary frowned, trying to remember what else he had been planning to ask before the news about Falco threw him off stride. "Captain Desjani, that other officer we discussed. Was that situation resolved in a satisfactory manner?" Given enough time in the fleet, you could learn to describe anything in official-sounding terminology.

"He was transferred to *Furious,* sir," Desjani replied in a routine-report sort of voice. "As you suggested, I ensured he was fully briefed on the situation and the reasons for his transfer before his departure."

"How did he feel about the transfer?"

"He seemed pleased by the opportunity it presented, sir," Desjani stated.

"Good." It all sounded so official that Geary had trouble remembering they were discussing personal issues. He hoped his advice resulted in a better outcome for Desjani and Lieutenant Riva than Geary had himself experienced. "Let's get out of here," he announced to no one in particular. With a last glance at the hours-delayed images of the Syndic light warships shadowing his fleet, then a careful look down the long list of his ships to see that all showed green ready-for-jump status, Geary ordered his ships to jump to Strabo.

•   •   •

THE transit to Strabo through jump space wasn't long, a mere five days. The jump to Cydoni wouldn't take a lot of time either, but the jump to Sancere would more than make up for that.

Jump space had always been odd, a strange, apparently endless emptiness of dull black marked only by rare appearances of splashes of light. What those lights were, what caused them and why, had been a mystery in Geary's time and remained unidentified to this day because there wasn't any known way to explore jump space. In a way that comforted Geary: something about his past and the present that had stayed unchanged.

But that was the only comfort he felt during the journey. Bad enough that the only person he'd felt able to partially confide in, Co-President Rione, hadn't come near him or sent any messages since their argument. Bad enough that he had to worry, as usual, that the Syndics would have a nasty surprise awaiting him and the fleet at Strabo. They could've thought past him, guessing that he'd guess where his current paths would lead and therefore doubling back like this. But if he surrendered to that kind of fear, then he'd be paralyzed, unable to make any decision because any possible course of action *could* have been anticipated by the Syndics.

No, there was something else bothering him this time. By the fourth day he'd narrowed the problems down to two. One was the new problem of Captain Falco, and the other the old problem of Captain Numos and the other disgruntled officers he represented. *I can handle one of those problems alone. But both of them . . . What if Numos seizes on Falco as the figurehead he needs to cause me serious command problems? When we arrive at Strabo, they'll have had almost a week to think up ways to make my life difficult and to imperil this fleet.*

Even more frustrating, a review of the mountain of communications between Alliance fleet ships before they left Sutrah had come up with none indicating Falco and

Numos had exchanged messages, but that meant nothing. With all the shuttle traffic that had been flying between ships, actual hard copy messages could've easily been transferred. The lack of detected messages from Falco to other officers stood out like a warning beacon in Geary's mind. Falco was obviously someone who thrived on attention and used his interpersonal skills to advance his career and what he thought were the best interests of the Alliance. He wouldn't refrain from trying to convince other officers to follow him, meaning that the messages Falco was surely distributing hadn't been detected by Geary or any of his firm allies among the ship commanders.

Am I being paranoid? But both Duellos and Rione warned me about Falco, and those two have proven the worth of their advice. Too bad I can't talk to Duellos since only simple, brief messages can be communicated while we're in jump space, and too bad Rione won't talk to me.

Geary watched the wandering lights, got more and more irritable, and wondered what would happen in Strabo Star System.

FOR a star, Strabo had very little to boast about. In terms of size, it had barely been big enough for the self-sustaining fusion reactions to trigger and turn it into a star instead of a very large planet. Strabo's satellites were well-suited for such a planet rather than a star, an assortment of bare rocks in close orbits. Geary had seen a lot of star systems and couldn't remember any as undistinguished and pitiable as Strabo. Little wonder the small emergency station the Syndics had once maintained here had been moth-balled long ago.

"Nothing," Captain Desjani remarked.

Geary nodded. "Are you talking about Syndic threats in particular, or just commenting on this star system?"

"Both." Desjani grinned.

"Are the fleet sensors scanning for anomalies that might indicate minefields anywhere in the system?"

"Yes, sir. The sensors are set to do sweeps automatically, though they're more effective when targeted on a specific area. No mines detected as of yet."

"Good." No Syndic ships visible in the system, either. Geary checked the display. The Alliance fleet spread out around *Dauntless*, every ship maintaining position as ordered. No threats. No apparent problems with Falco or Numos. Like the situations in Sutrah, it left Geary wondering what he might be missing.

Strabo also managed to be unimpressive when it came to the number of jump points it possessed. Even Sutrah had boasted four, but Strabo had only three. Relative to the one the fleet had entered the system using, the jump point to Cydoni was on the other side of the system. In order to get to that jump point, the fleet would swing past a third jump point, which led directly to only another hypernet-bypassed Syndic system before giving access to a couple of Syndic worlds that Geary believed would be defended by traps or mines because they were two of the same ones the fleet could've reached from Sutrah. Passing so close to the other jump point worried him, but there simply wasn't any good reason to swing wide of it. At its closest, the Alliance fleet would still be several light-minutes away. Taking a roundabout track to open the distance even more would surely feed rumors that Geary was too fearful.

Geary checked the maneuvering solution and ordered the fleet toward the jump point to Cydoni. Since Strabo was such a small star system, they would reach the other jump point in only a day and a half.

He took opportunity of the transit time to gather the fleet's ship commanders together for another simulated battle training session. Everything went off like clockwork, every ship doing exactly as Geary had directed. Which should have made him happy, but it didn't. His problem commanders were acting entirely too docile. He'd heard nothing from Falco, Numos, or any of the lesser figures who'd been most open about their distrust of Geary since he had assumed command. Occasional shuttles winged their

way between ships on what were identified as routine transfers of parts, materials, or personnel. Geary was positive
that they were also transferring appeals from Falco but
couldn't think of anything he could do about it. *I've already
checked with security, and they couldn't guarantee being
able to find any short video messages, even if they stripped
a shuttle down to component parts. Duellos hasn't heard
anything, but no one would talk to him, since he's known to
be an ally of mine.*

*I could preemptively order Falco's arrest. But that
probably would trigger mutinies on some of my ships, especially since I have no grounds for arresting the man. I
could order him back to* Dauntless, *but if he delayed or
simply refused to comply, I'd be stuck with either letting
him get away with it or arresting him.*

*I can't act now without certainly causing the problems
I'm afraid Falco might be creating.*

Geary put in a call to Captain Falco, figuring that facing
him was better than worrying about what Falco might be
doing behind his back. A nervous-looking Captain
Kerestes answered. "Captain Geary, I regret that Captain
Falco has been ordered to rest by fleet physicians on
Warrior."

"Captain Falco isn't well?" He wanted that set out
clearly in case anyone else was listening in.

"Just a temporary . . . illness," Kerestes advised, looking guilty as hell.

"I see." Any other attempt to get Falco would only emphasize Geary's inability to force Falco to talk. "Please inform Captain Falco that I hope he soon feels well enough
to continue working on behalf of the best interests of the
Alliance and this fleet."

"Yes, sir. Certainly, sir." After Kerestes broke the con-
nection, Geary had no trouble imagining the gasp of relief
that Kerestes must be producing.

Other than confirming that Kerestes was worried about
being noticed by his superiors, though, the call had accom-
plished nothing.

• • •

"MADAM Co-President." His pride had finally been overcome by his worries.

Her voice on the circuit was icy and detached. Rione had blocked the visual screen, leaving Geary wishing he could see her expression. "What do you want, Captain Geary?"

"I need to know if your sources within the fleet are aware of any problems."

Her answer took a moment. "Problems?"

"Anything concerning Captain Falco or Captain Numos."

Another pause before the reply. "There's a little talk. Nothing more."

"A little talk? That sounds like less than there used to be."

"It is less," Rione conceded. "But I've heard nothing else."

"I would be grateful if, should you hear anything, you tell me as soon as possible."

"What do you fear, Captain Geary? Your own commanders?" Her voice held a clear undercurrent of anger at him this time. "Such is the fate of heroes."

"I'm not—" Geary counted to five inside. "I'm worried that something may happen that will imperil the lives of many sailors in this fleet. I hope you can put aside your feelings about me and help me make sure no one does anything . . ."

"Stupid?"

"Yes."

"As opposed to heroic?" she inquired, as cold as frozen nitrogen again.

"Dammit, Madam Co-President—"

"I'll recheck with my sources. Out of concern for the well-being of the sailors of this fleet. Someone has to put concern for them first."

The circuit clicked off, leaving Geary barely restraining himself from slamming a fist into the wall next to the speaker.

• • •

"**CAPTAIN** Geary." Captain Desjani had her battle voice on, controlled and precise. "Something's happening."

The fleet was an hour from the jump point. Geary didn't waste time getting to the bridge, instead pulling up the fleet display above the table in his stateroom.

The "something" Desjani had referred to was all too obvious. The Alliance fleet's formation had developed gaps and holes as a lot of ships left their assigned positions. Based on the projected tracks the maneuvering system had estimated, all of the ships were headed in the same direction. Geary tallied them quickly. *Warrior, Orion, Majestic, Triumph, Invincible, Polaris,* and *Vanguard.* Four battleships and three battle cruisers. Six heavy cruisers, another four light cruisers, more than twenty destroyers. Almost forty ships.

Geary ran the course projections out and saw them heading for the other jump point. *Ancestors help them, they're going to try running straight for Alliance space, no doubt depending on their "fighting spirit" to overcome the odds they must realize they'll be facing.* He brought up the communications circuit, trying to think of the right commands to issue. "All units are instructed to return to formation." That was totally useless. They weren't likely to listen if they'd already decided to ignore his orders. "You are heading for heavily defended Syndic star systems. You will not be able to make your way through them."

No reaction. The rebel ships kept going, slicing across the fleet. *I can't convince them. Not now. They've placed their faith in Falco and what they imagine is their own superior moral strength. An appeal to reason won't work against that. But I need to make sure no one else joins them. What do I say?* "Your duties to the Alliance demand that you remain with this fleet and not abandon your comrades." That should sting. As it should, since they were running away from the rest of the fleet. "Return to your positions now for the sake of your ships and your crews, and there will be no disciplinary actions taken." There wouldn't have to be, Geary knew, since an abortive action would convince most of those inclined to follow Falco and Numos that they couldn't be trusted.

A reply finally came. "This is Captain Falco, commanding those ships willing to uphold the honor and glory of the Alliance fleet. I call upon—" A symbol popped up on Geary's communications display, and Falco's voice cut off.

"This is Captain Desjani," she called down to Geary using the *Dauntless*'s internal circuits. "I've activated the fleet command override. Any signals from other ships on the fleetwide circuits will be blocked. We'll hear anything sent directly to us."

"Thanks." If only he had a fleet full of commanders like Tanya Desjani. Geary himself had realized too late that he couldn't allow Falco a public forum to broadcast a plea to other ships to desert. He transmitted to the fleet again, keeping his voice firm and calm. "All ships, there is no honor in deserting your comrades, no honor in disobeying lawful orders. We fight for victory, for the safety of our homes, not glory. All units return to your places in the formation. You'll be needed when we strike the Syndics next." Maybe that appeal to being in battle would reach some of them.

But the thirty-nine ships making up Falco's force were rapidly forming their own small formation, heading straight for the other jump point and not far from it now. An irrational urge to open fire on the rebel ships grew out of Geary's anger at Falco, but he pushed the idea aside almost as soon as it surfaced. *Impossible. I won't give that order. Even if I did, who'd obey it? That's what the Syndics would do. But then what can I do? I can't stop them. They're only fifteen minutes from that jump point.* "All units that have left the formation, reconsider your actions for the sake of the Alliance and the sake of your comrades and the sake of your crews. You will not survive attempting to reach Alliance space along the paths available to you through that jump point."

The diverging ships were several light-minutes away

now. Even allowing for that time delay, it was clear that Geary's latest appeal had failed. There wasn't time for another appeal, really, just time for one more short transmission to be received by them before the other ships entered jump space. He took a deep breath, staring at the star display, his mind rapidly running through jump paths connecting the nearest stars. "All units that have left the formation. Ilion. I say again. Ilion."

Perhaps twelve minutes later, Geary saw the images of the fleeing ships vanish as they jumped out of the system.

He spent a while rearranging his fleet to cover the gaps left by the ships that had fled, then sat silently until they reached the jump point to Cydoni. "All ships, jump now."

HE had been dreading this sort of thing ever since being thrust into command of the fleet. Dreading a split in the fleet. It seemed obvious to him that dividing their forces while trapped deep inside enemy territory was insane, but it had been obvious from the first that not all of his ship commanders took a rational view of things. Now the precedent had been set. Almost forty ships had headed for an unknown fate under senior commanders whom Geary regarded with misgivings, distrust, and in the case of Numos no small measure of contempt. If only there had been some way for those commanders to meet the fates they deserved without those ships suffering the same fates.

But there is a chance. If they think, if they realize dying gloriously doesn't do much to protect their home worlds, if they are willing to take advantage of what I taught them while they were with the fleet. If they're willing to take advantage of what I told them before they left. And if the Syndics don't hear that information from them and have time to lay an ambush for the rest of us. I wish I knew.

Unable to stand the silence of his stateroom, which seemed to have grown much lonelier since Co-President Rione had ceased dropping by for visits, Geary forced himself to tour the compartments on *Dauntless* again, showing a confident face to a crew shaken by the departure of many comrades, telling them in a dozen different ways that once the fleet reached Sancere they'd give the Syndics a lesson to remember, trying to focus the crew on the future rather than events in Strabo Star System. He used the minimal communications available in jump space to send a brief variation on that to the rest of the ships in the fleet, hoping to do the same with them.

In the time that was left, Geary threw himself into designing more simulations to run. He kept hoping he could use them to impart some of the fighting skills he remembered from a century ago, skills lost to the fleet in the decades since, as devastating losses in ships and crews wiped out the institutional memory and skills of the smaller professional force Geary had once known. He didn't know how much longer he might have to try to pass on such lessons.

GEARY strode onto the bridge of the *Dauntless* as the Alliance fleet prepared to leave jump.

Captain Desjani glanced back at him and nodded in greeting, her concern for him impossible to miss. Geary nodded heavily back as he sank into his command seat. He hadn't realized how bad he must look in the aftermath of Falco's betrayal. Bad enough for Desjani to notice, anyway. Hopefully, the crew hadn't picked up on it. Or maybe he just looked particularly bad now, after an almost sleepless night wondering what might be in the Cydoni Star System. Wondering if any other ships would bolt the fleet there.

To cover the renewed anxiety he suddenly felt, Geary called up the fleet display and pretended to study it intently. He had been trying to come up with a plan for Sancere, given that he wouldn't know what was there until they arrived. An idea had occurred to him yesterday, prompted ironically by what had happened in the Strabo Star System, and he spent a few minutes thinking about it, checking on the names and records of some of his ship commanders.

"Preparing to leave jump," Desjani announced.

Geary hastily brought the system display to life and waited. All it showed now was the historical information the old Syndic Star System guides they had found on Sutrah Five had contained. As soon as the fleet arrived in normal space on the edge of Cydoni System, the sensors on *Dauntless* and every other ship in the fleet would start updating the display based on what could be seen from their arrival point.

Geary's insides jerked, and the drab, dull black of jump space was replaced by the glittering, star-filled universe of real space. He waited, watching, as system updates popped onto the display. No ships. No mines detected. Nothing. Captain Desjani was grinning triumphantly.

But Geary still stared at the system display, where the expanding photosphere of Cydoni's sun had been reaching out for the one habitable world this system had once boasted. The scene held the same sick fascination as a train wreck, though in this case the centuries-long process was playing out far slower than any human vehicle accident, and the wreck was of an entire world.

Most of the atmosphere of the formerly habitable planet had been stripped away by now. Empty ocean basins had long since been drained of their waters, also flung away into space by the bombardment of particles and heat from the swollen sun that had once made life possible on this world. Now that sun was slowly devouring the planet, and no trace of life in any form could be detected anywhere upon it.

"There's probably some extreme-environment life-forms still existing beneath the crust of the planet," one of the watch-standers reported. "They'll hold on a little while longer."

"How long until the photosphere actually envelops the planet?" Geary asked.

"It's hard to say, sir. The expansion of a star like this

takes place in fits and starts. Probably anywhere from fifty to two hundred years, depending on exactly what happens inside the star."

"Thanks." Geary took a look at a magnified image of the planet. *Dauntless*'s sensors had tagged some areas where ruins still existed, though badly battered and worn by the extreme environmental conditions they'd endured so that they seemed millennia old. One batch of ruins lay next to an empty sea, its partial walls almost submerged in dust dunes blown around before the atmosphere had thinned too much, the land glowing red from the light of the expanding star. Geary wondered what the city or town had looked like when there'd been waters rolling at its feet. The information from the Syndic system guides was at his fingertips, so Geary checked that. Port Junosa. Already completely abandoned before the outdated Syndic documents had been prepared. Lives had been devoted to that city, building it and sustaining it and making it a human community, but all that was left now were the battered ruins, and within another century even those would be annihilated by the expanding star. After seeing desolate places like Strabo and Cydoni, it would be a relief to see a bustling star system like Sancere, even if the robust human presence there was all enemy.

"We'll have to take a course that will remain well out from that swollen photosphere," Captain Desjani remarked.

Geary nodded. "Yeah. Do you have problems with the course recommended by the ship's maneuvering systems? It'll take us four days to reach the jump point for Sancere, but I don't see a good alternative."

"There isn't one," Desjani agreed. "This is the best option."

Four days. Four days for the less reliable among his ship commanders to think about what other ships had done at Strabo. Four days for them to consider heading for another jump exit. *I'll have to keep them busy. Keep them focused on Sancere. Keep them too involved with simulations*

*and maneuvers and plans to give them time to think about
anything but Sancere. It'll drive me to exhaustion, but I
don't see any alternative.*

He started setting up a limited fleet conference, involving only the commanders of roughly thirty ships. Who
should lead it? He hadn't quite decided before, but looking
at the list he'd compiled of able commanders, one name
stood out. Still, there was one question he hadn't looked up
yet, and the answer didn't seem readily available within
the *Dauntless*'s databanks. Either that or Geary wasn't asking the question right, and the artificial minds he was dealing with couldn't understand him. He'd run into that too
many times already. "How long will it take these intelligent agents to understand me?" he openly grumbled.

Desjani directed a glance to one of her watch-standers.
That woman cleared her throat before speaking. "Sir, the
intelligent agents have learned a pattern of responses based
on the ways of thinking and writing or speaking characteristic of the people they deal with." She hesitated.

"And I don't think like them, do I?"

"No, sir. Your unspoken assumptions, patterns of
thought, and ways of phrasing aren't quite the same
as . . . uh . . ."

"Modern minds?" Geary asked, unable to keep some
dry humor out of his voice this time. It made sense, he realized. A century built up a lot of subtle as well as not-so-
subtle differences in the way people thought and expressed
those thoughts. *Either I laugh at this or let it get to me, and
I've got too many other things trying to get to me.*

The watch-stander smiled nervously. "Yes, sir. I'm
afraid so, sir. The agents factor in your responses, but the
vast majority of people they deal with have, uh, different
ways of handling information, which means they aren't adjusting to you."

"Why can't you set up a subroutine for the intelligent
agents to use when dealing with Captain Geary?" Desjani
demanded. "Then they could reset to match his patterns of

usage while remaining attuned to the rest of the officers and crew."

"That's prohibited by fleet regulations on the use of intelligent agents, Captain. Intelligent agents on ship systems are never supposed to become personal agents for any individual. That could create conflicts of interest in the artificial minds."

Geary shook his head, wondering why even something like this had to be complicated. "Can the fleet commander override that regulation on an emergency basis?"

In response, the watch-stander looked troubled. "Sir, I'd have to look up what constitutes an emergency for official purposes."

"Lieutenant!" Captain Desjani rapped out. "We're deep in enemy territory and trying to get home in one piece. That meets my definition of an emergency."

"Me, too," Geary agreed. "Make it happen, Lieutenant. It'll make my life a lot easier."

The watch-stander smiled with relief on having clear instructions to a way out of the problem. "Yes, sir. Of course, sir. We'll get right on it."

"Thanks." Geary looked at Desjani. "It'll help with planning."

Desjani smiled, as confident in Geary as ever. "You have a plan for Sancere?"

"That's right. Sancere is unlikely to be lightly defended. I'm assuming we'll face a strong enough force to be a problem. If I'm wrong, we'll be able to adjust to less opposition."

"You'll strike for the hypernet gate?"

"Yeah." Geary looked down, frowning. "I've been trying to look up something about that. I assume the Syndics might try to destroy the thing. Just how hard is it to destroy a hypernet gate?"

Desjani looked surprised. "I have no idea. It gets talked about sometimes, but no one's ever actually done it, to my knowledge."

Geary shrugged. "Hopefully, it won't be an issue. If we

can draw any Syndic defenders out of position and lunge for the hypernet gate, we might be able to keep them from destroying it even if they want to. After wc have that, we can defeat the defenders, loot what supplies we need, and destroy every facility related to the Syndic war effort."

Desjani's eyes gleamed. "It'll be a nasty blow to the Syndics, hitting something so important where they surely never expected it to be seriously threatened."

"Right." *If they're not waiting for us with the kind of ambush that almost annihilated this fleet in the Syndic home system. And if my fleet doesn't fall apart any further before we get there.* Geary stood. "I'll be meeting with some of the ship commanders."

COMMANDER Cresida appeared to sit next to Geary, the other twenty-eight ship commanders ranked down the table, all plainly curious why they'd been singled out for this virtual meeting.

"You've been selected because your records and the records of your ships mark you as both brave and steady in combat," Geary explained. "We'll be arriving in Sancere with no idea what sort of forces the Syndics have on hand. It's not likely to be anything we can't handle," he stated confidently and hoped fervently, "but it might be enough to cause us losses if we don't deal with it well. Here's what I need from you. Commander Cresida on *Furious* will be in command of a special task force comprising your ships. Task Force Furious won't be broken out separately from the rest of the fleet when we arrive at Sancere. What you'll do is simulate breaking formation, *Furious* first and the others following, as if you were engaging in an undisciplined charge at the strongest force of Syndic ships we can spot."

Commander Cresida and the other commanders couldn't hide their puzzlement. "You *want* us to break formation?" Cresida asked. "To look like we're being so aggressive we aren't paying attention to orders?"

"Yes." Geary pointed to a representation of Sancere's system. "Charge headlong at the enemy. There's not enough of you here to deal with the likely number of Syndic ships guarding Sancere or just there getting refitted or undergoing repairs. That's deliberate. I want you to look like a small force that has rashly separated from the rest of the fleet and can be easily destroyed. You go racing down toward the enemy, but short of engagement range, I want you to turn, raggedly and still in an undisciplined fashion, and flee downward, away from the Syndics and the rest of the fleet." Geary traced the imagined tracks with his finger.

Cresida looked horrified. "As if we were running from the enemy?"

"Exactly." None of the commanders looked happy. "There's a good reason for that. The idea is—"

"Sir," Cresida interrupted, her expression concerned and earnest. "The Syndics won't believe it."

Geary had been momentarily upset at the thought that Cresida might act as bullheaded as Numos. But what she said nipped that anger in the bud because it seemed to have a good reason behind it. "Why not?"

"We don't flee battle, sir." The pride in Cresida's voice couldn't be missed. "Regardless of the odds." All of the other commanders nodded in agreement. "The Syndics know this. They won't believe a feigned retreat."

That was a problem, but Geary couldn't see any grounds for denying Cresida's assessment, especially with all of the other specially selected ship captains agreeing with her. It also matched the fighting-spirit-triumphing-over-all-odds nonsense that he had heard from Falco. How could he disregard the advice of commanders he had already decided were particularly trustworthy? "Then I want your advice. Any of you. How do we draw off Syndic defenders, get them chasing Task Force Furious instead of paying attention to what the rest of the fleet is doing?"

Commander Neeson of the *Implacable* shrugged.

"Captain Geary, if you want to get the Syndics chasing us, then I'd recommend a firing pass. Come in hard and fast, hit the outermost units with everything we can throw at them, then sweep onward."

Cresida nodded. "Yes. Get them mad. Even better if there's a follow-on target we seem to be aiming for. Something they can't let us reach. We hit them, then alter course to head for the high-value target."

"Sancere's got to be full of high-value targets," someone else observed. "We should be able to identify something on the fly."

Geary thought about the plan, gazing at the representation of Sancere's system. "What if you get too deep into the Syndic defenses? I don't want this to be a real suicide charge. I want you to be able to get out without being cut to pieces."

Neeson studied the system display as well. "We should be able to do that. Set off on a course aimed at something valuable, the Syndics get themselves onto an intercept and crank on the speed, then we swing out, leaving them out of position. What is it we're trying to distract them from, sir?"

"I want our fleet to get to the hypernet gate before any Syndic ships realize they need to flee through it and manage to get there. If we can seize the gate and block any departures, we'll have all the time we need to destroy Syndic facilities at Sancere and then ride the Syndic hypernet system back to the doorstep of Alliance space."

"If they destroy the gate . . ." Cresida began reluctantly.

"We won't have to worry about Syndic reinforcements rushing in," Geary replied.

"But the energy pulse might be dangerous."

It seemed he'd found that expert on hypernet gates that he needed. "Tell me about it."

Cresida gestured toward the representation of the Sancere hypernet gate on the display. "The gate is sort of a bound energy matrix. A hypernet key works by pairing the matrix of particles within a gate to the matrix of particles at another gate, establishing a path that ships can use. The matrix is held by these structures," she pointed to objects ranked around the gate. "As you can see, there's hundreds of them. They're called tethers, even though they're not really tethers, because in one sense they hold the particle matrix in the desired form. That's how a gate would be destroyed, by disabling or destroying the tethers. But when that happens, the matrix breaks, and the bound energy is released." A couple of the other commanders present nodded in agreement.

"Good description, Commander," Geary replied. Geary imagined that the actual science behind the gates was far more complicated than what Cresida had summarized. He wished everyone he needed technical descriptions from could render them so simply and concisely. "How much energy and in what form?"

Cresida grimaced unhappily. "That's a theoretical question. It's never been tested in practice. One extreme says the breaking of a gate matrix would generate a supernova-scale burst of energy."

"A supernova?" Geary questioned, incredulous. "A supernova puts out as much energy in one blast as a star puts out over a ten billion year life span. An explosion like that would fry not only everything inside the entire star system it's in but also surrounding star systems."

"Yes," Cresida agreed. "That'd be a negative outcome, obviously."

"Obviously," Geary agreed.

"But the other extreme says the energy in the matrix would, uh, fold in upon itself, like an infinite origami, getting ever smaller and tighter until it dropped into another state of existence and was lost to this universe. Energy output in this universe would be zero."

Geary sat down, looking around and seeing the other knowledgeable commanders agreeing with Cresida again. "Then our two extremes are that the destruction of a gate would destroy an entire star system and adjacent star systems, or it'd do nothing at all. But what level of energy release is regarded as the most probable outcome?"

Cresida looked to her fellows as she spoke. "Most scientists believe the energy output would fall somewhere between less than that of a supernova and more than nothing, but no one's been able to confidently predict how much that would be."

"You're kidding."

"No, sir."

"That's the best science can offer? And those gates got built knowing they could potentially blow the hell out of this part of the galaxy?"

"Yes, sir."

"They let you go really fast," Commander Neeson noted.

Geary stared at the representation of the hypernet gate at Sancere, wondering just how many disasters traced their origin to the human desire to travel faster than before. *I've been wondering if nonhuman intelligences might be tied somehow to this horribly destructive war we've been fighting for the last century. But I ought to know by now that humans don't need nonhuman intelligences to influence us to do something stupid.*

Hey. Wait a minute. "Why is it we don't know more about this? We designed and built the hypernet system. How could we be so uncertain about important characteristics of it?"

Commander Cresida exchanged glances with her comrades again. "I can't answer that exactly, Captain Geary. I know the practical breakthroughs that let us build the hypernet came ahead of the theories that explained it. A lot of the theory is still being worked out. That's not the first time that sort of thing has happened. People often figure out how to do something before they understand why it works."

"Us and the Syndics? We both made these practical breakthroughs at about the same time?"

She shrugged. "The Syndics stole the knowledge from

us, sir. That's what we assume, though I don't have the security clearances to know for sure."

Or we stole it from them. "The bottom line is, you're telling me the Syndics won't dare destroy that gate?"

"Uh, no, sir. We don't know. They may have decided the risk is acceptable."

Geary tried not to let his feelings show. *We don't know. What if the extreme guess is right, and this fleet causes the Syndics to do something that fries not only Sancere and this fleet but a lot of nearby star systems? And even just having this fleet appear at Sancere might cause the Syndic commanders to destroy the hypernet gate as soon as they spot us. But I can't afford not to go to Sancere and attack. This fleet needs the supplies there.*

There's no alternative. I have to hope for the best, that the energy release won't be so large it threatens anything, either nearby stars or just my ships.

Oh, hell. I know what they'll do.

"We have to assume the Syndics will plan on waiting until our fleet is near the gate, then destroy it," Geary announced. The other ship commanders stared at him. "They're going to hope the gate releases enough energy to fry us but not enough to fry Sancere or anything beyond it."

Cresida nodded in agreement. "And if it does fry Sancere, then that's just collateral damage in their eyes."

"But then what do we do?" Neeson asked. "We can't just ignore the gate."

"I'll think of something," Geary promised. *I hope.* "If this diversion plan works, we can keep the Syndics from having forces in place to actually blow the gate. Now, it sounds like we're in agreement on the best course of action for Task Force Furious. Break from the formation, charge at the Syndic defenders, make a high-speed firing pass, look like you're heading for something very valuable, but divert after the Syndics commit to an intercept." He paused. "I'll send orders what to do after that, based on the situation. The most critical thing is that I don't want you to actually dive into the heart of the Syndic defenses all by yourselves. Get back out of there so I can employ you in conjunction with the rest of the fleet." Everyone nodded. "I'll ensure orders are sent to each of you. Thank you. Commander Cresida, please wait."

After the virtual presences of the others vanished, Geary turned a serious face to Commander Cresida. "You're going to be a good ways away from the fleet after you charge the Syndics. You could easily be more than a light-hour distant from the fleet. That means I won't know if you get into trouble until an hour after the fact. I'm trusting you to fight smart, Commander. Keep the Syndics occupied, keep their attention on you, but don't get yourself shot up. Can you retreat when it's the best course of action?"

Cresida seemed to ponder the question for a moment, then nodded. "Yes, sir."

"I want you alive and fighting, not proud and dead."

She grinned. "Sir, you've demonstrated we can be proud, alive, and fighting. I'm still trying to figure out how you managed to bring everything together at Kaliban to smash the Syndics."

Geary smiled back at her. "Do a great job at Sancere, and I'll give you personal lessons on how to do it."

"That's a deal, sir." They both stood, and Cresida rendered a precise salute. She'd obviously been practicing. Geary didn't tell her that fleet salutes tended to be sloppier than that and as a result she looked more like a Marine. Come to think of it, maybe Colonel Carabali had been the one teaching her how to do it. Geary knew the Marines had been deriving considerable amusement from watching the sailors' attempts to deal with Geary's moves to reintroduce saluting to the fleet.

He sat down again after Cresida's departure, gazing at the display, especially the representation of the hypernet gate. It hadn't occurred to him before now that the gates were potentially dangerous. Potentially extremely dangerous.

Potentially by far the deadliest weapons mankind had ever built.

And he had no alternative but to charge most of his fleet right at the hypernet gate at Sancere.

FIVE

THE communications alert chimed urgently, bringing Geary to full wakefulness. He rolled and hit the accept-message control automatically, fearing to hear that some more of his ships had bolted the formation.

"Captain Geary." Commander Cresida seemed both anxious and excited. "I've been doing some thinking. Odd concepts. But it occurred to me that since the hypernet gate matrices are suspended between so many tethers, maybe a matrix would respond somewhat like a net or sail, which means exactly how it collapses would depend upon exactly how the tethers release."

Geary tried to get his mind around that. Fortunately, Cresida's analogy wasn't too complicated. "What does that mean for us?"

"Well, sir, if the way the matrix collapses affects the amount of energy released, which it should, and if the way the matrix collapses is dependent on how the tethers fail, then in theory it should be possible to use selective failure of the tethers to regulate the amount of energy released."

"Sort of like a nuclear weapon with a selectable yield?"

"In a way . . .though the physical processes involved and the science are completely different."

"What would you need to pursue this?" Geary pressed. "Can you get a workable answer?"

"Maybe." Cresida shrugged apologetically. "I'd need priority access to the entire fleet-distributed network, sir."

"The entire thing?" The amount of computational power in the network was far beyond Geary's ability to grasp. That gave him some idea of the complexity of what Cresida was proposing. "All right. You've got it."

He sat for a while after Cresida's message ended, wondering if he really wanted her to succeed. But if she was right, he couldn't afford to not find out.

THE combat simulations Geary ran as the fleet headed for the jump point to Sancere went well. But at the subsequent fleet conference, he found the absence of officers like Numos and Faresa to be jarring instead of welcome. Their absence only emphasized that forty of his ships had gone off to a fate Geary worried he could too easily predict. The way many of his remaining commanders kept looking around as if seeking familiar faces who weren't present made it obvious that a lot of his officers were also aware of the absences.

It couldn't hurt to try distracting people from that. "Has everyone received and entered the modified settings for their jump drives so we can make it all the way to Sancere?"

All of the officers ranged along the apparently huge table nodded, but their nervousness on those grounds was now easily apparent. He knew why they were worried. Leaping into battle against human foes was one thing, but jumping too far in the weirdness of jump space was another. Ships that jumped too far had never come out of jump space, though Geary knew sailors told stories about long-lost craft appearing suddenly at lonely star systems, their crews long ago dead in some particularly horrible ways, or simply haunting the ship still, changed by the strange nature of jump space into something no longer alive but unable to die. He'd heard the stories in bars and while standing watches late during a ship's night period, when the darkened and deserted passageways of a familiar ship somehow became eerie in their silence. Geary wondered if the old, cheap jump space undead horror movies of his youth were still around in newer versions.

"I assure you," Geary emphasized, "that the settings will work. I've personally made jumps of this distance more than once." That didn't seem to provide as much comfort as Geary had hoped. "You don't have to take my word for it. If you search the fleet database, you'll find accounts of it. I can show you the references." The accounts were otherwise too easily lost in the mass of information available. He'd only found them because he'd known exactly what to look for since he'd been on some of the ships involved. Geary sometimes wondered just how much accumulated knowledge mankind had hopelessly buried within databases collecting and endlessly storing everything possible. In ancient times, knowledge had been lost because copies no longer existed. Nowadays it was lost because copies of everything existed and finding a particular piece of information made the old needle in a haystack look like an easy task, even if you knew the information was there to begin with.

The knowledge that they could find proof of Geary's assertions cheered them up a little. "Believe me, the Syndics are going to be very unpleasantly surprised when we pop out of that jump exit at Sancere. As far as they're concerned, the Alliance fleet will have done the impossible." Geary finally saw smiles breaking out along the long, long virtual table. "We have every reason to believe we'll achieve total surprise. That will give us an important window to act before the Syndics command authorities in Sancere even realize we've brought the war to them."

"The shipyards at Sancere produce many Syndic battleships and battle cruisers," Captain Duellos observed.

Geary gave his ship commanders a grim smile. "It'll be a target-rich environment if even half of what we expect is there. That's why it'll be critically important that we coordinate our attacks. If ships start blazing away at the most attractive target they see, it could easily result in one Syndic ship getting blown to atoms while a half dozen other Syndics get away. We don't want any of them getting away." They liked hearing that, he could tell. It should go a long way to keeping them in check when confronted with a wealth of targets.

"Captain Tyrosian."

She nodded.

"The fast fleet auxiliaries in your division have done a fantastic job of fabricating new kinetic bombardment rounds and getting them distributed to the other combatants. The crews of *Titan*, *Witch*, *Goblin*, and *Jinn* are all to be congratulated on their hard work and dedication." Tyrosian looked pleased, which she had every right to be. *Thank the living stars none of the auxiliary ships was foolish enough to leave with Falco. I need those ships and what they can do for this fleet if I'm to get it home.*

Captain Tulev frowned. "While we have every reason to assume the Syndics will be caught totally unprepared, we have to also assume that defenses in the Sancere System are up-to-date and numerous."

"Agreed," Geary stated. "We'll have the fleet in a general-purpose attack formation when we jump, but we'll modify it as soon as I get a feel for the best way to take out the defenses. As you all know from the battle plan outline I provided, the ships in Task Force Furious will be pretending to break formation. They'll hopefully draw any Syndic warships after them and leave us free to seize the hypernet gate." He paused, not wanting to crush the enthusiasm he saw at the idea of reaching that gate. "We also have to assume that the Syndics will try to destroy that gate before we can use it."

"The gates are very robust," one of the other ship commanders pointed out. "They can take a lot of damage because of redundant components."

"Yes," Geary agreed. *Built that way, I now know, because if they did fail, the consequences could be huge, but if I tell everyone that, I might end up with panic at a crucial point.* "But they weren't designed to withstand deliberate attack. It may not be possible to get to that gate in time. But we're going to give it our best shot."

Several seconds of silence passed, then one of the destroyer commanders spoke up. "Sir, what about the ships that left at Strabo?"

Geary clenched his teeth before he could answer. "There's not much we can do. Hell, there's nothing we can do. We couldn't even go after them to help, because we didn't know which star they were jumping for." *Because I'd blocked their communications, in which Captain Falco was doubtless trying to tell everyone exactly that, along with his brainless call to battle.* "I believe they're going to run into a Syndic buzz saw and get cut to ribbons. Fighting spirit is all very well, it's absolutely critical in fact, but it's a lousy shield against enemy weapons." He paused, hating to have to say that out loud, but feeling he had to state a truth they all knew anyway. "But they do have one chance."

"Ilion?" Captain Duellos asked. "You gave them the name of that star system before they jumped from Strabo. I couldn't help noticing that it's within jump range of Sancere."

"Yes." Geary pointed at the star display over the table. *Of course Duellos has already researched that question.* "If we can't use the hypernet gate at Sancere, we'll jump to Ilion from Sancere."

"Why Ilion?" the captain of the *Terrible* demanded. "It's not the best route back toward Alliance space from Sancere."

"That's true," Geary stated calmly, "but it's the only star system those ships that left the fleet could reach if they turned back and tried to rejoin us. If they manage to escape

the Syndics, they can backtrack to Ilion and rendezvous
with us there."

Captain Tulev was gazing at the display, his face
somber. "You mean if *any* of them manage to escape the
Syndics."

"Yes. If they do, they know where to find us." Geary
looked around the table, meeting everyone's gaze. "That's
a risk to us. As noted, it's not the best route back to
Alliance space, and we'll likely need to hang around Ilion
longer than I'd like to give those other ships a chance to
meet up with the fleet again. But it's the only thing we can
do, and I made the decision to run those risks for the sake
of those Alliance ships and crews."

There was another pause, then *Terrible*'s captain nodded. "Yes, sir. Thank you, Captain Geary. I know you don't
have votes on decisions, but I'd have voted for that."

No one contradicted him. Geary nodded back.
"Thanks." *What else do I say? Please, no other ship captains take in your heads to run off for another star?*

But nothing else seemed to be needed. The uncertainty
Geary had felt earlier had been replaced by varying degrees of enthusiasm and resignation. The meeting broke
up, virtual presences vanishing until only Captain Duellos
remained. He gave Geary a stern look. "You should have
told them about Ilion right off the bat. I was going to bring
it up, having guessed what it meant, but *Terrible* beat me
to it."

Geary shrugged. "I wasn't sure how they'd take it, how
they'd take anything regarding those ships that followed
Falco."

"You're not the only one who's scared, Captain Geary."
Duellos smiled very briefly as Geary gave him a startled
look. "Oh, you hide it exceptionally well, but I know, because I know enough about you by now to read the signs.
Don't be fooled by the brave talk of my fellow captains.
We're all scared, all wondering if the next system will be
our last, all wondering if our best possible future involves

a Syndic labor camp like the one we found on Sutrah Five."

Geary sat down, rapping his forehead with one fist. "They needed to hear that I was still thinking in terms of everyone getting back, even the ones who took off."

"Exactly." Duellos exhaled a long, low breath. "That's the only hope for those forty ships, by the way. That they'll run."

"I know." Geary ran his hand through the star display, watching his forefinger spanning constellations. "But I've been told the fleet never runs."

"Ha! Let me guess. Desjani?"

Geary bent one corner of his mouth in a smile. "No."

"Ah, that's right. She's been watching you and learning. Let's see . . . oh, of course. Cresida. Our little firebrand from the *Furious*."

"The other captains seemed to agree with her," Geary pointed out.

Duellos smiled. "The ones from Task Force Furious? Naturally. Because you handpicked them for their quality. But if you weren't in command, even they would waver if things got bad enough, as they certainly will when Fighting Falco hits the Syndic ambushes you and I expect him to meet."

Geary toyed with the controls, his mind not on them. "What do you think will happen? What will Falco do?"

"Fall apart," Duellos stated matter-of-factly. "I mean it. Once he was a capable if unimaginative commander at his best. At his worst, Captain Falco assumed the enemy was as impressed by him as he himself was. The enemy didn't always accommodate that assumption, to the sorrow of the Alliance forces entrusted to Falco's command."

Geary nodded, thinking those descriptions did a good job of summing up what he had learned of Falco's battles before his capture. "But he wasn't totally incompetent. I still can't believe he was willing to charge into a certain Syndic trap with that small a force. For that matter, I can't believe that so many commanding officers were willing to follow him."

Duellos grimaced as if he were tasting something unpleasant. "Captain Falco's powers of persuasion haven't dimmed much. I finally acquired a copy of the message he had physically distributed among ships with possibly sympathetic captains. Even I found it to be actually moving and inspiring."

"Too bad none of those captains saw fit to tell me about it," Geary noted bitterly. "I might have saved some of their fellow officers and ships. But I can't say I'm surprised to hear it was moving. I had the impression that Captain Falco honestly believes he is the only one who can save the Alliance. He's not a fake in that respect."

"Oh, he cares about the Alliance," Duellos agreed. "Or, rather, he cares about what he thinks the Alliance is. His speeches have such power because they really do come from the heart. But because Falco also believes only he really understands what needs to be done and believes only he can do what needs to be done, he long ago convinced himself that saving the Alliance and advancing his career and power are one and the same thing." Duellos exhaled heavily. "He's spent twenty years driving himself in tighter and tighter rings of that mental circle, and he started out already convinced he was the savior of the Alliance."

Geary spent a while thinking about that before nodding again. "His arguments have such force because he really believes them, but they're even less grounded in reality now than they were twenty years ago."

"Much less grounded in reality." Duellos shrugged, looking unhappy. "On top of that, Captain Falco's spent a long time in a labor camp, where routine rules. Did you notice how hard a time he has now adjusting when something unexpected happens, even in a conversation? He hasn't dealt with emergencies, he hasn't been fighting battles. He's horribly out of practice at commanding ships. That's just the mental side of things. Physically, he's older and has been living under stressful conditions with poor food and poor medical care."

"It'd been a century since my last command when I took over this fleet," Geary noted dryly.

Duellos grinned this time. "For us. For you it had been a matter of weeks. And if you'll forgive me for being blunt, the only thing Captain Falco has in common with you is the rank insignia."

"That's nice to hear," Geary admitted, smiling to show he didn't take the implied compliment too seriously. "So you think Falco won't be able to command effectively at all?"

Duellos nodded, grim again.

"What will those ships do then? Make a glorious charge to the death into the teeth of the Syndic fleet?"

Duellos spent a moment gazing at the star display, his face serious. "Unlikely, I think. A glorious charge to the death has to be led by someone. Unless I miss my guess, Falco will be overwhelmed and incapable of doing that. The other senior captains like Numos and Faresa are neither inspiring nor emotionally suited to such an act of brave desperation. So, no leader to lead a charge. Worst case, they lose their heads and scatter, becoming easy meat for the Syndics. Best case, they remember Ilion and charge for the route back there, holding their formation together so they can protect each other. The Syndics wouldn't be expecting those ships to head for a jump point leading back into Syndic space, so that might leave a chance for them to make it. A small one, but it's there."

Geary nodded, his eyes on the same stars. "You sound like you've been listening in to my prayers to my ancestors. That's what I'm praying those ships will do."

"If they do come to Ilion," Duellos stated, "there may be Syndics in pursuit. A lot of Syndics."

"I know. We'll be ready if that happens. Ready to fight our way out of Ilion if the odds are bad enough, or to kick that Syndic force halfway out of this sector if the odds favor it."

"You should have told our ship captains that, too," Duellos advised.

"I will, in a message before we jump." Geary took a deep breath. "Do you think anyone else will leave?"

"Now? No. Even those who are scared to follow you are more scared of leaving the fleet. That's what held them from following Captain Falco."

Geary laughed. "I guess that's the best endorsement I can hope for."

Duellos stood and saluted. "I'll see you in Sancere, Captain Geary."

Geary came to attention and returned the salute. "Count on it."

To Geary's surprise, the instant Duellos vanished, Commander Cresida's image reappeared. She looked haggard as she saluted him. "We have something that may work."

"Really? We can limit the energy release from a gate failure?"

"In theory. If the assumptions made are accurate." Cresida made a helpless gesture. "We won't know if it really works until it's actually tried."

"And if it doesn't work, then we may not get a chance to try something else," Geary noted sourly. "Great job, though."

"Sir." Cresida hesitated. "There's something else."

GEARY cradled a data disc in one hand as the fleet went into jump, leaving the bloated shape of Cydoni's sun behind. The jump to Sancere would take over two weeks, a length of uninterrupted time in jump space that no one in the fleet but Geary had ever experienced. Nodding to Captain Desjani, he stood, knowing he probably looked distracted. "I'll be in my stateroom."

The walk to his stateroom seemed unusually short with his thoughts focused elsewhere. Reaching it with what seemed surprising quickness, Geary sat down, then gave a hard rap to his internal communications controls. "Madam Co-President, I need to speak with you."

"I'm afraid that won't be convenient." Victoria Rione's voice sounded not only colder than space itself but also tired.

"I'm afraid I must insist."

There was a pause before her answer came. "What is this about?"

"Something critically important."

"Am I supposed to trust your assessment of that?"

Geary fought down an angry retort. "I don't care whether you trust it or not. I need you here to discuss something. If you actually care about the safety of the Alliance, you'll come and talk to me."

"And if I don't?"

Geary stared at the bulkhead opposite him. He could threaten force, but that wouldn't predispose Rione to listen. It also might not work. Not with Co-President Rione. "Please, Madam Co-President. I swear on my ancestors' honor that this is something you must know."

The pause this time was longer. "Very well, Captain Geary. I still believe in the honor of your ancestors. I'll be there soon."

Geary slumped back, rubbing his eyes. *To think I once looked forward to Rione's visits. But this is too important. I can't avoid it.*

His hatch alert chimed, and Rione entered, her face impassive and her eyes glittering like ice. "Yes, Captain Geary?"

He nodded to the seat opposite him. "Please sit down."

"I'm comfortable standing."

"Just sit down!" His bark startled Geary as well as Rione. "Forgive me. The matter I need to discuss with you is an issue of critical concern." The formal words helped keep his voice level.

She eyed him narrowly but slowly sat down, her back stiff. "*What is it*, Captain Geary?"

Geary found it hard to look at her, his gaze wandering

away to rest on the starscape, imagining supernova-scale explosions ravaging it. "We've been planning on what might happen in Sancere, which has a hypernet gate, as you know. I assumed the Syndics would try to destroy that gate. I've since been informed that destruction of hypernet gates could liberate huge quantities of energy. Or perhaps none at all. It's all theoretical."

Her voice sounded as cold as ever. "Huge quantities of energy? Construction of the hypernet system was approved long before I joined the Alliance senate, so I don't know many of the technical details. What does huge mean?"

"Supernova scale." That finally provoked a change in Rione, her eyes widening in shock. Geary took a deep breath. "One of the ship captains, Commander Cresida, came up with a theory about the hypernet gates. If Cresida's theory is right, how the gate tethers are destroyed, the exact timing and sequence in which they lose their grip on the particle matrix, will calibrate the level of energy release. The fleet's network ran the math with some difficulty and came up with a weapons employment algorithm that might let us scale down any release of energy to minimal levels."

Rione's voice was still cold, but puzzled now, too. "Why does this have you upset, Captain Geary? I admit this news that hypernet gates were such a potential danger is surprising, but if you've learned how to control the danger, it seems like a good thing."

Geary looked down at the silvery disc in his palm. "It has me upset, Madam Co-President, because of the corollary. To work out a way to scale down the energy release, we also had to work out a way to scale it up." He held up the data disc, finally looking at her. "We would have the means to employ hypernet gates as by far the most destructive weapons in the history of mankind. We could in theory destroy not only entire individual star systems, but entire regions of space."

Victoria Rione was staring back at him, her face reflecting horror. "How could the living stars allow such a thing?

Humanity believed when we left ancient Earth that we'd removed the threat of racial extinction from disaster, that scattering among the stars would bring us safety from that. But weapons such as these—" Her eyes fixed on the disc. "What is that?"

"The algorithm for scaling up an explosion. The fleet network had to work up both, as I told you." He tossed it to her, and she caught it automatically. "I'd rather you have possession of this than anyone else. I ensured the work in the fleet system was wiped and overwritten. That's the only existing copy."

She was staring at the disc as if it were a deadly snake. "Why?"

He chose to interpret the question as being about her. "Because, Madam Co-President, that's too dangerous to be entrusted to anyone else. Including me."

Rione glared at Geary. "Why entrust it to anyone? Why keep even one copy?"

"Because if we can think this up, then someone else can, too."

This time Rione paled. "You think . . . but if the Syndics had this . . ."

"The Alliance probably would have already felt the results," Geary finished for her. "I agree. I don't think the Syndics have really thought it through. I don't think even Commander Cresida has, that the gates are potentially horrific weapons. But I think someone else does know that."

"I don't understand," Rione demanded, her ice turned to heat now. "If you don't think the Syndics have realized this, are you claiming the Alliance has?"

"No. Not the Syndics and no one from the Alliance." Geary spoke bluntly, knowing his words were brutal but feeling he had to make his case. "I've seen how the officers in this fleet think after a century of war and trading atrocities with the Syndics. If the Alliance knew the gates were weapons, it would have already starting blowing them, obliterating Syndic star systems wholesale. Right, Madam Co-President?"

Rione sat silent for a moment, then nodded. "I think there's a strong possibility you're right," she admitted, her voice quiet now. "Then who is it you believe knows this? There aren't any worlds that aren't part of the Syndicate Worlds or at least nominally part of the Alliance. There isn't anyone else."

"No one we know of," Geary corrected, his eyes back on the starscape. "No one human."

"You're serious?" Rione was shaking her head. "What evidence do you have?"

"Where'd the hypernet come from?"

She seemed startled by the question, her hostility momentarily forgotten now. "The breakthroughs were sudden. I know that much."

"And we still don't understand the theory behind it," Geary added. "That's what Commander Cresida said and the fleet database confirmed. When did the Syndics get the hypernet technology?"

"About the same time as the Alliance."

"Remarkable coincidence, isn't it?" He paused. "I heard the Alliance believes the Syndics stole the tech. That's certainly plausible."

Rione nodded, her eyes hooded. "Yes, but I happen to know from reports I've seen that the Syndics believe we stole the technology from them." She closed her eyes, thinking. "You are actually suggesting that some nonhuman intelligence provided that technology to us? To both sides? But why? The hypernet has greatly benefited us. The ability to travel so swiftly from one star to any other star on the net has been a tremendous boost to human civilizations."

Geary sank down lower into his seat, rubbing his eyes. "Have you ever heard of something called a Trojan horse? Something that seems like an attractive gift but is actually a dangerous weapon?"

Rione stared at him, her face white again. "You think someone, some*thing*, gave us those gates, knowing we'd build them, and knowing they could be used as weapons against us."

"Yeah." Geary waved at the display. "There's hypernet gates in every important star system in every human culture and grouping. Imagine what happens if every one of those systems has a supernova explode in it. Hell, just a nova. Even a mininova."

"But . . . why?"

"Maybe they're scared of us. Maybe they just want to keep us from bothering them. Maybe it's insurance if we ever threaten them. Or maybe that's how they fight, by hiding in shadows and luring an opponent into a trap." Geary shook his head. "This war started for reasons no one really understands, and it's kept going long past the point of making sense. There's nothing unique about that in human history, unfortunately, but this war has certainly kept the human race fully occupied with internal conflict for the last century. Neither the Syndics, as far as we know, nor any part of the Alliance have done any expansion into new star systems for most of that century. I checked."

Victoria Rione was gazing into the distance, her eyes narrowed. "Your ideas are still just speculation, though. Is there any proof?"

"No proof. Some strange stuff at Kaliban, where the Marines found the Syndic security vault had been opened using nonstandard tools and where no one could explain why the Syndics had done some of the things they had when they abandoned the system. But that's not proof of anything except the existence of something unusual."

She switched her gaze to the starscape. "How would anyone trigger all of the hypernet gates to explode at the right level of energy? Is it possible to send a signal of some sort through the hypernet? We don't know of any way to use them for that."

"But then we don't know a hell of a lot about how they work," Geary noted. "As long as neither us or the Syndics win the war, I think we're safe. If I'm right about what I admit is pure speculation."

"Awful speculation, Captain Geary."

He nodded, looking back at her. "I'd be grateful if you'd think about it, too. I'd be incredibly grateful if you could tell me I was wrong. But regardless, please keep that disc safe. Hide it somewhere and don't tell me."

"Surely even you wouldn't be tempted to use it."

"Even me?" Geary found himself laughing harshly. "Even me? Is there still something you think I wouldn't do, Madam Co-President? Should I be grateful?"

"As grateful as I am for being handed the instrument for the extinction of the human race!" Rione snapped back at him.

Geary bit his lip, then nodded. "I'm sorry. But there's no one else I'd trust not to use that."

"You claimed to want to avoid killing civilians and devastating planets." Rione seemed to be pleading with him. "Are you saying that wasn't true, either?"

His temper flared. "Either? Listen, Madam Co-President, you've yet to prove me false in anything! Until you do, I'd appreciate it if you didn't speak as if I were already without honor."

Her face tightened, but Rione nodded. "Very well, Captain Geary. I will refrain from calling you dishonorable until I prove otherwise." Her voice left no doubt that she expected that to happen at any time.

"Thank you," Geary replied coldly. "Now, as to your question, no, I hope I'd never want to use that. But I imagined being with our backs to the wall, the Syndics about to triumph, and I wondered. If everything seemed lost, would I give in to temptation to take that last chance despite the risk that an energy discharge aimed at destroying the Syndics would destroy a lot more? And I couldn't say with absolute certainty that I wouldn't. So I don't want the opportunity."

"Instead you want me to be so tempted!"

"I trust you more than I do myself, Madam Co-President. My focus is on saving this fleet. You've got a larger perspective." Geary stared at nothing for a moment.

"In case it hasn't occurred to you, I also just gave you the ultimate weapon against Black Jack Geary. You'd have the ability to stop him if it came to that."

He knew she was watching him. "So you now admit that Black Jack is a danger to the Alliance."

"I already admitted he's a danger to this fleet. I can't afford to ever let myself think I'm what too many people in the Alliance believe Black Jack Geary to be. But I'm sure you'll help keep me honest."

"I've been trying to do that since you assumed command of this fleet, though I believe myself a failure in that respect right now." She held up the data disc. "How do I know this is really the only copy? How do I know you don't have another?"

"Why would I lie about that?" Geary demanded. "What possible advantage would I gain from that?"

"I don't know. Yet." Rione curled her fingers around the disc, hiding it from sight again. "You fooled me once, Captain Geary. I thought I knew you. I won't be fooled again."

"Maybe the only person fooling you is yourself," Geary snapped.

"Maybe," Rione stated, though her voice and expression held no trace of agreement. "I know what I'll be doing for the long period until we reach Sancere. What will you be doing?"

"Why do you care?" Geary shrugged. "I won't be plotting taking over the Alliance or another attack on the Syndic home system, if that's what you're worried about."

"You seem to think you know my worries. What are yours, Captain Geary?"

To his surprise, the question seemed sincere. "My worries." He looked down, feeling the weight of command heavily again. "Worries that the Syndics have anticipated this move. Worries about forty ships from this fleet that I'm sure are charging straight into a trap under the command of that deluded fool Falco and his stupid friend Numos."

Rione nodded. "I'd add a worry to that. If what you guess is true about the origin and possible ulterior purpose of the hypernet gates, do you dare win, Captain Geary?"

"Win?" He laughed. "Do you believe I'm thinking in terms of winning this war? I'm out to get this fleet home safely, Madam Co-President. In the process, I may be able to inflict some blows to the Syndic war effort. But I'm under no illusions that anything I can do will break the stalemate."

"But you've come up with a weapon that could break that stalemate."

Geary took a deep breath, exhaling slowly before replying. "That's a weapon I will not use by choice. Hopefully never, but certainly not by choice. Keep it safe, keep it hidden, Madam Co-President. When we get home, I'm sure there's people you'll be able to trust with knowledge of it."

She shook her head. "There you are wrong, Captain Geary. No one can be trusted with this knowledge."

"You want to destroy it?"

"And if I do?"

He thought again for a little while. "I guess I wouldn't know. It's up to you."

Rione stood up, coming closer to peer at Geary. "I don't understand you. Every time I think I do, you do something that doesn't match what I know of you."

"Maybe you're trying too hard." Geary smiled humorlessly. "I'm not all that complex."

"Don't underestimate yourself, Captain Geary. You're far more complex than whatever theory underlies the hypernet. I just hope I figure you out eventually."

He nodded. "When you do, give me a briefing so we'll both have me figured out."

"I'll do that." Rione turned to go, then looked back at him. "You're either that most dangerous of demagogues, one who outwardly so perfectly pretends to be honest and honorable that others can't find grounds to hate or distrust him, or else I've misjudged you again. I sincerely hope I am in error, Captain Geary, because otherwise you are even more dangerous than I'd believed before this."

He watched her leave, feeling a sense of reassurance despite her obvious distrust and hostility toward him. If anyone in this fleet could be trusted with the contents of that disc, surely it was Co-President Rione. *Dangerous. I would've laughed at that description not so long ago. But now I know a weapon exists. What I do with that knowledge could doom more than the Alliance.*

What do the Syndics know? They started this damned war. Why? Did they know something that forced their hand?

GEARY had forgotten the itchy sensation that developed after too long straight in jump space, as if your own skin wasn't quite yours anymore and no longer fit right. But he barely noticed it now, sitting on the bridge of the *Dauntless*, waiting for the fleet to exit jump. Within a few minutes, he'd know if his gamble was going to at least partly pay off. Within a few days he was entirely too likely to learn what happened when a hypernet gate was destroyed.

The display for Sancere floated next to his chair. Alliance intelligence knew precious little about the system, and the old Syndic star system guide had offered only slightly more information since things like numbers and placement of defensive installations were all classified. Certainly Sancere was rich in resources as well as jump points. Eight significant planets orbited the star, two small ones in close orbits, two more within the habitable range, one of those almost perfect, then a colder but usable planet slightly farther out, and three resource-rich gas giants way beyond those. The Alliance fleet would drop back into normal space just outside the orbit of the last gas giant, about three and half light-hours from the star.

"One minute to jump exit," Captain Desjani reported calmly.

Geary glanced around the bridge. All of the watch-standers seemed slightly nervous, but in an excited way, not a frightened one. *Ignorance is bliss*, he thought. *No, that can't be right. What I don't know right now is driving me nuts. Ignorance is only blissful if you don't know you're ignorant.*

Geary was still pondering that when the hatch to the bridge opened again and Co-President Rione entered, going to the observer's seat she hadn't used since her argument with Geary back in the Sutrah Star System. He looked at Rione, and she gazed back steadily, her face rigid, her eyes watching him but revealing nothing of her feelings. Geary flashed back to his days as a midshipman, when evaluators would ride behind him in ship simulators, ready to pounce on any error he made.

Captain Desjani greeted Rione with formal politeness, her attitude unwelcoming. She'd picked up on the chill between Geary and Rione, and being Tanya Desjani, had rushed to stand beside Geary against anyone opposed to him. Not wanting open warfare to break out between the two women right there on the bridge of the *Dauntless*, with him in the middle dodging fire between the two sides, Geary searched for a diversion. "Captain Desjani, I'd like to make an announcement to the crew of the *Dauntless*."

Breaking her targeting lock on Co-President Rione, Desjani nodded to Geary. "Of course, sir."

Geary tapped the necessary control. He could've done that without asking Desjani, but it wouldn't have been proper to speak to the crew without doing the captain the courtesy of asking first. "All hands, this is Captain Geary. We're about to arrive at the Sancere Star System. I know you'll all do your utmost to uphold the honor of the fleet and the Alliance. May the living stars grant us a great victory, and may our ancestors look with favor upon us." In one sense, none of that needed to be said, but in another sense, it was the sort of pep talk that filled a real human need. Geary wondered, if his speculations about the hypernet were true, whether whatever had given humanity that creation also felt the need for speeches and sentiments.

"Our ancestors brought us this far," Desjani noted in a much softer voice. She glanced at Geary, leaving unsaid what he knew she was thinking, that they'd also brought the fleet Geary himself.

Her faith could be unnerving, but she was only one of thousands throughout the fleet who felt that way. *I wonder if Captain Falco has ever felt unequal to the faith others felt in him, or does he even worry about that as long as people agree that he's great? From what I saw of him and learned of him, Falco hasn't spent much time worrying about others or about his own ability to justify others' faith in him. I guess being certain of your own infallibility eliminates a lot of anxiety.* Last night Geary had spent a long time talking to his ancestors, expressing his fears and asking their help. At times like this not having faith would be a hard thing, he reflected, and wondered how others managed to face crises calmly without that support.

"Stand by for jump exit," a watch-stander reported. "Now."

Geary's guts wrenched slightly, his skin settled back happily into place, and the stars blazed forth on the external views. Objects on the display for Sancere System began multiplying as if in some insane video game where enemies flashed into existence in droves. Of course all of these Syndic defenses and installations had been there before. The fleet's sensors were just finding them now, as reports flowed in and watch-standers called out the most critical. The human interface might be clumsy and slower than the automated systems, but despite its flaws, the human mind had proved to still be the best way of filtering information and highlighting the most important.

"*Warhelm* reports a Syndic system monitoring satellite close to its position. *Warhelm* reports it has destroyed the satellite. Ships located twenty light-minutes to starboard in system plane, assess all to be unarmed mineral carriers. No mines spotted or encountered. Six, repeat, six F-Class battleships identified at shipyard orbiting fourth planet. Only one appears operational. Eight, repeat, eight D-Class battle cruisers at second shipyard orbiting fourth planet. Operational status undetermined. Syndic military base located forty light-minutes away on a moon of the eighth planet, appears fully operational, nine, no, ten mass accelerators in defensive positions around base—"

Geary scanned his fleet display quickly and stabbed a control with one finger. "Captain Tulev. Have your ships take out that Syndic base near the eighth planet with kinetic rounds. I don't want to give them time to get off a shot."

Tulev's voice took several seconds to reply. "Launching bombardment of weapons sites now. What about the rest of the base?"

There wasn't time for worries or second-guessing, now. Just time to act and react before the enemy took the options out of your hands. "Take it all out. We can't leave that kind of threat in our rear."

The next closest base seemed to be near the fifth planet, over three light-hours away. "Captain Duellos, have your ships launch kinetic rounds at the Syndic military base orbiting the fifth planet. I don't want it around when we get there."

"Duellos, aye. Launching bombardment within two minutes."

Geary bit back a curse as he saw his formation start to break, then realized he was seeing the ships of Task Force Furious faking an undisciplined charge just as planned. Hopefully the Syndics would be fooled as well as he had been. *Ancestors, please stand by Commander Cresida so she'll retreat when the situation calls for it.*

"Syndic warship flotilla sighted between orbits of fifth and sixth worlds, distance five point eight light-hours from current fleet position. Ten battleships, six battle cruisers, twelve heavy cruisers, ten, correction, eleven Hunter-Killers. Current position shown time-late, estimated real-time location based on time-late trajectory data now five point six light-hours from our current position."

"Nothing we can't handle," Desjani noted, smiling unpleasantly. "Not nearly enough light escorts for those high-value units, either."

"Enough that we can't take them lightly," Geary reminded her. "I'm guessing the big ships are conducting training, maybe with new crews or after extensive time in shipyards, so that isn't really a combat-ready formation, even though the Syndics probably also assign it system protection duties." His eyes were locked on the hypernet gate now. "There's nothing there. They don't have any ships guarding it." Then symbols flashed into existence. "What are those?"

Desjani frowned, studying the data. "Stealthy defensive units around the hypernet gate. Limited maneuverability, substantial defensive screens and so-so offensive firepower."

"They can maneuver some?"

She nodded to confirm her answer.

"That means we can't send some rocks on ahead to take them out. They'd see them coming and dodge." He checked the distance. Almost five light-hours to the hypernet gate. Even if they accelerated past engagement speed and slowed again when they approached the gate, the fleet was at least thirty-five hours' travel time from the gate. *Some dash. But then Task Force Furious is "charging" at a Syndic force even farther away that won't even see them coming for almost another six hours. That'll be a shock. Hopefully Task Force Furious will keep the Syndics' attention focused on them.*

But I don't want to head straight for the gate if I can help it. He tried various options on the maneuvering display, running courses toward other Syndic targets, bending them back toward the gate partway through the track. By arcing across the system toward mining installations clustered around a gas giant located a light-hour out from the star Sancere, then curving back toward the gate, the journey would take roughly fifty-three hours at engagement speed of .1 light. But the Alliance fleet's apparent objective wouldn't change from the gas giant to the gate until they were less than two light-hours away, or a little more than eighteen hours of travel time. That wasn't ideal, but it would leave little time for the Syndics to react if they hadn't already positioned extra forces at the gate.

"Here," Geary told Desjani. "We're going to follow this track as if intending to wipe out the mining facilities at the gas giant and then continue in system, smashing other things, but instead shift our course to head for the gate."

She nodded, studying Geary's plan. "We can toss out a bombardment as we reach the closest point of approach to the gas giant and take out a lot of those facilities anyway."

"Will we need anything from them?" Geary asked. "I can find out before we get to the firing point. I've got plenty of time to ask Captain Tyrosian on the *Witch*." The engineers in charge of the fleet auxiliaries *Titan*, *Witch*, *Goblin*, and *Jinn* would know what raw materials they needed to manufacture the things the fleet needed to keep going. He considered the display again, trying to decide if he should change the formation yet, then decided against it. It was still far too early to tell how the Syndic warship flotilla would react, and for a sweep against the shipyards and other targets in the system this formation would be fine.

Geary took a moment to gloat over the hulls of the battleships and battle cruisers under construction. Very dangerous threats when completed and crewed, under way with other Syndic warships, they were now sitting ducks that the Alliance fleet could destroy easily. Though there was always a chance the Syndics would try to get any nearly completed ones under way so they could flee. In addition to the assembled hulls, components of more battleships and battle cruisers had now been sighted. All of those would be easily destroyed as well as the shipyard facilities that were constructing them.

"It's so strange," Co-President Rione observed. Her

voice had lost its coldness, caught up in the unfolding situation. "Here we're at war, choosing our targets. Yet almost every Syndicate Worlds installation, ship, and individual in this system doesn't even know we've arrived yet."

"They will," Captain Desjani replied with a grim smile. "As the light from our arrival reaches them, a lot of Syndics are going to start praying to *their* ancestors."

Geary had to admit it was interesting to imagine the reactions of Syndicate Worlds leaders and citizens throughout the system to the arrival of the Alliance fleet. On his system display a bubble was radiating out from the fleet, indicating the movement of light on the scale of the Sancere solar system. He could see the bubble expand, its front covering the outermost gas giant now and moving on toward the inner planets. As light showing the fleet's arrival reached them, the Syndics in the mining ships and the orbital facilities would be reacting to sudden alerts on their warning equipment. They'd stare, not believing the information. They'd double-check and magnify the light images. Hopefully many would refuse to believe it and send messages that would take hours to reach their destinations. Others would believe it and also send messages, these asking for instructions.

All of the messages would be arriving at the offices of the main Syndic leaders in this star system at almost the same time as the light images announcing the arrival of the fleet, thereby adding to the confusion. And as everybody tossed out frantic messages to everybody else, the Syndic communications net would start bogging down under the strain of all that message traffic, slowing the Syndic ability to understand and react.

Perhaps enough to compensate for the advantages the Syndics had in defending their own system.

"All units," Geary ordered, "keep a close eye out for incoming kinetic projectiles and drifting minefields." He paused, evaluating the situation again for a moment, then finally deciding on the course feinting a close-in attack on the gas giant nearest the sun of Sancere. "All units in main body, this is Captain Geary. Come starboard to course three three nine, down four degrees, at time five one."

The representations of the ships in the fleet on Geary's display flared green in ripples spreading out from *Dauntless* as each ship received and acknowledged the order. It was so different from the mob he'd found himself commanding at Corvus that Geary found himself smiling.

An incoming message beeped for his attention. "This is *Furious*. Continuing attack. Follow-on target will be close-in attack on fifth planet."

Geary nodded absently, then noticed Rione giving him a suspicious look. "Not really," Geary explained. "They're going to feint at the fifth planet, then break away." *I hope.*

Captain Desjani spoke up, her voice diffident. "Our light units screening the port flank of the formation will pass not far from the mining ships off of the outermost gas giant."

"Yeah." *Okay, this time you're right. Those ships are legitimate targets and important industrial assets in this system.* "Fourth Cruiser Division, Sixth and Seventh Destroyer Squadrons, as we pass the outermost planet, engage merchant shipping traffic within range. Maneuver independently as necessary to engage targets. Inform crews of those ships they are to evacuate their ships now." That took care of military necessity and humanitarian obligations.

System display, still finding and evaluating new information, highlighted Syndic defensive systems on various moons and what were plainly headquarters and coordination centers on planets and in orbital locations. Geary gazed at the many targets either in fixed orbits or on objects with fixed orbits. Target-rich didn't even begin to describe it. He highlighted the Syndic battleships and battle cruisers being built in the shipyards, as well, then asked the combat system to recommend an engagement plan for everything military or military-related. Moments later it popped up, ships throughout the fleet tagged to hurl kinetic projectiles at the targets most favorable for their projectile load-out and geometry. Geary ran through the list quickly, seeing nothing that stood out as odd, then punched 'approve,' followed by 'execute.'

The ships of the Alliance fleet began throwing out many more projectiles, a rain of solid metal falling inward upon the Syndic defenses, a rain no shield would repel. Syndic command authorities, which in a few hours would be reeling from news of the Alliance fleet's arrival, would very soon afterward also see that bombardment on its way. In one sense it was unfortunate that the weapons would take a lot longer to reach their targets than the light advertising their approach, but since their targets couldn't avoid or block the projectiles, the sight of the incoming wave of devastation would have plenty of time to add to the panic.

Combat systems helpfully advised that *Witch*, *Jinn*, *Goblin*, and *Titan* should be told to prioritize fabrication of replacement kinetic bombardment projectiles. Geary tapped the control to pass that to Captain Tyrosian on *Witch*. It all felt so very smooth and simple, out here on the edge of the system. As the fleet raced inward, getting in among the Syndics where reaction times were measured in seconds and minutes instead of hours, it would start feeling a lot less smooth, he knew. And as those kinetic projectiles reached their targets, a wave of destruction would ripple across the worlds and human artifacts orbiting the star Sancere. Remembering the many Alliance ships the Syndics had destroyed in the ambush at their home system before he'd assumed command, Geary felt a grim satisfaction at the thought of how the Syndic leaders would react when news of the attack on Sancere finally reached them. *You thought we were scared, running so hard for our lives that we couldn't hit back. Now you're finding out just how wrong you were.*

One more thing had to be done. Geary straightened in his chair, adopting his best professional pose, then began broadcasting to the entire star system. "People in the Sancere star system, this is Captain John Geary, commanding officer of the Alliance fleet. We are engaging all military targets in this system. All other personnel, ships, citizens, colonies, off-planet facilities, and planets are directed to surrender immediately. Those who surrender will be treated humanely in accordance with the laws of war. Failure to surrender risks being targeted for elimination of military-related facilities and resources. Any attacks or attempts against ships of the Alliance fleet will be met with the full force at our disposal."

"To the honor of our ancestors, this is Captain John Geary, commanding officer of the Alliance fleet."

He ended the transmission, taking a deep, calming breath. "I'm not cut out to be an actor," he remarked to Captain Desjani.

"It sounded impressive from here," she replied. Desjani's attitude toward slaughtering Syndics had been moderated by association with Geary, but she'd still obviously been pleased by the threats of mass destruction that Geary had just broadcast.

About an hour and a half later the fleet swept by the outermost gas giant, the cruisers and destroyers on the wing nearest to the huge planet swooping over to slaughter the big, slow-moving mining ships. On the visual spectrum display, Geary could see dark shapes moving against the bright, pale green globe of the gas giant as his warships tore past, the charged particle "spears" of their hell-lance batteries ripping apart the unarmed mining ships. By bringing up more information, Geary could see representations of the survival pods fleeing from the mining ships, tiny objects scattering in all directions like seeds from bursting cases. Geary called up yet another set of data, and space was threaded with fine lines arcing in graceful curves, marking the projected paths of both his warships and the civilian ships.

From a distance, war could look remarkably beautiful. Having seen it close up, Geary had no trouble seeing past the attractiveness distance rendered, remembering instead torn ships and desperate crews, lifetimes of labor shattered in an instant's fire from a warship. Even a great victory didn't look pleasant from the deck plates of the ships involved.

Blossoming clouds of fragments marked the remains of orbital installations that had already caught the force of kinetic rounds hurled their way. "Light's coming in from our bombardment of the Syndic military base on the big moon of the eighth planet," Desjani remarked.

Geary switched to that. The optics of the *Dauntless*'s sensors provided remarkably clear pictures across vast distances, but in this case the clouds of dust and debris rising above what had once been a Syndic military installation were blocking much of the view. Having monitored the early impacts before the views were obscured, the ship's combat system had damage assessments posted next to every targeted location. All offensive weapons destroyed. All defensive systems eliminated. All communications and control facilities smashed by the impacts of unstoppable heavy chunks of metal traveling at a decent fraction of the speed of light. If something couldn't dodge the attack, destruction was certain. "This isn't war. It's murder."

Desjani gave Geary a surprised look.

"I know," he told her. "It's necessary. But the Syndics at those bases in fixed orbits don't stand a chance. I can't cheer the fact that those poor devils are dying."

Desjani seemed to be thinking, then nodded. "You prefer an honest fight. Certainly. There's honor to that."

"Yeah." One thing in which he and the minds of modern sailors could find agreement. Geary checked the display again. His light units had wiped out the Syndic shipping near the gas giant and were returning to formation. It would be hours yet before the Syndic command authorities saw the Alliance fleet. Like uncounted human military forces before them, the Alliance fleet had to endure the ancient ritual of hurry up and wait.

Geary studied the Syndic flotilla, its almost six hours time-late position meaning little now. If the flotilla had maintained the same trajectory through the Sancere Star

System, it would now be where the display predicted. Otherwise, it could have traveled a fair distance even loafing along at well under .1 light. He would have to be sure to handle that flotilla carefully. *If I get too confident about how easy destroying it will be, they might surprise me and inflict losses out of proportion to their numbers.*

Still, there's not enough there to threaten us. If Cresida's formation manages to capture their attention long enough, those Syndic warships won't be able to get to the hypernet gate before we do. This is looking very good.

Red symbols flashed into existence near the hypernet gate. Geary's eyes flew to that point, watching as the symbols multiplied, willing them to stop. *I spoke too soon. Did the Syndics figure out what we were up to after all? Did they hear from survivors of one of the ships that followed Falco? There shouldn't have been enough time for them to react to that and get reinforcements here.*

Not too many warships. Not too strong a force. Please ancestors make it small enough for us to handle. We can't run from this system without looting more supplies first.

SIX

"**LOOKS** like a dozen battleships and battle cruisers," Desjani remarked. She seemed happy at the prospect of a bigger battle. "Only five heavy cruisers, though, one light cruiser and nine Hunter-Killers. Why so few escorts?"

The answer to that question became apparent as *Dauntless*'s sensors evaluated what could be seen of the new Syndic force. "They've taken battle damage," the combat systems watch reported, "and were probably sent here for repair and refit. Most of their escorts were probably destroyed in the battle where the bigger ships took damage."

Geary nodded, his thoughts roving back toward Alliance space. Were these Syndic ships the victors of a battle in which the Alliance ships following Captain Falco had been annihilated? Or had they been mauled elsewhere by the portions of the fleet that had remained in Alliance space to guard it while most of the fleet had made the risky assault on the Syndic home system? "We need to find out where they got hurt and who did it," Geary stated out loud.

"Prisoners should be able to tell us that," Desjani noted

cheerfully. "We can pick up some Syndic survival pods after the battle." She gestured at the images of the newly arrived warships. "If they're coming here for refit after a battle, they may have little or no expendable weaponry on board. No missiles, no grapeshot."

"True," Geary agreed. "Can they reach any of the munitions depots we've identified before our kinetic bombardment hits the ammunition supplies?"

Desjani ran some calculations, her hands flying over the controls. "Maybe. If they haul ass for the farthest munitions depots from us as soon as they spot us. But they'd have little time, and they'd need to get clear before our bombardment hit."

Geary checked the solution. "And that would take them out away from our path to the hypernet gate. I hope they do make a run for that ammo dump." He added up the total operational Syndic forces in system now. Sixteen battleships and a dozen battle cruisers, thirteen heavy cruisers, one light cruiser, and an even twenty HuKs. A formidable force if they managed to join up and fight together. Formidable on paper, at least. The Syndic flotilla they'd seen in the system upon arrival, if engaged in training, might not have full load-outs of weapons and probably had inexperienced crews. The newly arrived Syndic force was likely as experienced as any warships tended to be when tactics led to bloodbaths with heavy losses, but those ships were already battered and almost certainly low or completely out of expendable weaponry. And, even combined, there were far too few light escorts for the bigger ships.

"What do you think, sir?" Desjani asked.

Geary sat silent for a few moments, using his finger to trace paths through the display before him, depending on instincts born of long experience to estimate how his fleet and the two Syndic forces would move relative to each other. "It's going to depend on what they do," he finally decided. "If they're stupid, they'll individually rush to battle, and we'll be able to overwhelm each of the flotillas with a very comfortable superiority in ships and firepower on our side."

"Will they dare risk trying to join?" Desjani indicated the hypernet gate. "If they know we might be able to use that . . ."

Oh, hell. Desjani had remained focused on the primary issue, while Geary had gotten lost in possible alternatives. "No. You're right. That newly arrived force will be told to reinforce the gate defenses." *Or to help destroy the gate. But what about the other flotilla?* He traced more paths, then shook his head. "The other flotilla could do any number of things. But my guess is that once they see we're headed for the gate, they'll charge that way, too, or else they'll be ordered there even though they'll get to the gate too late to stop us."

"We can handle that," Desjani noted.

Her calm confidence was infectious. "Yeah." Geary settled back in his seat. "I figure we've got a half hour window before anything else happens, then we'll have new information coming in for hours as we start seeing the Syndics react to us. I'm going to grab a quick bite to eat." Desjani nodded, her eyes on her own situation display. "Can I bring you anything?" Geary asked half-jokingly.

She tapped one pocket and grinned. "I've got ration bars."

"You're a better sailor than me." Geary smiled in reply. He stood up, turning to see Co-President Rione still seated and eyeing him, her expression impossible to read. Geary nodded to her. "So far so good."

"So far," Rione echoed, but he couldn't tell if her voice held humor or disdain.

MUCH of the action that unfolded over the following hours as the Alliance fleet fell deeper into the Sancere Star System was predictable. Nonmilitary shipping headed for nearby orbital ports or else began scattering into empty portions of the system in the hopes that the Alliance ships

wouldn't waste time hunting them down. Frantic activity
erupted in the orbital shipyards as tugs began hauling away
vital materials and a couple of the under-construction
major warships, but there weren't enough tugs to get all of
the battleships and battle cruisers being built out of the
way of the kinetic bombardment racing toward its targets.
The two unfinished warships being pulled out of the path
of the bombardment could be easily blown apart later
when the fleet swept through that area, but Geary still had
to admire the dedication of the Syndic work crews. They
were trying, even though the efforts must have seemed as
hopeless as they actually were.

Well behind the light announcing the arrival of the
Alliance fleet came the kinetic bombardment, spreading
out across the system, pummeling targets ever farther in-
system, heading inexorably for the inner system crowded
with industrial and military installations.

The Syndic force Geary had christened the Training
Flotilla in his mind even though the official combat system
designation was Syndic Force Alpha had turned toward the
fifth world almost four hours before it had sighted Geary's
fleet, closing the distance purely by chance. When he finally saw it yaw around and up, he knew that course
change had occurred five hours ago and realized he'd spent
more than ten hours on the bridge. He nonetheless waited
a little longer, until they could tell the Training Flotilla was
moving to engage Task Force Furious. A check of the
battle-battered Syndic Force Bravo showed it had, unfortunately, turned back toward the hypernet gate. Geary took a
moment to pray the Syndics in that force would use the
gate to flee the system and spare him the uncertainty of a
battle as well as the worry that they would destroy the gate
before he could reach it.

He rubbed his eyes wearily. It was still almost twenty-
four more hours until the fleet reached the vicinity of the
closest-in gas giant and altered course to sweep directly toward the hypernet gate. There were stimulants he could
take to stay awake and alert for days, but even the best of

those exacted a price, especially when quick decisions were needed under pressure. The human mind needed real sleep and wouldn't be happy with anything else. Captain Desjani was napping in her seat, apparently comfortable enough and able to sleep through routine sounds on the bridge. But nothing was going to happen fast now. New information might come in, but it was clear that any developing threat would be seen hours before it was a danger. Geary tapped his communications controls. "All ships ensure crews are rotated and given opportunity for rest." Geary stood, stretching, determined to provide a good example. "I'm going down to get some sleep," he advised the watch-standers on the bridge. "Call me if anything unexpected happens. I want to know about any changes in the movements of the two Syndic flotillas."

Sleeping for six hours in the middle of a battle seemed absurd, but when the battle was happening in slow motion over days of time, it just made sense. Staying awake to watch nothing happening would only leave him too tired to think straight when something did start taking place. So Geary told himself as he lay down in his bunk and stared at the overhead. It could have been a lot worse. The defenses were surprisingly weak despite the many military targets in the system. The Syndics obviously hadn't thought Sancere faced a real danger of attack, and why should they? But surprises could still happen, and he needed a clear head to deal with them.

Restlessness eventually drove Geary up to roam the ship, stopping to talk with officers and sailors at their duty stations or catching meals. Everyone seemed nervous and excited, worried about what might happen but also feeling the thrill of hitting a surprised enemy hard. A few wondered about the hypernet gate, and Geary offered vague assurances that the gate would be taken if at all possible.

Six hours from reaching the gas giant, the main body of the fleet finally had something exciting to watch besides the wave of destruction as the kinetic bombardment fell on targets ahead of the Alliance force. Task Force Furious had accelerated up to .2 light on its charge toward the inner planets and was now two light-hours away from the main body, braking back down to .1 light and closing fast on Syndic Force Alpha, the Training Flotilla.

Unable to direct the action from so far away, knowing everything he was seeing had already happened, Geary watched while trying not to reveal his nervousness. If those steady commanders of his gave in to temptation and lit into the Syndics, it would result in a bloody brawl. The thirty ships under Cresida's command were outnumbered by the thirty-nine in the Syndic Training Flotilla, and were also outgunned by the Syndic ships thanks to the ten battleships on the Syndic side. The odds were good enough to entice the Syndics to battle, just as Geary had hoped. He was certain Cresida wouldn't be dumb enough to get involved in a ship-to-ship slug out at close range, but mistakes on her part or clever moves by the Syndics could lead to just that.

It all came down to trusting the officer he had placed in command. After the mess Numos had made of his command of a formation at Kaliban, Geary had vowed not to put anyone else he didn't trust in charge of any part of the fleet. But it was far easier not to trust, to try to micromanage his subordinates, than it was to let them do their jobs. *Funny how that never changes. You have to learn that as a junior officer, and you have to stick to it as a senior officer. If you're going to be any good as a commander, that is.*

Two hours ago, but only now visible to the main body of the Alliance fleet, Cresida had played it smart, angling as if intending a direct clash, then altering course for a glancing engagement. With too little time to react, the Syndic ships reacted clumsily, confirming Geary's assessment that they were crewed by raw personnel. The Syndic formation tried to pivot around its flagship's axis, turning and changing heading to present a wall of firepower to Task Force Furious. But some of the Syndic ships turned late, shooting past their turning fellows, and others swung through the same space their comrades were trying to use. Ships twisted away from near collisions, further disrupting the Syndic formation and leaving the flank nearest Task Force Furious's approach hanging unsupported. As the Syndics tried unsuccessfully to concentrate fire on the approach of the Alliance ships, the Alliance force led by *Furious* tore past the unsupported flank of the Syndic formation and shredded it with overwhelming firepower directed by ship after ship against the Syndic warships making up the side of the flotilla.

Geary breathed a sigh of relief as *Dauntless* tallied the Syndic losses. One of the battleships raked repeatedly and left drifting and dead. Two battle cruisers severely damaged. All four heavy cruisers on that flank destroyed along with five of the Hunter-Killers. Status updates sent to *Dauntless* from the Task Force Furious ships and arriving now along with the light from the battle revealed the Alliance ships had taken little or no damage. "Nice job," Captain Desjani commented.

"Very nice," Geary agreed. Then he stiffened. On the two-hour-old time-late images, Task Force Furious had started bending around in a very wide turn, arcing up, over, and to the side as if intending another firing run at the flailing Syndics. *You're not supposed to do that, Cresida. Don't risk it.*

At the speeds the warships of Task Force Furious were traveling, the turn took a long time and a lot of space, even with the ships braking their velocity to reduce the turn radius. But eventually it became clear that Cresida had ordered another pass. *Damn. She should've known better.*

The Syndics had taken advantage of the delay to straighten out their formation and face their heaviest firepower toward the Alliance attackers. Apparently anticipating another blow to the flanks, the Syndic formation now clustered the surviving light units in the center, the remaining battleships and battle cruisers ranked in two vertically aligned planes, narrow ends facing the Alliance attack on either side like slices of bread enclosing the weaker ships. It was ironic to see the big ships escorting the smaller ships that were supposed to escort them, but Geary was impressed that the Syndics had so quickly figured out a counter to Cresida's tactic of hitting a flank.

"What do you suppose she did?" Captain Desjani asked, her voice intrigued rather than worried. The past tense sounded strange when they were watching events unfold, but it was a reminder that whatever had happened had already taken place, for better or worse.

"We'll soon see," Geary replied, trying not to sound furious himself at the actions of *Furious*. He couldn't stop it, couldn't change it, just watch history two hours old unscroll before his eyes as the light from the battle reached *Dauntless*.

Task Force Furious was now itself in an flattened pencil-shaped formation, long and thin. Geary stared at it, trying to figure out why Cresida had arranged her ships that way. The two forces closed rapidly, Task Force Furious accelerating at the best rate its handpicked force of agile ships could manage. The Alliance ships were now closing on the Syndic ships at a combined relative speed of just under .2 light. Both sides would have serious trouble getting effective fire control solutions at that speed with relativistic distortions confusing aim, but it was barely within acceptable engagement limits.

The speed and the difficulty that created with seeing the movements of other ships left the Syndics less time to react when Cresida changed her force's trajectory through space again, the warships of Task Force Furious bending the formation down and below the waiting Syndic defenders, aiming for one exposed corner of the rectangular plane formation on the port side of the Syndic force. The single Syndic battleship anchoring that corner found itself taking fire from the entire Alliance formation as it tore past, ship after ship hurling weapons at the beleaguered Syndic warship while it could only reply with single volleys at each individual Alliance ship. Even though a lot of Alliance shots missed because of the targeting difficulties, there were so many weapons hammering the same Syndic battleship that enough hits were being scored.

The Alliance formation passed completely under the Syndic formation, still diving down to open the range and leaving in its wake the spreading cloud of debris that had been a Syndic battleship.

Desjani was laughing softly. "They're going to be very angry with Commander Cresida. That was a good move, Captain Geary. She taunted them twice and hurt them both times. Now, look, they're coming around to chase her, but she's not heading for the fifth planet."

"No." Geary studied the track Task Force Furious was curving onto, *Dauntless*'s maneuvering systems quickly estimating the destination. "Cresida's decided to go for the shipyards orbiting near the fourth world." The huge industrial complexes were perhaps the most valuable targets in the star system. Geary had given Cresida orders not to destroy them because he wanted a chance to loot them first, but Task Force Furious could easily smash in passing the one nearly completed battleship and one battle cruiser being frantically towed out of their construction ways in an attempt to save them from the Alliance kinetic bombardment aimed at the under-construction shipping.

She handled it right. All of it. But if I'd had instant communications with her, I'd have ordered Cresida to do things differently, because I wouldn't have trusted her judgment. Remember that, Geary. There's good heads among these ship commanders and they're paying attention to you. You have to trust them in return. Knowing his message wouldn't reach her for hours, Geary tapped his communications controls. "To Commander Cresida and all ships in Task Force Furious, this is Captain Geary. Excellent work. Keep it up."

THERE'D been no reply to Geary's surrender demands by the time the Alliance fleet dove past the innermost gas giant, annihilating Syndic industrial targets unstruck by the kinetic bombardment and sweeping any remaining Syndic merchant shipping in the area from space. In-system ore carriers and other merchant ships had only a small fraction of the propulsion capability of warships. Over time they could build up substantial speed, but it took a long time, and these Syndic ships hadn't been granted that much time.

The kinetic bombardment was still a couple of hours from reaching the fourth planet, so the Syndic command structure was still fully operational in the inner system. Geary wished he knew just what orders were being issued by that command structure. "All units in Alliance fleet main body, execute course change two five degrees to starboard, down zero two degrees at time four seven."

"They'll have time to see we're heading for the gate and issue reaction orders before our bombardment hits," Desjani remarked regretfully.

"It can't be helped." Far off to one side, Task Force Furious was still bearing down on the shipyards orbiting the fourth planet. The battered, and no doubt enraged, ships of Syndic Force Alpha had piled on speed, edging past .2 light on an intercept course curving to meet up with Task Force Furious just short of the orbiting shipyards around the fourth planet. "What do think their odds are of getting hits on *Furious* at that speed?"

"With inexperienced crews and combat systems still aligning themselves? As close to zero as makes no difference," Desjani stated. "They'll need to slow to engagement speed, and if they slow, they won't make that intercept point."

Desjani's assessment matched his own. Geary nodded, then frowned, once again bothered by the thought that he was missing something. But whatever it was stayed hidden in the back of his mind, refusing to come forward, so Geary finally tried thinking of other things in the hope that would help. It didn't.

FIVE hours out from the hypernet gate, Geary frowned again. Syndic Force Alpha, the Training Flotilla, had kept accelerating to .25 light and adjusted its track slightly to cross the path of Task Force Furious before the Alliance ships reached the fourth planet. "Why do I get the feeling they're not planning on slowing down to engage Task Force Furious?"

Desjani seemed puzzled as well. "I don't see how many hits they can hope to achieve at that speed. There's no point in any intercept that isn't a threat. If Cresida's ships do any evasive maneuvers at all, they'll totally throw off firing solutions on the Syndic ships, and relativistic distortion will keep the Syndics from even seeing exactly what the Alliance ships are doing. Surely even if the commanders in the Syndic ships don't realize that, the more senior Syndic commanders on the planets do. They've had plenty of time to tell Force Alpha to do something different, but that hasn't happened."

"Why would they do something that will almost eliminate their chances of hitting our ships?" Geary wondered out loud. "Why would their superiors agree to it?"

He'd forgotten Co-President Rione was once again in the bridge's observer seat. Now her voice sounded like that of a teacher instructing a dull student. "Perhaps you should stop assuming you know their intentions."

Geary turned to look at Rione. "What do you mean?"

"I mean that you keep talking about what the Syndics must do to hit your ships. What if hitting your ships isn't the Syndics' priority?"

Desjani, looking reluctant to agree with Rione, clenched one fist. "If they can't hit us, that also means the same relativistic factors will keep us from being able to target them well. They're minimizing their chances of getting hit again."

Survival was the Syndic priority? But why? "What would be the point of keeping that formation as intact as possible while letting us run amok?"

"They expect something to change the odds," Desjani stated slowly.

Geary gritted his teeth. He and Desjani had been assuming they knew the Syndic intentions and then trying to make Syndic actions match those assumptions. The enemy's real intentions were obvious now that Rione had focused them back on what the Syndics were actually doing. "Do they expect more reinforcements?"

"It's unlikely but possible that a courier might have gated out without being spotted," Desjani agreed. "But even if they had done that, they couldn't possibly be expecting a reply already. We'd have to assume the Syndics had accurately guessed we were coming to Sancere."

"That doesn't match what we found here," Rione objected, again surprising Geary. "Everything reflected surprise at our arrival. That could be a very elaborate trick to lull us into overconfidence, but surely the Syndics wouldn't have avoided placing minefields at the jump exit if they believed we were coming to Sancere."

"You're both right," Geary agreed. "Which would mean the intercept apparently aimed at Task Force Furious is just a feint, trying to throw off *Furious*'s charge. That matches what the Syndics are doing. Let's assume no big reinforcements are coming within the next few days. What else could change the odds enough to make force preservation the primary goal of that Syndic flotilla?" Something big. That went without saying. Something big enough to drastically alter the balance of forces in this star system.

Geary looked at the representation of Syndic Force Bravo on his display. "Force Alpha is moving so fast we can't hit them, but Force Bravo is just sitting there near the hypernet gate, maintaining a fixed station, even though it's obvious that's our objective."

Desjani shook her head. "They must be planning on accelerating away soon. Just sitting there waiting for us is nothing but suicide."

"Yet they've clearly been told to do that. Just like the other formation has been told to avoid losing ships." Geary fiddled with the display, changing his perspective to view the Syndic formation from different angles. "What's the

latest on estimated damage to the Syndic ships in Force
Bravo?"

"They've all got some damage, but two of the battleships and three of the battle cruisers are so beat up that
they've probably got minimum combat capability,"
Desjani replied.

Geary highlighted the most heavily damaged Syndic
ships. All five were in the center of the Syndic formation,
which in turn seemed to be centered on the hypernet gate.
"Standard tactics, as I understand them, have been to
charge straight for the enemy, right?"

Desjani nodded.

"Why put their weakest units there, then? Why not tell
them to run for open space? All they can accomplish in that
station is absorbing shots from us."

Captain Desjani considered the display, her eyes narrowing in thought. "I can think of three possible reasons.
One would be simple stupidity if their commander is incompetent. Another would be that the five heavily damaged ships are intended as bait. A third would be that for
some reason the most capable ships are needed on the outside of the formation."

"I don't want to assume incompetence at this point.
That could make us too confident. Besides, why wouldn't
the Syndics have given coordinated orders to the two formations? It isn't like the Syndics to let commanders operate independently."

Desjani nodded.

Geary felt a sudden knot in his stomach. "I think your
reasons two and three are both right." He pointed. "We're
expected to charge straight for the center of the formation,
like Alliance forces usually do, and the most badly damaged enemies are there waiting for us to finish them off.
Bait, as you said." He remembered watching his fleet fall
apart at Corvus, where every ship had been scrambling to
get in on a few kills of hopelessly outnumbered light
Syndic warships. Syndic commanders who expected that
kind of behavior would know what a lure those damaged

ships would be to Alliance commanders seeking quick and easy kills. "And when we get close enough, these units," he indicated those on the outside of the formation, "with the best weapons capability, go after the gate itself. They want to sucker us in close, then destroy the gate and hope the resulting energy discharge is big enough to hurt a lot of our ships."

A moment of silence passed as Desjani considered his idea, then she rapped one fist on the arm of her command seat. "I think you're right, sir. If the main fleet got hurt badly enough at the hypernet gate, that changes the odds in the system, and Task Force Furious might find itself the only organized Alliance fighting force in Sancere."

Geary checked some ship statistics. "And even with the damage Task Force Furious did to Syndic Force Alpha, the Syndic flotilla still slightly outguns the task force. That's why they're trying to avoid further losses. So that they'll be in a superior position if their plan at the gate works."

"If the gate failure energy release is bad enough to hurt us," Desjani noted, "then it'll be bad enough to wipe out the Syndic ships there as well."

"Yeah." Trade a dozen big warships, about half very badly damaged, for three, four, or five times that many Alliance capital ships and who knew how many lighter combatants. To the bean counting minds of the Syndicate Worlds leadership, that probably looked like a very good business deal, especially since it might force the surviving Alliance ships to flee and leave a lot of the still-surviving installations in the Sancere Star System intact. "I wonder if the crews of those ships know?"

"I doubt it."

"Me, too." Geary played with his controls for a moment, then decisively punched one. "Syndicate Worlds warships at the Sancere Star System hypernet gate, this is Captain Geary, commander of the Alliance fleet in Sancere Star System. Be advised that the energy discharge as a result of destroying the hypernet gate is very likely to be so severe as to wipe out every ship nearby." He paused, wondering if he should mention the danger destruction of the gate might pose to the planets in the system and even the planets in surrounding star systems. But, no, if the Syndic leaders hadn't already figured that out, there was no way Geary wanted to be the one to tell them. "You face impossible odds. Your ships already bear substantial damage from earlier battles. There is no dishonor in surrender. You have my word that any personnel who surrender will be treated humanely in accordance with the laws of war."

Co-President Rione spoke again, her voice flat. "I hope you're not holding your breath waiting for them to surrender."

"No," Geary answered. "But there's a chance, and it'd make life a lot easier for us if they did."

"Don't assume the crews of those ships control their own fates," Rione added.

Geary gave Desjani a questioning look. She seemed to not understand the co-president's statement as well. "What do you mean?"

"I mean," Rione stated, her voice grim now, "that we believe the Syndics may have a remote command override on their ships, which would allow a Syndic CEO the means to input orders directly to the combat and maneuvering systems of ships, bypassing the crews."

"I'd heard rumors of that sort of thing," Desjani noted, "but nothing official."

Rione nodded to her. "Consider this an official confirmation. We don't know this is true for certain, but there's classified evidence available to support it. It's a sort of doomsday option for a Syndic CEO, rarely employed because if it was used often enough, we could detect and analyze the signals, then use the same override against them."

Geary felt a pain in his head and tried to push it away with his fingers against his forehead. "Unbelievable." *All right. Assume that's the case, that those crews are about to be deliberately sacrificed to lure us in and even if they try to do something about it won't be able to stop it. That means they won't be able to stop their ships from attacking*

the gate tethers. But this doomsday override can't be flex-
ible if it tells ships exactly what to do. "If we know what
the Syndics probably intend, then we can predict what orders those ships will execute."

Desjani's bared her teeth. "Which means we'll know
where they're going to be."

"Right." Geary called up the weapons employment system and began entering assumptions. If the Syndic ships in
the best shape were ordered to destroy the gate tethers, and
the destruction of the gate was supposed to be timed to
catch the Alliance fleet as close to the hypernet gate as possible, where would those Syndic ships go and when would
they go there? The system cranked through the math and
within a second projected courses and times flashed up on
the display. "We can target them. Send kinetic rounds to intercept the predicted courses, kinetic rounds heavy enough
to punch through their shields and take out the ships."

Rione was frowning. "I don't understand. You don't
normally employ such weapons against other ships."

"No, because the ships would just see them coming and
dodge." Geary pointed. "But if the ships have been locked
onto a certain trajectory and the crews can't override those
instructions, if the doomsday override doesn't allow for
enough maneuvering flexibility, we might be able to nail a
few."

"I see." Rione nodded. "This is the only way to keep
them from destroying the gate before we get to it, isn't it?"

Geary glanced at Desjani, who nodded as well. "I think
so. It's a chance, anyway. Captain Desjani, have your
weapons specialists double-check my work and set up the
engagement. I want the kinetic rounds to fire automatically
at the optimum point, giving us a one-minute heads-up and
countdown."

"No problem, sir." Desjani pointed at the appropriate
watch-stander, who bent to his task.

•   •   •

THE wave of destruction from the Alliance kinetic bombardment arrived at and swept over first the fourth planet and then, about an hour later, the third. Gazing at the highly magnified views, Geary could see explosions rippling in series across the worlds and installations orbiting them. The under-construction warships blew apart under the impacts, pieces hurled away to spin into space or get caught in the gravity well of the fourth world to tumble to their destruction. Syndic command and control centers on the planets vanished in intense flashes of light followed by towering mushroom clouds fountaining skyward. On the night-covered portions of the worlds that were visible, flickering lights from impacts rolled across the darkened surfaces in a show that would've been beautiful if it hadn't represented so much destruction.

Next to the images, *Dauntless*'s combat systems maintained a tally of results updating so rapidly it was hard to read at times. Irritated and not sure what the escalating numbers were telling him, Geary switched the display to tell him how many targets remained active. Now the tally scrolled rapidly downward. Communications hubs. Spaceports. Major airfields. Military bases. Antiorbital defenses. Military-related industrial facilities. Stockpiles of ammunition, spare parts, and equipment. Research facilities. In orbit, graceful arrays of satellites and facilities blew apart under impacts, changing into slowly spreading masses of fragments far above the atmosphere. Beneath that cocoon of wreckage, the rain of metal projectiles fell across the two worlds, leaving tangled debris and craters in its wake.

All of the numbers for targeted installations ran down to zero. "Like shooting fish in a barrel," Geary observed.

"More like dropping bombs into barrels full of fish," Desjani remarked. She seemed as cheerful as usual when watching destruction being worked on Syndic targets.

"There was plenty of time for the Syndics to evacuate

every one of those targets," Rione observed. "Do we know if they did?"

Desjani shrugged. "Madam Co-President, even *Dauntless* can't track that many human targets moving that far away beneath atmospheres or behind planets. We did see signs of evacuations under way, but if you're asking whether some Syndics died in that bombardment, I frankly can't tell you."

"You spared some of the raw materials stockpiles," Rione observed.

Geary nodded. "And some orbital facilities. We needed to leave the Syndics something to give us. Or rather for us to take. Since negotiations haven't worked well in the past, I'm planning on just sending in forces to grab what we want."

Rione gazed at Geary for a moment before answering. "That's probably a wise move."

He realized belatedly that his last statement could have been interpreted wrongly. "I don't blame you at all for the Syndic failure to abide by agreements. My decision was totally based on how untrustworthy the Syndics have proven."

Rione nodded. "Thank you, though like you, I hold myself accountable even for those things outside my power to control."

The statement sounded like a compliment. Geary wondered why Rione had suddenly said something to him that at least sounded nice.

"In any event," Rione continued, "I thank you for sparing civilian targets, Captain Geary."

"You're welcome."

"Captain Geary," a watch-stander announced. "Syndic Force Alpha is about to cross the projected track of Task Force Furious."

Which actually meant that the event had taken place some hours ago, the same as the bombardment of worlds that they had just witnessed. Geary focused his display there, seeing the arcing track of Task Force Furious curving toward the fourth world, the slightly flatter arc of the Syndic flotilla's trajectory crossing it almost a light-minute ahead of where Task Force Furious had been. "You don't think they tried to drop mines along that track, do you?"

Desjani shrugged again. "They might have tried. Surely Commander Cresida would have prepared for that."

She apparently had. Even before the Syndic force actually crossed the track of Task Force Furious, they could see the Alliance formation altering course, swinging farther and farther to the side. "Where the hell is she going now?" Geary wondered.

This time Desjani grinned. "Captain Geary, when you let loose a weapon like Commander Cresida and tell her to seek her own targets, you have to be prepared for some unexpected decisions."

Geary couldn't help laughing. "I guess since I have no idea what she's doing next, there's no possibility of the Syndics anticipating her moves, either."

Velocity and momentum carried Task Force Furious a long ways in the same direction it had been going, but its course kept diverging from the original projection. By the time it reached the region where the Syndic flotilla had crossed its track, Task Force Furious was several light-seconds away from where it would have been on that original course. "If the Syndics dropped mines, they were wasted," Desjani observed. "The region of space they would've had to cover is too huge."

Task Force Furious kept turning, now also diving below the plane of the system, forming a huge spiral as its ships came around through a full circle, only steadying up again when the task force was headed for the almost-completed Syndic battleship and battle cruiser that had been towed away from the orbital bombardment. Far beyond, Syndic Force Alpha was still charging across the Sancere Star System, putting tremendous distance between itself and the Alliance task force.

One half hour later, Geary watched as Task Force Furious swept by the already battered shipyards, taking out some unstruck targets with precision hell-lance fire. Ten minutes after that, as the Syndic tugs dropped their lines and ran frantically for safety, Task Force Furious tore apart the under-construction battleship and battle cruiser that the tugs had tried to save, the lightest units in the task force swinging farther out to blow apart the fleeing tugs as easily as if they were swatting flies.

Geary tore his attention away from Cresida's task force, knowing that whatever it did now was irrelevant to the ultimate outcome of the battle for Sancere system. That rested ahead of them, where Syndic Force Bravo still waited, unmoving, near the hypernet gate.

One and a half hours until contact, assuming the Syndics didn't stage a last minute charge and close the distance more rapidly.

Less than two hours, almost certainly, before everyone in the Sancere Star System discovered what happened when a hypernet gate was destroyed.

"Captain Desjani," Geary asked, "why *hasn't* anyone tried to destroy a hypernet gate before this? I know from the records of the war I've reviewed that star systems near enemy territory that contain gates have been attacked and captured. Why haven't the gates in those systems been destroyed?"

Desjani appeared surprised by the question. "The enemy couldn't use a friendly gate. This is the first time an enemy force has had a key to the other side's hypernet."

"Yes, but the enemy could still use their own gate to send in reinforcements quickly or mount a counterattack aimed at retaking the system."

"Yes, sir." Desjani seemed to think that didn't require explanation.

The reason dawned on Geary. He hadn't been thinking like these modern fighters. "You want the enemy forces to show up."

"Of course, Captain Geary. The point of offensive actions is to engage and destroy the enemy," Desjani explained as if discussing something everyone knew.

"Anything that makes it easier for enemy forces to arrive for combat furthers the goal of bringing the enemy to battle. A functioning enemy gate offers a guaranteed battlefield."

"Of course." Strip war down to its most basic element, and that was it. Kill the enemy. Looked at that way, it made perfect sense to leave the enemy hypernet gate intact, because that meant more enemies could be counted upon to arrive, and then you could try to kill them. Thanks to that functioning hypernet gate, the enemy would be reinforcing faster than you, but that just meant more targets. *No wonder they've taken such losses. It's not just the loss of battle-fighting expertise, it's an attitude that places killing above winning. They'd forgotten that winning smart can kill more enemies than slugging it out toe-to-toe.*

Geary studied his fleet formation for perhaps the one hundredth time in the last few hours. How did you best deal with a massively outnumbered enemy force that wanted your fleet to get close? He kept coming up with the same answer, even though it wasn't foolproof. "We'll have to split the fleet formation."

Desjani nodded, betraying no concern.

Geary made a decision, knowing he could otherwise spend endless time debating with himself because there wasn't any single obviously right way to do this. He worked the controls, setting up formations that broke the main body of the fleet into six sections, each composed of a mix of capital ships and escorts.

"Six?" Desjani asked, finally surprised.

"Yes. I want to avoid giving the Syndics the concentrated target they want. I also want to be able to employ our firepower against them, which I can't if we're in formations so much larger than our targets that a lot of our units are out of contact." Geary hesitated, then mashed the control sending the orders to the fleet. "All units in the Alliance fleet, this is Captain Geary. New formation assignments are en route to your units. Formation execution will be at time two zero. I intend having each formation conducting passes against Syndic Force Bravo until it either flees the area of the hypernet gate or is destroyed."

Desjani studied the information on her own display, eyes narrowed in thought. "Six formations. Each swinging past the Syndics in turn before arching out and coming around again. Like a huge wheel. We'll simply pound them to pieces if they don't move."

"That's the idea," Geary agreed.

"You've put *Dauntless* back in Formation Delta," Desjani observed.

"Yes." He could tell Desjani was a bit miffed about that, about being fourth in line. "I think the Syndics are going to hold out for the first three passes. By the time the fourth formation approaches, which will be Delta, I believe they'll do something. I want to have *Dauntless* there when they do." Desjani smiled, as did the watch-standers on the bridge. Geary felt slightly guilty, knowing he'd also held *Dauntless* back because of the likelihood that the Syndics wouldn't survive the first three formation passes and he was duty-bound to get *Dauntless* and the Syndic hypernet key safely home to Alliance space. Odds were that *Dauntless* would only be sweeping up the remnants of the Syndics.

Unless things went very badly and the Syndics started taking down that hypernet gate. In which case, key on board or not, Geary knew he had to be close to the scene.

"Kinetic rounds inbound," the weapons watch announced in an almost bored voice. They'd already easily dodged a half-dozen attempts to target them, seeing the rounds approaching from such a long distance that the tiniest course correction or change in speed guaranteed a miss. "Origin from hypernet gate defenses."

"We'll give them something to worry about soon enough," Desjani observed gleefully.

Geary briefly wondered what Captain Desjani would do for fun if the war somehow ended, and smashing Syndics was no longer an acceptable way to pass the time.

Dauntless's maneuvering systems kicked in at time two

zero, shoving her mass down and over to the place where she'd wait for the rest of Formation Delta to form around her. All around *Dauntless* the other ships of the fleet broke from the positions they'd held, as if an incredibly huge machine had just disassembled itself into component parts. The parts swung through space, weaving intricate patterns as they headed for new positions, the massive machine reassembling itself into six new machines, each a smaller version of the big machine they'd all once made up.

It took time for all of those ships to move across those distances, forming up so that the last formation in line was several light-minutes behind the first. The reassembly hadn't quite finished when the weapons watch called out again. "Weapons system recommends launching kinetic rounds at Syndic Force Bravo in one minute."

Geary nodded. "Do it."

Geary's rearrangement of the ships in the fleet had required the weapons system to rethink which ship should launch projectiles at what, but that required much less than a second of calculations. At exactly the optimum time, ships began automatically firing the barrage at the Syndic defenders of the hypernet gate.

Only three light-minutes still separated the leading Alliance ships from the Syndic defenders of the hypernet gate. At a velocity of .1 light, that meant thirty minutes, perhaps the longest half hour Geary thought he would ever experience. *Talk about relativistic distortion.* Time itself seemed to have slowed to a crawl.

"Syndic defenders conducting evasive maneuvers to dodge incoming kinetic rounds," the weapons watch reported. "Systems report four of the Syndic battleships are changing their positions along predicted tracks."

"They're doing it," Desjani murmured. "Just like you thought, Captain Geary."

"Let's see if they've got enough control of their ships to dodge," he cautioned, feeling his guts tightening.

"Formation Alpha commencing firing pass on Syndic defenders. Syndic forces are firing."

Geary centered his display on the action. Alliance destroyers and light cruisers swept in on either side, hammering the defensive units near the gate. With powerful shields, the units managed to shrug off the fire of the lighter units, but then heavy cruisers came past, tossing grapeshot out in tight firing patterns and following with barrages from their hell-lance batteries. The metal ball bearings of the grapeshot hit the weakened defensive shields, vaporizing on impact; then the charged particle spears fired by the hell-lance batteries ripped on through. Defensive unit after defensive unit reeled under hits, blown out of position and knocked out of action by impacts.

Meanwhile, the big warships in the center of Alliance Formation Alpha tore past the center of Syndic Force Bravo, the heavily damaged enemy battleships and battle cruisers still holding station opposite the center of the gate. The Alliance battleships *Fearless*, *Resolution*, *Redoubtable*, and *Warspite* hammered the hapless Syndics as they each passed closest to the enemy. The battleships had chosen to hold off firing grapeshot or specter missiles, depending instead on the massive hell-lance batteries they carried. Weak Syndic defensive fire glanced harmlessly from the battleships' powerful shields, while volleys from the Alliance ships tore into the already battered Syndics. First one battleship blew up, then another, then two battle cruisers, leaving a single crippled battle cruiser holding the center of the Syndic formation.

Geary watched, rubbing his chin, waiting for what he thought was the inevitable Syndic reaction.

Another cheer broke his focus on the center of the Syndic formation. Geary swung his gaze over and saw one of the Syndic battleships that had been in good shape had taken a heavy kinetic round amidships and was reeling off at an angle. Moments later a Syndic battle cruiser took another hit, shattering its forward section and sending it tumbling. The Syndic automated control systems had indeed left the crews no way to dodge an incoming round.

To Geary's surprise, Desjani wasn't cheering. She looked

angry, her face reddening. "They ought to be allowed to fight back," she muttered. Suddenly aware of Geary's eyes on her, Desjani shrugged in an embarrassed way. "As you said, sir, it's not right if it's just murder. Even if they are Syndics."

He nodded. "We've got three more battleships to worry about as well as two battle cruisers capable of fighting."

As Alliance fleet Formation Bravo lunged forward, the escorts from the Syndic flotilla leaped out to meet them. Geary held his breath, watching five heavy cruisers, a light cruiser, and nine Hunter-Killers charging straight at an Alliance formation holding four battle cruisers led by Captain Duellos in *Courageous*. With him was *Formidable*, *Intrepid*, and *Renown*, surrounded by ten heavy cruisers, six light cruisers, and a dozen destroyers. Still, Geary watched with concern, knowing the Syndics had enough firepower to cost him some ships if Duellos bungled it. Geary felt an almost overwhelming desire to punch his communications controls and tell Duellos what to do. But he was almost a couple of light-minutes from the unfolding battle, and those two minutes of time delay in his picture of events could prove critical. On top of that, of all his subordinates, he trusted Duellos, Desjani, and Cresida the most. *I need to keep my hands off the communications controls. I need to let good people do their jobs.*

Duellos justified that trust. As the Syndics curved down toward his formation, Duellos rotated it upward so that the firepower of every ship could focus on the area the Syndics were approaching. Minutes before contact, the Alliance destroyers and light cruisers accelerated forward as well, racing up and inward to rake the flanks of the Syndic attackers. HuKs flared and broke under the concentrated fire, then the heavy cruisers ran head-on into a carefully timed barrage of specter missiles, followed by grapeshot and hell lances. The leading three cruisers came apart, a fourth staggered and rolled away with some Alliance cruisers heading in pursuit, and the fifth tried to dive off in the opposite direction but ran into four Alliance cruisers that bracketed it and overwhelmed its shields on three sides simultaneously. As the wreckage of the fifth Syndic heavy cruiser tumbled off through space, the surviving Syndic light cruiser attempted to ram *Courageous* but disintegrated under the fire of all four Alliance battle cruisers.

"Very brave," Desjani murmured, acknowledging the doomed charge of the light cruiser.

Alliance Formation Bravo swept on up and outward. Geary, admiring how well Duellos had dealt with the attack, saw the surviving Syndic capital ships taking up positions around the hypernet gate and clenched his fists in frustration. The suicidal attack had done exactly what it needed to do, buying time for the other Syndic warships to prepare to destroy the gate.

"Formation Gamma, Captain Tulev, ignore the battle cruiser in the center of the gate. Hit the Syndic ships around the rim of the gate."

"Tulev, aye." He didn't sound nervous, but solid Tulev never did. Geary watched as Tulev altered the track of Formation Gamma, taking his battle cruisers toward the area where two of the surviving battleships were braking to glide slowly past sections of the hundreds of tethers holding the hypernet gate particle matrix in place. The heavy cruisers attached to Formation Gamma arrowed away, heading for the crippled Syndic battle cruiser opposite the center of the gate, while Tulev's *Leviathan*, along with her divisional sisters *Dragon*, *Steadfast*, and *Valiant*, swung up toward the two battleships.

Geary cast a grim eye on the last two unengaged Syndic capital ships, a battleship and a battle cruiser. He couldn't fault Tulev's decision. Splitting the Alliance battle cruisers in Tulev's formation would have left even odds facing the Syndics, which very likely wouldn't have been enough to stop the enemy ships. "Formation Delta. *Dauntless* and *Daring* will engage the Syndic battleship at ten degrees to port and six seven degrees up from *Dauntless*. *Terrible* and *Victorious* will engage the Syndic battle cruiser at one five degrees to port and four one degrees up from *Dauntless*.

Heavy cruisers accompany *Dauntless* and *Daring*. Light cruisers and destroyers accompany *Terrible* and *Victorious*. All units, come to new course up five zero degrees at time zero zero."

Geary leaned toward Captain Desjani. "We need a quick kill."

She nodded. "You'll have one, sir."

Tulev's ships were still short of engagement range when the weapons watch called out the words Geary had been dreading hearing. "The surviving Syndic ships have opened fire on the hypernet gate tethers."

SEVEN

GEARY stared at his display, watching the tethers blossom and shatter under the blows of the Syndic weapons. "How much damage can the gate take before it starts collapsing?"

"Uncertain, sir. We'll be able to tell when failure begins, but we won't know we're there until it starts happening."

Geary barely managed to keep from yelling at everyone on the bridge. *Next time you want to build something this dangerous, take some time to try to understand it first!* But he knew that wasn't fair. Under the pressure of the war, with the enemy also in possession of the hypernet technology, both sides had lacked the luxury of time to figure out the theory behind the technology.

He couldn't believe how quickly tethers were being destroyed. The Syndic ships were ignoring Tulev's oncoming attack, probably still fully under the control of their automated programs, fixed on trying to destroy the gate no matter the cost.

The cost came first for the last crippled battle cruiser in the center as a weak forward shield collapsed, leaving the hull open to bombardment by the hell lances on the four

heavy cruisers. The battle cruiser shuddered under the barrage, falling off and down, all systems apparently dead.

Minutes later Tulev's battle cruisers climbed past the
two Syndic battleships, making a dangerously close pass.
The first battleship took the full brunt of a volley of
specters that even its shields couldn't withstand, then fell
apart as grapeshot tore through it. The second battleship
managed to hold up briefly under the concentrated fire of
the hell lances of four Alliance battle cruisers, then blew up
as its shields collapsed and the lances ripped it open.

Tulev's ships were curving up and over, away from the
hypernet gate again, as Geary led Formation Delta up at
the last two Syndic ships.

Terrible and *Victorious* reached their slightly closer target first. The light cruisers and destroyers with them,
knowing the Syndic weapons were focused entirely on destroying the gate tethers, slashed past the Syndic battle
cruiser at insanely close distances, unleashing weapons as
they went. A battle cruiser's shields weren't the equal of a
battleship's, and at extremely close range even the light
Alliance warships pounded the shields dangerously low.

Behind the light units came *Terrible* and *Victorious*.
Volleys of grapeshot from both ships finally crashed the
Syndic battle cruiser's shields, then the hell lances did their
deadly work, leaving a broken wreck in their wake.

Geary's eyes kept switching from the status of the gate
to the shape of the Syndic battleship ahead. "Gate status.
Give me a guess."

The watch hesitated just a moment. "I think it's going,
sir," he reported in a voice higher-pitched by stress. "I
think we're too late."

Geary's hand triggered the communications switch.
"All units in the Alliance fleet with the exception of
Dauntless, *Daring*, and Cruiser Division Four, this is
Captain Geary. You are to accelerate away from the hypernet gate at best possible speed. Reinforce shields facing the
gate. We estimate the gate is collapsing and may produce a
very powerful burst of energy. *Dauntless* and the units with

her will destroy the remaining Syndic ship, attempt to sta-
bilize the gate, and if that fails, try to reduce the intensity
of the energy burst by further selective destruction of gate
tethers. I repeat, all units other than *Dauntless*, *Daring*,
and the heavy cruisers of Division Four are to accelerate
away from the hypernet gate at best speed."

He'd barely finished speaking when the heavy cruisers
got within range of the Syndic battleship and began pummeling it, throwing out every weapon they had. The battleship's shields held, of course, but shivered under the
blows.

Desjani spoke calmly. "*Daring*, this is *Dauntless*.
Closing to hell-lance range in conjunction with maximum
volley of grapeshot."

"*Dauntless*, this is *Daring*. Aye. Right beside you."

Geary couldn't know whether the Syndic battleship had
been released from its automated control now that the gate
seemed to be collapsing, or if the crew had managed to
override the controls on some of its weapons, but fire suddenly lashed out at the heavy cruisers. Two of them reeled
away from the hammer blows of the Syndic battleship's
massive main hell-lance batteries, damaged enough to be
out of the battle. A third cruiser arced up and back, curving away from contact. The fourth, *Diamond*, spun sideways and rolled in an attempt to confuse the Syndic aim
and kept firing.

The grapeshot from *Dauntless* and *Daring* hit the
Syndic battleship's shields, setting off a riot of flashing
lights as the shot converted its energy to heat and light. In
a few places, the shields thinned enough for grape to get
through and flare against the hull. Moments later, before
the shields of the battleship could recover, hell-lance fire
from *Dauntless* on one side and *Daring* on the other
pounded into them. The battleship trembled as the charged
particles ripped through its armor and on into its crew and
vital systems. "Specters," Desjani rapped. "Full volley."

Six missiles shot from *Dauntless*, taking just a moment
to lock onto the Syndic battleship and accelerate straight

into the stricken warship. Massive explosions bloomed and what was now nothing more than a derelict staggered away from the position it had held near the gate.

"They never stood a chance, being at almost dead stop," Desjani stated, shaking her head.

"The gate is definitely collapsing," the watch-stander monitoring it called out, his voice carrying a trace of fear now.

Geary entered a code and punched activate, calling up the program Commander Cresida had developed. *Ancestors, please let this work. It wants me to slave available warships to the program. Fine. Do it. I wish I had more than three right here, but how many do I need? The last two formations have already turned in accordance with my earlier order and are heading away.* "Dauntless, Daring, Diamond, this is Captain Geary. Your combat systems are being put under control of a program designed to try to control the collapse of the hypernet gate. Effective now." He punched in the authorization, pondering the irony of doing the same thing to his ships that the Syndic commanders had done to their Force Bravo flotilla. But then he was doing this to try to stop massive destruction, not to cause it, and if his commanders wanted to, they could override the program at any time.

Almost immediately Geary could feel *Dauntless* pivot and begin braking at maximum thrust to slow its movement across the hypernet gate. He could see *Daring* and *Diamond* also straining to kill their velocity and assume positions near the gate.

Geary looked up at the visual display, in which the hypernet gate now loomed. He had seen only one other hypernet gate, and that only for a few moments. Admiral Bloch had been eager to show it off to Geary, but Geary had still been half-dead from his extended survival sleep and the psychic shock of awakening a century in the future and therefore hadn't paid much attention. He vaguely remembered a shimmering in space, as if something wasn't quite right inside the gate.

Now he stared at something different. The destruction wrought by the Syndic ships had been limited by their losses, but it had clearly been too much for the particle matrix suspended between the tethers. The shimmering was gone, replaced by a waviness that rippled across space itself like spasms on the hide of some impossibly vast creature.

"Captain Geary," Desjani spoke as if discussing routine maneuvers, "the gate neutralization program is projecting positions for all three ships."

"Any problems with it?" Geary asked Desjani.

She shook her head. "We're already committed to the maneuver, sir."

Geary watched the image of the gate slide past *Dauntless*, the hypernet gate's size dwarfing even the Alliance battle cruiser. On his display, he could see *Daring* and *Diamond* also taking up positions called for by the program.

"Program reports gate collapse analysis complete," the weapons watch reported in a slightly baffled voice. "Stabilization impossible. Initiating destructive neutralization sequence."

Apparently that meant it was opening fire. The hell lances on all three ships hurled their charges at tethers spaced around the gate, taking them out in a pattern Geary couldn't understand. He found his eyes fixed on the gate itself again, appalled but unable to look away from the tortured death of the particle matrix bound within the gate.

The image of space through the gate now twisted and rolled as if reality itself were being bent. Something in the back of Geary's brain recoiled from the sight, repulsed by a vision that stripped bare the illusion of solidity which the universe normally held for human eyes. Inside the matrix of the gate, the fundamental nature of matter was being warped, and in the process literally unimaginable amounts of energy were being called into existence.

The hell lances on the *Dauntless* kept firing in apparently random sequences, vaporizing tethers singly and in groups. *Daring* had moved above and to port of *Dauntless*, and *Diamond* below and also to port, both of them firing their weapons as well under the coordination of the same program. It was impossible for Geary to tell from the visual display if the program was working or not. "What are the energy readings in that gate like?" he asked, his near whisper carrying clearly across the otherwise silent bridge.

"Rocketing all over the place, off the chart and then nothing, and then incredibly high again," the sensors watch reported, her voice strained by disbelief. "The changes are happening instantaneously. A lot of what's going on in that gate seems to be occurring in ways our instruments can't measure."

"Captain Geary, this is *Diamond*. What the hell is going on, sir?" The message was torn by some kind of static but still understandable.

Geary reached to push his controls without taking his eyes off the visual display. "*Diamond*, this is Geary. We're trying to leash a monster before it destroys everything in this star system. Make sure your forward shields are set to maintain at maximum. *Daring*, that goes for you, too. Do not, repeat, do not interfere with the firing pattern of your weapons."

A strange sort of humming seemed to be filling the air, a resonance traveling through everything near the gate. Geary felt it inside himself. He could hear someone whispering a prayer and didn't call for silence. The vision through the gate had twisted some more, into something almost impossible to look at because of the way his brain reacted to the sight. *The maw of the monster. The mythical beast that eats ships, leaving no trace of them in space. I've finally seen it. By the living stars, I pray I never see it again.*

A very low voice sounded near him. Co-President Rione, her tone reflecting the same awe and terror that Geary and everyone else must be feeling. "Captain Geary. Thank you for trying."

"We haven't failed yet," he managed to reply.

"Captain Desjani," the weapons watch called, his voice sounding too loud and with an undertone of panic. "Hell-lance batteries two alpha, four alpha, and five beta report overheating from the constant firing."

"Conduct emergency heat dumps," Desjani replied, her voice steady. "We have Captain Geary aboard, ladies and gentlemen. We won't fail him or the rest of the fleet counting on us."

Even through his fear Geary felt a rush of gratification at her words and admiration for Desjani's ability to project control even in the face of what was happening inside the gate.

The strange humming had grown to a moan running through and tearing at everything. Geary felt the sort of strange instability that came with being very drunk and realized his nervous system was being pummeled by whatever was happening inside the gate. He hoped that *Dauntless*'s electrical systems were better shielded than his own body was at the moment.

"Captain Geary, this is *Diamond*. Experiencing secondary system failures. Primary systems remain operational on backup circuits. We've lost one hell-lance battery to overheating. Holding position."

"This is *Daring*. We're suffering the same. Remaining on station and continuing to fire."

"Captain Desjani, failures to secondary systems throughout the hull, hell-lance battery two alpha nonoperational due to overheating."

"Very well," Desjani replied in the same steady voice. "Hold station. Continue firing."

Geary had been proud to command this fleet when he wasn't feeling overwhelmed by the responsibility. But now he felt such a strong sense of honor in commanding ships and sailors like this that he had to fight back tears. "Damn, you're all good," he stated roughly. "May the living stars reward such courage."

"This is *Diamond*. My weapons have stopped firing. All

combat systems nonoperational. Request further instructions."

Geary slammed his hand onto the control. "Withdraw, *Diamond*. Maximum acceleration. Keep your shields facing the gate as strong as possible."

"*Diamond*, aye. Unable to comply. Inertial compensators are still working but main maneuvering controls have just failed. Looks like we're staying at the mouth of hell with you."

"I couldn't ask for better company there than you, *Daring* and *Dauntless*," Geary replied. "Captain Duellos, if *Dauntless* is destroyed, you are to assume command of the fleet by my order."

It would be a while before Duellos heard that order, assuming the strange static emanating from the gate didn't mask it completely at a distance. Geary took a deep breath. "How much longer can we hold out, Captain Desjani?"

"No telling, sir," she stated in a soft but firm voice that left Geary marveling at Desjani's self-control. "The ship is undergoing a unique set of stresses."

The pace of firing from the hell-lance batteries had finally slowed, with pauses of varying length occurring before the firing program ordered new shots to blow apart more tethers at locations all around the gate. The hell mouth inside the gate was fluctuating wildly, one moment swelling as if to burst the bounds of the gate and the next dwindling to a point almost too small to see.

Geary felt his body pulsing in time, wondering how long humans could endure whatever was happening to the structure of reality in this part of space.

The hell mouth shrank into nothingness in the blink of an eye, vanishing from sight. "What—?"

Geary's question was cut off as a shock wave hit the *Dauntless*, traveling so fast that there'd been no warning time this close to the gate. He'd seen time-lapse images of the shock wave from a nova, and this seemed like that, though happening in real time the event was so fast his senses didn't really register it. *Dauntless* shuddered under the impact, the inertial compensators whining as they dampened the effects of the force.

"Forward shields being reinforced." The lights overhead dimmed. "All nonessential power being diverted to forward shields."

It ended as fast as it had come. Geary blinked at the visual display, which showed nothing but normal space. The remaining gate tethers had been vaporized by the energy release from the gate collapse. "*Diamond*! *Daring*! Report your status!"

"Sir, communications are down. Systems being restored now. You have communications, sir."

Geary punched the control again. "*Diamond* and *Daring*, request your status."

The delay was agonizing, but a reply finally came. "This is *Daring*. A lot of equipment is off-line, but we haven't taken serious damage. Estimate we can restore full capability given time. We'll have a time guesstimate for repairs for you as soon as possible."

"This is *Diamond*. We should be able to get moving again, though it will take a minimum of several hours and possibly much longer. We've lost a lot of vital systems. *Diamond* is in nonoperational status for an indefinite period."

Geary let out a breath he hadn't known he was holding. "*Daring*, remain with *Diamond*. Captain Tyrosian, designate one of your auxiliaries to close on *Diamond* and render assistance." Geary checked the system display, stunned to realize that the shock wave they'd ridden out was only now hitting the next-closest Alliance ships. "How much was that? Not a nova."

"We wouldn't be here if it'd been nova strength," the sensor watch agreed shakily. "It was sort of a minor fractional nova. Even then we couldn't have survived that kind of energy bombardment for any length of time, but there was just the one shock wave."

Geary collapsed into his seat, weak with reaction. There wasn't any way to get a message to any of the Alliance ships before the shock wave reached them, but they should be already facing the gate with their shields ready, and the energy at any point in the shock wave would be weakening rapidly as it expanded away from the gate. Cresida's program hadn't managed to eliminate the energy discharge completely, but it had kept it to a level low enough that everything remaining in the Sancere Star System should be able to ride it out. "Very good job, Captain Desjani. You and your crew. *Dauntless* is a great ship."

"Thank you, sir." Even now Desjani didn't seem as rattled as everyone else. Apparently she really had believed that having Geary along would keep the worst from happening.

He heard a deep intake of breath behind and looked to see Co-President Rione there. She was looking down at the deck, her fists clenched, but as if aware of Geary's gaze, Rione slowly raised and turned her head to face him. Rione's eyes were haunted. Geary thought he knew why. They had just seen the sort of forces that could be deliberately unleashed using the program Geary had given her for safekeeping. Until now, even Geary hadn't appreciated how terrible a burden that could be. "I'm sorry."

She nodded, understanding exactly what he meant. "As am I, Captain Geary. We will speak later." Rione inhaled slowly, straightening herself and standing erect, regaining her composure by an exercise of pure willpower. Even through his lingering shock from the destruction of the gate Geary found himself impressed by her.

Desjani seemed to have been impressed as well, despite herself. She watched Rione leave, then turned to Geary. "Orders, Captain Geary?"

"Return to the fleet, Captain Desjani." He studied the fleet display, fighting off a wave of fatigue such as he hadn't felt since the lingering effects of his long survival sleep had worn off. "All units with the exception of Task Force Furious, this is Captain Geary. After passage of the shock wave assume standard fleet formation Sigma. Task Force Furious, maintain screening position between

Syndic Force Alpha and the rest of the fleet. Well done, everyone. Very well done. Sancere is ours."

The Alliance fleet wouldn't be flying home on the wings of the Syndic hypernet. Not from Sancere, anyway. But it had survived and was striking a major blow at the Syndics. Not bad for a fleet that had once seemed doomed to destruction.

IT took twelve hours to get the fleet back together in a tight formation after the shock wave from the collapsing hypernet gate passed. The subformations Geary had put together had followed his orders to run for it in what he had to admit was a gratifying fashion. Slowing, turning, and rejoining took a while, especially since Geary didn't want to get too distant from where *During* was now towing *Diamond* toward the rest of the fleet.

With the thirty ships under *Furious* still close to two light-hours distant, much too far away to participate in a conference, the number of ship commanders around the virtual conference table seemed to have shrunk dramatically again. In this case, though, the missing ships would definitely be back. Geary nodded in greeting. "Excellent work, everyone. We have two major tasks remaining in Sancere system. The first is to acquire as much of what we need as we can. The fleet logistics system has matched Syndic stockpiles to our needs where possible. I've transmitted another message to the Syndics warning them to comply with any demands we make."

"They probably won't get it," Captain Tulev noted. "That energy wave seems to have fried most of the Syndic systems that we'd left untouched."

Desjani shrugged. "Then they won't be able to coordinate any actions against us."

Geary nodded. "The second task is to destroy those targets we left unstruck in the initial bombardment, after we've looted them to our heart's content. Unfortunately, Syndic Force Alpha is lurking around the outer edge of the system. We can't just scatter the fleet to maximize the speed and efficiency of our looting while those Syndic warships are around, even though they're too far off to be an immediate threat. I was thinking of breaking the fleet main body into six subformations again. Task Force Furious will remain on station for a while guarding against Syndic Force Alpha, but we'll rotate them in-system after a while so they can restock and resupply, too." His suggestion was greeted by a lot of nods and no objections. "Captain Tyrosian, I need to know whether I should have your auxiliaries broken up into four of the formations or if they should be concentrated."

"Pairs would be best, Captain Geary," Tyrosian replied as soon as possible given the five-light-second delay between her ship's position and the *Dauntless*. "*Titan* and *Jinn*, and *Goblin* and *Witch*."

"Good. You tell me where in Sancere they need to go to pick up what we need. After I have that, we'll work up a schedule for other ships to swing near them to pick up new weapons and fuel cells."

"We're manufacturing as fast as we can," Tyrosian assured Geary. "The primary need is materials for fabricating new fuel cells, but the Syndics have what we want."

"Colonel Carabali," Geary ordered. "Your troops will provide escort for exploitation teams from the auxiliaries and other warships."

Carabali nodded, looking concerned. "Sir, even limiting the number of subformations to six will still leave my Marines with a lot of responsibilities for their numbers. We have to assume any Alliance personnel who leave their ships or shuttles are subject to attack by regular or irregular Syndic ground forces."

"Would it help if we armed some of the sailors?"

The Marine colonel hesitated. "Sir, with all due respect, I'm not sure handing weapons to sailors will enhance the security situation." Carabali relaxed as Geary and the other fleet officers smiled. "No offense intended, but dealing with these situations requires a lot of specialized training and experience."

"I understand," Geary assured her. "That'll slow us up some more, then. We need to make sure we only land on as many sites as we can guarantee security for. I don't want the Syndics grabbing hostages."

"We've got a lot more hostages than they do," the captain of the *Terrible* laughed. "About a billion."

"True. But even if we exacted vengeance on every one of those Syndics, it wouldn't necessarily get our own people back alive." Everyone nodded again. They agreed with that logic, at least. "Any questions?"

A long pause followed while Geary let the officers think about that. He wanted anything else brought out now if possible.

The captain of the *Vambrace* spoke with visible reluctance. "Captain Geary, I would like you to address a terrible rumor I have already heard being passed around the fleet. Anonymously, of course, since those passing it don't have the courage to show themselves." A ripple ran around the table as the other commanders reacted to that. "There are those saying that the hypernet gate here was deliberately destroyed."

Geary stared, trying to understand the question. "Of course the gate was deliberately destroyed. All of your ships should've seen the Syndics open fire on it."

"No, sir. The rumor is that the gate was still functional, but was destroyed by you." The captain of the *Vambrace* grimaced. "You should know people are saying this."

"Why would I have wanted to destroy the gate if it was still functional?" Geary wondered, too amazed to yet be angry.

"According to the rumor, sir, because you want to retain command and fear it would be taken from you upon our return to Alliance space."

Torn between incredulous laughter and anger, Geary slapped his palm upon the table. "Unbelievable. Let me assure you, and everyone else, that no one here desires the safe return to Alliance space as quickly as possible more than I do."

On the heels of his words another officer spoke, his voice harsh with emotion. "Who the hell could believe that?"

Geary, shocked, looked over and saw the commander of the *Diamond*, then realized that since *Diamond* was still twenty light-seconds away that the comment wasn't addressed to Geary's last statement, but rather to the one before.

"That rumor is beneath contempt!" *Diamond*'s captain continued. "My ship was there, and anyone who wants to look at *Diamond*'s logs is welcome to it. That gate was collapsing when we reached it." He looked toward Geary. "I'll admit something. I'd been among those worried about Captain Geary, about what he was doing and how he was doing it. A lot of you know that. I was worried whether he was aggressive enough. But we charged that gate! We charged it hell-bent for leather, and we took down those Syndics as fast as we could, but they'd done too much damage. Check *Diamond*'s logs if you don't believe me. And while you're at it, look at the readings from inside the gate while it was collapsing. Unbelievable, that's all I can say. Captain Geary did all that could be done. I've stood at the doorway to hell with him, and I will stand there again if need be."

Silence fell at the end of that statement. Geary took a long, slow breath, realizing there was something else he needed to say. "Ladies and gentlemen, I've told you before that I admired the courage of the personnel in this fleet. I freely admit that I've had difficulty grasping some of the changes in the Alliance fleet from my time to now, the changes wrought by a century of time, a century of war. But I tell you now that I had not fully realized one thing before this day."

He paused, finding the right words. "The fleet I knew was smaller, professional, more highly trained. But we had not been tested in battle. Not like you have. And when

Dauntless, *Daring*, and *Diamond* stood at that gate, standing their ground without a moment's hesitation even
though they were facing something so terrible I had never
imagined the like, that's when I truly realized just how
courageous you all are. Every officer and sailor of this fleet
has the right to stand among the finest the Alliance has ever
seen. You could not possibly bring more honor to your ancestors than you have by your dedication to duty, your per-
severance in the face of a seemingly endless war, your
willingness to bear any burden in the defense of your
homes. I am honored beyond all measure by having been
granted the right to command you. I will bring this fleet
home, if for no other reason than that such people as you
deserve that your exploits be known to your homes, and
you deserve to return safely to them. I will bring you
home. I swear it."

He stopped talking, worried that he had let too much
emotion into the impromptu speech as the words tumbled
out, worried that he had sounded foolish or patronizing.
But everyone was watching him silently, their own faces
solemn. Finally the commanding officer of *Vambrace*
spoke again. "Thank you, sir. The honor is ours." No one
contradicted him. Not out loud, anyway.

Geary sat down after the meeting had ended and the virtual presences of the other officers had vanished, only
Captain Desjani remaining. She smiled, saluted, and left,
letting her expression and the gesture speak for her.

He had often wondered why fate had put him in this position, why he had lost all he had known and been thrust
into a command far beyond his old responsibilities. The
idea that he would ever be grateful for any part of that had
never occurred to him. But, remembering the steady presences of *Dauntless*, *Daring*, and *Diamond* at the gate,
Geary breathed a prayer of thanks for having such ships
and sailors at his side.

•   •   •

THE ship's night had begun, with Geary sitting in his stateroom staring at nothing, his mind filled with memories of the hell mouth within the hypernet gate, when his hatch alert sounded. Expecting Captain Desjani, he was startled when Victoria Rione entered, her face betraying some deep emotion. *I probably ought to be mad at her for making my life even more difficult since Sutrah, but compared to what Falco did, it's nothing. Rione isn't going to cause the loss of a lot of ships.* So Geary stood and spoke politely. "Madam Co-President. I admit to being surprised by this visit. You haven't been by here for some time."

"Not unless you insisted, you mean?" Rione stated calmly.

"Yes. I hope you're not planning to hand me the sort of problem I handed you at our last meeting here."

"No." She paused, apparently steeling herself to do something. "Captain Geary, I wish to apologize."

That was a surprise. "Apologize?"

"Yes." She indicated the star display floating above the table. "Since our argument at Sutrah I've done as I said I would. I ran simulations. I took this fleet along every possible path from Sutrah using the jump points we had planned on employing." Rione hesitated, her jaw muscles tightening. "They all ended the same. Minor losses in system after system adding up while options kept being limited more and more by Syndic defensive moves, until the fleet ended up pinned between superior forces."

Geary couldn't help saying it. "So I was right."

"You were right," Rione agreed in a sharp voice. "I admit it."

"What I told you that I'd worked out in my head was accurate enough to predict exactly what the simulations predicted."

She nodded tightly, her expression hard. "You spoke the truth. I admit that as well. I apologize for questioning your motives."

He shook his head, letting frustration show. "My motives? Hell, Madam Co-President, you all but called me a traitor to this fleet and the Alliance. You actually did use the word *betray,* didn't you?"

"I did, and I admit I was wrong." Rione's eyes were flashing with resentment now. "Will you not accept my apology?"

"Yes. I will. Thank you." Geary struggled not to lash out at her again, knowing he was actually angry at Falco and people like him. "The last several weeks have been difficult ones."

"I know." Rione shook her head. "It must have been very difficult to face Captain Falco's betrayal."

"It would've been easier if I'd had you to talk to." Startled that he had actually said that, Geary looked to Rione, seeing her face composed again, carefully not betraying her feelings. "I've missed your counsel."

"My counsel. I'm glad you find my counsel welcome." Her voice was flat. "But you obviously don't need it. Your judgment was superior to mine on where this fleet should go."

Now what was she mad about? "Madam Co-President . . ." Geary struggled to find the right words. "I do need it. I don't have many people to confide in. I don't have many people I trust the way I trust you."

Her expression was hard to read, but her eyes searched Geary's face. "I can't be the only person in this fleet you can trust."

"No. It's not just that. It's . . ." Geary looked away, rubbing the back of his neck with one hand. "I like having you around."

Silence stretched for a few moments. He finally looked back at Rione, to see her still watching him. "Do you think I'm your friend, Captain Geary?"

He hadn't gone there. Hadn't been willing to consider it. "My last friend died a very long time ago."

"Then accept new friends, Captain Geary!" Her renewed anger startled him.

"You don't . . . Madam Co-President, if I . . ." Geary

felt the words sticking in his throat, surprised to realize how hard it was to actually speak of his fears, of how it had felt to wake up from survival sleep and learn every friend, every acquaintance, everyone he had known, was long dead.

"Is this the man daring enough to take the Alliance fleet to Sancere?" Rione asked in a mocking voice. "The hero of the fleet? The man who stood facing the mouth of hell? And he cannot bring himself to risk accepting a friend for fear of the possibility of loss?"

"You have no idea what this is like," Geary stated angrily. "When they revived me, every single person I'd known was dead. All of them."

"Are you the first to ever lose someone they cared about? Or everything they cared about? Let yourself live again, Captain Geary!"

"You don't know—"

Her face turned furious for a moment. "A man I loved more than life itself died, Captain Geary, one more victim of this endless, ugly war! It happened more than a decade ago, but I can still see him clearly if I close my eyes. I had to decide whether to let myself die inside or try to live again. I knew what he would've wanted. I won't deny it was hard, but I have lived."

Geary just stared at her for a moment. "I'm sorry. Very sorry."

The fury faded, replaced by weariness. "Damn you, John Geary, no one else has ever been able to make me lose control. Not since he died."

"Why do you care?" he asked, feeling bewildered now. "Why do you care what I think? Why do you care what happens to me?"

She took a moment to answer. "I do care. You're a remarkable man, Captain Geary. Even at your most infuriating."

"You hate me!"

"I have never hated you!" Rione shot back at him. Then she grimaced. "That's not quite true. When I thought you'd betrayed the fleet, believed that you'd lied to me and used me, I did hate what I assumed you were doing."

"You accused me of betraying you personally, as well as the fleet."

Rione nodded. "I told you that I thought you'd deliberately manipulated me. It wasn't just my pride that was hurt by that. I'd let myself believe in you. I'd let myself . . . grow to care for you."

Geary shook his head, feeling baffled again. "Do you actually *like* me, Madam Co-President?"

Rione looked upward as if beseeching aid. "You are so wise in the movements of fleets and such a dolt in reading the feelings of others. I've liked you for some time, Captain Geary. I wouldn't have been so angered by what I thought was your betrayal if I hadn't become fond of you, despite my instincts that warn me away from someone like you. My instincts that tell me you are not to be trusted, that you cannot be sincere."

Geary wondered if his puzzlement showed. "You don't trust me but you like me?"

"Yes. I will never trust Black Jack Geary," Rione explained. For some reason she was smiling wryly at him. "But I've come to like John Geary. When he isn't driving me insane. Who are you?"

"John Geary, I hope, Madam Co-President."

"Madam Co-President? Is that who you wish to be here? If you care for me at all, if you consider me a friend, call me Victoria, John Geary!"

He stared at her again. "Care for you? I do. I hadn't realized how much I'd grown to enjoy your company until I was deprived of it for a while."

"I'm waiting," she stated.

"Victoria."

"That wasn't so hard, was it?"

Geary uttered a small laugh, then sat down again. "It was very hard."

"Try saying it again. It may get easier."

He watched her, trying to figure out what Rione was doing. "All right, Victoria."

She sat down next to him, her face somber now. "You're not the only lonely person in this fleet, John Geary. Not the only person in need of comfort with few places to turn."

"I know that. But I only knew my feelings. I missed not seeing you and not talking to you."

"Why didn't you ever tell me that?"

Geary shook his head, smiling ruefully. "You know the reason as well as I do. Aside from the fact that you were refusing to talk to me, I'm the commander of this fleet. I can't do anything with anyone that isn't professional and business-related, not unless I know they want it. I have too much power for it to be otherwise, even if every person under my command isn't already off-limits for other reasons."

"And every single person in this fleet is under your command," Rione noted. "Save one. I'm not off-limits."

"No, but . . . even you can't forget the authority I wield. No one can look at me and see just me. They see the fleet commander. They see someone who could misuse their power to coerce or to reward for the wrong reasons. I have to avoid even appearing to misuse my authority that way. That's just the way it is."

"Many of them look at you and see Black Jack Geary," Rione noted.

"Yeah." Geary shrugged. "Being perfect in every way, Black Jack wouldn't even consider doing the wrong thing, I'm sure. No matter how much he liked a woman."

"Oh? Do you like me so much, John Geary?"

He couldn't help grinning. "When you're not driving me insane."

"Then why do you fear to show it even now? Will you just talk, or will you act?"

He had thought there had already been plenty of surprises, but that startled him even more. Geary stared at Rione again. "What?"

To his further surprise, she smiled. "We've already

agreed that I'm not off-limits to you. We've already agreed that we're both lonely people in need of comfort, people who have both lost those we cared about. We're both people who have responsibilities that they cannot share. Therefore, I'd like you to show me how much you like me."

Geary had been prepared for many things to possibly happen while the fleet was in Sancere Star System, but this hadn't been one of them. Caught totally off guard, he just stared at her.

Rione shook her head, still smiling. "You act like you've never kissed a woman before."

There couldn't be any doubt. She meant it. He'd resigned himself to a lack of physical contact to match his emotional isolation, but it seemed he had been wrong about that. "I have, but it's been a century since I did that last."

"I trust you haven't forgotten how."

"I hope not."

"Then show me. For a dashing hero, you can be very hesitant at times."

Oddly enough, the kiss did feel to Geary as if it was the first in almost a century. "What's going on, Madam Co-President?"

Rione shook her head, looking upward again, this time in apparent despair. "Madam Co-President will not answer."

"I'm sorry," Geary stated with mock formality. "Victoria, what's going on?"

"I'm trying to seduce you, John Geary. Haven't you figured that out yet? How can you be so oblivious with me when you can guess what the Syndics are going to be doing three star systems down the line?"

He gazed at her for a moment longer before he thought of an answer. "The Syndics are easier to figure out. Why, Victoria?"

She sighed. "You must be the only sailor in the universe who'd ask a partner that before the act instead of after. I don't know why. Maybe because we both gazed into infin-

ity today and ended up surviving the experience. Why does
it matter?"

Geary took another moment to answer. "I guess it matters because I think you matter." Rione smiled in a very
genuine way, which made her look very nice, so he kissed
the smile. Before he could pull away again, her arms were
around him, and he decided that he didn't want to move
away.

As it turned out, kissing wasn't the only thing Geary remembered how to do. By the time Victoria Rione's body
arched beneath his, Geary had recalled a few other things
well enough to satisfy his partner. As they collapsed together, spent, Geary realized that this was the first time
since being thawed out from the survival pod that he
couldn't sense any trace of ice inside his body or soul. The
discovery both elated and frightened him.

EIGHT

HIS communications alert sounded and Geary jerked awake, rolling to slap the control and remembering only at the last instant to keep the video off so no one would see he wasn't alone. "Geary here."

"Sir, Captain Desjani sends her respects, and wishes to inform you that Colonel Carabali is expressing concern regarding the movements of Alliance fleet Formation Bravo."

"Concern?" Every time to date that the Marine had been worried she had been proven justified. "I'll talk to her in a minute. Ask the colonel to hold on."

"Yes, sir."

Geary sat up carefully, trying not to make noise.

"Did you actually think that didn't wake me up?" Victoria Rione asked.

"Sorry."

"I'll have to get used to it, I suppose."

Geary paused in his movements and looked over at her, seeing her lying on her back and gazing at him as calmly as if they had woken up together like this a thousand times before. "You want this to be long-term?"

Rione raised an eyebrow at him. "Are you saying you don't?"

"No. I'm not saying that. I'd like to try it. I think long-term could make me . . ."

"Happy? It's all right to be happy, John Geary. It took me a long time to realize that after my husband died, but in time I did."

"How long did it take?" he asked quietly.

"Until tonight. Now go speak with your colonel and for the living stars' sake make sure you're dressed before you do."

"I'm sure the colonel has seen worse," Geary noted. But he hastily pulled on his uniform as he went to the desk in his stateroom and activated the communications terminal there, trying to shake his mind clear of what had happened with Rione earlier that evening so he could concentrate on his job. "What's bothering you, Colonel?"

Carabali bore signs of fatigue, which made Geary feel guilty about his own rest. The Marine commander pointed at a display next to her. "Sir, your ships are moving close to the fourth world. That's not my business normally, but it's my job to warn fleet officers about planetary threats."

"Planetary threats? We bombed the hell out of that world. There shouldn't be any functioning antiorbital weapons left."

"Shouldn't be," Carabali agreed. "That's not the same as aren't. Sir, we hit everything we could see from a few light-hours out. But that's a densely populated and heavily built-up world. It's not as easy to see things when there's so many other buildings and installations around. On top of that, the impacts stirred up a lot of dust and water vapor into the upper atmosphere, so we can't see the surface worth a damn right now. We don't know what we haven't seen, and we don't know what's down there now."

Geary studied the display, rubbing his chin. "Good point," he conceded. *Fighting in space makes it too easy to*

*assume you can see any threat long before it reaches you.
That won't apply in this case. I should have realized that.
The victories over the Syndics so far in Sancere Star
System, and surviving the collapse of the hypernet gate
made me too confident. I haven't been paranoid enough
about what else might be lurking in this system.* "Can they
target us through that stuff in the atmosphere if they do
have surviving weaponry?"

"We definitely didn't get every possible air- and spaceport, sir. All they have to do is get something high enough
to relay a view down to the surface. It could be an un-
manned drone that would be very hard to spot."

Geary called up the exploitation plan, checking to see
what Formation Bravo was getting. "Our ships are heading
for the Syndic orbital shipyards, what's left of them anyway, and some big orbiting civilian installations. We need
what's on those, Colonel, especially the food and raw materials stockpiles."

"Sir, I don't like it."

"Can you give me a plan, Colonel? Something that
would let our ships loot those locations and keep the
Syndics from targeting us with any weapons surviving on
the surface?"

Carabali frowned, looking down as she thought. "We've
got scout ships we can send into the atmosphere. Recce
drones. But there's no telling how low they'd have to go to
get a decent look around, and the lower they are, the less
area they can monitor or search."

"How many of those drones are with Formation
Bravo?"

The colonel frowned again, checking something outside
Geary's view. "Ten, sir. All operational. But if we send
them down into that, there's no guarantee they're coming
back up, and as far as I know, your auxiliaries can't make
new ones for us."

"They can't make me new ships, either." Geary took a
moment to think. "I'll talk to the commander of Formation
Bravo. That's Captain Duellos. We'll use the recce drones

to check beneath the junk in the atmosphere, and we'll keep ships out of low orbits. I'll see what else I can think of and get back with you soon."

"Thank you, sir." Colonel Carabali saluted, and her image vanished.

Geary sighed heavily and stood, turning to say good-bye to Rione. He discovered her near the bunk, standing leaning against the bulkhead, still naked, watching him. "No rest for the weary?" she asked.

"I've gotten more rest than a lot of people," Geary muttered, looking away.

"What's the matter, Captain Geary?" Rione asked, her voice sounding mildly amused.

"I'm trying to concentrate on my command responsibilities. You're a little distracting."

"Just a little? I'll see you on the bridge in a while."

"Okay." Geary paused before leaving, then set his state-room access to allow Rione entrance at any time, knowing she was watching. On the way up to the bridge, he felt an odd sense of disquiet. Rione had been extremely passionate during their lovemaking but now once again held that attitude of cool detachment toward him, even while standing before him naked. Geary couldn't help thinking of a cat, one that had taken the affection it desired but reserved the right to walk out the door at any time with no regrets. He had never seriously considered the possibility that Victoria Rione would want a relationship with him and so had never thought about what that might mean. She had said she liked him, but the word *love* certainly hadn't come up. Was Rione only using him for her own comfort? Or, worse, was she positioning herself close to him for her own political advantage, either against the Black Jack Geary she feared or other politicians back in the Alliance?

What would it be worth for an ambitious politician to be the consort of the legendary hero who had miraculously brought the Alliance fleet home to safety?

How can I think that? Rione's never shown any sign of that kind of ambition.

But then there's a lot of things she's never shown. Not to me, anyway. Like wanting to bed me. Say she's still devoted to saving the Alliance from Black Jack Geary. How hard would it be to rationalize gaining power for herself by close association with me so she would be better able to control whatever I did? How do I know that beneath that dedicated exterior there isn't a very ambitious woman ready and willing to use me to further her own career?

Ancestors help me. For all I know Rione is totally sincere. Why do I have to try to second-guess this? Why do I have to be suspicious of her?

Because I'm so damned powerful, and if I succeed in getting this fleet home, I'll be a lot more powerful. She's the one who made me realize that in the first place.

On the other hand, if she is using me, I might as well enjoy it while it lasts. And if I'm just a means to help her attain rank in the Alliance governing council, there's worse fates. I've no reason to think she's unethical or power-hungry.

Right, Geary. You're such a good judge of women that she had to practically drag you into bed before you got the hint.

Not for the first time, Geary found himself baffled by what Rione was thinking and looked forward to the relative simplicity of dealing with an enemy he knew was just trying to kill him.

CAPTAIN Desjani yawned and nodded in greeting as Geary entered the bridge of the *Dauntless*. "You spoke with Colonel Carabali?"

"Yeah," Geary replied, taking his seat and calling up the display. He studied it for a moment. He had been either sleeping or otherwise engaged with Co-President Rione for about five hours. Against the scale of a star system, not a lot changed in that amount of time. But Formation Bravo was bearing down steadily on the fourth world and the supplies it offered. *Courageous* was just over thirty light-minutes away from *Dauntless* now, so any conversation with Captain Duellos would be a drawn-out affair.

Geary organized his thoughts, then keyed the personal command circuit. "Captain Duellos, this is Captain Geary. There's some concern here about the dangers posed by bringing your ships close to a heavily built-up world that might still have some functioning antiorbital systems under that dust blocking our views of the surface. Please deploy the Marine atmospheric recce drones on your ships to search beneath the high dust layer for any signs of a threat. Ships should be kept out of low orbit. Maintain a tight scan of the upper atmosphere for any signs of Syndic drones or other reconnaissance activity that might provide targeting information to weapons on the surface. Please employ whatever other safety measures you feel are prudent and keep me advised." *Should I add anything else? No. Duellos knows what he's doing. He doesn't need me preaching to the choir about the need to be careful and avoid losing ships.* "Geary, out."

He slumped back, rubbing his forehead. *I forgot when I broke up the fleet that it would mean I'd lose real-time communications with most of my ships. At least I don't need to worry about Numos messing something up.* Unfortunately, that small comforting thought reminded Geary of the almost forty ships that had followed Falco and might already have been destroyed.

Desjani shook her head. "With your leave, Captain Geary, I'm going to go below and grab a couple of hours of real sleep. I'm wasting my time up here right now."

Geary automatically checked the display again. Formation Delta, once again formed around *Dauntless*, was close to a day away from the facilities orbiting the third planet, which were its objective. There wasn't a trace of Syndic shipping under way in the system, except for the battered Force Alpha, which remained out between the orbits of the seventh and eighth planets, maintaining a very large distance between itself and the closest Alliance ships in Task Force Furious. Geary wondered how long it would be before the Syndic commander realized that it wouldn't be a career-enhancing move to survive with the rest of his or her flotilla intact while the Alliance leisurely trashed the star system. "Why not make it more than a couple of hours? I'll stay up here for a while."

Desjani grinned. "Thanks, but even with you on the bridge, I'm still the captain of this ship."

"How about if I order you to get at least four hours' rest?"

"I guess I can't refuse a direct order," Desjani admitted with clear reluctance. She stood, stretching again. "You seem to be feeling better, sir, if you don't mind my saying so."

"Rest helps." Co-President Rione chose that moment to arrive on the bridge. She nodded coolly to Desjani and then inclined her head in another wordless greeting to Geary. He nodded back, more pleasantly than he had been greeting Rione for some weeks. As Geary turned back, he caught Desjani's eyebrow raised as she looked from Geary to Rione. Realizing Geary was watching, Desjani rapidly hauled down the eyebrow, assuming a noncommittal look. *Desjani can tell? How could it be that obvious?* Geary wondered. *We didn't even say anything.*

Captain Desjani faced her senior watch-stander. "I'll be in my cabin. Resting." On the last word, she gave a sidelong glance to Geary and one corner of her mouth twitched as an effort to suppress a smile didn't quite succeed. As Desjani left, she paused by Rione. "It's a pleasure to have you aboard, Madam Co-President." As far as Geary could remember, Desjani had never offered that kind of sentiment to Rione before.

Geary felt a headache starting again, even though Rione looked amused as Desjani left. "How?" he asked Rione in a very low voice.

"I'm afraid that information is on a need-to-know basis," she informed Geary in a matter-of-fact voice.

"In other words, it's a woman thing."

"If you care to think of it that way."

He leaned back, indicating the display. "What do you think? Colonel Carabali was concerned about Formation Bravo getting close to the fourth planet. Does anything else set off alarms for you?"

"I'll take a look. Surely you don't think I have the skill to make a military assessment?" Rione asked.

"No. But sometimes someone with military training can overlook even something obvious to a layperson. I notice you don't seem all that worried. Whenever we're in Syndic systems I'm used to having you toss out warnings about everything that can go wrong."

"And you like that?"

"Well, I'm used to it, anyway. Besides, you've often been right."

Rione gave him a very small smile, then nodded and bent to study the display before her seat. Geary checked the time. Twenty more minutes before Duellos would even get his message. Probably an hour, at least, before an answer came.

Who could have guessed war could be boring? Right up until it starting scaring the bloody hell out of you.

DUELLOS rogered up for Geary's instructions, adding that he would keep his ships positioned with Syndic orbital facilities between them and the surface of the planet as much as possible. Presumably even the Syndics wouldn't deliberately shoot through their own installations.

The formation of which *Dauntless* was a part coasted past the orbit of the fourth world, heading farther inward toward the third world. At their closest point, Geary was within four light minutes of Formation Bravo. On his display, small images reflected relayed data from the Marine recce drones over the fourth world, their transmissions occasionally fuzzed by static from the dust filling the upper atmosphere of the planet.

On visual, the images revealed what seemed a pleasant

enough world, with large cities, abundant towns, and big areas of wilderness marred by occasional scars of mining or other resource extraction. It seemed a nearly deserted world from the images, though, with streets and roads almost empty of people and vehicles. The few vehicles sighted were clearly official, often traveling in convoys. The rest of the population was apparently hunkered down, though hiding in buildings or cellars or even shelters wouldn't offer any protection if the Alliance decided to bombard the planet in earnest.

Here and there, craters marked the sites of impacts from the kinetic bombardment. All of the images from the parts of the planet receiving sunlight had a grayish, washed-out quality, as if seen on a very cloudy day, because of all of the dust in the upper atmosphere. The night-side images were pitch-black, the dust blocking any starlight from reaching the surface.

By tapping controls Geary could make the images shift from visual to infrared, to radar of various kinds including ground-penetrating, to scans of the electromagnetic spectrum. He could see other functions available but left them alone, afraid that he would inadvertently order one of the drones to do something. Occasionally a drone would report coming under fire as the Syndics tried to shoot it down, but they made difficult targets at the best of times, and with the dust cover in the upper atmosphere to duck into for extra cover when necessary, the drones were even harder to hit.

"Captain Geary, this is Captain Duellos. Whatever remains of the surface defenses is trying to get a picture of us." Accompanying the message was a link that showed Syndic drones popping up above the dust for brief moments to get a good look at the situation above the planet before dropping down again and being lost to the Alliance sensors before they could be targeted themselves. "There's no obvious pattern. If they're trying to get targeting data for something, we can't tell where it is. I've ordered all of the ships in my formation to institute random changes in position and track."

Duellos wouldn't hear his answer for over four minutes, but Geary responded. "Thanks. Let's hope—" He broke off as his display sounded an alert.

"Weapons fire from the surface of the fourth world," a *Dauntless* watch-stander reported. "Particle cannon. It looks like an entire battery."

Four minutes ago. "Can we tell if they got any hits?"

There was a pause that seemed to last far too long before the watch-stander reported back. "Near misses on *Falchion* and *Renown*. No hits."

Desjani, back on the bridge and looking considerably more rested, shook her head contemptuously. "They're practically firing blind, and now we know there's ground defenses still active."

"Duellos ordered random evasive moves just before those cannon fired," Geary pointed out. "If he hadn't done that, the Syndics might have gotten hits." Unlike the ship-based weapons, the planetary particle cannons could be much larger and draw on tremendous power supplies. Even a single hit from one of them could slash through shields and rip into a ship.

Even as Geary spoke, *Dauntless*'s sensors reported another volley fired. He itched to order counteractions, having to remind himself that this had all happened minutes ago and Duellos had surely already done something. "That should be enough to determine the location of the cannon on the surface of the planet," Desjani noted.

Sure enough, a half-dozen kinetic bombardment rounds shot from Duellos's battle cruisers, arcing down into the atmosphere as the Alliance ships continued making random changes in position and track, and the Syndics fired yet a third volley, this one managing a single near miss on *Gauntlet*. "It's a good thing those cannon take a while to recharge," Geary commented.

"They'll probably only get one more volley off," Desjani agreed. She was right; the shots all going wide this time.

One of the Marine recce drones had been swung over to

observe the position where the cannon were located, providing a long-range view of the spot near the horizon of the drone's viewing area. The kinetic rounds launched by Duellos's battle cruisers flashed down, leaving tracks of intense brightness in their wakes, the impacts creating huge bursts of light and throwing out fountains of debris. As the light faded, mushroom clouds rose above the site, merging into one titanic grave marker for the cannon battery.

Geary sighed. "Let's hope that was all they had."

"Unlikely," Desjani advised.

"I know." Geary tapped his communications controls again. "Captain Duellos, congratulations to you and your ships. Well done. Keep an eye out for further attempts." He grimaced at the images from the recce drones. *I can understand why it's tempting to just bomb the hell out of a planet to minimize the chance of anything surviving to threaten us. But what would give me the right to kill millions of civilians in the hopes of hitting some concealed defenses? It wouldn't even ensure eliminating those defenses if they were hardened and concealed, and they're probably both.* He looked at Desjani. "Do you think we'll have to deal with that at the third planet?"

"Possibly. We have to assume the threat exists."

Geary leaned back, shaking his head. "Why can't they be rational about this? They don't have much chance of hurting us, and they're inviting retaliation every time they shoot."

Desjani gave a questioning glance his way. "Sir, we've been fighting a war with them for a century. I think things like 'rational' went out the window quite a while back."

"Good point. Do you think it would do any good to broadcast another demand not to attack our ships?"

She shrugged. "That's hard to say. The energy pulse from the collapsing hypernet gate must have fried every unshielded receiver in this star system, but some might still be operational to hear you."

"Unfortunately, those probably belong to the government and the military."

"Yes, sir. And they're unlikely to listen to reason."

Geary nodded, then studied Desjani. "Captain, when I first met you I think you wouldn't have hesitated to wipe all of these planets clean of human life. You don't seem interested in doing that now."

She looked straight ahead for a while before answering. "I've listened to you, sir, and I've had some long talks with my ancestors. There's no honor in killing the helpless. Besides, what we've done here will require a massive investment from the Syndics to repair, whereas if we wiped out the system, the Syndics would just write it off." Desjani paused. "And no one can accuse us of behaving like the Syndics here. We're not them. I realized I don't want to die doing things the Syndics would do."

"Thank you, Captain Desjani." Between honor and practical considerations, Desjani had decided Geary was right. It made him feel much better than having her agree with him just because he was Black Jack. Geary had wondered what would happen if he dropped dead tomorrow, if the fleet would return to the tactics and practices he had seen when he arrived. But it seemed at least some of the officers were returning to even older practices, the ones Geary was familiar with. He wasn't fool enough to believe that everything from the past was better than now, but surely abiding by the laws of war, the dictates of true honor, and fighting wisely instead of just bravely were good things.

Over the next several hours as Geary's formation headed for the third planet, Captain Duellos had to bombard the fourth planet three more times. None of the Syndic attempts to hit his ships had succeeded, which wasn't surprising, given the fact that the surface-based weapons couldn't directly observe their targets and had to depend on data provided by drones popping up briefly to take snapshots of the Alliance ships. On the other hand, two of the Marine recce drones ceased transmitting, indicating they had been shot down. Colonel Carabali wouldn't be pleased about that, but Geary thought two drones was a small price to pay for avoiding hits on his ships.

As Formation Delta closed on the third world, shuttles launched, carrying Marines to their objectives. Most of the shuttles and Marines headed for a big orbiting complex with a large population. The rest aimed for orbiting warehouses containing raw materials and supplies that would have been taken down to the surface or sent onward to other places in the system to outfit Syndic warships under construction. Now they would be taken to the Alliance fleet to take care of its crews and go into manufacturing the supplies it needed.

Geary kept a wary eye on the third world as his ships closed on the planet. The third world hadn't been quite so densely covered with Syndic defense and defense-related targets, so fewer targets had been hit there, so the upper atmosphere wasn't as heavily clouded with the dust and water vapor debris from those impacts. It still wasn't very easy to see the surface, though. A bit warm by human standards, the world was still nice enough to be tolerable. Or at least, it had been. For the next several months it would be a bit more uncomfortable thanks to all of that dust in the atmosphere. But compared to the damage the Alliance could have done, rendering the world completely uninhabitable and smashing every city, the inhabitants of the third world really didn't have strong grounds for complaint.

The sensors of *Dauntless* and the other ships in the formation were scanning every piece of surface visible beneath the dust tossed up by the Alliance bombardment, but no defenses missed by that bombing had been detected. "All units in Formation Delta are to avoid entering low orbit around the third world and are to initiate random course and speed changes while within range of weapons based on the planet."

The order was still being acknowledged when very powerful particle beams tore up through the atmosphere of the third world, aiming for *Daring*. Fortunately, the Syndics had been overeager, firing at extreme range, and

as a result their shots narrowly missed the Alliance battle
cruiser. Geary punched his controls savagely. "*Daring*,
take out those guns."

"It'll be a pleasure, sir," *Daring* responded. A second
volley from the Syndic planetary battery ripped through
the space *Daring* would have occupied if she hadn't jogged
slightly to one side and up. The second attack gave *Daring*
the targeting data she needed. The battle cruiser began spitting out kinetic projectiles, the solid metal rounds racing
downward through the atmosphere. This time Geary could
see the flashes of light on the planet's surface when the kinetic bombardment tore apart the particle beam battery as
well as a fair amount of real estate around it.

By now all of the Alliance ships were jinking errati-
cally, changing courses and speeds by the tiny amounts,
which were all that was needed to throw off shots aimed
from the planet's surface at targets in high orbit. Geary
tried to relax, knowing they would be worried about more
such attacks the entire time they were near this world. "I
hope that's all we have to deal with," he remarked to
Desjani.

On the heels of his words a small window appeared before him, showing the worried face of Colonel Carabali.
"Our troops on the orbiting city are under fire," Carabali
reported.

*Serves me right for saying something that stupid. I was
just asking for trouble.* "The orbiting city." Geary called up
the information. With a population of around fifty thousand, the big orbiting complex did qualify as a city by the
standards of space installations. It also had a gratifyingly
large amount of food stockpiled or otherwise available to
feed those fifty thousand and to provision Syndic warships
stopping in for supplies. The Alliance fleet could use that
food, though Geary had insisted enough be left to avoid
starvation. "What exactly is going on?"

"We've secured most of the food warehouses and the
areas adjacent to them. But Syndic special forces are firing
on us from outside our perimeter, using the civilian popu-

lation for cover. They're popping out, firing, then fading into the populace."

It stood to reason that there would be lots of Syndic military forces among the population here, not merely to defend the system but also to provide internal security, a nice way of saying they kept the local population in line. At least some of those military forces weren't adverse to doing things that could cause the deaths of the civilians they were supposed to be protecting. But he was thinking in Alliance terms. Those troops weren't really there to protect the citizens of Sancere. Their job was to protect the Syndicate Worlds and the interests of the Syndicate Worlds' leaders. If a few citizens of the Syndicate Worlds got in the way, or a few million, that was just too bad for the innocent bystanders. "What do you want to do?" Geary asked.

Carabali looked unhappy. "We've got three options. One, we fire back as necessary, which will undoubtedly kill a lot of bystanders. Two, we pull back and abandon our efforts. Three, we keep taking casualties with little chance of responding. You'll notice that under all three options, the Syndics win in one way or another."

"Hell." Should he threaten to retaliate against the planet? Would that stop people who had already demonstrated a lack of concern for civilian casualties? And if it didn't stop them, would he be willing to go through with his threat? "We need that food. Has it tested safe?"

"So far. They didn't realize we were coming here for that reason, so they didn't have a chance to poison it."

Options. There had to be a fourth. Compromise was usually a dangerous course in military actions, but in this case it seemed like the only choice. "What about ordering all civilians out of a buffer area around our troops? Tell them to clear it fast, because after a certain time anything moving in that area is a target. Would that work?"

Carabali nodded slowly. "It might. But if you're thinking all of the civilians will get clear, that won't happen. Some always stay. Some because they're too stubborn or stupid or scared, some because they can't move for one reason or another. There will still be some within the kill zone."

"But not nearly as many."

"No, sir."

Geary shook his head. "I don't see that we have any choice. Those Syndic special forces are backing us into a corner. Too bad we don't have a smart bullet that homes on evil."

"I think commanders have been wishing for that since the dawn of time, sir," Carabali noted. "Except for evil commanders, of course."

"Get it done, Colonel. Give the civilians as much time as you consider prudent to evacuate, but don't unnecessarily risk your troops." As soon as Geary had said that, he realized he had given one of those frustratingly contradictory orders that had driven him crazy when he had received them. He owed Carabali something clearer than that. "Do you think half an hour is good?"

"I'd prefer fifteen minutes, sir. That ought to be sufficient for the area we need cleared."

I won't second-guess the person with primary responsibility for those troops. "All right. Fifteen minutes."

"And after that we're authorized to use necessary force in the buffer area?"

"As long as you don't punch holes in the outer skin of the city. I don't want the atmosphere all venting to space."

Carabali grinned, her earlier upset replaced with apparent good humor. "Yes, sir. I'll pass on those orders now. Thank you, sir."

"You're welcome." Geary leaned back after the transmission ended and noticed Rione had arrived on the bridge and was watching. "I seem to have made a Marine happy," he explained.

"Oh? Is she going to get to kill something?"

"Probably." Geary hesitated, scanning the system display for evidence of other threats. But Syndic Force Alpha hadn't shown any signs of heading inward yet, and nothing else seemed active. Reassured, Geary pulled up the landing force display, seeing the ranked images that represented the views seen from each of the squad leaders currently on the orbital city. He picked one at random, touching it to make the image grow in size.

The lieutenant whom Geary had chosen to monitor was gazing out across a small courtyard to a cluster of buildings on the other side. Curving upward and into the distance behind the buildings, Geary could see more of the city, which was arranged in the classic and functional rotating cylinder design to remove the need for artificial gravity.

Something flashed within the buildings, and the lieutenant's view jerked as he pulled back. Fragments flew as a piece of the structure the lieutenant was behind got chipped by a solid metal slug of some kind. Geary keyed the sound and heard the echoes of the shot reverberating. Other shots could be heard sporadically to either side. Then a voice boomed across the buildings. "This area is to be evacuated immediately. All Syndicate Worlds citizens are ordered to withdraw immediately to an area behind Fifth Street. Anyone present in the area this side of Fifth Street is subject to attack as enemy combatants."

The announcement began repeating. Geary, watching from the lieutenant's view, saw men, women, and children erupting from buildings and racing away. The distant figure of a man holding a gun stepped out and made threatening motions that halted the exodus near him. "Get him," the lieutenant ordered. Geary heard the sound of a weapon firing nearby, and moments later, the armed man jerked to one side as if he had been punched, then fell to lie unmoving. The civilians surged into motion again, stampeding past the body.

Geary checked some other views, seeing the same thing. Shots still came from the buildings across from the Marines, but after the fifteen-minute grace period expired, the buildings began exploding as the Marines started targeting them with heavy weapons. *Did I approve that? I did, didn't I?*

Syndic civilians might well be dying in those buildings, but that was a choice forced upon him. Somehow that knowledge didn't make him feel better. Fighting an opponent who kept inviting atrocities, who kept trying to force him to commit atrocities, was an ugly thing. *I'll do what I have to do but not one thing more, you cold-blooded bastards. You won't be able to blame the deaths of innocents on me or the fleet I command.*

It took most of a day to off-load as much food as the Alliance wanted to take, as well as material from the separate warehouses, shuttles distributing it all among the fleet while the warships dodged occasional shots from the planet's surface and retaliated against the attacks. No surface battery got any hits, and none of them survived the attempt. But there always seemed to be another hidden battery somewhere.

Twenty hours after arriving at the third world, Geary gave the orders to pull away from the planet, happily though wearily reviewing the lists of supplies they had "requisitioned" from the Syndics. The orbital city, somewhat battered from the extended battle between Alliance Marines and Syndic special forces, was nonetheless safe now. But the orbiting warehouses were another matter. Geary confirmed that all of the personnel had been evacuated from them and then ordered their destruction. Anything the Alliance hadn't taken wouldn't be used by the Syndics. The warehouses themselves wouldn't be used anymore, either.

Sancere hadn't been the only system supplying the Syndics with warships. There were plenty of others churning out capital ships and hordes of lighter units, drawing on the resources of an interstellar power that spanned many star systems. But losing Sancere's shipyards would make a difference. For a while, at least, the ability of the Syndics to replace their losses would be curtailed.

"All ships, well done." He yawned as he confirmed that

the formation was heading for a new position outside the orbit of the fourth world. "Ladies and gentlemen, I'm getting some sleep." Desjani grinned tiredly as he left the bridge of *Dauntless*, making obvious preparations to leave herself.

Geary headed for his stateroom, weary but pleased, wondering if Victoria Rione would be there.

"GEARY here." He blinked away sleep, checking to make sure he had also remembered to block the video again.

"You asked to be informed when Alliance Formation Bravo began withdrawing from the fourth planet, sir. We've been told the withdrawal is under way and confirmed it with sightings of the ships in motion."

"Thank you." Geary lay back, grateful that for once the information was good news and wouldn't require immediate action, as well as knowing he could stop worrying about particle-beam batteries for a while.

"You know," Rione's voice came from beside him, "they can tell you're hiding something."

"You think so, huh?"

"I know so, John Geary. Have you always blocked video in the past? I thought not. And you're keeping your voice pitched low. They're surely wondering who it is you don't desire to wake."

"Damn." Her words suddenly awoke an anxiety in him. "They might think it's someone from the fleet." One of his officers. Or worse, one of his sailors. Exactly the sort of thing he was required to avoid doing because of his command authority.

Rione raised herself on her elbow and gave him a thin-lipped smile. "And so I must ensure the fleet knows their hero is sleeping with me. I wonder how I should make the announcement?"

He winced. "I never intended you becoming a public issue. This should be private."

"Nothing about you can be private, John Geary. If you didn't realize that already, you should now."

"This is about you, not me."

"Are you protecting my honor?" Rione seemed amused again. "I'm old enough to handle that myself. In case you're wondering, I also realized going into this that it would become a public matter."

The statement had the unfortunate effect of reminding Geary of his speculations that Rione might be attracted to his power rather than to him. But if that was the case, she would never admit it, and if it wasn't, he would be crazy to bring up the possibility with her.

"Our relationship isn't improper or illegal," Rione noted. "In the morning, I'll inform the commanders of the ships from the Callas Republic and the Rift Federation. I know in the past they've been asked about rumors of your and my association, and have denied them. I must let them know we now do have a relationship if only to keep faith with them. Once they're informed, the entire fleet will probably know within a span of time too brief to measure."

Geary couldn't help sighing. "Does it have to be the fleet's business?"

"Yes." She favored him with a stern look. "You know it, too. Attempting to hide personal ties between us would make it look like we believed we were doing something wrong."

"It's not wrong."

"Are you trying to convince me, John Geary? While I'm in bed with you? That's a little after-the-fact."

"I'm trying to be serious here. Listen, there is one thing that concerns me. There's something I've counted on from you in the past, and I want that to continue."

"What would that be?" she asked idly.

"I want you to remain skeptical of my plans. I need you to be skeptical and questioning and demanding. You're the only person in the fleet I could see as being able to take an outside view of my plans. I need that to continue."

"You want me to continue to be demanding?" Rione

asked. "That's a bit unusual in a man, but I'll be happy to try to be as demanding as ever."

"I'm serious, Victoria," Geary repeated.

"Victoria may not be able to help you, but Co-President Rione has every intention of continuing to regard you with a worried and skeptical eye. Does that make you feel better?"

"Yeah."

"Then I'd like to get back to sleep. Good night, again." She rolled over, leaving Geary with a view of her back that was breathtaking, though he thought she didn't realize it.

Geary tore his eyes from Victoria Rione's back with considerable effort, then spent a while staring at the overhead. *So she's going to tell the galaxy that we're sleeping together. But she's right that we have to do that. If rumors spread that I'm sleeping with anyone else, it could create serious problems. I'm not sure how I feel about the fleet knowing, because I'm not sure how I feel about her. Am I just attracted to her because I need someone strong beside me now? Or is this just physical and I'm fooling myself about caring for the person? No, I can't believe that. She's one hell of a woman, and I know I like a lot of things about her. But she's not exactly warm and cuddly when we're not having sex. She's holding something back. That's an understatement. She's holding a lot back. By the time we get home, Victoria Rione might decide I've gotten boring and walk away, or might decide Black Jack needs to be stopped, or might not really give a damn about me but still want to be standing beside me so she can use that status to her benefit.*

Or she might really care about me.

Face it, Geary, you have no way of knowing how you and she will feel when you reach Alliance space, whether you'll go off to Kosatka together to get married or if you'll shake hands and walk away from each other for the rest of your lives.

I guess I'll make that jump when we get there. If we get there.

• • •

INTELLIGENCE gathered in Sancere so far seemed to be both massive in quantity and frustratingly uninformative when it came to the most important issues. Marine landing parties had downloaded a huge number of files from abandoned Syndic terminals, but none of them held information of immediate use. Several surviving escape pods from the destroyed ships of Syndic Force Bravo had been picked up, but the sailors inside only knew they had been in a battle at Scylla near the border with the Alliance. Syndic officers could have told the Alliance interrogators more, but any of the escape pods carrying officers had been destroyed by the energy release from the collapsing gate. The battle at Scylla seemed to have been fought to a bloody draw, with both sides withdrawing from the star system afterward. The minor installations Geary had remembered being at Scylla a century ago had long since been destroyed or abandoned as the two sides fought incessantly over an otherwise worthless star system.

They pounded the hell out of each other and then broke contact. It wasn't a big battle. What we saw arrive here at Sancere was the majority of the Syndic force, and the Alliance side was about equal in numbers. But I can't draw any conclusions from that, because I don't know what's happening elsewhere on the front lines of this war.

Frustrated, Geary searched through the communications links to find the intelligence center on *Dauntless*. "This is Captain Geary. I'd like to personally speak to the senior surviving Syndic sailor we picked up. Can I do that now?"

The reply took a moment. "I'll have to check—" The voice broke off as Geary heard someone yelling in the background. "Uh, yes, sir! Immediately, sir. Do you want to do it by virtual contact or actual physical interview?"

"Actual interview." Geary had never been able to shake a nagging suspicion that the virtual meeting software didn't convey every movement and nuance exactly right. In his experience software had a tendency to smooth out things that didn't match its parameters, even though humans frequently betrayed minor, seemingly contradictory behaviors. What software thought of as anomalies to be eliminated could be the most important things a person was showing. "I'll be down in a few minutes."

The intelligence section rested behind some impressive security hatches. A slightly nervous lieutenant was waiting outside them and quickly led Geary though into the high-security area. For some reason it always felt hushed in there to Geary, even though to the eye it just seemed a regular office space with a few more pieces of equipment crammed onto desks and into odd corners. In keeping with ancient tradition, the intelligence section was a world unto itself, part of and yet also separate from the rest of the ship's crew. The tighter security world in which they operated was matched by a somewhat looser working environment.

One of the desks actually had a plant on it, a small splash of living greenery. Geary cocked a questioning eyebrow at the lieutenant, who looked a little more nervous as he responded. "That's Audrey, sir."

Of course. If a spaceship had plants on board, one was usually called Audrey. The reason for that, if there was a reason, was lost in the mists of the past, but it made Geary feel a little better to see something that hadn't changed from his time to now. Geary smiled reassuringly and followed the lieutenant toward the interrogation room.

The interrogation room followed a design that outwardly at least probably hadn't changed for centuries. Geary looked through the one-way mirror into it and saw that a Syndic noncommissioned officer sat in a single chair, apparently unrestrained. She seemed dazed and scared but trying not to show it. "If she makes a move for you, we'll drop her with a stun charge," the lieutenant assured Geary.

"She doesn't seem the suicide-charge type," Geary remarked. He studied the instrument readouts before him. "These are all related to your interrogations?" He had been down in this area before, but there hadn't been prisoners then.

"Yes, sir." The lieutenant indicated the devices. "We can do remote scans of brain activity while asking questions. That way we can spot deception on things we need to know."

"And what do you do then?"

"Confrontation sometimes works. Once they realize we know when they're lying, some people crack. For the tough ones, the best process is the use of drugs to eliminate normal inhibitions. We ask, they talk."

"That sounds more humane than beating them up," Geary noted with another smile.

"Beating them up?" The lieutenant seemed startled by the suggestion. "Why would we do that, sir? It produces unreliable information."

"Does it?"

"Yes, sir. Not as bad as outright torture, but still unreliable. Our job is to find out accurate information for you. Physical and mental abuse might get people talking, but it wouldn't provide accurate information."

Geary nodded, secretly relieved that in the case of intelligence collection simple pragmatism had avoided the atrocities he had seen elsewhere. If he had learned his intelligence people were depending on torture, it would have meant they were as dysfunctional as the fleet's tactics had once been. "Okay, let me in."

The Syndic sailor jerked her head to look as the heavy door opened. Geary walked in, the Syndic sailor staring at his rank insignia, and stopped near her. "Who are you?" he asked. The intelligence types could have told him, but it seemed a good way to start a conversation.

The woman spoke steadily enough. "General Service Sailor Rank Seven Gyal Barada, Syndicate Worlds Self-Defense Forces, Mobile Space Forces Directorate."

Geary sat down in the other chair, grateful that he worked in a fleet rather than a "mobile space forces directorate." "I'm Captain John Geary." The woman blinked in confusion. "I used to be called Black Jack Geary. That's probably how you've heard of me. I'm the commander of this fleet."

Confusion changed to fear. "That's how—" the Syndic sailor blurted, then choked off further words.

Geary kept his voice calming and conversational. "How what?"

She was staring at him in near terror. "I heard the officers talking before our ship was destroyed. The enemy fleet couldn't be here, they said. It couldn't have got here. But it was."

Geary nodded. "I did have something to do with that."

"They told us this fleet was destroyed. In the home system. And you died a century ago." The Syndic sailor had gone so pale that Geary feared she would faint.

"Were you injured in the battle?" he asked.

She shook her rapidly. "No. I don't think so."

"Have you been treated in accordance with the laws of war since being made prisoner?"

Confusion had returned again. "I . . . yes."

"Good. How's the war going?"

She swallowed and spoke the way someone did when reciting something. "The Syndicate Worlds are going from triumph to triumph. Final victory is within our grasp."

"Is it?" Geary wondered for how long Syndic propaganda had been declaring final victory was nearly achieved. "Do you ever question that?" The woman shook her head, not saying anything. "I didn't think so. It's probably dangerous to question that sort of thing." Still no answer. "Would you like to go home?" She stared at Geary for a long time, then nodded. "So would I. But then my home is free. Yours isn't. Does that ever bother you?"

"I am a citizen of the Syndicate Worlds, living in prosperity and security thanks to the sacrifices of my leaders," the sailor recited.

Amazing. That little piece of nonsense the Syndics get drilled into them hasn't changed in a century. But then how

do you improve on something that simple and misleading?
"Do you actually believe that?"

"I am a citizen of the Syndicate Worlds—"

"I heard the first time. What would it require to get you to question that? To do something about it?"

She stared back at him, plainly terrified again. "I will not answer your questions."

Geary nodded. "I didn't expect an answer. I'm just curious what it would take for someone like you to turn against a government that enslaves you and mistreats you."

The Syndic sailor stared back for a long while before speaking. "I have a home world to defend." Another pause. "I have a family on that world."

Geary thought about that, then nodded again. Old motivations, but strong ones. Defend your home from foreign invaders. And keep your family safe from your own government. It had worked for countless totalitarian states throughout human history. For a while, anyway. "I'm going to tell you something. I don't expect you to believe it, but I'll tell you anyway. The Alliance doesn't want to attack your world. It doesn't want to cause harm to your family. No one in the Alliance is fighting because we fear our own government. Everyone in the Syndicate Worlds has the choice of continuing to support their leaders in this ugly war or calling for it to end on terms of mutual safety."

Her face had closed down like a true believer being told that her ancestors weren't watching over her, but the Syndic sailor said nothing. Remaining silent in the face of authority even when you disagreed with it was doubtless a survival tactic in the Syndicate Worlds.

Geary stood up. "Your ships fought bravely. I regret the fact that we had to destroy them. May our children meet in peace someday." Those words finally drew a startled reaction, but the Syndic sailor just stared, not saying anything as Geary left the room.

"You can't talk them into working against their leaders," the lieutenant commented. "We try. You'd think self-interest would motivate them."

Geary shook his head. "Lieutenant, if self-interest motivated humans, then you, I, and every other Alliance and
Syndic soldier, sailor, and Marine would be sitting on a
beach back on our home worlds drinking beer. For better
or for worse, people believe in things they'll fight for. In
our case, better, in their case, worse."

"Yes, sir. But you planted an interesting seed there, sir.
We didn't realize how that would play out."

"What do you mean?" Geary asked.

"She thinks you're dead, and she thinks this fleet was
destroyed. Did you see how scared she was? Her metabolic
readings went sky high. She thinks that we're a ghost fleet
commanded by a ghost." The lieutenant grinned. "That just
might impact Syndic morale a bit."

"It might." He studied the Syndic sailor through the
one-way mirror. "What are the plans for her and the other
prisoners?"

"We'd been trying to decide. They don't have any intelligence value. But if we can use them to spread rumors,
that might benefit us," the lieutenant said carefully, "perhaps we should . . . consider . . . releasing them."

"Do we still have their escape pods on board?"

"Yes, sir." The lieutenant seemed surprised that Geary
hadn't been outraged at his suggestion. "We searched the
pods for anything of value that might have been brought
off their ships, but there's nothing worthwhile in them either."

Geary looked at the Syndic sailor, thinking that a few
changes in events would have left him in her place. A century ago if the Syndics had picked up his pod after the battle. A few months ago if this fleet had been unable to run
from the Syndic home system, the ships all destroyed, the
crews captured. "All right, then. Here's my orders. There
wouldn't be any sense anyway in hauling around Syndic
prisoners of no value that we have to feed and guard and
keep confined. I think you've made a very good suggestion. We can use these prisoners to our benefit. Make sure
the other prisoners know who's in command of this fleet.

I'll make personal appearances for any of them who don't believe it. Then I want them returned to their escape pods and relaunched so they can land on one of the worlds in this system."

The lieutenant grinned. "Yes, sir. They're going to be surprised."

"I like surprising the Syndics," Geary noted dryly. "Don't you?" The lieutenant smiled wider. "Make certain the pods have sufficient life support and fuel remaining to get those people home. They may need to be restocked. Have system checks run on them, too, to make sure nothing critical got broken by the energy release from the gate." Intelligence types might not pay attention to that kind of detail if not reminded. "Understood?"

"Yes, sir." The lieutenant hesitated. "This may not work, sir. And they're not going to be grateful for being released. We may just end up fighting them again."

"Maybe. Maybe not. A few sailors more or less shouldn't make a big difference to the Syndic war effort."

"That's true, sir."

"One other thing," Geary added. "I could tell that you were reluctant to suggest this course of action to me. I want to know when the Intelligence section has ideas. If I don't want to follow them, I'll decide that after I've heard them."

"Yes, sir."

"And you never know, Lieutenant. On the one hand, those sailors may spread rumors that we're all demons. On the other hand, we treated them decently. If enough Syndics learn that we're *not* demons, maybe that will help, too." He left, thinking that in a few more days the fleet could leave Sancere, having taken everything it could carry and destroyed everything it couldn't. About a billion Syndic citizens would be looking up at the stars and breathing easier. They would also be worrying about the Alliance fleet possibly reappearing someday. That wouldn't be possible, their leaders would assure them, but then it should have been impossible for the fleet to show up here even once. One way or another, this fleet had given a lot of Syndics a lot to think about.

Of course, Syndic Force Alpha was still out there. Sooner or later, Geary was sure Force Alpha would try something. It couldn't let the Alliance fleet leave without trying an attack of some kind, not if the CEO in charge of it wanted to keep his or her head on their shoulders.

NINE

"**SYNDIC** Force Alpha's moving." The warning from a *Dauntless* watch-stander came almost simultaneously with an alerting message from Alliance Formation Echo, which was currently charged with blocking any attack by the surviving Syndic flotilla.

Geary rubbed his chin, studying the sightings coming in. The Syndic flotilla had been cruising along the outer edges of the star system for days now, watching from very long range as the Alliance fleet systematically looted supplies and repaired damage to its own ships. Now it had finally come around and begun accelerating toward the inner system. "Too early to tell where they're aiming for."

"Yes, sir," Captain Desjani agreed.

"But even after the damage Task Force Furious inflicted, they've still got eight battleships and four battle cruisers." Geary checked the display again. The two battle cruisers shot up by Task Force Furious had jumped out using different jump points over the last two days, doubtless going to notify the Syndic leadership that the Alliance fleet had shown up at Sancere and to call for reinforcements. One of the HuKs had also jumped out, heading for a third destination. It would be about a week's transit time for all of them to their objectives, plus time to gather more warships, then a week back. More Syndics would be coming, but Geary planned to have the Alliance fleet long gone before they arrived. "Plus eight heavy cruisers and five HuKs. They outgun any one of our subformations, even though they don't have nearly enough escorts."

He pondered the situation. The Syndics had been about three and a half light-hours out from the star Sancere when they turned inward. Alliance Formation Echo was outside the orbit of the fifth world, only thirty light-minutes from the sun. The Syndics had been accelerating toward the inner system for three hours before any Alliance ship had seen them. Three hours' time delay left a lot of room for as-yet-unseen changes.

On the other hand, even if the Syndics ramped all the way up to .2 light, it would still take them at least fifteen hours to even reach the area where Alliance Formation Echo was located. If they were aiming at any other Alliance formation, the time required to intercept at even .2 light ranged from twenty hours to well over a day. Nothing was going to happen immediately. But eventually things would happen quickly.

Don't act too fast. But don't put off acting, either. Do I want to stop all exploitation activity in this system to confront Syndic Force Alpha? But if I do, what's to stop the Syndics from just racing through the system at .2 light or even higher? How long could they keep that up, denying me the chance to engage them and keeping my forces from continuing to loot the supplies we need? It would be the smartest thing they could do. Good thing they didn't think of something like that sooner. "Captain Desjani. Assume the Syndics are planning to hit a smaller Alliance force, but will avoid action indefinitely if confronted with a larger force. What would you recommend?"

She considered the question, gazing at her display. "We can try seeding mines in their path, but at the speeds we would need to be going to ensure intercepting their track, the odds of planting a decent minefield are pretty low."

"What about high-speed engagements? Could we manage to inflict much damage that way?"

Desjani grimaced. "If they're going point two light and we're coming in fast to meet them? Then the combined velocities would be, maybe, point two five light to point three light or higher. The relativistic distortion would be ferocious. Even the tiniest errors in compensating for it would mean clean misses."

"So we have to slow them down to engagement speed and meet them with a more powerful force," Geary concluded.

"I don't think that's going to happen," Desjani suggested unhappily.

Co-President Rione's voice came from behind them. "Why do military minds always focus on one alternative?" Geary looked back at her. "The way to slow them down is to offer a target that seems attractive."

"I don't care for sacrificing units that way," Geary stated flatly, earning an emphatic nod of agreement from Desjani.

Rione leaned forward. "You're too honest in your thinking, Captain Geary. You, too, Captain Desjani. Make it a trap."

Geary exchanged a glance with Desjani as he spoke to Rione again. "What kind of trap?"

"I'm not a military expert, Captain Geary. Surely you can think of something."

Desjani's eyes had narrowed as she studied the display. "There might be a way."

"Even with the Syndics able to see everything we're doing?" Geary asked.

"Yes, sir. The trick would be making it look like we're doing one thing when we're actually planning another."

Rione nodded. "Yes. Excellent. Present one image to the enemy while keeping your true intentions hidden."

Geary kept his expression controlled while nodding

back. Hearing Rione recommend that course of action was a little unsettling, given his doubts about her intentions toward him. "We can't make the force we'll use to bait the Syndics too powerful. They'll spot that without fail."

"I am thinking," Desjani stated slowly, "of a star named Sutrah."

Geary frowned at her, then his expression cleared. "That would be poetic justice, wouldn't it?"

In the end, it required an awesome amount of analysis for the maneuvering systems to come up with the movement plan needed to implement Desjani's idea. All six Alliance fleet formations had to swing through space, in some cases trading ships that would follow their own tracks for a while, some of the ships and formations passing through certain small areas where the Syndics were judged most likely to transit given the movements of all of the Alliance ships, most particularly Alliance Formation Gamma. This all had to be done without making it apparent to the Syndics why they were moving in that particular way, and presenting a credible image of part of the Alliance fleet girding for an engagement with the Syndics while other portions tried to continue looting Syndic assets. Formation Gamma had to be maneuvered in such a way as to present an attractive target while looking like it was unaware of the fact that it was exposed to Syndic intercept if the Syndics altered course away from battle with the larger force being assembled to meet its current path.

Captain Tulev's battle cruisers had been joined by the fast fleet auxiliary *Goblin*, and were now to be dangled as the necessary bait even though Geary hated the idea of risking one of the auxiliaries. "They won't bite without one of the auxiliaries in the target force," Desjani had insisted, and Geary had reluctantly agreed.

Now he stared at the intricate web of tracks his ships were to follow for a long moment before authorizing the orders to be sent. "All units. Maneuvering orders to follow. Every unit must carry out these orders exactly as sent."

It was far too complex to pass by voice. The detailed orders went out to all ships, and at the ordered times they began moving, though with the time delays involved in seeing his widely scattered formations, Geary had plenty of time to worry about whether everyone was acting as ordered. It was the sort of thing no human or command staff could have put together or executed. Without the substantial superiority in ships that Geary had over Syndic Force Alpha, it wouldn't even have been possible.

Now he sat, watching the ships move at various distances and time delays, as the Syndics pressed onward toward the inner system.

"You'll be exhausted if you stay up here until the battle," a voice murmured.

Geary roused himself and looked back at Rione. "I know. But this entire thing depends on everyone doing what they're told."

"And if they don't," she replied, "you won't even see it until some time after they didn't. Watching makes no difference. Get some rest."

He gave Desjani a glance. *Dauntless*'s commanding officer was catnapping in her command chair. Geary envied her the ability to do that. He checked his display again. If the Syndics kept on their current track, they would be approaching engagement range in eight hours. If they slowed or turned, engagement range to any other Alliance formation would be at least ten hours. Engagement time to Formation Gamma, if the Syndics had already turned, was ten and half hours. *Rione is right. I'm an idiot to stay up here.* "I'm going below for a while," Geary informed the watch-standers on the bridge. "Please inform me immediately if any ship deviates from their ordered tracks or if we spot changes in the Syndic track."

He stood, looking at Rione. "How about you?"

She shook her head, looking past him. "I don't want any rumors about the way you spend your time preparing for battle, Captain Geary," Rione said in a very soft voice. "You're going down to sleep. Do it."

"Yes, Madam Co-President," Geary responded. "You're not going to stay up here the whole time, are you?"

She shook her head. "In a while I'll go to my stateroom."

That would surely be remarked, Geary knew, by the many eyes that just happened to notice such things. He also knew Rione was right about it looking bad if his fleet believed Geary was enjoying himself while battle loomed. "Okay. I'll see you back here in a while."

This time Rione nodded. "I confess I feel partly responsible if this plan doesn't work. I suggested it, in a way."

"You did. But I approved it. It's my responsibility. No one else's."

Rione looked straight into his eyes. "John Geary, I've had moments of wondering if I should've succumbed to my feelings for you, if I shouldn't rather have kept my distance for the sake of the Alliance and for my own long-term happiness. Statements such as that reassure me."

There didn't seem any good, simple answer to that, so Geary nodded to her and smiled. He left the bridge, taking a meandering path to his stateroom so he could be seen by the crew of *Dauntless,* stopping at a few places to speak with the crew and repeat the now-familiar lines about his certainty that they would defeat the Syndics in this battle, that the fleet would get home safely, and that he was proud to serve with them. No matter how false he sometimes felt about promising the first two things, Geary always knew the last statement was true. Knowing that helped him sleep when he finally got to his stateroom, though he was surprised to discover that the absence of Victoria Rione from his bed already felt noticeable.

He woke to his communications alert, seeing that six hours had passed. "Geary here."

"We've spotted Syndic Force Alpha maneuvering, sir. They're heading for Formation Gamma."

The bait had been taken. "I'll be up there in a few minutes."

There had been a lot of options for the Syndic flotilla as

it charged into the inner system. Too many to produce any meaningful prediction of what particular spots in space it would pass through. The Alliance plan had been aimed at luring the Syndics into a particular course of action, in this case an attack on a smaller formation that appeared to have accidentally been left out of supporting range of the rest of the fleet. As Geary settled into his seat on the bridge of the *Dauntless* and checked the display, he saw the probability cone for the Syndics' course still had a huge diameter at its base where the Syndic flotilla had just changed course. But that cone necked down inexorably toward a tight channel near the track of Alliance Formation Gamma, which the Syndics would have to traverse if they wanted to engage the ships in Gamma. *Beautiful. If they do it, we've got them. If they decide not to hit Gamma, then those ships will be safe. Either way we've won except for some wasted ordnance.*

The rest of the Alliance fleet was still re-forming. Another small formation accompanied by *Witch* but too far off for the Syndics to target without sweeping around through the system, and two larger formations, one built around *Dauntless* and the other centered on *Courageous*. Task Force Furious was almost two light-hours distant on the side away from the Syndics, where it had been returning from smashing some Syndic installations on the two innermost worlds. Geary was gratified to see that a good number of the ships making up both formations were still on the way. Part of the plan involved letting the Syndics think the Alliance was taking its time getting ready to meet the Syndic attack, and as a result the Alliance would be forced to be slow in reacting to the changed Syndic course.

All theater, preplanned to lure the Syndics into going where the Alliance wanted them to go.

It was nonetheless increasingly nerve-racking to see the Syndics heading toward Formation Gamma, which was holding its track but had accelerated from .05 to .075 light speed. To the Syndics, that would look like an attempt to escape, but it was actually aimed at adjusting the location where the Syndics would intercept Formation Gamma. It all came down to simple physics now. In order to get within striking range of Gamma, the Syndics would have to go where the Alliance wanted them to go. The trick was to keep the Syndics from changing their minds and veering off. Accordingly, Gamma made a show of trying to accelerate past .075 light, only to have *Goblin* fall behind as if she couldn't keep up. The rest of the ships in Gamma slowed to rejoin *Goblin,* having put on a hopefully convincing show for the Syndics.

His own formation finally assembled, Geary swung it around and down to head for an intercept with Syndic Force Alpha. He had retained the name Formation Delta, even though he now had more than twice as many ships. On the far side of Formation Gamma was the new Formation Bravo, also bulked up to twice its former strength, thirty light-minutes away but hopefully getting into motion itself now. A much smaller force, Formation Echo with *Witch*, was playacting as if returning to the third planet to loot more supplies or destroy more surface installations. Finally, Task Force Furious had been told to remain on the far side of the system, a last piece of insurance against the Syndics getting away clean. If all else failed, Task Force Furious might get in some good shots as the Syndics tried to climb out of the system again.

"Surely they're going to figure out what you're doing now," Rione noted.

"I sure as hell hope not," Geary replied. "It shouldn't be as obvious to the Syndics. To them, it's going to look as if we're bending on speed but won't be able to reach them at engagement speeds before they reach Formation Gamma. Same for Formation Bravo, since its intercept location is even farther off than ours. The Syndics are thinking they've caught a weaker formation that we let get too far from supporting formations. They're planning to come in fast, brake hard, rake Gamma with everything they've got, then accelerate away and frustrate our planned intercepts by this formation and Formation Bravo."

"You're a more devious man than I'd thought, Captain Geary," Rione observed.

"Captain Desjani helped come up with the plan."

Desjani grinned.

"Anyway, if all goes right, the Syndic plan won't even survive until contact with Gamma. It'll start falling apart well before then. The really hard part in setting this up was getting enough ships to cross through the area where the Syndics will have to transit to intercept Gamma, without the Syndics figuring out those ships were dropping strings of mines along a single relatively narrow channel."

"And," Desjani added, "since the Syndic plan clearly requires them to come in fast, maintaining close to point two light as long as they can before braking hard to engage Gamma, relativistic distortion is going to make it very difficult for them to see the mines, especially since it's not a single, dense minefield but a diffuse series of strings."

Now it was just a matter of watching again. Everyone remained several hours away from any contact, the representations of the various formations seeming to crawl through the display of Sancere Star System. Geary took advantage of the time to arrange his formation for what he expected would work best. Assuming the Syndics would seek to avoid a fight with him, Geary arranged his ships in a rectangular block, the battleships and battle cruisers clustered by divisions down the center, the escorts around the outside. If he only got one firing pass, he wanted to ensure his heaviest units could all hit the Syndics in succession.

Increasingly restless, Geary finally stood up. "I'm going to walk around the ship." The crew undoubtedly thought his walks were a sign of his interest in them, and they certainly were that, but at times like this, the walks were also a way to work out nervousness and kill time during the long, slow approach to combat.

The crew members he met all seemed tired from the long days at increased alert while in Sancere Star System, but cheerful and confident. The hopeful and certain expressions they turned on Geary still had a tendency to unnerve him, since he knew how fallible he really was, but at least he also knew he hadn't let them down yet. As he walked around, Geary noticed crew members looking past him as if expecting to see someone with him, and realized they were looking for Co-President Rione, even though none of them mentioned her. That was a little unnerving, too.

At some point, he went past the worship area and walked into the area set aside for ancestors, entering one of the small rooms and lighting a candle before saying a brief prayer. The living stars knew he needed all of the help he could get. But tempting as it was to linger and speak for a while to the one audience he felt sure of, his dead ancestors, Geary knew he couldn't hide in here while the fleet headed for battle.

All of that didn't kill nearly enough time. Geary confirmed that nothing had changed in the situation, everybody rushing toward their respective intercept points and the Syndics still closing in on the path to the mines, then forced himself to go by the meal areas and pretend to eat. Most of what they had now was Syndic rations looted from places like Kaliban and now Sancere. The best thing about the Syndic food, Geary and the sailors he spoke with agreed, was that it made the usual fleet food seem good by comparison. "If we offered the Syndics decent meals, they'd probably surrender in droves," one of the sailors suggested as she choked down something that was apparently supposed to be hash, though made up of unidentifiable meat and some very odd looking potatoes with the texture and taste of blocks of cardboard.

Geary returned to the bridge. Rione wasn't there, and Desjani was asleep in her chair again. A captain who spent that much time on the bridge could drive her crew insane, but Desjani wasn't a screamer or a micromanager, so her presence didn't wear on her watch-standers. She woke up as Geary entered and nodded to him. "One more hour until the Syndics reach the first mines. They're still heading right down the chute."

"When do you think they'll start braking?" Geary asked.

"In about half an hour. That'll leave them a very slight margin for error." Desjani indicated the projected track on the display. "If they brake too early, they'll slide off the path to the mines, but we'll have a much better shot at catching them with this formation. But if they want to hit Formation Gamma, they'll have to start braking at this point."

Geary settled in, relaxing as best he could. To kill time, he began rechecking the supplies the fleet had picked up here at Sancere, and how the auxiliaries were doing on manufacturing replacement items. There had been a lot of maneuvering here in Sancere, burning through fuel cells, so Geary tossed off a quick message to Captain Tyrosian on *Witch* to make sure new fuel cells were a priority. All of the grapeshot, mines, and missiles in the world wouldn't provide enough help to ships that couldn't maneuver.

Co-President Rione returned, surveying the bridge of the *Dauntless*, Captain Desjani, and Captain Geary with her usual unruffled and challenging attitude. Nodding in greeting, Geary realized there was little chance of him ever accidentally calling her Victoria while on the bridge. The Co-President Rione who occupied the observer's seat on the bridge might look like the Victoria who shared Geary's bed, but her attitude was so different that she seemed to really be another person, one who retained distance and distrust toward Captain Geary. *I did ask her to stay challenging, after all. But I have a feeling she'd be like this whether I'd asked it of her or not.*

Desjani also nodded in almost-friendly greeting. Being involved with Geary had clearly made Rione more trustworthy in Desjani's eyes, though he suspected Rione would react pretty negatively to the idea. He certainly wasn't going to mention it to her. But then she probably already had realized that, which might be contributing to the frosty way Rione was treating Geary on the bridge. Maybe he should put off mentioning to Rione that the crew seemed to be expecting to see them together. Or maybe she wanted to be seen with him, to make as public a spectacle as possible of their association.

Geary turned back to the much less complicated situation playing out between the Syndic flotilla and his five formations. His display indicated every Alliance ship had come to full battle readiness. He and thousands of other officers and sailors had nothing to do for a while yet but watch the time scroll down to the moments when the Syndics would encounter the first mines.

The Syndics pivoted up and over in place almost exactly when predicted, bringing their propulsion units to face forward so they could brake the Syndic formation's velocity down to engagement speed. A few minutes later, Geary saw Formation Gamma increase speed a fraction to move the Syndic track to intercept exactly back onto the path through the mines. Surely the Syndics would get suspicious? But, perhaps because they were fixed on their intended targets, the Syndics adjusted their course just as the Alliance needed them to.

Fifteen more minutes crawled by. "Here they come," Desjani murmured.

The intricate maneuvers that had set up the trap had sent ships or formations across the space the Syndic flotilla was now braking through. The result hadn't been so much a minefield as a lattice made up of multiple rows and strings of mines spread across light-seconds of distance along the track. The Syndic warships were now rushing stern first into the area holding those mines. Any hits would fall on their main propulsion units aft, which was exactly where the Alliance wanted those hits to strike.

The Syndic formation braked through the first two lines of mines without encountering any. Frustrating, but the odds didn't favor a lot of hits. The third line lay right across their path.

A Syndic HuK took a direct hit on the stern. The mine collapsed the rear shields and blew the HuK's propulsion units, leaving it unable to maneuver. One of the battle cruisers took two hits, losing a single propulsion unit. There was a pause as the Syndics swept onward, until they hit where the fourth and fifth lines crossed. This time several hits sparked on the Syndic ships, sending a heavy cruiser stumbling out of formation and taking out a couple of propulsion units on another battle cruiser.

By this time the Syndics had figured out they were running into something. The most effective counter would be to pivot their ships so they were facing forward and would take any further hits on their bows. But pivoting would mean the warships couldn't use their main propulsion systems to brake anymore, which would prevent them from slowing enough to intercept Formation Gamma. Geary had guessed that the Syndic leader would chose to continue taking occasional hits rather than give up the chance to strike the Alliance ships in Gamma. If the Syndics had hit all the mines at once and sustained the damage in a single burst, it probably would've caused the leader to call off the attack, but instead the hits kept coming in ones and twos, adding up in a way that the Syndic commander might well miss until too late while focus remained on the Alliance warships in Gamma.

More hits occurred as the Syndics encountered successive lines of mines, each one doing a little more damage, weakening even the shields on the battleships. By this time the Syndic commander had to be worried. The damaged ships were already losing their places in formation and might have to be left behind when the Syndic flotilla accelerated away after hitting Gamma.

"Captain Tulev has fired specters," Desjani observed. "It looks like he's firing every specter he's got. They'll intercept the Syndic formation just as it's clearing the last string of mines."

"Good move," Geary agreed.

A final flurry of three mine strikes marked the last string of mines, then the Syndic ships were sweeping down on Formation Gamma with no more obstacles between them. Moments later the specters from Gamma flashed into contact. The high relative speed caused some to miss, but others hammered at ships that in many cases had already seen their shields drained by mine hits and hadn't recovered yet. Another battle cruiser took hits to its propulsion systems, another HuK vanished into a ball of debris, and two of the remaining heavy cruisers were badly battered. Even better, two of the battleships lost a couple of propulsion units.

"Adjust course as necessary to intercept the Syndics," Geary ordered Desjani, passing the same command to Captain Duellos in Formation Bravo. The rest of the ships in the formation would conform to *Dauntless*'s moves as Desjani made minor adjustments to course and speed to manage the best intercept.

"We'll have to start braking ourselves, soon," she advised.

Geary checked his display and nodded. "All units in Formation Delta, adjust ships' headings one hundred eighty degrees now." That would bring the Alliance ships around so their main propulsion units faced aft. "Begin braking down to point one light at time three one."

Tulev had formed his battle cruisers facing the Syndics and close around *Goblin,* making as close to a physical shield for *Goblin* as it was possible to construct. The Syndic formation, though increasingly spread out as damaged ships fell out of position, was still aiming for intercept and still had more than twice the firepower available to Tulev's forces.

Geary blinked, trying to understand what he had just seen.

Desjani was grinning broadly. "Brilliant!"

Tulev had pivoted his ships and accelerated at maximum when it was too late for the Syndics to react but just in time to throw off the Syndic intercept. The maneuver had required perfect timing, and Tulev had carried it off. He'd also thrown a barrage of grapeshot at the leading Syndic ships, which were firing on the place Tulev's ships should have been if they hadn't changed speed, only belatedly shifting aim to target the actual positions of the Alliance warships. The two leading battleships seemed to flare incandescent as the Alliance grapeshot hit their shields in a concentrated volley. "He got them!" Desjani exulted as *Dauntless*'s sensors provided damage reports that both battleships had been badly hurt.

But that left a lot of Syndic capital ships rolling past Tulev's formation. The shields on the Alliance battle cruisers around *Goblin* sparked and flashed with hits as the Syndic battleships poured fire onto them. "*Leviathan* has taken several hits," a watch-stander reported. "*Dragon* has lost two propulsion units and main maneuvering control. *Steadfast* reports hell-lance batteries one alpha and three alpha out of commission and numerous hits. *Valiant* has taken serious damage amidships but is continuing to fire."

Geary clenched his fists, trying not to think of the sailors dying on those battle cruisers. If he lost one or more of the battle cruisers, it would be a bitter price for whatever losses were inflicted on the Syndics.

"Most of the Syndic capital ships have passed out of range of Formation Gamma," a watch-stander reported.

It dawned on Geary as he read the updates on damage to his battle cruisers that they had been saved by the damage inflicted on the Syndics earlier as a result of mines, specters, and grapeshot. The cumulative effect of those hits had spread out the Syndic formation so that their fire wasn't concentrated on the battle cruisers in one short, overwhelming barrage but rather dispersed enough to allow the screens on the Alliance ships to hold longer than they would have otherwise. "What about *Goblin*?"

"Several hits, none critical."

Geary let out a breath he hadn't known he was holding. Tulev's battle cruisers had hit back as the Syndics roared past, inflicting more damage. And unlike the Alliance warships, the Syndics didn't have massive reinforcements rushing to the scene. They had to run, but many of them couldn't run fast enough anymore.

Unfortunately, plenty of them could still run.

Geary made a fist and softly pounded the arm of his chair. He had occasionally wondered why that part of the chair's arm didn't have controls on it and finally realized it had been deliberately left bare so that frustrated and worried commanders could beat on it. "He's still got five battleships with only minor damage and three heavy cruisers." The Syndic formation was stretching out as the warships with full propulsion capability accelerated away from the damaged units. "We can't catch those. Blast."

"We won't have to," Desjani stated in a flat voice. "Unless I miss my guess."

"What do you mean?"

She pointed at the front of the Syndic formation. "There's a commander out there who's now lost half of their force, or will once we catch those damaged ships. The remaining units won't be able to threaten us enough to prevent us from completing whatever we want to do in this star system. That commander knows the best fate they can hope for is a labor camp. A firing squad is more likely, though we've heard of punishments that amount to torturing someone to death under the guise of 'volunteering for medical research' and other euphemisms."

Geary studied the display. "You think that commander will choose death in battle?"

"Or at least fighting to the death of their ships. It might not seem the best option, unless you're a commander facing death anyway." Desjani gestured again. "There they go." The undamaged and lightly damaged battleships were braking, falling back to rejoin their damaged sisters. "Despairing or not," Desjani acknowledged, "it's a brave move by all of those ships."

Hearing Desjani describe Syndics as brave startled Geary. She was starting to think of the enemy as human. He would have to warn her that such feelings could help her understand the enemy's actions but also make it harder to do what needed to be done. Like killing the brave sailors on those brave ships.

Intercept points were updating rapidly on his maneuvering display as the Syndics' speed dropped lower. "I'm going to bring this formation across the bottom of the Syndics and have Formation Bravo come across the top here. They should be able to hit the Syndics about fifteen minutes after our pass. We'll come around and hit them again after that." Geary gave the orders, angling Formation Delta slightly to port and down, telling Formation Bravo to also turn to port a bit and angle up.

Tulev had sent his escorts after the departing enemy, and now one of the damaged Syndic heavy cruisers at the rear of the formation blew up under the fire of the Alliance light forces snapping at the heels of the Syndics. Geary frowned, studying the movements of the Syndic battleships. "Task Force Gamma, get your escorts back. They're going to be facing battleships soon unless they break contact. Have them take up position outside of enemy effective range, ready to hit any units that fall back outside the protection of the rest of the force." Like wolves racing behind a fleeing herd, ready to pull down any animal that faltered.

But it would be several minutes yet before the escorts got that message. Hopefully the Syndic attempt to concentrate their formation would take longer than that.

The Syndics were settling into a roughly cubical formation when Geary took Formation Delta beneath them, unleashing an avalanche of fire on the ships on the bottom of the enemy force. Two damaged battle cruisers were riddled and three battleships took heavy damage, while the heavy cruisers and few surviving HuKs simply disintegrated under the Alliance fire.

Fifteen minutes later, as Geary was bringing Formation Delta around in a wide curve, Formation Bravo swung across the top of the Syndic formation, smashing two battleships and one of the remaining battle cruisers.

Geary pressed his communications controls as Formation Delta steadied on another firing pass. "Commander of the Syndic flotilla under attack, your situation is hopeless. Surrender your ships. You and your crews will be treated in accordance with the laws of war."

There wasn't any answer, but Geary hadn't expected one. As Desjani had said, the Syndic commander had likely decided that death in battle was preferable to the fate his superiors were likely to inflict.

The Syndic cube was shrinking into a flat square, its speed reduced even more as less damaged ships slowed to stay with their damaged sisters, when the second pass from Formation Delta ripped through it and left only two battleships functional. The second pass from Formation Bravo finished them, smashing the remnants of Syndic Force Alpha into scrap. As Formation Bravo drew away, one of the broken Syndic battleships blew up from a core overload.

Geary blew out a long breath, gazing at the cloud of escape pods heading for refuge. "What do you think the odds are that the Syndic commander went down with that last battleship?" he asked no one in particular.

Desjani just nodded.

Rione gestured toward the display, which showed Alliance ships closing on the Syndic wrecks to ensure they were all completely destroyed and unsalvageable by the Syndics. "Congratulations on your victory, Captain Geary."

"You gave us the idea," Geary responded.

Desjani nodded again. "An object lesson in what happens when you do what the enemy wants you to do."

"Yeah. The trick is figuring out what the enemy wants you to do, and doing something different." He pondered the state of his fleet. "All units, rejoin *Dauntless* in fleet general purpose Formation Echelon. Captain Tulev, I want your battle cruisers and escorts with the auxiliaries division so they can provide support to you. Give me estimated repair times for your ships when possible. To all ships in Formation Gamma, very well done."

Desjani gave him a glance. "Are we leaving Sancere soon?"

"That's right." Geary ran his eyes across the system display, remembering the mass of installations and shipping that had greeted the Alliance fleet when it had arrived here. Very few of those were left. *Let's see if the Syndics can try to spin this into a victory.* "We've done all the damage we need to do here. And we're going to be needed at Ilion. If we're lucky, there'll be some ships rejoining us there."

"And some Syndicate Worlds forces right behind them," Rione noted.

"Yeah. I'd better make sure the auxiliaries are manufacturing more weapons as well as more fuel cells during the transit. I'm assuming we'll need both at Ilion."

BEFORE they went into jump, Geary took the time for a private conference with Commander Cresida. "If not for your ideas on controlling that hypernet gate collapse, there's a good chance none of us would be here. As fleet commander, I can authorize the award of a Silver Nebula, and that's what I'm giving you. I hope you don't mind that the wording on the citation may be a little vague."

Cresida flushed with pleasure. "Thank you, sir. Hopefully we won't need that firing algorithm again."

"Let's hope not," Geary agreed. "You've done outstanding work as an independent formation commander." He paused. "I'm also granting a battlefield promotion to captain. Congratulations. You earned it. We'll have a proper ceremony at Ilion if time permits."

"Captain?" Cresida smiled, looking stunned. "Thank you, sir. I don't know what else to say."

"You don't have to say anything. Like I said, you earned it. Task Force Furious has proven to be a very valuable asset to this fleet." Geary leaned back, relaxing in a way he knew communicated that the formal portion of the conference was over. "Commander Cresida—excuse me, Captain Cresida, there's something I've been wondering." She gave him an attentive look even as she smiled at the first use of her new rank. "When that hypernet gate here was destroyed, what happened to any ships heading for Sancere?"

"There's two possibilities, sir," Cresida stated. "One is

that when the pathway between the Sancere gate and whatever gate they come from was broken, everything in it was destroyed in one manner or another."

Geary nodded, thinking of ships suddenly dying without any warning. Enemy ships, but still . . . "What's the other possibility?"

"It's actually considered by far the most likely, sir," Cresida assured him. "It's believed that when the path ceases to exist, any ships affected simply fall back into normal space."

"That's all?" On the heels of his statement, Geary realized what that meant. "They drop into normal space. Somewhere between whatever star they came from and Sancere."

"Yes, sir."

"Which could be a long, long ways from any star," Geary added.

"Yes, sir." Cresida grimaced. "With luck, and rationing, and some creative attempts at converting compartments into growing areas to recycle waste, grow food, and regenerate oxygen supplies, they should be able to make it to a star from which they could use jump points to get somewhere safe."

"It'd take years, though, even if they were only a light-year from the nearest star."

"At the sort of economical cruising speed they'd have to use, yes, sir. Probably at least ten years. Possibly a lot more."

Geary shook his head. "I guess it beats dying. Oh, hell, they could use some of their escape pods. Put most of their crews into survival sleep without launching the pods. That would stretch all of their supplies a lot. I wouldn't want to be one of the guys left awake, though. That'd be a long time staring at a star getting bigger very, very slowly."

"It's not like we're going to be home tomorrow," Cresida pointed out wryly.

"True. And if we caused a lot of Syndic warships to get stuck between stars for a decade, that ought to help out the

Alliance a bit." He smiled somewhat, too. "Maybe they'd finally get to a star and find out the war had been over for years. I wonder how that would feel?"

Cresida didn't reply for a moment. "Some of us wonder if the war will ever be over, if we and the Syndics will just keep fighting no matter what happens."

Geary looked at her, recalling that the war had been going on for Cresida's entire life and long before then. "I suppose sometimes it must seem like it'll last forever. But there must be a way to bring it to an end in a way that preserves the safety of the Alliance and ensures the Syndics won't attack again." The ability to use hypernet gates as means of unparalleled destruction came back to him, then. That would end the war and eliminate the Syndic threat. Would he ever come to believe that was the only thing to do? Or, worse, that it was the right thing to do? "I'll see you at Ilion, Captain."

TEN

AFTER the riches of Sancere, Ilion seemed bare and bereft. A single marginally habitable world boasted a few enclosed cities, one of them already apparently shut down for lack of inhabitants. The only shipping to be seen were a few aged in-system ships running between the habitable world and some old industrial facilities near an asteroid belt. No warships to be seen, and the Syndic military base that had occupied a moon of a gas giant about two light-hours out from the star had also been mothballed.

Geary decided not to bother communicating with the inhabitants of the Syndic planet. He had no intention of bringing the fleet near them and couldn't imagine they had anything he needed. Indeed, careful examination of the closed Syndic military base showed that it been stripped of supplies, with even some of the equipment cannibalized. "It looks like they've been taking that base apart for a couple of decades, at least," Desjani observed. "With Sancere so close, everybody who could leave must have already left."

"Why do you suppose the Syndics haven't already evacuated the planet, then?" Geary wondered.

"I'd bet because moving all of those people would cost a fair amount of money. They've probably been left there to fend for themselves because on a Syndic corporate balance sheet they're not worth moving."

"Abandoned in place." Geary nodded, wondering how that would feel. It was something sometimes done to equipment. He had never expected to see it being done to people. How long could these people keep going on what they could grow, manufacture, and cannibalize? It was a good bet the population left here was still shrinking. Would the day arrive, centuries from now perhaps, when the last human in Ilion died? He had seen a number of systems bypassed by the hypernet before this, but Ilion carried the worst impact. "Let's get the fleet moved to cover the jump point from Strena." If any of those almost forty ships with Falco survived, they would have to come here through Strena. "I want us ten light-minutes from the jump point. If anyone comes through, they may need very fast rescue."

Geary took another look at the display. At their current speed it was about two days to the jump point he wanted to cover. "I guess it's time for another fleet conference."

It felt good to have the thirty ships from Task Force Furious back at the table. It felt good to see everyone pleased with how well Sancere had gone. For the moment at least, no one seemed ready to openly display hostility or dislike. Once again, Co-President Rione had chosen not to attend. Geary wondered what she was up to, why she was depending on secondhand accounts of these meetings rather then being at them to raise questions and objections. Surely she knew that as long as the objections were reasonable he wouldn't take them wrongly.

The days spent in jump space between here and Sancere had been mostly given over to resting and recovery after the extended pressures of the operations at Sancere. With no alerts in the middle of sleep periods, Rione had been able to actually sleep while sleeping with him and seemed to have enjoyed that. But she hadn't told him anything to explain why she wasn't present at this conference. The woman remained an enigma.

"We can only estimate what the ships that left the fleet have been doing," Geary told his assembled ship commanders, deliberately avoiding loaded terms like *mutiny* and *fleeing*. "The best guess our simulations have generated show that any that survived their certain encounter with vastly superior Syndic forces at Vidha would have retreated through these stars to reach Ilion, with their last waypoint at Strena." He laid that out bluntly. It was the simple truth, and if none of those ships had survived to reach here, he didn't want anyone wondering why. "If these estimates are correct, any ships seeking to rejoin the fleet will arrive sometime between tomorrow evening and the next four days."

"How long will we wait?" the commanding officer of *Dragon* asked.

Geary gazed on the display for a moment before answering. "At least through the end of those four days. How much longer, I haven't decided. We can't stay indefinitely, but if anyone shows up, I want to be here."

"What if the Syndics show up first?" the captain of *Terrible* wondered.

"If it's within those four days, we'll fight," Geary confirmed. "After that will depend on a lot of factors. It will be my decision." Heads nodded, some in agreement and others just in acknowledgment that he was in charge. That was something, anyway. "If the Syndics come through on the heels of any ships trying to rejoin us, we'll have a fight on our hands. I expect to have to protect the ships arriving, since they'll probably have sustained a lot of damage, plus we'll have to do our best to wipe out the Syndic force."

Geary gestured toward the star display. "Once we've recovered our missing ships and dealt with any Syndic pursuers, my plans are to leave here for Tavika." That brought some smiles. Tavika would bring them back toward Alliance space. "Tavika will give us three options for the next jump. If it looks like Baldur is safe, we'll jump there next." More smiles. Between Baldur and Tavika the fleet would have made up the distance to Alliance space lost jumping toward Sancere. "At this point the Syndic command structure at a lot of places, including their home system, still hasn't heard that we paid a visit to Sancere. Which means they have no idea where we are. Once they hear we were at Sancere, they're going to start looking, but they won't find us soon."

He paused, looking around the table. "If any ships rejoin us, we'll have to evaluate their damage. It's possible I'll have to order one or more to be evacuated if the damage is too great. Be ready to take personnel on board in case that happens. Ideally, we won't leave any ships behind. We will *not* leave any people behind regardless of the circumstances. Are there any other questions?"

There weren't. Everyone was being too compliant. Maybe he was being paranoid, but Geary found it hard to believe that every one of the commanders who had regarded him skeptically was now willing to simply accept whatever he said. Or maybe they were just tired. It was pretty late in the official day. "Thank you."

When the others had "left," Captain Duellos's image remained, his eyes on the display. "It's frustrating, not being able to do anything but wait and hope for some of those ships to show up, isn't it?"

"Very," Geary agreed, flopping down into his seat. "Why is everybody being so quiet and accepting? Why aren't I getting more questions?"

Duellos bent a enigmatic look toward Geary. "Because everybody else is frustrated, too. They want to help those fools who ran off with Falco, but they can't think of any way to do it better than what we are doing, waiting here and hoping some of them make it to Ilion. Even the worst skeptic with the fleet approves of the risk you're taking in waiting here. If Falco was around to rally them with some fool plan to charge back and forth among Syndic star systems looking for our missing ships, then it might be different. But Falco didn't want to wait to build up more support."

"Lucky for me, I guess," Geary noted gloomily.

"Lucky for all those ships that didn't go with him as a result," Duellos corrected. "Cheer up, Captain Geary. Things are going well."

"They could be worse." Geary paused. "Okay, I've got a personal question. About me."

"About you? Or about you and the iron-jawed Co-President of the Callas Republic?"

Geary smiled. "Iron-jawed?"

"She's a tough woman," Duellos explained. "The sort who makes a valuable friend and a dangerous enemy."

"That describes Co-President Rione," Geary agreed.

"But I understand you're on friendly terms with her at the moment."

"You might say that. The entire fleet knows, right?"

Duellos nodded. "I haven't personally polled every sailor in the fleet, but I think it would be hard to find one who hasn't heard."

"No one's saying anything."

"What are we supposed to say?" Duellos asked. "Congratulations? Ask you what tactics you employed to achieve your objective?"

Geary laughed as Duellos grinned. "That's a good point. I just want to know if it's causing any problems. I know Numos and his friends wanted to make an issue of my relationship with Rione back before there was any substance to the rumors."

"I've heard little," Duellos admitted. "As I once told you, it's your business and doesn't reflect on your professionalism. As long as you and Co-President Rione refrain from acting out in public, I expect no one will say anything. Openly that is. Those opposed to you will try to find a way to paint it in a negative light. I can't see the issue gaining much traction, though, if you two continue to carry on as you have. The most damaging rumor would be that you've compelled Co-President Rione to become a sort of concubine, debasing her, but no one who has ever met that woman would believe such a rumor. Nor would rumors that you two are plotting against the Alliance hold up. Aside from the legend of Black Jack Geary's devotion to the Alliance there's also Co-President Rione's well-known loyalty to her world and to the Alliance as a whole." He gave Geary a questioning look. "How serious is it, if you don't mind my asking?"

"Frankly, I don't know."

"Not that you've asked, but I personally wouldn't toy with the affections of a woman like Co-President Rione. I wouldn't be surprised to learn that the expression about 'hell hath no fury' was coined about a woman very similar to her."

Geary smiled again. "I'm pretty sure that's not going to happen."

Duellos frowned down at his hand as if examining it. "On the other hand, the woman standing beside Black Jack Geary when he returns this fleet safely to Alliance space will be in an enviable position for a politician."

"That's true," Geary stated, keeping his voice carefully neutral.

Duellos glanced back at Geary. "You're riding a tiger. You know that."

"Yeah. I know that." The old saying had already occurred to him, that someone riding a tiger is fine except for the fact that the tiger is taking them where it wants and they don't dare get off, because the instant they do, the tiger can turn on them. *She's powerful and can be dangerous. I wonder if those are some of the things that attracted me to Victoria Rione?*

GEARY was still musing over that when he got back to his stateroom and found Victoria Rione waiting for him there. "Did the conference go well?"

"Your spies haven't reported in yet?" Geary replied.

It didn't faze her in the slightest. "Not all of them, no.

It's rather inconvenient for them when you hold fleet conferences in the evening." She indicated the star display over the table. "I have something to show you."

He sat down, his eyes on the region of stars shown. He could usually guess which general area of space he was looking at by spotting particularly noteworthy stars, nebulas, or other features, but not this time. There wasn't a single thing he could identify from memory. "Where is this?"

"The far side of Syndicate Worlds space. It's not surprising you can't recognize it since no one from the Alliance has ever been allowed there, except perhaps as prisoners en route to labor camps." Rione's fingers danced delicately across the controls, rotating the view. "I've been studying some of the Syndic records we acquired at Sancere. This is the latest information available in them on the far side of the Syndicate Worlds. Do you notice anything?"

He watched the stars swing past slowly as the star field pivoted under Rione's commands. The boundary with unexplored or uncolonized star systems was a lumpy thing, of course. The arrangement of stars in the cosmos didn't lend itself to the neat lines that human minds liked to see. Something about the view teased at him, but he couldn't figure out what it was. "What am I supposed to be seeing?"

"Perhaps if I highlight star systems abandoned within the last century," Rione suggested. "And by abandoned I mean not left to wither, but rather star systems in which all human presence was withdrawn." She pushed another control, and several stars glowed brighter.

The picture clicked into place in Geary's mind. "It doesn't look like a frontier. It looks like a border."

"Yes," Rione agreed calmly. "It shouldn't look like a border, because there's not supposed to be anything bordering the far side of Syndicate Worlds space, but it does. The region of occupied star systems doesn't bulge and extend as it should to cover particularly rich stars. There's no gaps where much poorer stars have been left unoccupied."

"Just like the boundary between the Syndicate Worlds

and the Alliance." Geary leaned closer, studying the region. "Isn't that interesting." He moved one finger to point to the abandoned star systems that Rione had indicated. "And these places would've penetrated beyond that 'border' that isn't supposed to be there."

"I was put in mind of the buffer zone you had the Marines create in that orbital city," Rione remarked. "A place no one is supposed to occupy to separate the Syndicate Worlds from . . . who or what? Now, I'm going to superimpose a representation of the Syndic hypernet in that region." Stars glowed a different color, forming an intricate lattice. "What do you see?"

"Are you sure of this?"

"Absolutely."

Geary stared at the depiction. He had been told hypernet gates had gone into the systems rich enough or unique enough to justify the expense, places people wanted to go, stars whose resources and populations generated enough wealth to make the gates worthwhile there. But the hypernet had a military use as well, of course, allowing forces to be shifted very rapidly to where they were needed. A poor star, but one strategically placed, could earn a gate on that basis. There were a lot of poor stars with hypernet gates on the far side of Syndicate Worlds space. "They seem to be worried about something, don't they?"

Rione nodded. "But if your speculation is correct, whoever or whatever gave humanity the hypernet technology has simply given the Syndicate Worlds the means to build nova-scale bombs in every system facing this unknown-to-us threat. It looks like a wall of defenses. It's actually a minefield on an unimaginable scale, aimed at the people who think it's defending them."

"It's more than that," Geary replied. "I talked to Commander—blast it, Captain Cresida about what happens to ships headed for a hypernet gate that ceases to exist. Those ships might be lost, or they might be dumped into interstellar space a decade of travel time at least from any star. If the Syndics tried to rush reinforcements to that area, anything actually there would be destroyed by the energy discharge from the gates, and anything on the way would either be destroyed or eliminated as a threat for years."

"Thereby eliminating a very large proportion of the Syndicate Worlds' military capability? A retaliatory strike would be rendered impossible."

"Yeah." Geary tried to get his mind around the potential scale of destruction those hypernet gates represented and couldn't manage it. "How are they keeping this quiet, Victoria? How can even the Syndics keep knowledge of this from spreading?"

"It's a society that tightly controls information anyway," she pointed out. "Add in the war to justify telling people to keep their mouths shut. On top of that, add the sheer volume of information available. It's easy to bury important facts in a mountain of trivia. We picked up a tremendous amount of material at abandoned installations at Sancere. I've only skimmed small parts of it. I'll keep looking, but I don't honestly expect to find some information that proves all of this. The records we seized are all at or near the lowest level of classification. Anything regarding a nonhuman intelligence, especially a threat from such, would be very highly classified."

"Meaning we probably vaporized any copies of those records when we bombarded the Syndic headquarters sites at Sancere. I almost wish we could go to this far frontier ourselves to find out for sure, go beyond that border to see what lies on the other side." Geary realized he had been mentally tracing possible paths to the far side of Syndicate Worlds space without realizing it.

"That would be suicide," Rione stated crisply. "Even if the fleet would follow you."

"Yeah. I know. They wouldn't follow me. At least, I hope not." Geary leaned back, closing his eyes. "What can we tell anyone else about this?"

"Nothing, John Geary. Because, really, we have nothing but speculation."

"Do you believe it?"

"I fear it."

"Me, too." Geary opened his eyes again, gazing upon the unfamiliar star systems of the far side of Syndicate Worlds space. "As if we didn't have enough to worry about, already. I was told there isn't recent intelligence about the progress of the war in the captured files. Have you found any?"

"No. It's all old."

Geary nodded, wondering again what had been happening on the border between the Alliance and the Syndicate Worlds. It occurred to him, looking at the picture from deep within Syndic space, that from the perspective of the Syndicate Worlds they might see themselves as being pinned between two other powers. Did that viewpoint cause the Syndicate Worlds' leaders to feel menaced on two sides? "The Syndics told their own people that they'd destroyed this fleet in their home system. They surely announced the same thing to the Alliance, and the Alliance doesn't have any way of knowing that's a lie. Do you think they'd sue for peace?"

"No." Rione let pain show momentarily. "Many in the Alliance warm themselves against the cold of endless war with hatred of the Syndics. They wouldn't trust any peace terms offered."

"We've seen they have grounds for that distrust. The Syndics have broken every agreement we reached with them and laid traps everywhere they could."

"Which has worked against them in the long run despite any temporary advantage they gained, because now they can't even get an agreement favorable to them because they aren't trusted to abide by it."

Geary nodded, his eyes on the star display. "Since we're keeping a lot of Syndic warships tied up trying to catch us, the Syndics hopefully haven't been able to exploit the current military situation."

"You've destroyed more than a few Syndic warships as well," Rione noted.

"This fleet has," Geary corrected, "but still . . . I wonder what kind of battles are being fought near the border with the Alliance right now? Those Syndic sailors we captured who had fought at Scylla couldn't tell us anything." Were there elements of the Alliance fleet that had been left behind fighting desperate battles against long odds while the Alliance frantically tried to construct replacement warships and train replacement crews? How many of the warships guarding the border would be lost while the fleet under Geary fought its way home? "I've got a grandniece on the *Dreadnought*."

Rione raised her eyebrows in surprise. "How do you know that?"

"Michael Geary told me just before *Repulse* was destroyed." Just before his grandnephew sacrificed himself and his ship to help the rest of the fleet escape from the trap in the Syndic home system. "He gave me a message for her." *"Tell her I didn't hate you anymore." Not that I could blame him for hating Black Jack Geary, the impossible-to-match hero whose shadow had dogged him his entire life. Thank the living stars we had a few brief moments for him to learn I wasn't really the Black Jack he had grown to resent. Does my grandniece hate me, too? What could she tell me of the family I lost to time?*

"I hope you find her," Rione stated quietly.

"You've never told me whether you have any family back home," Geary noted.

"I have a brother and a sister. They have children. My parents still live. I have everything that was taken from you by chance. I hope you understand why I don't speak of them much to you. I'm uncomfortable with the idea of forcing you to recall your own losses."

He nodded. "I appreciate that. But feel free to discuss it if you want. Denying what you and other people have won't bring back what I've lost."

"You're not very good at denial?" Rione asked with a small smile.

Geary snorted in self-derision. "I imagine I'm as good at it as anyone can be."

"I disagree." She indicated the star display. "You've found something the rest of us have missed. Or found reasons to avoid seeing."

This time Geary shook his head. "We haven't found anything. As you pointed out, there's no proof here. Do you think people in authority in Alliance space will believe it?"

"That worries me less than the fact that we might have to tell them about the potential to use hypernet gates as weapons in order to explain it."

He stayed silent for a moment. "You still think they'd use those weapons?"

"I'm not certain, but if the Alliance governing council knew, I couldn't swear a majority wouldn't agree to use the Syndic hypernet gates as weapons. My instincts tell me they would decide to use them." Rione gazed at the star display, her face bleak. "And the Alliance senate would very likely muster a majority in favor if given the opportunity for a vote. Think of it, John Geary. We could send task forces to every Syndic star system within range of our frontier and blow the gates in them, then proceed on deeper and deeper into Syndic space, leaving a trail of utter devastation behind."

"That wouldn't work," Geary corrected. "You saw what the collapsing gate was like at Sancere. The energy burst released would destroy the ships that destroyed the gate. It would be a one-way mission."

She nodded, her eyes distant. "So we would construct robotic warships, crewed and controlled by artificial intelligences, and send them to destroy star systems. And because space is vast, the Syndics would have time to realize what we were doing, time for their spies to report, and they would retaliate in kind. Fleets of artificial minds shattering star systems and wiping mankind from the galaxy. What a nightmare we could unleash."

He felt a tight, sick feeling in his gut and knew Rione

was right. "I'm sorry. I didn't mean to dump this kind of thing on you."

"You didn't have much choice, and your intentions were good." She sighed. "I can't ask one man to carry every burden in this fleet."

"I didn't even ask you if you wanted to share those burdens."

"Ah, well, you're a man, aren't you?" Rione shrugged. "It's worked out all right."

"Has it?"

Rione tilted her head slightly and regarded Geary. "What's bothering you now? Unless I miss my guess, that last wasn't about Syndics or aliens or robotic slayers of mankind."

He returned her look. "It's about you and me. I'm just trying to understand what's going on between us."

"Good sex. Comfort. Companionship. Are you looking for anything else in our relationship?"

"Are you?"

"I don't know." Rione considered the question, then shook her head. "I don't know," she repeated.

"You're not in love with me, then."

She had that cool, amused expression again. "Not as far as I know. Are you disappointed?" Geary's face or body language must have betrayed his feelings, because Rione dropped the amusement. "John Geary, there has been one love in my life. I told you that. He's dead, but that hasn't changed my love for him. I've dedicated myself since then to the Alliance, trying in my own way to serve the people my husband gave his life for. What's left over is currently yours, for what it's worth."

Geary found himself laughing softly. "Your heart can't be mine, and your soul belongs to the Alliance. Just what is left over?"

"My mind. That's no small thing."

He nodded. "No, it's not."

"Can you be happy with that part of me, knowing the rest belongs to others?" Rione asked calmly.

"I don't know."

"You're too honest, John Geary." She sighed. "But then so am I. Perhaps we should try lying to each other."

"I don't think that would work," he stated dryly, unable to keep from wondering if she was being honest, if there wasn't still some agenda here that he didn't know about. In many ways, Victoria Rione's mind seemed as unknown to him as the far frontier of the Syndicate Worlds.

"No, lying probably wouldn't work." Rione gazed past Geary. "But then, will honesty work?"

"I don't know that, either."

"Time will tell." She reached to turn off the display of stars, then stood up, regarding him with an expression Geary couldn't interpret. "I forgot that there's one more part of me available to you. My body. You haven't asked, but I'll tell you. That has been offered to no one else since my husband died."

He couldn't see any trace of insincerity in her and wouldn't have been fool enough to question her statement even if he had. "I really don't understand you, Victoria."

"Is that why you're keeping your emotional distance from me?"

"Maybe."

"That may be for the best."

"You're not exactly opening up to me," Geary pointed out.

"That's true enough. I haven't given you any promises. You shouldn't give me any. We're both veterans of life, John Geary, scarred by the losses we've endured because we cared for others. Someday you should tell me about her."

"Her?" He knew exactly who Rione meant but didn't want to admit it.

"Whoever she was. The one you left behind. The one I see you thinking of sometimes."

He looked down, feeling an emptiness inside born of might-have-beens. "I should. Someday."

"You told me you weren't married."

"No. I wasn't. It was something that could have happened and didn't. I'm still not sure why. But there was a lot left unsaid that should have been said."

"Do you know what happened to her after your supposed death in battle?"

Geary stared at nothing, remembering. "Something happened before my battle. An accident. A stupid accident. Because her ship was a long ways off I didn't even hear about it until she'd been dead for three months. I'd been planning on getting back in touch and apologizing for being an idiot, rehearsing what I was going to say."

"I'm very sorry, John Geary." Rione looked at him with eyes filled with shared sorrow. "It's not easy for dreams to die, even when they've remained only dreams." She reached down to take his hand and pull Geary up to stand next to her. "When you're ready, you can speak more of it. You never have spoken of it to anyone, have you? I thought not. Open wounds don't heal, John Geary." She stepped close and kissed him slowly, her lips lingering on his. "That's enough companionship for one night and far too much thinking for both of us. I'd like to enjoy the other benefit of our relationship now."

Her body was warm and alive in his arms, and for a short while at least the concerns of the present and memories of the past were forgotten.

THE right formation had been the dilemma. The Alliance fleet was pretty close to the jump point from which any Syndic force would exit. That meant he would have little time to adjust his formation and would probably have to fight from whatever formation he had the fleet in when the enemy arrived. But he wouldn't know how the enemy was formed up until they got here.

The one thing he did know was that if the Syndics were in hot pursuit of a small, badly battered Alliance force, they wouldn't be wasting time. It was a safe bet that there would be fast, light units coming in right behind any fleeing Alliance ships. Those would be easily disposed of no matter what formation Geary adopted. The problem was what came next. Heavy cruisers would be quickly annihilated, but if the Syndics had battleships coming in soon after the light units, Geary had to make sure those capital ships couldn't take too many of his own ships with them.

In the worst case, the Syndics would have a superior force, in which case the Alliance would have to strike fast and hard to take advantage of any element of surprise and any momentary numerical lead as Syndic ships exited the jump point.

"It could be very ugly," Geary remarked after discussing options with Captain Duellos. "But we'll be close to the gate, which means they can't be spread out. I'm going to keep us in a modified cup formation." On the display floating between them, the formation resembled its namesake, with a thick circular bottom formed by over half the fleet in a matrix with interlocking fields of fire, the remainder of the ships arranged in flat, semicircular formations extending outward toward the enemy. "We'll be able to hit them hard in one spot, then come back and hit another part of whatever formation they're in."

"If they're truly superior in numbers to us, we will beat the hell out of them even if we're destroyed in the process," Duellos replied. "Not the best outcome, but combined with the losses we inflicted at Kaliban and Sancere, it will leave the Syndics without numerical advantage in the war."

Geary nodded, gazing at the star display. "So the war would just go on."

"The war would just go on," Duellos agreed.

"I'd like to manage a better outcome than that."

Duellos grinned sardonically. "You can count on the fleet. Everything's coming together here. The pride of the fleet, the need to rescue our fellow ships, the confidence born of recent victories, and the training you've given us. We've got a chance, even if the odds are bad." His grin widened. "And I just thought of something else we can do to even the odds a bit."

• • •

YOU *would think someone who had spent so many years in the fleet would be used to waiting by now*, Geary thought as he wandered the passageways of *Dauntless*. A very large amount of time in the fleet was spent just waiting. Waiting to get somewhere, waiting once you got there, waiting for an emergency or crisis that might not happen, waiting to find out how long you would have to wait. That seemed to be as much a part of military life as risking your life and bad food.

None of which made waiting to find out if any ships would rejoin them here any easier. The fleet had been positioned facing the jump point from which any of the missing ships would have to come, hanging in space with its movements slaved to the slow progression of the jump point around its star. The auxiliaries were busy enough building new weapons and parts, and every other ship needed routine upkeep and repair, but Geary had done everything he personally could do to prepare. Too restless to address other tasks, he went through *Dauntless* seeing the crew, finding his increasing ability to recognize the sailors and officers he encountered to be a source of comfort. Slowly, very slowly, he was beginning to feel like he belonged here.

In one passageway he encountered Captain Desjani, surprised to see that she was demonstrating the sort of cheerfulness that usually only appeared after Desjani had watched a lot of Syndic ships be destroyed. "You seem in a good mood," he commented.

She smiled back. "I recently had a long conversation with someone on *Furious*, sir."

Furious was a ways off, with her once-again reconstituted task force, ready to carry off another special mission. Geary spent a moment wondering why Desjani would have had a long talk with Captain Cresida, given the time delay involved, then realized that hadn't been who she had talked to. "How is Lieutenant Casell Riva?"

Desjani actually blushed slightly. "Very well, Captain

Geary. He's impressed by Captain Cresida and the new sensors and weaponry we have."

"I see. I'm glad he's pleased by the new weapons in the fleet."

"Actually, he's happy to be liberated, and seemed pleased to talk to me," Desjani confessed.

"I suspect he really is pleased, Tanya. He's fitting in okay, then?"

Her smiled faded a bit. "There's been some rough moments, he said. That much time in a Syndic labor camp with no hope of release or rescue will take a while to overcome. Sometimes he wakes up in a panic, fearing that his liberation was only a hallucination. But of course he has hope now." Desjani paused. "Cas—Lieutenant Riva was surprised to see the way you're directing the fleet. The tactics you're using. He's still puzzled and torn by Captain Falco's departure from the fleet. But he watched everything that happened at Sancere and was astounded, sir."

Geary felt embarrassed himself. "A lot of things worked right. We were lucky."

"You make much of your own luck, sir, if you don't mind my saying so." She paused again. "He's still the man I remembered. Perhaps something will come of it."

"I hope so. War messes up enough lives. It's nice to think that two of them can have a chance to get back on track."

Desjani nodded, her eyes distant with memory. "We'll see. There's a lot of time to make up and experiences to share. Did you know that among the records we downloaded at Sancere there was a huge database of Alliance prisoners of war? It's not up to date, the latest information is about three years old, but it has a lot of names of people who for all we knew were dead. If—excuse me, sir—*when* we get back to Alliance space, a lot of people will be happy to see some of the names on that list."

Geary gave her a curious look. "How long has it been since the Syndics shared captured personnel lists with the Alliance?"

"Decades at least. I'd have to check. At some point they decided not knowing if lost personnel were alive or dead would harm Alliance morale and stopped providing lists of prisoners. The Alliance did the same in retaliation, of course."

That wasn't a pleasant thought. Sending friends, lovers, and family off to battle was bad enough, but not knowing afterward what had happened to them was a form of slow torture. "We'll have to get that list back, and maybe convince the Syndics to swap up-to-date lists."

Desjani nodded. "If anyone can do that, you can," she replied. "I've just started to look at the list. There's so many names and the list is organized in an odd way, so I'm stumbling through it usually getting results I didn't ask for. But there's some people whose fates I'd like to check. Some of them were supposedly captured, some supposedly killed in battle. Maybe I can confirm those things now."

"I guess you and a lot of other people will be doing that," Geary noted, thinking that a list three years old wouldn't tell him if some miracle had allowed his grand-nephew to escape from *Repulse* before its destruction in the Syndic home system. That would remain an unknown for him, but best to assume Michael Geary was dead and be very pleasantly surprised if he turned up alive. There really weren't many grounds for assuming he had survived the death of his ship.

Which brought his thoughts back to the thirty-nine ships that had accompanied Captain Falco at Strabo. How many of those had survived? He wished he already knew the answer, as terrible as that was likely to be. The uncertainty was almost as bad as the nagging, ugly conviction that few if any of them would survive to reach Ilion.

"THEY'RE here."

Geary bolted from his stateroom without bothering to check his own display. He ran down long passageways and up ladders until he reached the bridge, gasping for breath as he dropped into his seat. Only then did he call up the display with a silent prayer for as many survivors as possible.

Amazingly, three battleships were there. *Dauntless*'s systems quickly identified them as *Warrior*, *Orion*, and *Majestic*. And a single battle cruiser, *Invincible*, so badly damaged that Geary had to double-check the assessment before he believed it. Of the six heavy cruisers that had accompanied the capital ships, only two remained. None of the four light cruisers were there, and of the nineteen destroyers only seven had survived.

"Those stupid bastards," Geary muttered. A battleship and two battle cruisers lost, along with a lot of lighter ships. Of the thirty-nine warships that had followed Falco, only thirteen had made it to Ilion.

Captain Desjani's face was white with anger. "*Triumph* didn't make it. I'll lay you any odds you care to name that *Triumph* stayed behind to hold off the pursuit while the other big ships got away."

"That didn't do *Polaris* and *Vanguard* any good," Geary noted, knowing how much fury his voice was showing. "Look at *Invincible*. How is she still functioning?"

"I have no idea, sir. But all of those ships are beat up. I don't know if even *Titan* can restore those ships to full service no matter how much time she's given."

"We'll find out." Geary finally punched his communications controls. "Colonel Carabali. Get in touch with your Marine detachments on *Warrior*, *Orion*, and *Majestic*. Captains Kerestes, Numos, and Faresa have been relieved of command effective immediately and are to be placed under arrest. Captain Falco is also to be placed under arrest for the negligent and criminal loss of ships of the Alliance fleet." Charges of mutiny could wait until later. What really mattered to Geary was knowing that Falco's stupidity had caused the loss of so many ships. He pushed another control. "*Warrior*, *Orion*, and *Majestic*, this is Captain Geary, acting commander of the Alliance fleet. Your commanding officers are relieved effective immediately. Executive officers are to assume temporary command." Another push, this time on the fleetwide circuit. "All units that have just arrived in the Ilion system are to accelerate at your best speed, passing through the fleet formation and joining up with the fast fleet auxiliaries and their escorts in the rear. We assume pursuit is coming in after you and want a clear field of fire. Task Force Furious will be executing Operation Barricade in your wake. Please remain clear. All other units in the Alliance fleet, prepare for battle. We've got a lot of shipmates to avenge."

· "Operation Barricade?" Rione had arrived on the bridge, breathing heavily from what must have been a run of her own up here. She was gazing at the display, her face bleak as she realized the extent of the losses.

"Operation Barricade is a little idea from Captain Duellos," Geary explained. "We loaded out the ships under *Furious* with most of the mines in the fleet. They're moving across the jump point exit now, planting as dense a minefield as we can manage in whatever time remains."

Captain Desjani was grinning in anticipation of the Syndics hitting those mines. "What makes it especially sweet is that we're able to expend those mines because the matériel we picked up in Sancere will let the auxiliaries manufacture replacements. The Syndics themselves provided us the means to replace the mines we use here."

On his display, Geary could see the time-late images of *Furious* and the other ships in the task force accelerating across the jump exit to lay their mines as Rione spoke again. "What happens if a large number of Syndic ships exit the jump point as *Furious* and her sisters are crossing in front of it?"

"There's a substantial risk there," Geary conceded. "Even though having Task Force Furious sitting next to the jump exit ready to go minimized the chance the Syndics can arrive before our ships are done crossing in front of the jump point. That's why I asked Captain Cresida to volunteer for the task." At least he was finally remembering to refer to her using her new rank.

Rione gave him a flat look. "Do you honestly believe that Captain Cresida would treat a request to volunteer as any different from an order to take part?"

Desjani shot Rione a sour glance while Geary tried not to grimace. There was enough truth to Rione's accusation to sting. "Madam Co-President, if I refrained from doing or asking anything that might lead to the deaths of some of the people under my command, then I would be paralyzed with indecision, and then *all* of the people I'm responsible for would surely die or be condemned to Syndic labor camps."

"As long as you are keeping consequences in mind," Rione stated.

This time Geary glowered at her, wondering why Rione was being so contrary. Perhaps she was trying to emphasize that she remained the voice of his conscience. "If you're trying to keep me honest," he stated in a low voice, "you've made your point."

Focusing back on the display, Geary saw that at least the dispute had distracted him for a few minutes from worrying that Syndic pursuers would erupt into the middle of Task Force Furious. The gate exit was ten light-minutes away. His orders relieving the commanding officers of the three battleships would just be arriving at those ships. The Syndics could have appeared in force several minutes ago, ravaging Task Force Furious, and he wouldn't have seen it yet.

His display updated, showing where mines were being laid like deadly eggs as of almost ten minutes ago. The field was gratifyingly dense, since Geary had held almost none of his mines back. There would be a price to pay for that later. His ships were certain to expend a lot of grapeshot and specters as well, in addition to taking damage that would need to be repaired and losing equipment that would need to be replaced, and four fleet auxiliaries couldn't manufacture replacements for all of that at once, no matter how many resources had been plundered from Sancere. It would take a while to make up the expenditure.

But at least the auxiliaries could keep working during jump space transits. By the time they reached Baldur a lot of replacement weaponry would be available.

If his fleet reached Baldur, Geary reminded himself. They were a long ways from that star, with very likely a major battle between them and it.

"*Invincible*'s really lagging," Desjani remarked.

"I'm surprised she's still moving," Geary muttered in reply, taking another look at the amount of damage the battle cruiser had sustained. He studied the display, mentally evaluating the progress of the fleeing Alliance ships, trying to guess when the Syndic pursuers would appear. *I can't be too close to the jump exit when the Syndics arrive, but if I don't move now, there's a growing chance we won't be able to cover* Invincible *in time.*

I had to leave Repulse *to her fate. I'm not leaving* Invincible. "All units in the Alliance fleet, accelerate to point zero five light speed at time zero four. Maintain position relative to fleet flagship *Dauntless*." He turned to Desjani. "Captain, please keep *Dauntless* on a course centered on the jump point exit."

"Yes, sir." Desjani gave the necessary orders, outwardly as calm as usual.

Geary thought a moment longer. "Task Force Furious. Upon completion of Operation Barricade take up position behind and above the exit." Did he need to do anything else? *Warrior*, *Majestic*, and *Orion* had almost reached the rest of the fleet. Several of the surviving destroyers accompanied them, but the two surviving heavy cruisers and the rest of the destroyers had stayed with *Invincible*. He would have to remember that they had done that. In the heat of battle Geary couldn't afford to bother replacing the commanders of the surviving cruisers and destroyers that had gone with Falco. Maybe he didn't need to do that at all, not if their commanders were displaying the courage and discipline to stick with the badly damaged *Invincible* when the safety of the rest of the fleet beckoned.

Well behind the Alliance formation the auxiliaries were

guarded by a disgruntled group of escorts built around the Second Battleship Division, four powerful ships, which should be enough to fend off or repel any attack aimed at the auxiliaries. No one wanted to miss a battle. But Geary had assured the escorts that in the next battle, and there would surely be a next battle, they would be allowed to occupy the front ranks of the fleet.

Majestic, *Warrior*, and *Orion*, moving as if the devil were at their heels, passed through the Alliance formation without a pause. "I would have joined the line of battle," Desjani grumbled in disgust, clearly unhappy that the three battleships hadn't turned to help fight their pursuers. She had a point, Geary conceded to himself, despite the damage the three battleships had suffered. *Simply replacing their commanding officers isn't going to turn those three ships into reliable parts of the fleet. Their crews are acting scared and beaten even when the rest of the fleet is here to protect them. I shouldn't be surprised that ships commanded by the likes of Numos and Faresa don't have highly motivated crews. Getting those crews retrained and reinspired is going to be a major project.*

Once we've finished the battle I'm sure is coming.

As if they had heard Desjani, the destroyers accompanying the three wounded battleships turned and headed for the squadrons they had abandoned back at Strabo, trying to take their places in the fleet formation. Geary took a look at the damage they were reporting to the fleet net and shook his head. "*Claymore* and *Cinquedea*, this is Captain Geary. Your willingness to continue the fight is noted with pride and pleasure, but you've sustained too much damage. Join up with the auxiliaries so you can assist their escorts and they can start fixing you." He paused, thinking there was something else that needed to be said. "If any Syndics get near the auxiliaries, I know I can count on you to defend them gallantly." That sounded awkward, but it should satisfy the pride of the destroyer crews. They deserved that much courtesy for volunteering to keep fighting. Fighting spirit did indeed have its place.

The jump point exit remained more than eight light-minutes away. No signs of Syndic pursuers had appeared yet. Task Force Furious had finished its work and was headed for its ordered position. Desjani was eyeing the distance to the jump point exit with concern. "Should we slow, sir? If we're too close when the Syndics come through . . ."

Geary shook his head. "Not yet. We don't have *Invincible* covered yet."

"Yes, sir." Desjani grinned.

If he ever lost Desjani's approval, Geary reflected, he would know for sure that he had messed up as badly as any human possibly could. "We'll hold our speed until we're within a light-minute of *Invincible*, and if the Syndics haven't shown up at that point we'll—"

"Enemy forces at the jump exit," a watch-stander cried as alarms wailed.

Geary blinked in amazement at the images on his display as the Syndic vanguard flashed into normal space. Not a swarm of light units, but twelve battle cruisers, arranged in three vertical diamond formations. It made sense, he realized, if the Syndic commander thought he would be facing four battered capital ships with very few screening units surviving. Why send light units through to be destroyed by a potential desperate ambush when losses could be minimized by sending through a force capable of overwhelming the four damaged Alliance capital ships if they had chosen to make a stand at the exit?

Unfortunately for the Syndic commander and the twelve battle cruisers, this side of the jump exit actually held the rest of Geary's fleet and a dense minefield.

The Syndic battle cruisers sailed majestically away from the exit at .1 light speed for a few seconds, doubtless seeing the waiting Alliance force and having those few moments to realize the tables had been turned on the pursuers. Geary watched the images of the Syndic battle cruisers begin to turn, pivoting to alter course downward. He had a second to wonder why fleeing ships almost always sought to "dive" down instead of "climb" up, as if they were aircraft or even people running on the surface of a world, even though the two directions were purely arbitrary and required exactly the same effort in space.

In this case, as the Syndic battle cruisers pivoted their bows downward, it meant they ran into the minefield not bow on, but broadside on, offering even bigger targets for the waiting Alliance mines. If their escorts had been leading the way, the deaths of smaller units on the mines would have warned the battle cruisers, but instead the first warning the capital ships received was when they hit the mines themselves. Explosions rippled down their lengths, collapsing shields so that other mines could strike the hulls. The battle cruisers reeled as the mines blew holes in them and sent fragments flying into space. One of the battle cruisers blew up as its power core overloaded, then two more in quick succession, the three ships turning into fields of shrapnel blossoming out from the scenes of their deaths. Of the nine remaining battle cruisers, eight were drifting away out of control, rocked by occasional new explosions as an outlying mine battered them or as damage set off internal explosions.

The last Syndic battle cruiser, in even worse shape than *Invincible*, staggered on past the minefield with most of its propulsion blown and combat systems out of action but still managing to hold a course. Geary checked the geometry of the battlefield. "*Warspite* is just within maximum specter range of that battle cruiser. Is it worth trying to get hits?"

Desjani nodded. "That Syndic isn't going to be dodging any missiles. He's a sitting duck."

"Just like *Invincible* would've been for them," Geary agreed. "*Warspite*, this is Captain Geary. Engage the leading Syndic battle cruiser with specters. All other ships hold your fire. This can't be the entire Syndic pursuit force. You'll have plenty of targets to play with soon."

Forty seconds later the answer came back from *Warspite*. "Aye. Engaging lead battle cruiser." On his display, Geary could see four specters leaping out from the Alliance battleship and heading in long, shallow curves toward intercepts with the crippled Syndic.

"No matter what they've got left, twelve battle cruisers gone is going to go a long ways toward evening things up," Desjani observed.

"Yeah. Where's the rest?" Geary wondered.

His words were answered almost immediately. The jump exit, now barely seven and a half light-minutes away, was suddenly filled with ships. Geary forced himself to carefully study the enemy formation. A deep rectangle, broad face toward the Alliance fleet, capital ships arranged at each corner and in the center, the gaps filled with lighter units.

"Twenty capital ships," Desjani noted. "Sixteen battleships and four battle cruisers. Thirty-one heavy cruisers. Forty-two light cruisers and HuKs."

"More than enough to wipe out the Alliance ships they followed here," Geary observed.

"Why didn't they send more?" Desjani asked. "If there was a chance the fleeing ships would rejoin us they must have known what they could end up facing."

"Because they didn't know where the rest of the fleet was. They had to find us and protect every other place we might have gone. Trying to protect against all of the options they expected meant they committed insufficient forces to this mission. If we hadn't been waiting for them, that might have worked out because they could have run from an engagement, but we're too close for them to get away without a fight." Geary tapped the fleet communications control. "All ships accelerate to point one light speed at time one five. Task Force Furious, adjust course and speed as necessary to block the rear of the Syndic formation. Don't let them turn back toward the jump point. All units, target the capital ships first." He checked the distance to *Invincible*, seeing she was still a light-minute ahead, between the charging Alliance fleet and the sur-

prised Syndics. At current closing speed they would meet
and pass *Invincible* within seven minutes.

The main body of the Syndics hit the minefield, many
of the ships sweeping unscathed through the gaps swept by
the hulls of the twelve battle cruisers in the first wave. But
a lot of mines remained.

Syndic HuKs exploded and broke under the force of
mine explosions, their pieces tumbling across space. A
half-dozen light cruisers shattered into fragments. Three
heavy cruisers reeled out of formation, two completely destroyed and the third out of the battle. The Syndic battleships and battle cruisers took the blows on their bows,
having had time to reinforce their forward shields, thanks
to the sacrifice of the lighter units, and blundered through
the minefield with weakened shields but no apparent damage. "That's for *Anelace*, *Baselard*, *Mace*, and *Cuirass*,"
Geary announced. A low-key cheer sounded around him as
Dauntless's bridge crew acknowledged that Alliance mines
were avenging the ships lost to Syndic mines at the jump
point at Sutrah.

Invincible staggered through the Alliance fleet formation. Geary winced as he took a moment to stare at the
damage to the ship. *Invincible* had taken so many hits that
Geary marveled the battle cruiser had kept moving. He
wondered if it would be appropriate to issue a fleet citation
to the crew of a ship that had fled the fleet, then decided he
didn't care whether or not it was appropriate.

Past the Alliance mines, the Syndic formation began
curving upward, aiming to pass over the Alliance fleet so
it could hit the topside ships and remain out of range of
most of the Alliance warships.

"That won't work," Geary stated out loud. "All units in
main body, alter formation course up three five degrees at
time four seven." At the ordered time, the cup-shaped formation swung around the axis formed by *Dauntless*, aiming the center of the Alliance cup-shaped formation to
once again intercept the middle of the Syndic formation,

coming up on the Syndics from ahead and beneath now. "Let's see if he spots that in time to try avoiding us."

"Estimated time to contact twenty minutes."

The specters from *Warspite* finally reached the Syndic battle cruiser badly hurt by the mines, racing in to strike unimpeded by shields. Four massive explosions blossomed on the Syndic ship, smashing any remaining working systems and reducing the ship to a wreck tumbling off to one side.

The surviving Syndic forces were substantially outnumbered but in a more spread-out formation. The Alliance formation aimed at it would only strike half of the Syndic formation if neither Geary nor the Syndic commander changed anything. Geary couldn't see how the Syndic commander would allow that to happen, since it would grant the Alliance overwhelming firepower superiority at the point of contact.

"The Syndics are moving again. Looks like they're adjusting course to port and down."

On Geary's display, the Syndic formation pivoted up and away, trying to position itself so one side of the Alliance formation would rush upward past the flat side of the Syndic formation. It wasn't a bad move, Geary conceded to himself. This Syndic CEO obviously wasn't a fool. "All units, roll starboard nine zero degrees, change course down six zero degrees at time zero six. Task Force Furious, adjust course as necessary to block the Syndic formation from turning toward the jump point to Tavika." He had to assume the Syndics would break and run, and with the jump point they had used to arrive still blocked by Alliance mines, the jump point to Tavika was the next best option.

"Eight minutes to contact."

The Syndics had finished rolling, each ship turning within the formation to present its bows to the oncoming Alliance fleet so that the Syndic warships were now coasting sideways within their rectangular formation. The flat side of the Syndic rectangle was now positioned almost vertically "up" and "down," facing the Alliance formation.

Geary pondered whether to try some fancy use of his ship's firepower and decided against it. "All units employ weapons at your discretion. Primary targets are the capital ships. Maintain formation except to maneuver as necessary to avoid enemy fire. Permission granted to open fire when favorable engagement opportunities are presented."

"Six minutes to contact."

The Syndics were still settling into formation, doubtless worried about being caught in the middle of another maneuver when the Alliance fleet swept into range. Geary watched on his display as the two fleets rushed toward each other, the Alliance cup overlapping the back half of the Syndic formation. He had positioned his ships and positioned his fleet, given his commanders authority to fire, and now had nothing to do but watch as the Syndic warships and the Alliance fleet raced to contact.

"Enemy is firing," the weapons watch reported unnecessarily as Geary's display lit up with warnings. Grapeshot, concentrated on the points where some Alliance warships would soon be. It had been fired at extreme effective range. Geary hoped the commanders of those ships would use the very brief time available to alter course slightly to avoid the worst of the barrage. More warning symbols sprang to life. Syndic missiles.

On the visual display, spots of bright light began flaring as Syndic grapeshot struck Alliance shields. Geary could see his own ships firing, their data up to several seconds time-late for the farthest-off ships.

Captain Desjani had her eyes fixed on her own display. She highlighted a Syndic battleship. "That's our target," she informed her watch-standers. "Let's hurt him."

The sides of the Alliance cup were plunging into the Syndic rectangle, each Alliance ship only briefly exposed to enemy fire as it tore through, while the Syndic ships in those areas were battered by ship after ship. The lighter Syndic units were ripped apart under the repeated blows, flaring and dying around the stronger islands formed by the surviving Syndic capital ships.

Then the main strength of the Alliance fleet reached the Syndic formation.

After long, slowly passing minutes as the final huge distances were closed, the actual moments of fighting were so swift as to be disorienting. If not for the capability of the combat systems to target and fire at speeds far greater than humans could achieve, there probably would never be hits scored as two opposing fleets flashed by each other at decent fractions of the speed of light. Geary felt as if the moment of combat had come and gone between one blink and the next, *Dauntless* still quivering from the impacts of weapons on her shields and tallying the damage from an occasional hit that had made its way through a spot failure of the shields.

Behind him, the Syndic battleship targeted by Desjani had also taken fire from many other Alliance ships, including *Daring*, *Terrible*, and *Victorious*. Under that hail of fire, the mighty Syndic warship, an S-Class dreadnought, had first lost its shields then taken an onslaught of hits. Something had hit in the wrong place, and the Syndic battleship's power core blew while some of the Alliance ships were still closing in.

They were too close when it happened. Geary stared at the display, seeing that the trailing battle cruiser in the Alliance formation, *Terrible*, had been shooting past close to the Syndic ship, battering it with close-range hell-lance fire. *Terrible* had already taken a lot of hits, substantially weakening her shields. The shock wave from the explosion of the Syndic ship reached out and slapped the Alliance battle cruiser like a huge hand, sending it tumbling. That alone would've been recoverable, but one of the surviving Syndic battle cruisers was too close and traveling on exactly the wrong trajectory. Even the ultrafast computers responsible for maneuvering ships to avoid collisions couldn't avoid the result. *Terrible* and the Syndic ship collided as Geary watched in horror.

The collision, at a relative velocity of perhaps .06 light speed, or roughly eighteen thousand kilometers per second, turned both ships into a single titanic ball of heat, light, and scattered fragments that blossomed brilliantly against the dark of space, a human-made nebula that would briefly light the void of Ilion Star System.

A collective gasp of shock and dismay went up on the bridge of *Dauntless*. Geary heard a voice saying "Damn, damn, damn," and realized it was his own. "May your ancestors protect you and the living stars welcome you," he murmured to the dead crew of the *Terrible*.

Desjani, finally seeming shaken for the first time Geary recalled since they had escaped from the Syndic home system, called out commands to refocus her crew. "Damage report!"

"Minor hits on hull. No systems lost," one of the watchstanders reported in a stunned voice.

Geary got a grip on himself as well, forcing himself to look away from the grave of the *Terrible* and evaluate the entire situation. There had been eight Syndic battleships and two battle cruisers in the part of the Syndic formation the Alliance fleet had met. Three of the battleships still survived, but all had taken damage. The Syndic light cruisers and HuKs around them had been wiped out, and only a few heavy cruisers still accompanied the surviving battleships. He took a deep breath, focusing on the front half of the Syndic force, which had turned hard to port and was accelerating away toward the jump point to Tavika. They obviously weren't planning on fighting if they could possibly get away. "All units, come right one two zero degrees down one zero degrees and accelerate to point one five light at time two nine." The huge cup pivoted again, turning to face the fleeing Syndics.

"We won't get them," Desjani grumbled.

"Yes, we will." Geary pointed to Task Force Furious, slashing in from above and to the side of the Syndics. The Syndic maneuver, necessary as it was to reach the jump point, had turned their force toward Cresida's formation and made an intercept of the leading Syndic elements possible.

Desjani didn't so much grin as bare her teeth as *Furious* and the ships with her cut across the front of the Syndic formation, concentrating their fire on the lighter warships and stripping the remaining capital ships of their escorts. Diving below the Syndic formation with a speed advantage, *Furious* led the formation back up to hit the bottom of the Syndics. Another Syndic battleship reeled out of the formation, racked by secondary explosions.

Geary studied the situation, evaluating the geometry of the battle and reaching a decision as he watched the three damaged battleships that had survived the first Alliance pass falling farther and farther behind the rest of the Syndic formation. "Second Battleship Division. You are released from escort duties for the auxiliaries. Intercept and destroy the three Syndic battleships trailing their formation."

Due to distance, the reply took almost a minute but made up for the delay in enthusiasm. "Second Battleship Division, aye! We're on our way."

Geary took another look at the battered Syndic formation still trying to accelerate away as Task Force Furious made repeated passes, curving up and down and side to side to keep hitting the front of the Syndics, whose own speed was falling off as undamaged ships reduced speed to stay with their damaged sisters. But Geary could see that the frequent passes were wearing down the shields of the ships in Task Force Furious. "All units, accelerate to point one eight light." That might not be enough, though. He paused, hating to give the next order but seeing no alternative. "All units, general pursuit. Get those Syndics before they get away. We need to slow down those battleships."

Geary had seen it before but was still amazed at how quickly one of his carefully built formations could dissolve when he unleashed his ships. A swarm of destroyers and light cruisers jumped ahead at maximum acceleration. Individually they wouldn't stand a chance of hurting a battleship, but their sheer numbers would be more than the shields of even battleships could endure. And once the propulsion systems of the Syndic battleships had been damaged, they'd be slowed enough for first the Alliance battle cruisers and then the Alliance battleships to catch them, and that would seal their fates. "Task Force Furious, concentrate on slowing down the surviving capital ships."

The Syndic formation technically still existed but had stretched out as it was hammered by Alliance hits. The sole surviving battle cruiser had pulled ahead of the rest, but that meant it was too far away for the battleships to support it when Task Force Furious swung past, unleashing a rain of hell-lances on its stern and knocking out most of its main propulsion systems.

As the battle cruiser began drifting back, the Alliance escorts drove into range of the trailing Syndic battleships and began slamming every available weapon at their sterns. Within ten minutes those battleships had lost enough propulsion to begin losing ground as well, their own hell lances flashing out impotently at the mass of light Alliance forces sweeping past.

The pursuing Alliance ships swept implacably up the rear of the Syndics, some of the destroyers and light cruisers reeling away with damage but the rest pounding at ship after ship in turn. *Falcata* got too close or got unlucky and took a series of hits that smashed her into wreckage.

"Heavy cruisers, avoid the battleships and get me that battle cruiser," Geary ordered. He didn't want to lose any heavy cruisers in an outmatched slugging contest with still-dangerous battleships. With an obedience that Geary would never have expected a few months ago, the heavy cruisers sidestepped the Syndic battleships, aiming to intercept the battle cruiser, which was still dangerous enough to keep Alliance destroyers and light cruisers at a distance.

Fearless, *Resolution*, *Redoubtable*, and *Warspite* dove at a slight angle toward the farthest-back Syndic battleship. The battleship unleashed a barrage of missiles, grapeshot, and hell lances at *Fearless*, but all four Alliance battleships kept coming, holding their fire until close enough for their own hell lances to pound the Syndic shields. The aft shields, heavily reinforced, held until *Fearless* got close enough to hit the side shields as well.

Its shields collapsed, the Syndic battleship was riddled by close-range hell-lance fire, most of its weapons falling silent and the majority of its systems registering as dead on Geary's display. *Fearless* fired a null-field charge that bored a large hole right through the battleship, gutting a portion of it. Escape pods began bursting from the battleship, first in a scattering of twos and threes, then in a mass. By the time *Dauntless* and her sisters roared past, only an occasional escape pod was coming out of the stricken ship. "Finish him," Desjani ordered calmly.

Dauntless's own hell lances rained down on the length of the Syndic battleship, punching holes and destroying any remaining functional systems. By the time *Daring* made its own pass, the Syndic ship was definitely dead.

Captain Duellos's *Courageous*, along with *Formidable*, *Intrepid*, and *Renown*, bore down on another damaged battleship and raked it so badly that the after section broke off, leaving the two pieces tumbling along their last trajectories.

The last Syndic battle cruiser, its remaining propulsion systems knocked out, started spitting out escape pods even though many of its weapons still seemed functional. Geary guessed they had been set to fire on automatic, which worked well enough for attackers to respect but didn't select targets or concentrate fire as well as human-directed weaponry. Under fire from more and more heavy cruisers, the battle cruiser's shields failed, and it took hit after hit, until the last weapons fell silent long after the final escape pod had left.

Geary took a moment to check on where the Second Battleship Division was closing on the three damaged Syndic battleships. To his surprise, one of those Syndic battleships had already begun throwing out escape pods as well.

"So much for fighting to the death," Desjani commented.

"What would be the point?" Rione demanded. "They know they're doomed."

"You still fight," Desjani insisted, her eyes on the next Syndic battleship *Dauntless* was overhauling.

"Why?" Rione asked.

Desjani threw a despairing glance at Geary, who understood what she meant. How to explain the strange logic? That sometimes you had to fight a hopeless battle for reasons that might seem to make no sense, for reasons that had nothing to do with any hope of winning? "You just have to," he told Rione quietly. "If you don't understand why, there's no way to explain it."

"I understand fighting when there's a chance, but when it's hopeless . . ."

"Sometimes you win even when it seems hopeless. Sometimes you lose there but cause something that helps elsewhere, like hurting the enemy bad enough while they kill you, or keeping them busy for a critical period of time. I told you, I can't explain. You just do it."

"Like you did," Rione stated, eyeing Geary. "A century ago."

"Yeah." Geary looked away, not wanting to remember that hopeless battle. He had been the one facing a far superior force that day. He had known he had a chance of delaying the surprise Syndic attack on the convoy he was protecting. He had hoped the convoy would get away, hoped the other warships with him could escape as well. But he hadn't had any hope of his own ship getting away, even though he had pretended to himself there was a chance. He had tried to remember how it had felt, the numbness inside that let him keep going while his ship was destroyed around him, while his surviving crew members escaped. But most of it was a blur now, fragments of memory in which his ship was torn apart around him, in which the last weapons stopped firing, and he had set the power core to self-destruct, in which he raced through passageways made alien by destruction to reach an escape pod he hoped hadn't been destroyed. It had been there, damaged, and with no other hope and no time left, he had climbed in and ejected.

To drift for almost one hundred years in survival sleep, his pod's beacon knocked out so no one found him. Not until this fleet came through the same star system en route to the Syndic home world and thawed him out.

In a sense he had died that day. When he woke up, the John Geary he knew was gone, replaced by the impossibly noble and heroic image of Black Jack Geary, legendary hero of the Alliance. "Yeah," Geary repeated. "Sort of."

Rione gazed back, her eyes deep with some emotion he couldn't quite figure out.

"Fire grapeshot," Captain Desjani ordered as *Dauntless* rolled in on another damaged Syndic battleship, the low relative speed allowing a long, slow firing run. The grapeshot formed a pattern of dancing lights as it impacted on the battleship's shields. *Daring* and *Victorious* pounced from the top and bottom, their own fire helping to overwhelm the battleship's shields. The Syndic battleship poured out a hail of hell-lance fire, concentrating on *Dauntless*. Geary could see the shields weakening even as the defensive systems on *Dauntless* automatically shifted power from the unengaged sides of the ship. The Alliance battle cruiser returned fire, its own hell lances digging holes in the battleship's armor to wreak havoc inside the ship. Null fields shot out from *Dauntless* and *Daring*, vaporizing parts of the battleship. With *Victorious* also pounding away, the already stricken battleship was hopelessly outmatched. Its weapons fell silent one by one, atmosphere venting from compartments holed by Alliance fire, the huge craters left by the null fields looking like bites from an unimaginably large monster.

Dauntless and her sisters cruised past the now-silent battleship, which began tossing out escape pods as it tumbled helplessly, pieces of it breaking off and spinning away. "That's for *Terrible*," Desjani muttered.

Geary checked the overall situation again. The Second

Battleship Division had caught up with the two wounded Syndic battleships that were still trying to flee and was methodically pounding them into scrap, while the lighter Alliance units with them continued on to make sure the abandoned Syndic battleship was destroyed. Only one other Syndic battleship was still firing, and as he watched, it shuddered under fire from half a dozen Alliance capital ships.

The Syndic HuKs and light cruisers had already been wiped out, and now the last heavy cruiser succumbed to a flock of Alliance destroyers and light cruisers. A cloud of Syndic escape pods was slowly heading toward the refuge offered by the barely habitable world. Geary gazed at his scattered fleet and the drifting wrecks of the Syndic force that had come charging to Ilion in pursuit of the ships under Captain Falco. *We won. How much longer can we count on fighting forces we outnumber enough to win like this? How many more ships can I afford to lose?*

Invincible and the auxiliaries force had almost joined up, but Geary didn't see how the battle cruiser could be saved. *Triumph*, *Polaris*, and *Vanguard* hadn't even made it this far, along with a bevy of lighter units lost at Vidha. *Warrior*, *Orion*, and *Majestic* had all taken heavy damage and lost a lot of crew.

Escape pods from *Falcata* were broadcasting requests for rescue, and a few of Geary's other destroyers were headed that way. But the pieces of what had been *Terrible* and her crew were too small for even the best sensors on *Dauntless* to identify. There had been no chance for escape from that ship.

The Alliance fleet had won, but they had paid a bitter price.

It didn't help Geary's attitude to recall that this battle wouldn't have occurred if not for the self-centered certainty of Captain Falco.

•   •   •

THE conference room seemed more heavily occupied than usual. It wasn't just that thirteen surviving ships had rejoined them. It was also that the figures of Captains Falco, Kerestes, Numos, and Faresa were standing to one side. The Marine sentries guarding them on their own ships weren't part of the program and so were invisible here, but somehow their presence was still obvious in the way the four officers held themselves.

Down the table, the image of Co-President Rione sat with the commanding officers of the ships from the Rift Federation and the Callas Republic. She had finally chosen to be at a conference again but had elected to attend the conference in virtual mode from her stateroom rather than be here in person. Geary wondered what significance that decision held, or if Rione was simply ensuring that she was seen with the ships from her own Republic for purposes of politics or morale.

Falco had his head up and was gazing around confidently as if expecting to assume command of the fleet at any moment. Geary had to wonder at the state of the man's mind. He didn't seem concerned at all, not even showing signs of awareness that he was under arrest. Captain Kerestes, on the other hand, appeared almost frozen with fright, everything about him conveying shock and incomprehension. His long and careful career of avoiding doing anything that might backfire in any way had come crumbling down around his ears after he deferred all decisions to the wrong man. Numos and Faresa, though, were standing with angry expressions but not concerned ones. They had something up their sleeves, Geary thought. They should be worried. Numos wasn't the brightest star in the heavens, but he was clever enough to know when there was hell to pay.

Geary stood, drawing everyone's attention. "First of all, congratulations to every ship and the officers and sailors of the fleet on an outstanding victory. The loss of *Terrible* and *Falcata* was an awful price to pay, but the Syndics paid a lot more. Unfortunately, we now have to also acknowledge the loss of *Triumph*, *Polaris*, and *Vanguard* as well as a number of smaller units. I've also been informed that *Invincible* is beyond our capability to repair and will have to be abandoned." Everyone flinched at that. "The acting commanding officer of *Invincible* isn't present because her ship's systems are too badly torn up to allow her to participate in this conference. Those who knew Captain Ulan will be distressed to learn that he died in fighting in the Strena Star System as *Invincible* covered the retreat of her sister ships." This time a lot of officers turned to glower at Kerestes, Numos, and Faresa. A battle cruiser shouldn't have been screening its comrades. That was a job for a battleship, better able to absorb hits for a longer period of time. But obviously *Warrior*, *Orion*, and *Majestic* had left that task to *Invincible*.

"I disagree with the decision to abandon *Invincible*," a sharp voice announced. Geary stared in disbelief at Captain Falco as that officer continued, displaying his trademark confident, comradely smile. "We'll fix up *Invincible*, then proceed back to Vidha to assist *Triumph*—"

"Silence." Geary could feel as well as hear the stillness that followed his command. "The only reason you're present is so you can hear along with everyone else the reasons for your confinement. I'm still considering whatever charges may be appropriate for a court-martial when this fleet returns to Alliance space." No matter how popular Falco might be, Geary couldn't let him go uncharged for something like mutiny.

"Why wait?" Captain Cresida demanded. "Hold a tribunal and shoot the son of a bitch. It would be a better fate than he inflicted on those foolish enough to follow him."

That caused a reaction to ripple around the table. Some of the commanders present appeared to wholeheartedly support Cresida's suggestion, but many others seemed either shocked or disapproving. Geary took a deep breath before replying. "Your suggestion was inappropriate, Captain Cresida. Captain Falco has a long and distinguished record of serving the Alliance. We have to assume the stresses that prisoner status placed upon him as the senior Alliance officer at the labor camp have led to long-term problems that must be addressed." He had spent a long time thinking about what to say about Falco, how to balance the lingering respect so many officers and sailors felt for the man with the need to ensure no one would question keeping Falco under arrest. "Captain Falco appears to be suffering from serious difficulties with judgment and command ability. Preliminary reports from those ships that survived the engagement at Vidha indicate he was unable to offer effective leadership. For his own safety, and for the safety of the ships of this fleet, Captain Falco needs to be kept in custody."

A lot of officers looked unhappy, some visibly flinched at the news, but no one seemed willing to dispute what Geary had said. Oddly enough, though, Captain Falco only gave one of his customary frowns in response. "Victory remains within our grasp if we act boldly. This fleets needs my leadership. The Alliance needs my leadership." Silence followed the statement. "When the Syndics arrive in this system, we can be ready for them."

Geary glanced at the other officers before replying. "Captain Falco, the Syndic forces pursuing the ships with you have already arrived. They've been destroyed by this fleet. I'm at a loss to understand how you can be unaware of that." What was Falco thinking? Charisma was one thing, and self-confidence was important, but speaking as if recent history hadn't even occurred?

Falco blinked and smiled again. "Good. Exactly as I'd planned. I'll review the behavior of all ships in the battle and issue commendations and promotions where appropriate." Captain Falco gazed around, frowning once more. "Why are we holding this conference on *Dauntless*? *Warrior* remains the fleet flagship," he lectured. "Where's Captain Exani?"

It took Geary a moment to remember that Exani had

been commanding officer of *Triumph*. "He's most likely dead."

"*Triumph* will need a new commanding officer, then," Falco stated crisply, giving another smile, this one saddened but resolute, to everyone in the meeting. "Any officers who aspire to the command should contact me directly after this conference."

"Ancestors save us," someone whispered.

Captain Duellos spoke in a somber voice. "I fear Captain Falco may be more badly impaired than we suspected."

Geary spoke carefully. "Captain Falco, *Triumph* was destroyed covering the retreat of the ships with you from Vidha Star System."

Falco blinked, his smile crumbling. "Vidha? I haven't been to Vidha. That's deep in Syndic space. Why was *Triumph* there?"

That brought a few gasps from the table.

"Following you," Captain Tulev stated shortly.

"No," Falco corrected, then stood silent for a moment before speaking crisply. "I need to address the Alliance senate. There's a way to win this war and I can do it."

Geary tasted something bitter as he activated a special circuit to speak with the Marine guards on *Warrior*. "Remove Captain Falco from the conference and return him to his quarters." The figure of Falco, frowning once again at everyone, vanished. Geary closed his eyes briefly. How could he try a man who had obviously lost his mind? Duellos had been more right than he realized when he said Falco would fall apart when faced with the ruin of the dreams that must have kept him going in the Syndic labor camp. Fantasy had met reality at Vidha, and as fantasy had fallen apart, Falco's reality had shattered as well. Perhaps Falco couldn't handle a reality in that he wasn't the savior of the Alliance.

Painful as watching Falco's behavior had been, at least it had made it obvious to everyone here that Captain Fighting Falco wasn't in any shape to exercise command.

Opening his eyes again, Geary focused on Kerestes, Numos, and Faresa. "Do you three have anything to say?"

Numos answered, speaking with all of his usual arrogance. "We followed orders given by a superior officer. We've done nothing wrong. Nothing to justify this."

"Nothing?" Geary felt a stirring of the rage he was keeping bottled up just beneath the surface. "You knew full well that Captain Falco was not part of this fleet's command hierarchy. You knew the fleet was proceeding to Sancere. You heard my commands to return to the fleet."

"Captain Falco informed us we were participating in a diversion, and any orders heard from you were part of that," Numos replied. "He insisted we must keep this secret, sharing it only among the captains of the capital ships."

Captain Tulev's voice was as cold as the emptiness between stars. "All of whom are dead except for you three, and the man who you claim told you this is insane. How convenient."

Numos actually looked outraged. "We had no way of knowing a superior officer had lost his grasp upon reality and followed his orders to the best of our ability as our duty required. How dare you question my honor?"

"Your honor?" Geary demanded, knowing full well how harsh he sounded. "You have no honor. Not only did you break your oath to the Alliance, not only did you violate orders in the face of the enemy, but now you lie about it, depending upon the sealed lips of dead officers and the broken mind of another officer to protect your lie."

"We demand a court-martial," Captain Faresa insisted, speaking for the first time, her expression somehow even more acidic than Geary had remembered. "That is our right under Alliance law."

"A court-martial?" Captain Duellos marveled. "So you can claim innocence based on secret orders supposedly given by Captain Falco? So you can deny the responsibility you share for what happened to twenty-six warships of the Alliance? So you can deny any role in the deaths of their crews? Have you no shame?"

"We have nothing to be ashamed of," Numos stated with every trace of his old pride.

"I should have you shot now." It took Geary a moment to realize he was the one who had spoken those words. And even as he realized he had said it, he knew he could do it. Officers accused of mutiny in the face of the enemy would find few defenders and no friends back in Alliance space. Numos and Faresa at least seemed to have no friends left here, though Geary had learned from bitter experience that the friends of people like Numos could hide from his sight. But they weren't Falco, who had a reservoir of hero worship from the past and a current spate of horror and pity to win him sympathy.

He could do it. He could give the order. Not even bother with a court-martial, let alone a tribunal. This was a battlefield. As fleet commander, he could order summary justice. Who would try to stop him here and now? And when he brought this fleet safely back to the Alliance, who would raise any questions about one of his actions? Who would debate his decisions when he, and he alone, had brought this fleet home? No one in the Alliance would dare.

He could have Numos shot. And Faresa. Maybe Kerestes, too, though the man didn't seem worth a bullet. No one could stop him. Numos could get what he deserved. Justice would be done and done quickly and damn the legal niceties.

It was so very tempting because it felt so very right and because it was what his anger wanted him to do.

Geary took a long, slow breath. *So this is what life as Black Jack Geary could be. Do what I want. Make my own rules. I'm a hero. The hero of the Alliance. The hero of this fleet. And I want so badly to make Numos and Faresa pay.*

Badly enough to use the sort of power I swore I had no interest in? Badly enough to act like a Syndic CEO? Badly enough to become the man Victoria Rione believed me to be? Is that what all my lectures to these people about doing what is honorable come down to? Myself breaking the rules because I can when the reason matters enough to me? At least Falco genuinely believed he could break the rules because he was special and the only one who could save the Alliance. I wouldn't even have that excuse. I'd be doing it because others thought I was special when I didn't believe it myself.

He looked down the table to where Rione sat. She was watching him, her face devoid of expression, but her eyes bored into him like a battery of hell lances. She knew what he was thinking, knew what he was feeling.

Geary did not look at Numos, not sure he could refrain from giving an order for an execution if he kept seeing Numos's ugly pride. "I won't. This will be handled in accordance with the letter and spirit of fleet regulations. Charges will be preferred. If opportunity permits, court-martials will be held before our return to Alliance space. If not, you'll be handed over to Alliance authorities with charge sheets signed by me."

"We demand to be released," Faresa insisted. "There's no grounds for this unlawful detention."

"Don't push me," Geary warned, realizing as he did so that both Numos and Faresa would probably derive a last satisfaction from driving him to compromise his principles by having them executed. *You won't get that from me. I won't grant you that victory. Not today. Every day I'm going to wake up and go to sleep knowing I could make them pay. May my ancestors help me avoid the temptation to inflict vengeance upon those two and that idiot Kerestes.* "You have the blood of Alliance sailors on your hands," Geary stated. "If you had honor, you'd resign your commissions in shame. If you had courage, you would've stayed and let *Triumph* escape." He was using his power to browbeat them now, when they had Marine guards standing nearby and had to just take it. Abuse of power was too damned easy. Calling the Marines guarding Numos, Faresa, and Kerestes, Geary had them dropped from the conference circuit.

He took a moment then to run one hand through his hair, looking at the surface of the table and trying to let his anger drain away. Looking up at the other officers again, Geary spoke in what he hoped was a calm voice. "It will take a little while to properly evacuate *Invincible*. Her crew performed in an outstanding fashion. *Invincible* and her crew will receive a fleet citation for courageous action prior to the crew being evacuated and the ship abandoned. We'll blow up the wreck afterward to keep it out of enemy hands. I deeply regret the loss of that ship, as well as the other ships lost recently. I want us to be ready to leave this star system tomorrow, subject to the readiness of *Warrior*, *Majestic*, *Orion*, and the lighter units that have sustained damage to make the jump. I'd like to be informed of any problems on any of those ships that might prevent us from leaving. Our objective will be Tavika. Are there any questions?"

A commander with a haunted expression spoke in a steady voice. "What are your intentions toward the commanding officers of the other ships that accompanied Captain Falco, sir?"

Geary studied the woman. Commander Gaes of the *Lorica*, one of the surviving heavy cruisers. Her ship had stayed with *Invincible* while that ship limped to safety. "What do you think I should do?"

Her mouth worked silently for a moment before words came out. "Hold us accountable for our actions. Sir."

"How bad was it at Vidha?" Geary asked.

Commander Gaes bit her lip and looked away for a moment. "Very bad. Overwhelming odds. We'd already lost two light cruisers and a destroyer at a mined jump point on the way to Vidha. As soon as we reached Vidha, we lost four more ships to mines right out of the jump point, and *Polaris* took enough damage she couldn't keep up. The Syndics were sweeping in. We were asking for orders but none came. *Triumph* told us to run while she acted as rear guard, otherwise none of us would have made it out." She paused. "My executive officer is ready to assume command of my ship."

Gaes was no less guilty than Numos, perhaps, but had the courage to accept the consequences. And she had stayed with *Invincible*, doing what a damaged heavy cruiser could do to protect a crippled sister ship. "Not yet," Geary replied. "You made a grave error. So did the commanders of the other escorts. Unlike certain fleet captains, you're willing to admit that, and willing to take responsibility for your actions. You also had the courage and honor to remain with *Invincible*. I'm not blind to that. On that basis, I'm willing to give you another chance. Will you stick with this fleet from now on, Commander Gaes?"

"Yes, sir."

"Then show me how good a commanding officer you can be. You and the others. I won't pretend I won't be paying particular attention to you and them. Can you live with that?"

Gaes looked back at Geary, her expression still haunted. "I'm going to have to live with memories of Vidha, sir."

"So you will. May it make you and the others better officers. If you or any of those others decide you can no longer bear the burden of command, let me know. Otherwise, carry out your orders, Commander Gaes."

She nodded. "I will."

"Then I'll see you all in Tavika." Geary waited as the images of the other officers vanished rapidly. Rione's image disappeared as fast as the others. Desjani, shaking her head and giving Geary a sympathetic look, left with a quick apology about duties she needed to be seeing to.

In a very short time, only Captain Duellos's image was left, looking pensive. "I never cared for Captain Falco, but it's a sad thing to see, isn't it?"

Geary nodded. "How do we do justice to a man who no longer lives in this world?"

"Perhaps the fleet physicians can cure his ailment."

"Cure him so we can try him? Cure him so he can use his skills to contest command of the fleet again?" Geary gave a bitter smile. "Or just cure him so he can realize what he did to the ships and crews who followed him? That would be a form of vengeance, wouldn't it? Would Falco ever be able to recognize and accept guilt? Or would he rationalize it all away?"

"I don't pretend to know what justice would be in a case like this," Duellos noted. "But Captain Falco has lived in a universe centered on himself for a long time. On devotion of a sort to the Alliance as well, to be sure, but in Falco's mind he and the Alliance are one and the same. I don't think he'll ever be capable of understanding his role in the loss of those ships."

"What about the others?" Geary asked.

"Contemptible, aren't they?" Duellos noted with a sour expression. "Maybe that little show of theirs, seeking to avoid all responsibility for their actions, will eliminate the remnants of their support. But maybe not. Some people can find ways to get around anything. I think you handled Kerestes, Numos, and Faresa right, but as far as the commanders of the lighter warships go, you should know that not all of them seem to have learned the lessons that Commander Gaes has."

"I know. I'll keep an eye on them. I just hate wholesale sacking of commanders. That's a Syndic thing to do."

"Sometimes it's necessary." Duellos paused, giving Geary a searching look. "But I imagine you erred on the side of mercy after too nearly erring on the side of vengeance."

Geary tried to push away a headache. "You could tell?"

"I could. How many others could, I don't know. There you definitely made the right decision. I say that even though for a moment I was ready to volunteer to be a part of the firing squads for both Numos and Faresa."

"Thanks." Geary stared at the system display still floating above the table. "Why do people like the commander and crew of *Terrible* die while people like Numos and Faresa survive?"

"I fear the answer to that is beyond my knowledge,"

Duellos confessed. "I know I'm going to be speaking to my ancestors about it tonight."

"Me, too. May they grant us the wisdom we need."

"And the comfort. If you begin to focus too much on those who died here, Captain Geary, remember the sailors who survived this battle, and who escaped from the Syndic home system under your command."

"You'd think that would balance out, wouldn't you?" Geary stated. "But it doesn't. Every ship, every sailor we lose is a blow."

"And it is nonetheless what we must do." Duellos nodded and departed.

Exactly sixteen hours later, Geary watched on his display while the drifting wreckage of *Invincible* blew into fragments as its power core overloaded. There would be no trophy left for the Syndics, and at least the surviving crew members had all been safely transferred to other ships, but it was still a sad moment that called to mind the fate of the *Terrible*. "All units, accelerate to point zero five light speed and come to course down one three degrees, port two zero degrees at time five one." It was time to head to the jump point for Tavika, time to bid farewell to Ilion.

HE had to be seen on the ship, had to let the crew know he appreciated their efforts and cared about them, even though their welfare was primarily Captain Desjani's responsibility. Geary walked slowly through the passageways, exchanging brief greetings, occasionally pausing for a short conversation with sailors who seemed to be daring to really believe that they would get home. Their faith in him was still unnerving, but at least Geary could find comfort in knowing that while he had made his share of mistakes, he had also brought them this far in the face of some serious obstacles.

Voices that were low but sounded angry came to him. Geary turned a corner and saw Captain Desjani and Co-President Rione standing almost nose to nose in an otherwise deserted short passageway, their expressions intense. The moment he came into view, they both stopped talking. "Is something wrong?"

"No, sir," Desjani replied in a crisp voice. "Personal business. By your leave, sir." She rendered a precise salute to him and walked quickly away.

Geary shifted his gaze to Rione, whose narrowed eyes were watching Desjani leave. "What's going on?"

Rione glanced at him, her expression smoothing out and hiding any emotions. "You heard your officer, Captain Geary. Personal business."

"If it concerned me—"

"Do you think we were having a catfight over you, Captain Geary?" Rione asked mockingly.

He felt his temper rising. "No. But I have a right and responsibility to know if there's bad blood between you and Captain Desjani for any reason."

Rione was giving him that cool look again, betraying nothing. "Oh, no, Captain Geary. Captain Desjani and I are on the best of terms." She said it so it sounded like a lie, and he knew Rione had done that on purpose. But why, Geary couldn't imagine.

Geary tried to control his temper. "Victoria—"

She held up a hand to forestall him. "Co-President Rione has nothing further to say on the subject. Interrogate your officer if you're not willing to let it lie. Good day, Captain Geary." Rione turned and walked away, her back and her movements betraying a stiffness of anger he could spot thanks to the time they had spent together.

They were still several hours from reaching the jump point to Tavika, and he already had another problem to deal with. But what was the problem? Desjani had seemed if not welcoming at least more tolerant of Rione lately. Rione, on the other hand, had managed to avoid him since the fleet conference. He still didn't know how she felt about the events at the conference, and in their brief conversations since then Rione had begged off on the grounds that she was busy on research and other duties.

Geary reached his stateroom, sitting down and staring at the star display for a while before reaching for the internal communications control. "Captain Desjani, I'd appreciate seeing you in my stateroom at your convenience."

"I'll be right down, sir," Desjani replied in a professional voice that revealed nothing. Within a few minutes she arrived, outwardly composed but with troubled eyes.

"Please sit down," Geary offered. Desjani sat stiffly, her back straight, relaxing not at all. While she normally sat at attention in his stateroom, she was definitely more rigid this time. "I'm sorry if I'm prying, but I needed to ask again. Can you tell me what you and Co-President Rione were arguing about?"

She stared over his shoulder, her face betraying nothing. "I must respectfully decline to answer, sir, as the matter deals with personal issues."

"That's within your rights," Geary agreed heavily. "But I must insist on knowing one thing. Whatever it was about, can you still work effectively with and regarding Co-President Rione?"

"I assure you that I am fully capable of carrying out all of my duties in a professional manner, sir."

He nodded, letting his dissatisfaction show. "I can't demand more than that. Please inform me if you think that changes, and please see fit to tell me at some future date if you consider whatever you discussed to concern the safety and welfare of this fleet and its personnel."

Desjani nodded as well, her expression still controlled. "Yes, sir."

"You understand I'm in a very awkward position here."

"I'm sorry, sir."

"Okay, then." Geary was about to tell Desjani she could leave when the door to his stateroom opened, and Rione walked in, either deliberately or inadvertently blatantly advertising the fact that she had personal access to Geary's living area. It was certainly a remarkable coincidence that Rione had chosen this moment to visit his stateroom again after avoiding him since the conference.

Rione eyed them dispassionately. "Am I interrupting anything?"

Desjani stood up and returned the same expression. "Not at all, Madam Co-President. I was just leaving."

Geary watched them, fascinated in spite of himself. It was like seeing two battle cruisers circling each other, all shields at maximum, every weapon ready to fire, but both maintaining tight control over their every move so that the situation didn't escalate into a bloodbath. And he had absolutely no idea why the two were at the brink of hostilities. "Thank you, Captain Desjani," he stated carefully, wondering if the wrong word from him could somehow lead to open warfare. He wasn't egotistical enough to think the women were sparring over him, which left him baffled as to what had happened between them.

Desjani left, the hatch somehow seeming to close with extra force behind her. Geary exhaled heavily and looked at Rione. "I've got a lot of things to worry about, you know."

"That has come to my attention more than once," Rione agreed in the same detached tones.

Geary studied her for a moment, wondering at the way she could be both familiar and unknown, sometimes at the same instant. "Who's here right now? Am I talking to Victoria, or to Co-President Rione?"

She gave him that cool look back. "That depends. Am I speaking with John Geary, or Black Jack Geary?"

"I'm still John Geary."

"Are you? I saw Black Jack the other day. He was preparing to order someone to be shot. He wanted to do it."

"He wasn't the only one." Geary looked away. "Maybe you did see Black Jack. But Black Jack didn't make any decisions."

"He came close, didn't he?" Rione was keeping more than an arm's length away, maintaining both physical and emotional separation from him. "How did it feel to know what you could do if you wanted to?"

"Frightening."

"Was that all?"

He took a long, deep breath and exhaled slowly, recalling the emotions that had filled him then. "Yes. It scared the hell out of me, because it looked so very attractive. Because I wanted those idiots to pay for what they did, and I knew I could get away with it if I wanted. And knowing I could get away with it scared me." Geary fixed his eyes on Rione. "And what is it you're feeling?"

"Me?" Rione shook her head. "Why should I feel anything?"

"Does that mean we're over? Did you come here to tell me that? Is that why you've avoided me since the conference?"

"Over?" Rione seemed to need a minute to think about the question. Then she shook her head again. "No. There are . . . some other issues I need to deal with. However, I want to stay close to John Geary. I think he may need me."

"What about Black Jack?" Geary asked, recalling that Rione had bluntly declared that her first loyalty was to the Alliance, not to him.

"If he shows up again, I'd like to be close then, too." She said it calmly, in a voice still almost devoid of emotion, her eyes meeting Geary's gaze.

To keep me honest? he wondered. *Or to make sure you're in a position to take advantage of the power Black Jack wouldn't hesitate to use?*

Or to ensure Black Jack doesn't hurt the Alliance by slipping a knife into him while he sleeps? Did I ever imagine I'd be sleeping with a woman who might literally kill me if she thought it was best for the things she believes in? Things that I also believe in?

At least this way I can keep an eye on her, too.

"It's a very long ways back to Alliance space," Geary stated. "We will get there, though, no matter how much the Syndics throw at us. This fleet will get back. And

Captain John Geary will get back. Any help you can offer is always welcome. Your company is always welcome." Almost always, anyway.

"I believe now that this fleet will make it back," Rione agreed in a quiet voice. "We'll see if John Geary does."